BADD APPLE

A BADD BROTHERS NOVEL

Jasinda Wilder

BADD
APPLE

ONE

Delia

IGNORED PRESTON'S HOPEFUL GAZE ON MY ASS AS I TUGGED, shimmied, and stuffed myself back into my stretchy gray *T-shirt* material romper.

"You're sure you have to go?" he said, flopping across the bed to run a finger over the curve of my ass cheek. "I can rustle up something to eat and we can watch something and then go again."

I batted his hand away and then ran my fingers under the elastic around my thighs and under my booty cheeks. "Yes, Preston, I have to go. I have work to do."

He shifted so he was sitting on the edge of the bed behind me, running his hands up my torso toward my boobs. "Awww, c'mon, *Dee-Dee*. I didn't see you all break."

I batted his hands away—the first time, I did so gently and almost playfully, darting out of his reach; when he followed me and tried to cop a feel anyway, I gave him a sharp wrist block followed by a *palm-strike* shove.

He stumbled backward, rubbing his chest. "What the hell was that, *Dee-Dee*?"

I whirled on him, letting him see the full force of my fury. "That was a warning, Preston. I've trained in Brazilian *Jiu-Jitsu*, MMA, and kickboxing with my Uncle Bax since I was a toddler. Don't fuck with me."

He shook his head. "*Dee-Dee*, c'mon. I was just playing."

"No, you weren't," I snapped. "I told you no. You grabbed me again anyway, and I knocked your hand away. I'd have thought that was a pretty clear signal that we're done. Yet, even after I moved out of your reach, you tried to grope me again."

He gave me a perplexed frown that somehow managed to come across as whiny. "You're my girlfriend, *Dee-Dee*. It's not groping. Jesus."

And cue the ick.

I stepped into his space, letting my temper seethe out of me just a little bit—I keep that monster on a tight leash, but it seems my *about-to-be-ex*-boyfriend needs to see a hint of the beast that lies within.

"*Any* unwanted touching is groping, Preston. I made it clear I didn't want you to touch me. Boyfriend, fiance, husband, stranger—*any* unwanted touching is considered sexual assault. The next time you push my boundaries like that, you'll wind up in the ER with a broken bone." I glared up at him, starting to wonder what I'd ever seen in him. "That's number one."

"*Dee-Dee*, I'm—"

I cut in over him. "Save it, Preston. Your apology doesn't mean dick in a bag. Number two, I've told you roughly a hundred times, I hate it when you call me *Dee-Dee*. I *hate* it. I mother*fucking* hate it. Like, *stab-you-in-the-eyeball-with-a-rusty-fork hate* it. We clear on that?"

"Yeah, got it, but—"

"Save the buts for your boyfriend," I snapped, earning a hurt wince from him. "I'm not interested in anything you have to say at this point."

"What the hell is going on, Delia?" he asked. "Where is this coming from? I come back from spring break in Hawaii with my family, you show up unannounced at seven in the goddamn morning, fuck my brains out, and then the second you come, you roll out of bed and start dressing. And then you don't let me touch you, and now you're acting like you hate me. Sorry, but I'm not following."

I inhaled deeply, held it— rolling my eyes when his gaze cut down to my breasts as they swelled with the breath—and then turned away and let it out, summoning patience. "Okay, buddy, I'll break it down for you."

"Buddy?" he said, more confused than ever.

"Yeah—*buddy*. Here's what's going on since you're

clearly too dense to follow, and don't worry, I'll use very small words."

He shook his head. "Now you're just being mean."

"You disrespected my boundaries and then tried to play it off. When a woman stops you from touching her, that's it. You keep your slimy mitts to yourself, fucktard."

"Jesus, Delia, I'm sorry, I—"

"I said, save the fucking apology. I was planning on breaking up with you anyway, to start off with. And then you went to Hawaii for the entire month of March without telling me at any point that that's what was happening." He opened his mouth, and I held up a hand to forestall him. "Still talking, shut the fuck up. As I said, I was planning on breaking up with you anyway, but you ghosted me before I could. The reason I was going to break up with you was because you started acting weird. If you weren't frantically and surreptitiously texting someone, you were hiding your phone—taking it into the bathroom with you to take a shower, changing your passcode, and disappearing to make mysterious phone calls. You were gone a lot with vague and *thinner-than-tissue* paper explanations—not just once or twice, but regularly. And when you were gone on these mysterious outings, you didn't text, didn't call, and didn't answer my calls or texts." I shrug and hold out my hands at my sides, palms up. "To me—shit, to *anyone*—that says you're cheating. Or being dishonest in some way. And honestly, I don't care. I don't want to know if and who you were fucking on the side or if you were just…I don't know, gambling or…or whatever. I don't know, and I don't care. You act sus, you're done. My last boyfriend did the exact same thing, and he was cheating on me, and I swore I'd never let that shit slide again. Therefore, you're fucking done."

"Delia, I swear to god I wasn't cheating."

I shook my head. "I don't care. And that's the problem, Preston. I don't. I genuinely *don't care*. I'm apathetic to whether you were screwing someone else."

I let out a breath and push the *temper-beast* back into its cage, forcing myself to soften a little bit. I squeezed my eyes shut, wincing as I realized how harsh I'd just been.

I sighed again and looked at him—Preston isn't a bad guy. He's really not. He's decently attractive, in a *boy-next-door* sort of way, with wavy *sandy-blond* hair and puppy dog brown eyes, and the tight, hard, lean body of a *twenty-one-year-old* lacrosse star.

"Look, Preston." I took his hands and gave him full eye contact. "We were never going to be anything but a few months of fun and companionship. I thought you understood that. I'm not in love with you. I never was and never will be. And I don't think you're in love with me either."

He blinked, sighing and thinking. "No, I'm not. But I do really like you. I'm sorry I ghosted you over break. It's just that my parents have rules and expectations for us when we're all together like that. I had to leave my phone in the room. And then I just…" he did a weird *head-roll-shake* thing of frustration. "Got caught up and…I didn't forget about you, I just…"

"I get it," I said. "I didn't call or text either. At first, I was waiting for you, but then things got busy. So it's not entirely on you." I took my hands back and rubbed my face. "I was a bitch just now. I'm sorry. I've enjoyed our time together, and I guess my instinct was to make it easier on me to break up with you by being a raging *bitch-hole*. That wasn't fair to you, and I am sorry."

He nodded. "I get it… It's cool. So…this is it?"

"Yeah, this is it." I shrugged. "Sorry?"

He laughed. "Don't be sorry. I just…okay, two things. One, I wasn't cheating. I want you to know that. My friend, who is a girl, was going through something and was leaning on me to get through it. We're just friends, and we've never hooked up, and we never will. But I felt weird and guilty about it, and instead of talking to you about it, I made it weird. I can show you the texts if you don't believe me."

"Thanks—I do appreciate the truth. And for the sake of your future girlfriends, next time, just be honest. I would have understood. I'm not jealous. I mean, I *am*—but only if I need to be. If you have a friend who's going through something and you tell me you're just talking to her and helping her, I'd have been cool with it. Lying and being sus never gets anyone anywhere good."

He winced, pinching the bridge of his nose. "I

know, and I'm sorry. Lesson learned, not that it makes a difference here, with us."

"And number two?" I asked.

"If you were going to break up with me, why sleep with me first?" He asked.

I grinned—a cheesy, apologetic, *all-teeth*, simpering grin. "I didn't get laid all of March. I figured once more for old time's sake can't hurt." I sighed, passing my hand through my long auburn hair. "And, honestly, I guess I was seeing if there was anything there to hold on to."

"I can respect both reasons," he said. "And I assume, obviously, there isn't?"

I shrugged. "No, not really. I mean, it's nothing personal. You're good in bed, Preston. Truly. We had fun. And you're a good dude. You're sweet and cute. I dunno…I guess whatever it was we had has run its course."

He nodded. "I can't say I'm surprised." A little laugh burst from him. "I guess I always expected it. You're out of my league, Delia. Shit, you're out of *everyone's* league. Everyone in Ketchikan, at least. I always did my best to keep up with you, but fuck, man, you're *a lot*, and I say that with every ounce of respect I have."

I couldn't help but laugh. "Yeah, you know, you're not wrong. I mean, I don't know about being out of your league, but I know I'm a lot. I guess that's where some of my frustration comes from. I feel like I always have to hold back or…or something. I dunno."

"Someday, some guy is gonna come along and he's gonna know exactly how to handle everything that you are." He took my hands. "But until then, just promise me you won't put yourself in a box for anyone. Okay? Don't hold back. Hold out for the guy who can handle you." He leaned in and kissed my cheek. "And I'm sorry about disrespecting your boundary earlier."

I shook my head. "Nah, it's okay. I mean, you did, but I sort of went from zero to a hundred on you, so it's not entirely your fault. It's not unrealistic to think you're allowed to touch me five minutes after we boned."

He nodded, letting go and stepping back. "So. Now what? What's next for the great Delia Badd?"

I shrugged. "Fuck if I know. For right now, finish getting dressed and go to work. You?"

He rubbed the back of his neck. "Well, actually, I got an offer from Johns Hopkins to come there and play lacrosse. The scholarship beats the shit out of what I've got going on here, plus that ties in nicely with my plans of going to med school, so...I'm transferring there."

"Hey, that's awesome, Preston, congratulations. You've worked your ass off for that. Good for you." I crossed over to him and hugged him. "I am happy for you. You deserve it."

He smiled at me. "Thanks, Dee. Sorry—Delia. I will miss you."

I winked at him. "Nah, you'll just miss my lack of a gag reflex."

He blushed, the li'l cutie. "Well, yeah. That and the thing you do when you're on top—"

I held up both hands. "Aaaand enough. I'll miss you

too." I glanced at his alarm clock. "Shit, I really have to go. I'm gonna finish getting ready in your bathroom, okay?"

He nodded. "Sure. I'll put some coffee on and you can take it with you."

"You're sweet, thanks."

I took my clothes into his bathroom and dressed, ran my fingers through my hair, and put on a touch of makeup. Examined myself in the mirror.

I'm *five-eight* and run to extra curvy, thanks to a double helping of parental genes. Dad's side of the family, while all male, tends to be beefy, which I assume plays a hand in my build. Mom is curvy as hell, and always has been, and I take after her—to the point that when we're out together, people question if we're *mother-daughter* or sisters. Mostly, I'm happy with myself. Sometimes, usually in the spring when I first start trying on bikinis, I get down on myself for the inevitable winter surplus, but I just wheedle Uncle Bax into whipping my ass, literally, back into shape. I have Mom's hair— dark red, auburn, whatever you want to call it. Depends on the lighting, really. Indoors, it's more *brownish-red*, but outside in full sun, it's more *reddish-brown*. I have bright blue eyes and a few freckles across the bridge of my nose and cheekbones.

I should go home and change, but I only wore this outfit for a couple of hours yesterday and then this morning, so I see no point in changing it. Plus, I look cute AF. Dark blue jeans so tight they fit like leggings and do *quasi-miraculous* things for my admittedly rather large ass, with my gray romper under a *blue-and-black* plaid flannel. The romper isn't exactly a bra, so the girls are all but hanging out, with the flannel buttoned up just enough to keep them from playing swing low sweet chariots in the Alaskan sunshine.

I hate bras. I'll wear a sports bra to work out, and if an outfit absolutely demands one, I'll wear it, but only for as long as I have to. Otherwise, fuck those *titty-prisons*. A lot of people, Mom especially, like to tell me my boobs are way too big to be running around without one, but I don't give a shit. So they sag when I'm older—if I'm ever lucky enough to find the kind of love Mom and Dad have, my man will love me even if my tits hang to my knees later in life…and he'll appreciate the view in the meantime. As for what people around me think? Who gives a fuck? Not me. Yeah, I have big, thick, prominent nipples that like to play headlights no matter what I'm wearing or not wearing. Don't like seeing my nipples? Don't look. Not my problem.

One last glance in the mirror—hair looks decent, makeup is decent, boobs are even. Good enough.

I exited Preston's bathroom and shouldered my purse, a Louis Vuitton Neverfull that was a gift from Auntie Eva. It's vintage, in mint condition, worth a small fortune, and my prized possession. Plus, it fits a change of clothes, a full makeup set, my wallet, charger, a water bottle, phone, keys, and all the other shit a woman has floating around in the bottom of a big purse.

Preston, true to his word, had a *U-of-A* Southeast *to-go* tumbler full of freshly brewed coffee ready for me, just the way I like it—black with two packets of Splenda. "Here you go."

I accepted it and lifted on my toes to hug him. "Thanks. I can run this by after work." I lifted the tumbler.

He waved me off. "Don't worry about it. I have like four of them. They give them out for free all over campus every year during orientation."

An awkward silence ensued. I flapped my free hand out. "So...bye?"

He hugged me again. "Bye, Delia."

"When do you transfer?" I asked.

"Working on it now. I start at Johns Hopkins next week."

"Oh, well...I guess I probably won't see you again anytime soon, huh?" I bit my lower lip. "So this is good-bye for real."

"Nah, probably not." He opened his apartment door and ushered me out. "It's been real, Delia Badd."

I gave him a saucy *two-finger* salute and tromped down the stairs to the exit, my *calf-height* leather boots noisy on the uncarpeted stairs. My car was at the Kitty—I parked it there this morning and walked to Preston's place. I made the short walk back to work. It was only just now nine—I called Preston at seven, was at his place by *seven-thirty*, and we were naked by *seven-thirty-five*.

The one thing I can say about Preston's bedroom abilities is that he's not quick. Our last romp in the sack was a good long one, resulting in a pretty decent little O for me. Which isn't easy to accomplish—I don't come easily, and sometimes not at all. I'm used to that and don't expect to come every time I have sex. I still enjoy the fun, but it's always a nice bonus if I do get an O out of the process. Preston, to his credit, always understood that. He didn't take it personally if I couldn't get there, but always did his best to make sure I did, and if I didn't, he made sure I felt damn good along the way. He understood that I like to play—not just a quick *wham-bam-thank-you*-ma'am penetration session. I liked to think I taught him a few things, honestly.

I let myself in through the rear door into the kitchen, lock it behind me, and set about opening. We don't open till eleven, but I like to have the front of the house ready to go first, and then get the back of the house prepped for the opening crew, and then I start on the office work.

I lost myself in the familiar process of opening, but my mind was still whirling in the background.

I felt bad for how cunty I was to Preston. I mean, I did wake him up for a booty call, and I did give him an O he wouldn't forget any time soon, so I don't feel *that* bad, but I did go full bitch on him for no reason. I mean, not *no* reason, but it was an *over-the-top* reaction that he didn't deserve. It's just easier to break up with someone when you're pissed off.

What I'm stuck on, though, was his statement that I'm a lot, that he felt like I was out of his league. What? I hate that shit. There are no leagues. Dating is not a sport. And he's a good dude. Good looking. Funny. Athletic. Popular. Decent in every way. I knew going in I was never going to be in love with him, which meant the whole thing always had an expiration date, and we both knew it. But I don't like the idea that he felt like I was out of his league. I don't know what to do with that.

Once the FOH and BOH were both good to go, I went into the office and called Emerson, my best friend and adoptive sister. It rang and went to voicemail. I left a *two-word* voicemail: "Call me."

I went through last night's receipts, counted the cash, got the deposit ready, and balanced the drawers. I was just getting started on the paper stock inventory when Emerson called me back.

"Hey, bitch," I said, putting it on speaker and setting it on the rack as I kept counting. "How's soccer camp?"

She was out of breath. "Kicking my ass, but good. I only have like ten minutes, though, so what's up?"

"I broke up with Preston."

Silence greeted this. "I thought you already did?" she said, finally.

"No, he was in Hawaii with his family, I guess. I *booty-called* him this morning, and we ended up breaking up afterward."

She snorted. "Only you, Delia. So...you're just calling me to tell me, or there's something else?"

I sighed. "He told me he always thought I was out of his league, and that's bugging me."

"You are," she said, pausing to guzzle water noisily, causing me to frown at the phone in disgust—I have a pretty gnarly case of misophonia.

"He said I was out of everyone in Ketchikan's league."

"You are. Why do you think no boyfriend lasts for more than a few months?" She laughed. "Delia, *honey-buns*, you're a handful and a half. You're sexy as hell, you have the sex drive of a teenage boy, you're an actual, factual boss of a whole bar, you can kick ass in three martial arts disciplines, and you're funny as fuck."

"But…"I sighed, annoyed. "I'm not trying to be in any league or out of a league. And who determines the league? Preston is a good guy. I just…" I moved the phone to the next rack and flipped the page of my inventory. "I dunno. It was an offhand comment on his part, but I'm stuck on it. He said I'm a lot. And that someday, some guy is going to come along who knows how to handle me."

Em snorted. "Ohhhh, honey. You *are* a lot. And yeah, Preston is a good dude. But he's…he's a puppy dog and you're a *she-wolf*. He can run around after you and all, but at the end of the day, you're not gonna end up with a cute little golden lab; you're gonna end up with a big alpha wolf."

"You're just calling me a bitch, aren't you?" I teased.

"Oh, absolutely. But you're *my* bitch." She yelled

something muffled and then addressed me again. "I gotta go. But babe, Preston was right. And I know you're not asking, but if you were to ask me, my advice would be to spend a bit of time not dating or anything. If you *have* to get your rocks off, I dunno…maybe Preston will let you booty call him again. But just wait for the right guy to come along. I truly believe that the Badd Family Love Charm has its sights on you next."

I faked a gag. "Don't make me nauseous."

"Oh, shut up with that. You're a romantic, deep down. You're just prickly and defensive about it because the idea of falling in love scares those giant tits right off of you."

"You're mean," I groused.

"But not *wro-o-o-o*-ng!" She *sing-songed*. "Okay, gotta go kick ass. Love you bye!" She was gone before I could get another word in.

"Yeah, bye to you too, bitch," I mumbled under my breath. "Bad Family Love Charm my big fat ass. It's not real and it's not coming for me."

I wasn't sure who I was trying to convince: myself, or the Badd Family Love Charm that I pretended not to but totally did believe in, and was absolutely scared shitless of.

TWO

Hunter

I LET THE DRIVER GET MY BAGS OUT OF THE TRUNK AND SET them on the bottom step of my new Alaskan property. I'd had to get an actual taxi, which was after having to take a ferry from the airport to the city itself. I haven't taken a cab in years—I've either been driven by my personal driver or by a hired driver. In a *worst-case* scenario, I get an Uber Black.

This guy is, as far as I can tell, about as Alaskan as a human can get: as wide as he is tall, with long gray hair in a ponytail and a beard down to his chest, wearing a red flannel shirt and a ball cap so dirty and battered it's a miracle it's still intact. If he were to wash it, it would disintegrate. The cab itself was a twenty- or *thirty-year-old* minivan that smelled of grease, fish, and chewing tobacco. The rear bench was full of tackle boxes, fishing rods, bright orange life jackets, and a rattling assortment of other fishing…stuff. On the seat beside me on the *second-row* bench was a large mason jar full of dirt, in which wriggled dozens of fat worms.

"Here ya go, *Fancy-Pants*," the driver grumbled. He took a look at the house and property, managing to look impressed and derisive at the same time. "Wondered who bought this eyesore."

I followed his gaze—he was not wrong. It was… well, it was certainly something. A lot of words came to mind as I looked at my new home away from home: eyesore, monstrosity, tasteless exercise in excess.

Look, I'm worth almost a billion dollars—that's just my own personal fortune, earned under my own power, with no more than a *half-million-dollar* seed fund from my father the day I graduated high school. If you factor in the trust fund established by my grandparents, not to mention my cut of what I'll get when my parents pass, I'm worth well over a billion. So, I know how to spend money. I'm intimately familiar with excess. I have properties in New York, Colorado, Florida, Switzerland, and the Caribbean. All of them are ostentatious and excessive. I have cars at every property. Full wardrobes, watches, belts, ties, shoes, everything. I only pack the necessities I need to feel at home—toiletries, my phone and chargers, laptop, and my favorite loungewear and jeans and such.

Point is, I know excess.

This?

This place takes the concept of ostentatious excess, bends it over what I imagine will be the *gold-flecked* marble counter, and fucks it into next week.

In the ass.

Without lube.

I hate it.

It's not modern, and it probably fits the whole "rich guy buys a house in Alaska" aesthetic, but good fucking god, is it ugly.

With its two stories of log and stone and glass, it's probably been featured on the cover of some magazine or other. I could see right through the glass front door to the backyard, which was more stone—probably travertine. Probably has an elaborate outdoor kitchen that's never been used. Probably a *built-in* hot tub that could fit the whole Jets offensive line. The master suite probably features trayed ceilings, a *walk-in* closet I could get lost in, and at least six balconies picked to have all the best views—which are, admittedly, *awe-inspiring*.

It's just…soulless.

It's a museum, not a home.

I glanced at the cab driver. "Thanks for the ride." I handed him a *hundred-dollar* bill. "Keep it."

"Mighty generous of ya, *Fancy-Pants*." He hobbled back to the van and was gone in a cloud of blue exhaust, leaving me alone with my new house.

I unlocked the lockbox, retrieved the key, let myself

in, and gave myself a tour. It was exactly what I expected in every way.

I peeked into the garage to check out what kind of wheels Elara had procured for me. Here, at least, I'm pleasantly surprised: a Ford *F-150* Raptor, not new, in black, with tasteful mods to make navigating Alaskan roads more palatable. Or something. I wouldn't know.

Tour done, I called Elara, who answered on the second ring. "Good afternoon, Mr. Hawkins. Is everything to your satisfaction?"

I reminded myself that she followed my instructions to the T, and the fact that I absolutely hate this house is not her fault.

"I hope you didn't pay more than a couple million for this eyesore of a house," I growled, only partially successful in my attempt to be nicer to her.

She was silent for a moment. "Um…you didn't specify a price range, sir. Is it…is there something wrong with the property?"

I sighed, rubbing the bridge of my nose, biting back half a dozen asshole replies. "No, there's nothing wrong with it. It's just ugly."

"You said not modern, sir. That property is the most expensive one in the entire region. It was *custom-built* and cost over…"I heard paper rustling. "Three million dollars to construct. It was for sale for over four years. You paid *two-point-five* for it."

I bit my tongue until I tasted copper. "You were merely following instructions, Elara, and you're brand new, so I cannot very well expect you to know the intricacies of how I approach business matters. Therefore, I shall give you some tips. I may be extraordinarily wealthy, but I do not believe in purchasing the most expensive of anything simply because I have a lot of money. Personally speaking, if I deem something to be valuable to me, cost is no object. But in business, we must be smart. It is not smart to own the most expensive home in a region. It would have been better if you'd found something tasteful that's near the upper end but not the apex. This place is…well, it's overdone in every way. It has no soul. You couldn't have known that because I didn't ask you to vette the properties in person. But once I'm done with this Alaskan project, we need to figure out what to do with this place, because quite frankly, Elara, I fucking hate it."

I heard her gulp. "I'm sorry, sir."

"Not your fault. Consider it a learning experience. Never pay top dollar for a property. Never. No exceptions. Always drive a hard bargain. If the seller won't budge, they're not motivated, and you're wasting your time. We do not negotiate with terrorists, which in this case means unmotivated sellers. If this place was for sale for that long, you should have been able to get it for much, *much* cheaper than you did." I forced my tone to soften. "I'm putting you in charge of dealing with this property on the back end of this whole process. Recoup my investment one way or another. I don't want to know the details; just get my money back out of this tasteless monstrosity. Rent it, lease it, sell it, renovate it, use it for corporate motivational retreats, I don't give a fuck what or how. Understood?"

"Yes sir. Again, I'm sorry. I should have asked more questions."

"An excellent takeaway, Elara—always ask more questions. I'll never fault you for getting as much information as possible before pulling the trigger on something, especially when it comes to spending money. That's how you get rich, and that's how you stay wealthy."

"I have a question, sir."

"Ask away."

"What's the difference between rich and wealthy?"

"Ah, an excellent question. Rich is quick. Some lucky schmuck who develops an app at the right time and sells it for seven figures is rich. Someone who makes seven figures and turns into enough wealth that their *great-grandchildren* will never have to work a day in their lives...*that's* wealth."

"But if those *great-grandchildren* never have to work, won't the wealth stop accruing?"

I chuckled. "Now we're entering philosophical territory, Elara. Yes. Which is why I personally, if I were to ever have children of my own, would not simply pass untold millions on to them. There would likely be a stipulation that you have to make your own first million before you get more than a certain percentage of my money—meaning, I'd provide seed funding, but if you blow that on trivial shit, you don't get more. If you make a million, I'll match you million for million for a certain period of time after that. I don't know. I'm not sure I even want children, so I'm not sure why we're even talking about this."

"My father is rich. Not wealthy, but rich. He made some good investments and got promoted at the right time." She paused, sighing. "He paid for my education and provided a nice place to live and a fairly generous stipend to live on while I was an intern, but he's not paying my way beyond that. I have to make my own way. That's why this job is so important to me, sir. I have a trust fund, but I can't touch it until I'm thirty and have at least a quarter million in total assets. And that's not whichever comes first—I have to satisfy *both* stipulations."

"Seems to me like your father is a smart man who has your best interests at heart, then. You're motivated to succeed. If I were you, I'd hang up and call him and thank him," I said. "Now, I have to unpack and get to work. While I'm gone, unless I give you an assignment, you answer to Harriet. You're doing fine, Elara. If you pay attention, listen to me and Harriet, and keep honing those instincts of yours, you'll be just fine. Goodbye for now, Elara."

"Goodbye, sir."

Funny how I have zero interest in the girl, sexually. Once upon a time, she'd already be back in the hiring pool because I'd have fucked her and gotten bored. I'd never have seen the potential in her as an employee and a human.

In fact, when was the last time I had sex? A month ago? That British lingerie model. What was her name? Fuschia? Something idiotic like that. Sweet girl, truly. Not the sharpest crayon in the toolbox, but sweet and eager. Mouth like a goddamn Hoover vacuum and naturally perky tits, but outside of sex, there was zero connection. The pillow talk was about as interesting as watching paint dry. She wanted to talk about shoots and give me all the gossip about which models were banging who, and who has anorexia and who's on the coke diet, and who gives a fuck? The only good thing was I didn't have to contribute to the conversation because she never shut the fuck up.

I may have been a bit cruel about kicking her out. The words "vapid *cum-receptacle*" may have been used. There were tears and imprecations. I felt bad immediately and sent her a BMW 4 Series convertible with an apology note. She sold the car, the note, and the story. Whatever.

I guess now that I'm thirty, my interest in empty sex has begun to wane. I have money. I have all the trappings of success. I love my work. I'm just...not happy. I am successful. Satisfied.

Mostly.

Sort of.

I have goals, still. I'd like to get into the aerospace field. Rocketry, perhaps. Work with someone like

Valentine Roth or Xavier Badd—who, rumor has it, is *part-owner* of the very establishments I'm attempting to buy—Badd's Bar & Grille, and the rest.

But romance? I don't know. I wouldn't know where to begin looking for something real. What does that even mean? My parents were, and still are, a business arrangement. They are friends, business partners, and occasional lovers, but they're not in love. My father has his lovers and my mother hers, and if they sometimes shag, as my British mother likes to put it, then very well. But they're not a love match.

I've never been in love. I know no one who is happily married and truly in love.

So, where did this leave me? No longer interested in fucking the models, socialites, and actresses. Clueless about love. Distrustful at best—because at my level of wealth and fame, you have to be.

I sighed, disgusted with the maudlin, meandering direction and substance of my thoughts.

Enough, Hunter. Focus on the business at hand.

Do I go in as myself? I think not. I think I have to play this very carefully. Go incognito, assess the lay of the land, and develop a plan. I truly do not want to simply buy them out and take over, but my concern is that they won't believe me. They've built a successful business, and they're rightfully proud of it. They'll be skeptical and suspicious of a New York billionaire coming in waving around his checkbook.

I unpacked my bags, which contained my

personal capsule wardrobe and effects; the rest of the closet is stuffed with the usual suits, slacks, ties, and *button-downs* as curated by Sofie, my stylist. I change out of my Brooks Brothers suit and into a pair of jeans, a black *T-shirt* with a forest green flannel, and a pair of Timberlands, with my favorite ballcap—a faded, battered thing I've owned since I was sixteen. That hat has seen every phase of life. I've worn it everywhere— yachting in the Mediterranean, mountain climbing in Nepal, backpacking in Thailand. Everything else I own is new, except that hat.

It was the last thing my grandfather gave me before he died. It was once red with tan mesh around the back, but now the red has faded to near pink, and the logo has long since faded into obscurity—an oil and gas company my grandfather invested in or something. The brim is perfectly curved to frame my face, the rim is torn and tattered, the band is sweatstained, and I wouldn't trade it for my fortune doubled or even trebled.

I intentionally haven't shaved all week, so my stubble has grown into almost a beard, which I hope disguises my rather recognizable jawline. Or, at least, that's what the gossip rags liked to write about—Hunter Hawkins and his rugged jawline.

I slipped a pair of mirrored aviators on my face and headed for the garage, feeling rather excited about driving myself for the first time in years. Despite the millions of dollars in cars I own around the world, I rarely get the opportunity to drive myself anywhere. Usually,

I'm accompanied everywhere by drivers and bodyguards and PAs and secretaries and PR and who the fuck knows who else. True solitude? A rare blessing.

I got into the truck and started the motor—it caught with a loud snarl, and I backed out. I input the original Badd's Bar and Grille into my phone's GPS and headed that way.

I saw the appeal.

The original Badd's had the feel of a comfortable, simple local watering hole. The floors were worn and smooth and aged, the tables scratched and battered but sturdy, the lighting low, the TVs playing sports clips, and the decor rustic without being chintzy or Cracker *Barrel-y*. The bartender was a beautiful blonde woman in her *mid-to-late* forties—dark blond hair, brown eyes, and a killer figure. She moved behind the bar with the ease and grace you only get from decades of experience. The servers were all young women, attractive but professional, dressed in black jeans and a black polo with the bar logo on the left breast. The clientele was a mix of obvious locals and just as obvious tourists, and the two did not mingle. Despite being barely four in the afternoon, it was hopping, with only a single spot open at the bar, and that was at the very end near the service bar.

I took that spot and slid my sunglasses up onto the

brim of my hat, keeping the brim tugged low and my head ducked.

"Hey there," a friendly female voice said. "What can I get you? All Alaskan Brewing Company drafts are half off until five, and everything on this menu—" she slid a small square of paper toward me, "is also half off until five."

I perused the menu—chicken tenders, burgers, chili, cheese fries, and some sort of salad with everything on it but the kitchen sink. "How's the chili?" I asked.

"Made *in-house* fresh every day, and *nine-time* winner of the Ketchikan chili *cook-off*," she answers, with a friendly but not flirty grin.

"Bowl of that and the stout," I said, smiling back without exactly making eye contact. "Thanks."

She nodded, rang up the order, and then pulled my beer. She set it on a napkin in front of me. "So. What brings you into town? You're not on a cruise. Business?"

I frowned at her. "How do you know I'm not a local?"

She just snorted. "Okay, buddy."

I sipped the stout and nodded in approval. "Good beer. Fine then—how do you know I'm not on a cruise?"

She glanced pointedly at a cluster of *middle-aged* men and women; they were all dressed in pastels and beach attire, with loafers and no socks for the men and strappy *wedge-heeled* sandals for the women.

I couldn't look any further from belonging to that crowd if I tried. "Ah. Point taken."

She laughed. "Also, if you *are* on a cruise, either you're a weirdo who goes on cruises by yourself, or you misplaced your wife. She shopping or something?"

I held up both hands. "You got me. Not on a cruise, and no wife. Here on business, sort of."

"Sort of?"

I shrugged. "Prospective business."

She nodded. "Well, welcome to Alaska. If you value your hearing and your privacy, I'd be out of here by six."

"Why?" I asked. "What happens at six?"

She pointed over her shoulder with a jerked thumb at a poster taped to the wall by the service bar: "Myles and Lexi LIVE in an intimate concert, ONE NIGHT ONLY!"

It was only then that I noticed the stage in the back corner, set up with a pair of mics and stools and minimal audio equipment.

"Myles and Lexi?" I asked.

She frowned at me. "Myles and Lexi North? Grammy- and *CMA-winning* recording artists? Husband and wife duo?"

I nodded as if that meant something to me. "Ohhhh, right. Them."

She rolled her eyes. "You must live under a rock, dude. Jesus."

"Something like that, yeah." Now that she mentioned it, though, I did seem to remember Good

Morning America recording some show or other outside my building back in New York with this particular
pair. The crowd was insane. "So, if they're so famous,
why are they doing some acoustic set *here*, of all places?"

"Because they're family," she answered. "Lexi's
mom is married to the uncle of the people who own
this bar. And that same uncle also happens to be my
father-in-law."

"You're one of the Badds, then?" I asked.

She nodded, grinning. "Guilty as charged." She extended her hand to me, and I shook it. "Kitty Badd."

"Hawk."

She frowned at me. "Just Hawk?"

I shrugged. "Just Hawk." I eyed her, putting two
and two together. "Heard about another place your family owns. Badd Kitty. That have any connection to you?"

Her grin widened. "My husband may have named
it after me, yes."

"So you're *the* Badd Kitty, huh?"

She shrugged. "Guilty as charged again." The
printer spat out a ticket; she grabbed it and began pouring. "Your chili should be up in a minute."

I spent the next half hour or so observing. I'm not a
restauranter, so I don't know the details involved in running a place like this, but I do know quality, efficiency,
and taste, and this place has all three. I observed the
food as it arrived at each table, and every plate looked
appetizing, if not downright mouthwatering. It was simple, classic bar fare but done extraordinarily well. Every

table seemed thrilled to receive their food, and I observed no impatience, no complaints, only high spirits. The staff seemed comfortable with each other, and in between tasks, the waitresses—sorry, *servers*—huddled together and laughed and showed each other things on their phones, but as soon as there was work to be done, they got to it. Kitty, behind the bar, watched everything that happened with an expert, watchful eye. When one waitress got saddled with more tables than she could handle, Kitty came out from behind the bar to alleviate her load and keep things running. All in all, Badd's Bar & Grille has all the hallmarks, in my estimation, of a *well-run* establishment. Considering the profit I know they pull in, any offer I make is going to have to be *eye-watering*. But it won't be the dollar figure that's going to sway them; it's going to be the terms.

I paid my tab with cash, leaving a healthy tip, and headed out on foot to explore the area before popping into Badd Kitty to assess the situation there.

This is an interesting place, that's for sure. Tourists swarmed the sidewalks, pouring in and out of shops and stores and bars in groups and gaggles. I ducked between them, head down, praying I didn't get recognized. So far, so good. Perhaps I was even overestimating my own fame. That'd be nice, in a *hubris-popping* sort of way.

I slowly made my way toward Badd Kitty. Inside, it had a totally different atmosphere from the other place. Here, it was more of a frat party. The TVs played clips of people doing extreme athlete things—snowboarding off mountains, skateboard tricks, skydiving, parkour, BMX, all sorts of unlikely feats of athleticism and daring, along with more comical offerings along the lines of America's Funniest Home Videos. The music was modern pop and *hip-hop*, loud, unedited, and relentless. The crowd was younger, mostly singles and people trying to stop being single—for the night at least. The servers were male and female here, and all attractive and dressed in casual blue jeans and plain *crew-neck T-shirts* with the bar logo large and centered.

The food caters to the crowd and atmosphere, all finger food, snacks, and appetizers served in paper baskets lined with wax paper. The drinks seemed to be mostly mixers and bottled beer—which lined up with the happy hour specials listed on plastic *A-frame* holders on each table.

Once again, the only spot open was a stool at the bar at the far end, near the kitchen entrance. A young man with long black hair and a scraggly goatee worked at a frantic pace at the service bar, pouring, shaking, and mixing with freakish speed and efficiency, each hand doing something different simultaneously. The bartender had her back to me, facing the opposite end of the long bar as she popped the top off of beer bottles and accepted a card from the douchebag on the other side.

I say "douchebag" because he was leaning against the bar with a skeezy, smarmy grin that said he thought he was god's gift to womankind, wearing a tight pink *collar-popped* polo and white slacks, hair permed and coiffed in that idiotic broccoli thing. I want to punch him in the face on principle. The bartender seemed to agree, if her body language was any indication: she was careful to allow no part of his hand to touch hers as she handed him the bottles and took his card. He said something to her, grinning a stupid, irritating, *shit-eating* grin. She rolled her eyes at him and turned away without a word in response to whatever he said.

He leaned over the bar, grabbing her wrist.

Oh, fuck no.

I left my stool and marched that way, intending to eviscerate the poor little fuck. It turned out my evisceration services were unneeded, however—before I got two steps, the bartender broke his hold on her wrist, reversing it so she had his hand bent backward, elbow turned inside out and his shoulder twisted, with his douchey face pressed into the bar.

Within seconds, all activity in the bar stopped, even the music. Two huge men with brown hair and dark eyes hovered nearby, eyes spitting fury, their mammoth muscles bulging as they only just barely restrained themselves from interfering.

"Listen closely, you slimy little *cock-gobllin*." The bartender's voice was a low, vicious hiss, which I was just barely close enough to hear. "You are *not* hot. You are *not* sexy. You are *not* cool." She twisted harder, and he screamed like a little bitch, but she only increased the pressure until he shut the fuck up. "You are a loser.

You are desperate. You are pathetic. I wouldn't fuck you if you were the last living creature on earth, and there weren't any goats. You understand?"

"Aaaahhhh——gah, ahhh, gahhh, ahhh!" He couldn't manage any real words, not with his face smashed into the bar.

"I'm gonna give you a refresher on how this works, okay, SparkleFarts? I take your request. I give you your drinks. I'm a professional, so I smile at you. I'm a woman, which means I have tits. Thanks for noticing. Get a good look and move on like an adult. Give me your money. Go back to your fucktard friends, and that's it. I'm not flirting with you. I don't want you. I don't like you. I'm not going back to your cabin with you. I'm not giving you my number. I'm not giving you my socials. *That's* how this works. You don't put your hands on me or any waitress, bartender, barista, or anyone, anywhere, ever, unless they clearly and specifically give you verbal consent. Are you following along so far?"

"Yes. Yes. Ow. Yes!" his voice was small and pained.

"Good." She picked up one of the bottles of beer he'd set down in order to grab her; she upended it over him, dumping the entire contents into his ear. "Now. Fuck off. Take your friends and get the *fuck* out of my bar. Leave all the *one-star* reviews you want. I don't give a fuck. If I see you again, I'll *really* hurt you. Got it, SparkleFarts?"

"Got it. Got it."

She released him, shoving him hard enough that he went sprawling. "Now fuck all the way off."

He rose, *beer-drenched*, *red-faced* with shame and rage, and scurried out, not waiting for his friends.

One of them, a young woman wearing a skirt so short her ass cheeks played peekaboo, tottered on *four-inch* heels to the bar. "I don't have to leave, do I? I don't even like Paul. He gives me the creeps."

The bartender eyed her. "Behave like an adult, and sure, you can stay. Act like that, and you'll get the same treatment."

The girl tittered a ditzy laugh. "I'll be a good girl, I promise."

The bartender gave her a puzzled, disgusted frown. "Cool. You need a drink?"

The girl sucked her drink down with a loud, slurping crackle. "Sure, thanks!"

"Vodka Redbull?"

"Ohmygod, you're so good! How'd you know?"

An eye roll. "Because I poured it for you five minutes ago, princess."

I suppressed a snicker as I returned to my seat. I waited another couple of minutes before she made her way to my end of the bar.

Finally getting my first real look at her, I discovered a heretofore unknown anomaly: my jaw dropped open, literally, and my palms went clammy, and my words dried up faster than a mirage in the desert.

Fuck me.

She was the single sexiest creature I'd ever seen in my life. I couldn't have stopped staring at her if I had a gun to my head. I didn't even try to look away, and the thought that she might recognize me never even entered my brain.

A touch above medium height, her hair was a dark red, the color of the richest, darkest Burgundy wine. Wavy to the point of almost being curly, it was an explosion of loose spirals around her shoulders and down her chest, the tips trailing just above her tits. Which were, simply put, fucking epic.

The plain, *heather-gray, V-neck T-shirt* bore the logo of the bar, but the sheer size of her cleavage left the logo wildly distorted. There was only a hint of decolletage above the V of the shirt, so it's not like she had it all hanging out. They were just that fucking big. I gave myself a man moment to appreciate them, and then, with the fate of the young douchebag firmly in mind, I ripped my gaze away and met her eyes.

Vividly dark blue, wide and deep and fierce, glinting with intelligence, sparkling and amused. The rest of her was hidden below the level of the bar, but I had no doubt the rest of her curves were just as epic as her cleavage.

"You gonna order a drink or just ogle me?" She planted her palms on the bar opposite me, giving me an *I-dare-you* grin. Friendly, so far, but one that could turn deadly in a heartbeat.

This one was all fire.

She was young—not much over twenty—but her gaze and energy was all woman, someone who's packed a lot of life into a few short years.

I slid a hundred out of my pocket and slapped it on the bar. "Both."

She snagged a test marker from beside the register and swiped it across the bill. "Let me guess… *top-shelf* Manhattan?"

"Not a bad guess, but no. Your best scotch, neat."

"Best is subjective. Most expensive? Best reviewed? Most awards?" She raked me with her eyes, subjecting me to every bit as much of an ogling as I'd given her.

The smirk on her plump red lips was amused, playful, teasing. Her lips glistened scarlet, contrasting with her creamy skin.

She was daring me to make the wrong choice. And there was a wrong one, make no mistake about that. If I got this right, the possibilities were endless. If I got it wrong, the game was over before it could begin.

"The best according to you. Amaze me."

"Amaze you, huh?" She nibbled on her lower lip, letting her eyes flick over my face, a flutter of recognition sparking and then dissolving there. "Good answer."

She turned away, facing the shelves stacked to the ceiling with an infinite variety of scotches, whiskeys, bourbons, and ryes. She lifted on her toes, reaching for something on the very top shelf—just out of reach.

And my god, her ass. There must be a god, because

an ass that perfect can only be an act of artistic creation by a higher power.

I openly ogled her as she danced on her tiptoes for a moment and then sank to her heels with a huff.

"Motherfucker. Zeke!" The *long-haired* bartender hurried over, and she pointed at the bottle she wanted.

He grabbed it, handed it to her, and left for the other end of the bar without a word—which said a lot about how much they must work together.

She grabbed a rocks glass from a stack below the bar, tossed it airborne, flipping end over end, and then poured two generous fingers. "Get a good enough look at my ass, or should I turn around again?"

"It's a start," I said, not quite smirking, daring her to decide if I'm playing along or if I'm really this much of an asshole. "But if you were to turn around and bend over…"

"Yeah, you wish." She slid the rocks glass to me. "Try that."

I picked up the glass, swirled, and sniffed. I didn't recognize the label. I swirled again and took a test sip—my eyes went wide. "Damn. That's impressively good. What is it?"

She shoved the bottle toward me. "Fuck me if I can pronounce it. Some obscure scotch Uncle Rome swears is the best in the world. He and Aunt Kitty went on a *month-long* tour of Scotland and Ireland, and he came back raving about that stuff."

Uncle Rome, is it? Roman Badd—owner and

founder, with his two brothers, of this place. Cousins of the eight brothers who own the original Badd's, making this girl the daughter of one of those eight brothers.

A family affair, indeed. Her aunt, who owns this place with her husband, is bartending at Badd's while this *foul-mouthed*, *fire-haired* siren with an attitude bartends here.

I took another sip. "Not sure if it's the best in the world, but it's damn good. Very damn good."

Her eyes fixed on my lips as I took a nice long drink, swallowed, and licked my lips. Her pupils flared as her eyes darted back to mine, and she realized I'd caught her staring.

"See something you like?" I murmur, giving her the grin that an obsessed novelist, in her steamy fanfic, once described as "arrogant, *panty-melting*, and infuriating."

Her eyes blazed as she yanked the *hundred-dollar* bill off the bar, held it in front of my face in both hands, crumpled it together, and snapped it apart. "Yeah, I do."

She turned away, shoved the bill into the tip jar, and scurried off to pour more drinks.

I caught her looking my way as I sipped my scotch—which, in fact, may be the best I've ever had.

I don't mind her looking.

Because I'm staring just as much.

This could be fun.

Dangerous, but fun.

THREE

Delia

FUCK ME.

What the fuck is wrong with me?

I can't stop my stupid eyes from going over to the arrogant city boy at the service bar.

Well, *boy* may be the wrong term.

The *man.*

The fine as fuck, sexy as hell, mouthwatering, *heart-stopping*, arrogant man.

I marked him the moment he walked in. Clocked him when he got up to intervene when that little pissant grabbed my wrist—and it didn't escape my notice that he didn't just charge in, but held back when he realized I had it under control.

It's been an effort to keep my focus on my work.

As it is, I've already messed up twice—both times when I made the mistake of going over to that end of the bar where he sat.

Those fucking eyes.

Light brown, the color of coffee with a splash of milk, shot through with streaks of green. Piercing, viciously intelligent. Arrogant. Confident. The kind of eyes that take ownership of everything they see. Eyes that I feel carving over my body, no matter where I am.

Zeke sidled up beside me, dunking pint glasses in the sink full of soapy water before shoving them into the washer. "You're off your game, boss lady." He grinned at me. "Have anything to do with the cheechako at the end of the bar?"

"Mind your own goddamn business, Zeke." I didn't look at him as I counted the cash left on the bar by the departing customer. "I'm not off my game."

"You gave Al Bud Lite."

Al, a local who comes in every day at *four-forty-five* on the dot to get shitfaced on Coors Banquet, is *extremely* loyal to his preferred brew. Giving him a Bud Lite is the gravest of offenses. Only the fact that he's scared of me kept him in his seat with no more than a disgusted glare, his arms crossed in refusal to so much as sully his fingers by pushing the bottle away.

I sighed. "Sue me. I comped his next two."

"You poured four shots of Jameson instead of Crown Royal."

"Zeke." It was a warning.

He held up his hands, dripping sudsy water every-where. "Just sayin'. Want me to handle the service end?"

Yes.

But no.

I kept getting drawn over there as if by some mag-netic anomaly.

The anomaly was over six feet tall, with tanned skin, the aforementioned *green-streaked* tan eyes, and dark blond hair beneath a battered and *well-loved* red ballcap that was at odds with the clean, new, expensive cloth-ing he wore. The anomaly had a jawline you could use as an anvil, shadowed by a thick, dark stubble of beard.

The anomaly had a presence I simply was unable to ignore.

"No. I'm good."

Zeke just shrugged. "Whatever you say, *boss-lady*. Good luck with the cheechako."

I filled a few more orders and then let magnetism have its way with me, drawing me back to the anomaly.

I leaned over the bar on my elbows, giving him a nice little downshirt angle, watching to see how he re-acted. He met my eyes first, to make sure I was pay-ing attention, and then he let his eyes slide down. You can't fake his reaction—one of pure male appreciation. Unfiltered, unvarnished. A long, greedy look, and then he brought his eyes back up to mine.

Flicked the empty rocks glass with a fingertip. "Excellent scotch. Your uncle has great taste."

I nodded. "I know." I grabbed the bottle. "Another?"

A blinking moment of consideration. "Only if you'll drink it with me."

"I don't think so."

He clapped a fist over his heart. "You wound me."

"You'll live."

He shook his head. "My fragile ego cannot withstand this rejection. I'm doomed."

"Well, you're certainly *self-aware*. At least you have that going for you." I smirked because good, witty banter is like catnip for me.

He snorted. "You're merciless. My mother would approve."

I blinked at this and at the fact that I was momentarily without a comeback.

He gave me that grin again—the one that made me so irrationally angry I wanted to punch it in, and yet at the same time, it also made me want to climb on his face and ride that grin until he was begging for air.

"Cat got your tongue?" He knew damn well the effect it had on women, I'd wager.

"If I wanted your mother's approval, I'd try out for the rodeo."

He frowned, trying to work that one out. "I know that's an insult, I just can't work out what it is."

I bit my lip, but the laugh spluttered out of me anyway. "Yeah, that one sounded better in my head."

He snorted. "We'll have to work on our banter. What time do you get off?"

"Smooth. You haven't even asked my name yet." I

glanced at the printer as it spat out the ticket, and then uncapped the correct beers and handed them to Stacey.

I crumpled the ticket and rolled it into a ball in my hands, trying like hell to keep my eyes off of his damned sexy mouth, and away from those wicked eyes that seemed to see my every little secret.

"You have a point," he conceded. "My apologies. Would you do me the honor of telling me your name?"

"Delia Badd," I said. "And you are?"

"My friends call me Hawk." He extended his hand to me, and I took it.

Instead of shaking my hand, however, he rose from his stool, bowed over my hand, and kissed the back of it like a medieval courtier.

The move should have been cheesy, lame, and cringey…at best.

Instead…it was fucking hot. I don't know why. Maybe it was those stupid eyes of his, the way they seemed to fuck me six ways to Sunday every time he looked at me. Maybe it was the strength in his hands, the scratch of callouses on his palms from lifting weights. Maybe it was the soft, warm, damp touch of his lips.

"Hawk?" I repeat, sounding as stupid and silly as I feel.

"That's what my friends call me."

"Bold of you to assume you have friends," I said, hoping to get my equilibrium back once I'm on the more familiar ground of *insult-based* humor.

He still had my hand in his, and his eyes were fixed

on mine with laser focus. "What time are you done working, Delia Badd?"

"A quarter past never."

"Delia."

"Hawk?"

"What time?" It was a demand. His eyes blazed, roiling with confidence.

"I close."

"What time?" he repeated the question impatiently.

"*Two-thirty*," I whispered, the answer dragged out of me against my will.

"Back door or front?"

"Back."

His thumb grazed over the knuckle of my forefinger, and then he kissed where his thumb had just been. "See you at the back door at *two-thirty*, Delia Badd."

He swaggered away without a backward look, slipping his aviators on his face.

I watched him go, mainly because the man's ass was divine.

Even after he was gone, I was stuck in place, wondering what had just happened.

Zeke nudged me. "Earth to *boss-lady*."

I jolted, startled. "Jesus, Zeke."

"I called your name twice." He grinned at me. "Cheechako has your number, *boss-lady*."

"No, he doesn't. I didn't give him my number."

Zeke just laughed, which is when I realized he didn't mean literally.

Yeah, I don't know what just happened.

I'm not sure I like it, either.

Hours later, the house lights were on, the last few stragglers were tossing back the dregs of their drinks, and Zeke was restocking while I put up chairs and stools. It was a killer day. Zeke and I made mad tips, the bar sold a shit ton, and the servers all left happy, their aprons stuffed with cash.

Once the doors were locked, I left Zeke to do the rest of the closing work while I counted out the drawers and dealt with the credit card batches.

By 2:30, I was exhausted but pleased. Zeke and I were the last two out, as usual; he waited as I shut off the lights, did one last check to make sure things were clean and properly closed down, and then we exited to the alleyway where we parked.

Zeke's lifted Wrangler was behind my *pimped-out*, late 90s eggplant purple Ford Ranger. Zeke hesitated in his Wrangler, engine running and the door propped open by one foot. "You good, *boss-lady?*"

I nodded. "I'm good. Thanks. See ya."

He always waits to leave to make sure I'm good, the sweet boy. We've established a detente after the awkwardness that ensued when I originally hired him. He developed a major crush on me, which made things weird, and I told him either he got over the crush and acted like an adult because I would never date him, or he could find a new job. He chose door number one, and we've been cool ever since. I don't know if he's still harboring the crush, but if he does, he keeps it under wraps.

Zeke pulled away from the alley, giving his horn two short honks. I waved at his departing taillights, dawdling before leaving myself. I made a production of checking the time on my phone: 2:28 am. So, "Hawk" as his friends call him, wasn't late. I was early.

I unlocked my truck and started it, wishing for the first and probably only time in my life that I was a smoker so I'd have an excuse to hang around waiting.

Which was idiotic. I didn't even like the man. Sure, I was pathetically attracted to his arrogant ass…and his arrogant eyes, and his arrogant jawline. But he was a tourist. It'd be a fling for a night or two, and then he'd go back to wherever absurd specimens like him lived.

No point in getting attached.

I checked my phone again: 2:31. Fuck it. I'm tired and I want to go home.

I shoved my phone into my purse, tossed the purse onto the passenger seat, and slid behind the wheel. Flicked on my headlights…

And screamed exactly like a scream queen from a *black-and-white* King Kong flick.

Why?

My headlights illuminated a tall, *broad-shouldered*

male silhouette at the mouth of the alley, which hadn't been there a split second earlier.

"Oh my god, fuck you," I gasped, one hand clapped to my chest. "You *cannot* sneak up on a girl like that in a dark alley at *two-thirty* in the fucking morning. You're lucky I don't carry a gun. This is Alaska, buddy, you're taking your life into your hands pulling a stunt like that."

Hawk swaggered toward me, hands loose at his sides, green flannel shirt straining around his biceps, lean hips swaying. "I'm sorry, I didn't mean to scare you."

"Then you should do something about that face," I quipped.

He just snorted, shaking his head. "You can't help yourself, can you?"

"No, I cannot. I operate exclusively on caffeine, inappropriate humor, and insults."

"And let me guess, you've long since run out of caffeine?" Hawk asked, now standing in the opening of my door.

"Oh, I ran out of caffeine at like nine this morning. I'm running on sheer stubbornness and psychotic rage at this point."

"Then maybe I should take a rain check," he said, smirking. "I wouldn't want to end up dead in the harbor."

"Passage," I corrected.

He frowned at me. "Pardon?"

"It's not a harbor or a bay, it's a passage. The Inside Passage, to be specific." I waved in the general direction of the water. "So. Why are you here?"

He frowned. "Here, as in Ketchikan? Or here, as in this alley at this particular moment?"

"Both?"

He shrugged. "I'm here on prospective business. Checking out a possible investment. As for here, this particular moment? I'm here because you're hot as fuck, and your attitude turns me on."

Hot as fuck.

Nice.

I mean, it was not the most romantic or *swoon-worthy* compliment I've ever received, but still, it felt nice.

"My attitude turns you on?" I gestured at the passenger seat. "You gonna stand in my door all night, or are you gonna get in and let me give you the *locals-only* tour of town?"

"Don't have to ask me twice," he said and circled to the passenger side.

I slid my purse toward me to make room as he sat down. "So. What's the prospective business?" I asked as I pulled out of the alley.

"I didn't show up in that alley at *two-thirty* in the morning to talk business."

"Oh no?"

"Nope."

"I'm not taking you back to my apartment if that's what you think is happening. *Locals-only* tour was not code for sex." I glanced at him, watching his reaction.

"Of course not. I wouldn't expect that until the

third date at the soonest." There was no grin or laugh to indicate he was joking.

I frowned at him. "Are you for real? You really ascribe to the whole *third-date-sex* thing?"

He eyed me, considering. "Well, no. It's a situational decision. If a girl I'm interested in shows indications that she's down for it, I'll make a move before the first date is half over. I've also waited over a month before making a move."

"Ooooooh, a whole month. Did you survive?" I grinned at him because I was joking. Mostly.

Sort of.

"When was the last time you waited a month before having sex with a guy you're dating?" he asked. "Truthfully."

"Wait, we're *not* lying to each other?" I shook my head. "Weird. I thought we were."

"Why would I be lying to you?"

I rolled my eyes. "' My friends call me Hawk,'" I mumbled in a deep voice, mocking him. "Right. No one calls you Hawk."

He blinked at me and then pulled his phone out. Hit a speed dial and put it on speaker.

It rang six times before someone answered. "Jesus Christ, asshole, don't you ever fucking sleep?" The voice was male, sleepy, and irritated.

"What's your nickname for me?" he asked.

"Hawk."

"Thanks. Sorry, buddy. Go back to sleep."

"Yeah, fuck you too, *ass-clown*."

Hawk hung up, shoved his phone back into his back pocket, and shrugged at me. "I don't lie. I may not always tell the whole truth, but I never lie."

"Never?"

"Never. Not an actual falsehood."

"Just lies by omission."

"Correct."

"So what lies by omission are you telling me?" I asked.

He eyed me. "My real name, my business in Alaska, and my intentions where you're concerned."

I blinked at him, shocked. "Wow, you...you told the truth." I snickered. "About what you're lying to me about."

"Not lying, just not giving you all the information... yet."

"So you will? At some point?"

"At some point, yes."

I narrowed my eyes at him. "I'm not sure how to feel about the fact that I now know you're not telling me things."

"There's a lot you're not telling me. No one ever tells anyone the full truth all the time. We all lie by omission all the fucking time. It's part of the human condition." He shrugged. "We're just not always honest about that with ourselves or each other. I am."

I thought about this.

The Passage rippled in the late spring moonlight, a

field of black and silver. Hawk's eyes took in the view. Flicked to me. Back to the view.

"Sure is pretty out here." He rolled his window down, letting in the cool night air.

"You think *this* is pretty?" I glanced at him. "You down for a bit of a drive?"

"I showed up in your alley at *two-thirty* in the morning, Delia. What do you think?" His eyes held mine, sparking with interest, attraction, and secrets.

I headed north, taking him to one of my favorite turnouts a good fifteen or twenty minutes out of town. It's a place I go to a lot, actually, usually alone, to think. Occasionally, I'll bring a boy there to make out, but usually, it's a solitary spot.

Today, I'm not sure which one it'll be. Depends on how Hawk plays his cards, I guess.

I pawed blindly through my purse, found my watermelon lip gloss and applied it, hoping it came across casual rather than communicating some sort of intent. Which was there, but I didn't want him to know that.

Or maybe I did.

Fuck, I'm confused.

I felt his eyes on my lips as I rolled them in and then popped them with a kissing noise. I gave him a look. "Chapped lips. Don't get any ideas, buddy."

He snorted and shook his head. "Methinks the lady doth protest too much."

I kept quiet, testing his comfortability with silence; he passed the test easily, letting the silence hang, seeming content to take in the view. Which, occasionally, included me.

We reached my favorite turnout, a short length of dirt road that *dead-ended* at the Passage. I did a *three-point* turn so my tailgate faced the water and shut off the engine and headlights. I snagged my hoodie from the bench seat and then shrugged into it as I let down the tailgate and hopped up onto it.

Hawk followed me, settling his ass down next to me—close enough that our arms brushed. Close enough that I could smell his cologne—spicy, smooth, rich, and intoxicating. A very, very expensive scent.

We sat together in companionable silence for a while, taking in the expansive view of the passage, the moon full and round above us, the stars glittering in countless millions. Wind sighed through the pines around us, and an owl hooted somewhere.

"This is an amazing spot," Hawk said after a while. "Appreciate you sharing it with me."

"Tell me something true," I said.

"Something true? Regarding what?" He eyed me, curious.

I shrugged. "Anything, as long as it is one hundred percent the full truth."

He was silent for a long time, thinking about his answer. "I have never, in my whole life, been as attracted to someone as I am to you."

My heart flipped, and my stomach did somersaults. "Not what I meant."

"You meant like secrets?"

I shrugged. "Sure."

He snorted. "You want one of my secrets, you're gonna have to give up one of your own."

"Fine. Deal." I held out my hand, and he shook it, yet again holding on too long, his thumb gently grazing over my knuckles.

I yanked my hand free. "Don't be weird."

He just shook his head, returning his gaze to the water. "I have a lot of secrets."

"I get that impression," I said. "You don't have to tell me a sensitive one."

"My very first business opportunity was a complete mistake." He chuckled. "I was a kid. Eighteen, just out of high school, with a head full of dreams and a heart full of ambition, and not much sense or experience to back it up. I started talking to this older guy in the locker room at my fitness club, mentioned an idea I had for a business, and the older guy said he'd invest. What makes it a lie is that all I had at that exact moment was the idea. And this guy literally wrote me a check right there on the spot and made me write him a promissory note that I'd pay him back with five percent interest within one year."

"But you made it sound like you had the whole idea more fleshed out than you did?" I surmise.

"Hell no. I *flat-out* lied. Told him I was weeks from taking the business live, I just need a bit more capital to get me over the hump. To this day, I don't know if he believed me or if he was just…I don't know. Paying it forward or something."

"So what did you do?" I asked.

He grinned at me. "Spent the next year working twenty hours a day to make the idea I'd lied about a reality."

"And? Did you succeed?"

"Of course I did. I never fail."

I stared at him. "Never? You *never* fail?"

"Nope."

"You *always* win, always succeed—*always.*"

He smirked at me, a cocky tilt of his lips. "Always."

"You always get what you want."

"Always."

"And no one ever tells you no?"

"Rarely. Not never. My secretary tells me no all the time. It's why I hired her."

"So you'd have someone who tells you no?"

"Correct."

I laughed. "Does it work?"

He snorted, nodding. "Yes, it does. I get a hell of a lot more done."

"What kinds of things does she tell you no about?" I ask.

"Oh, all sorts of things. Usually, my impulses."

"Such as?"

He blinked at me. "Such as my predilection for fucking my personal assistants."

A cackle burst out of me. "Wow, okay. Now we're getting somewhere."

"I don't do that anymore. I tasked Harriet with hiring PAs who I won't fuck."

"So…gay men and ugly women?"

He shook his head. "I don't fuck men, Delia. That was weirdly specific."

"But you will fuck an ugly woman?"

He frowned. "I feel attacked."

"Have you?" I pressed.

"Have I what? Had sex with an ugly woman?"

"Yes."

He looked away. "Ugly is rather subjective."

"To a degree. Some people are, objectively, just ugly."

"I don't like the direction of this conversation, Delia."

I cackled. "You have!"

"I neither confirm nor deny the allegation. I do not disclose any information regarding past sexual partners." He said it so smoothly that it almost sounded like a prepared statement, one he'd given before.

I shoved him playfully, and it was roughly akin to shoving a brick wall. "I'm kidding."

He arched an eyebrow at me. "No, you weren't."

"Oh, come on, Hawk. I was playing."

He didn't grin or laugh with me. "Delia, I wouldn't do that. I wouldn't have sex with someone I wasn't attracted to."

"You're very serious, Mr. Hawk." I gave him an exaggerated grumpy face. "I was joking around. Relax. Jesus."

"Your turn," he said. "A secret."

"Just to prove a point, I'll tell you something salacious about me." I wiggled my eyebrows at him.

"Okay."

"The longest I've dated someone before sleeping with them was three weeks and two days. And he was on a business trip for half of that. We...um... *video-called* each other while he was gone, if you know what I mean. But I didn't actually hook up with him for three weeks after we first went out."

"So my month beats your three weeks, especially since you only had a week and a half of *face-to-face* interaction." he grinned at me. "My month was weekly dates, in person."

"Why did you wait so long?" I asked. "I'm genuinely curious."

"Because she wasn't that type of girl. It was an *ill-fated* attempt to do things...differently." He shook his head, snorting.

A cold wind blew, and I pulled my hood up. "So, it didn't go well, is what you're saying."

"Not at all."

I waited, but he didn't elaborate. "Oh, come on. You can't leave me hanging like that. What happened?"

"She had much different expectations than I thought I'd communicated. We dated for a month. I took it slow. Didn't pressure her. Didn't even try anything, not even a kiss, until the third date. When she finally gave me indications that she was ready for more, I let her set the pace."

"What indications did she give, incidentally?" I asked.

"Oh, nothing much. Just, you know, shoving her hand down my pants."

"Oh," I said, laughing. "I guess that's a pretty clear sign."

"I thought so." He sighed. "We slept together, and it was...not bad. But she clearly wasn't very experienced. Which was fine. But I think a lot of her expectations for how sex should go was based on some serious misinformation."

I snickered. "Oh boy. That sounds interesting."

"It certainly was. She thought we were supposed to switch positions every thirty seconds. I'm not sure if her one previous partner taught her that or if she watched too much porn or what, but it was fucking annoying."

"Annoying fucking, you mean," I said, laughing. "So...then what?"

"Then...she told me she loved me. And confessed that she'd lied about being on birth control."

I stared at him. "No!"

"Good thing I didn't take her at her word and insisted on using protection anyway."

"You think she was trying to trap you?"

He nodded. "Oh, for sure. Maybe not trap, but she was certainly delusional."

"And that was when you swore to only go for the easy girls who put out on the first date?"

"Exactly," he said, without any hint of a joke in his tone or expression.

I frowned his way. "I can't tell if you're joking or not."

"I'm not."

I made a show of shifting away from him. "Well, if you think that's happening here, please, allow me to disabuse you of that misapprehension."

His *green-streaked* eyes bored into mine. "I never thought that, Delia."

I rolled my eyes. "Oh, come off it. I know I give off 'easy' vibes."

"You do not." He said it with a straight face, I'll give him that.

"I do too. I've been told that to my face." I cupped my boobs. "It's these. Men seem to think big boobs on a more slender frame is some sort of indication of hyper-sexuality. Or something. I don't know."

"Bullshit. The men who said that were just inse-cure assholes who thought you owed them sex simply because they're a man and you're a woman." He shook his head. "Men like that ought to be castrated."

I stared at him for a moment. "You really believe that?"

"Do you really believe you give off easy girl vibes simply because of the size of your chest?"

"I didn't say I believed it, just that I've been told that."

"But yet, you've gone out of your way to make sure I know you're not going to sleep with me tonight, even though I've given you precisely zero reason to think I think that's gonna happen."

"Why, I do believe you're calling me out, sir," I said, feeling pissed off and embarrassed. "How am I supposed to know you're not hoping I'm gonna fuck you right here in this truck bed?"

He leaned close, face inches from mine, his cologne making my head swim; his scent, his heat, his proximity—shit, his mere presence left me dizzy and aroused and disoriented. "Because if I thought that was a possibility—if that was my intention in any capacity—you'd be naked right now, riding my cock and screaming my name."

An image flashed through my mind—me, naked, riding his cock, and screaming his name. I saw it, damn near felt it. And fuck, but it felt real, for a split second. His hands would be powerful and rough, digging into my hips. Or, more likely, grabbing my big, bouncing tits.

My core went slick and wet as the unwanted image slashed through me, making me squirm on the tailgate as arousal seeped out of me.

Goddammit.

"Bold of you to assume you can make me scream your name," I whispered, the foolish, stupid, *ill-advised* words tumbling out of me, because I am, in fact, a complete and total dumbass.

Don't poke the bear, Delia.

"Do not challenge me, Delia Badd," Hawk whispered, his voice hot against my ear. "You're one wrong move from finding out exactly how hard I can make you come."

My core clenched, my nipples turned to diamonds, and my lungs froze solid, even as my skin burned. I've never been affected like this—by anyone, ever.

It honestly terrifies me.

His nose slid against the side of my neck, his words hot whispers against my skin. "You're about to combust, aren't you?"

"No," I lied.

"Yeah, you are." He leaned against me, his hard body too close, too hot, too solid. He rested a hand on my knee, and my thighs pressed together involuntarily. "One touch, and you'd come apart. Wouldn't you?"

"You wish," I whispered. "And wouldn't you like to know?"

"Both are true. But that doesn't make what I said any less true." He nuzzled behind my ear, and I shivered, gasping. "You're about to come and I haven't so much as touched you."

"Am not."

He laughed. "Don't be petulant just because I can read you like a book." His hand on my knee slid higher, and I pressed my thighs together even tighter. "See? The way you're closing up tells me how turned on you are. You just don't want to be."

"Cocky bastard, aren't you?" I whispered.

"Absolutely I am. But I'm not wrong. Am I?" He nipped my earlobe. "We're not going to lie to each other, are we, Delia? I don't promise to always tell you every-thing, but I *do* promise I'll never lie to you. Can you do the same?"

"Yes. No."

"Which is it?"

"I don't know." My voice was breathy, vapid, and stupid.

What the hell kind of sorcery was he using on me?

His hand inched higher up my thigh, callouses scrap-ing over denim. He was mere inches from my core, and I was shaking all over, core pulsing, nipples aching. I couldn't pull in a full breath. Couldn't think straight.

I had to get away. I couldn't take this any longer. I wasn't about to let this man know how affected I truly was.

I pushed off the tailgate, and my shaky legs nearly gave out—I caught myself before I went sprawling, lurch-ing like a newborn colt before regaining my balance. Embarrassment burned on my face as I stormed away from the truck and him.

I went down to the water's edge, letting the cool wind carve across my face, cooling the burn, settling my nerves.

Fuck, fuck, fuckity fuck.

What the actual hell was *that*?

I scraped my hand through my hair. Now that the irrational arousal was gone, anger welled up in its place. I stormed back to my truck, jerked open the driver's door, and got in, gunning the engine. "You want a ride back to town, better get in now or I'll leave your ass here."

He hopped down, shut my tailgate, and slid in beside me. I barked my tires on the gravel, fishtailed onto the tarmac, and headed back for town.

"Delia," Hawk started.

I held up a hand. "Nope. Not a word."

He lapsed into silence, and I resolutely refused to look at him.

For at least a whole minute.

When I did finally sneak a glance at him, the bastard was smirking. Which only pissed me off further.

"You think you're funny, don't you?" I snap.

"No, I think *you're* funny." He eyed me, the smirk fading. "What are you so pissed off about?"

"Nothing. Never mind."

He rolled his eyes. "Suit yourself."

In my experience, when you give a man the 'never mind, whatever, nothing' *brush-off*, they can't leave it alone. They have to know.

Hawk seemed immune. Which only bothered me more.

"Really?" I asked. "You're just gonna leave it like that?"

"You said never mind. I'm taking you at face value."

Well, if it isn't me, hoisted by my own petard.

"You're obnoxious," I snapped.

"I know."

"And cocky."

"Very much so. Although, I prefer to think I'm merely confident. Because I'm only cocky when I know I can back it up." He gave me that damned smirk yet again.

The conflicting, competing desires to punch the smirk off his face and ride it until I screamed was renewed with increased fury.

And he seemed to damn well know it, the bastard.

I don't speak to him the rest of the way back to town. He pointed out his truck, the only vehicle parked in the bar's lot—a black pickup with muddy tires, a lift, bullbar with a winch and KC lights, and windows tinted to the very edge of legality.

It doesn't fit him at all, for a reason I couldn't explain—it's a perfectly reasonable truck for a man like him to drive in a place like this.

He opened his door but didn't get out. "I had a good time, Delia. Thank you."

I snorted. "You enjoyed the tense ride back, did you?"

He grabbed my hand, the one resting on the console between the seats, and kissed the back of it again, sending a thrill shivering through me. "Yes, in fact, I did. Because I know exactly why you were pissed off at me."

"And why, pray tell, is that?" I demanded.

He flipped my hand over so my palm faced up and nuzzled my palm, kissed my wrist, my forearm—soft, delicate, damp, warm, nuzzling little kisses that sent heat blasting and billowing through my body, centering at my core, making my sex weep with incoherent, undeniable arousal.

"Because you're turned on and you don't want to be." His voice is low, and rough, and close. "I affect you, and you hate that."

"You do not," I hissed.

"We said we wouldn't lie."

"You said that, not me." Oops. I just admitted to lying.

His lips brushed my ear. "So you're saying your panties aren't soaked right now?"

Fuck.

I gulped. "Nope."

"You're a shitty liar," he murmured. "See ya 'round, Delia Badd."

And with that, he just fucking left.

The cocky asshole got into his big stupid truck, started the big, stupid, noisy engine, and drove his stupid, sexy, obnoxious ass away from me.

It left me so turned on that I didn't know which way was up, with absolutely drenched panties and a terrible attitude.

This was a very serious problem.

FOUR

Hunter

Back at my *ugly-as*-fuck house, I sat alone on the back deck, a glass of scotch in my hand that I didn't drink.

Why?

Because it was wholly inferior to the obscure stuff I had at Badd Kitty.

And because I'm too lost in thought about Delia.

She was a complication I didn't need. At fucking all.

I mean, how the fuck was I supposed to handle this situation? It wasn't immediately obvious what her role in the larger Badd collection of companies was, but I wasn't sure how much that mattered—regardless of her official role, she obviously had sway. Which meant I had to be very, very careful with her.

I stopped mixing business with pleasure because it caused problems. I'd bang my assistant, things would go sideways when I got tired of her or she wanted more than I'd clearly defined at the outset as nonnegotiably not happening, and then things would get messy, and I'd have to fire her, and then Harriet would have to hire a new girl, and rinse and repeat.

Now, I find my pleasure strictly outside of work. No exceptions. The problem that has arisen lately is that I've been increasingly bored with and uninterested in the women I've spent time with. They're all the same. Wealthy, privileged, vapid, and boring. They want the trappings. The billionaire. The attention. The fun. For a long time, I was content with that. See and be seen, gallivant around Manhattan with beautiful women with the right pedigrees and resumes. The sex was good. But…

I'm bored.

It's deeper than mere boredom, though.

It's not just that everything and everyone is the same. That is true enough—the women I've dated the past few years have all been pretty well interchangeable. And honestly, that's true of my life as a whole. One day is the same as the next and the last. Making money has become rote. It's not fun anymore. It's not challenging.

I guess that's at the root of why I'm here in Alaska.

And more to the point, why I'm so interested in Delia Badd.

She's unlike anyone I've ever met. She's not the tall, willowy model type that is so prevalent in the circles I frequent in NYC. She's not vapid or clueless. She's got bite. A sharp mouth and quick wit. She's not blinded by who I am. I mean, sure, she doesn't seem to *know* who I am, not really. I guess I take that for granted—being known on sight. The hat, casual clothes, and nickname wouldn't fool anyone back home. So either she doesn't realize, or she doesn't care.

It's refreshing. Frustrating in a way because she doesn't respond to anything I do or say in a way I'm accustomed to. But that makes it a challenge.

She's a challenge.

And the issue is that I'm already losing sight of why I'm here—to purchase or invest in the Badd's Bar spread of companies.

My phone rings; it's Givey.

I answered it and put it on speaker. "What's up, Givey?"

"You're being weird."

"I've always been weird," I answered. "That's not new."

"Weirder than usual. You're in fucking Alaska? And I had to hear it from The Hatchet?"

I sighed. "It was a *last second* decision."

"One you need to explain because I'm fuckin' lost. What the hell business could you possibly have in motherfucking *Alaska*, Hunter?" His perplexed frustration is apparent, if nothing else, in his use of my actual name.

"A restaurant acquisition, or at least an investment." I sipped the scotch, grimaced, and set it aside.

"In Alaska."

"Yes. Not a restaurant, though, a bar. Or, rather, a few of them. Owned by a very interesting family."

A long silence. "What's her name?"

"What are you talking about?"

"The girl. What's her name?"

"Givey."

"Hawk?" He laughed. "Sure, a bar. A few bars. *In Alaska*. Except for vacation, you haven't set foot outside Manhattan in your life. Sure, you own businesses and companies all over the world...through intermediaries, umbrellas, and shells. You didn't go to fucking China when you bought that telecom company. You didn't go to Colorado when you invested in that medical startup. You own a whole fucking *thirty-story* skyrise in Chicago that you've never laid eyes on, let alone set foot in. And now, suddenly, you decide you're investing in some random company in motherfucking *Alaska*, and you have to go there in person for...what reason? You could have, and probably did, look at the details in a *write-up* put on your desk by that Elara girl you asked me about, decided you wanted to invest or purchase, and then all you do is send an email or make a few phone calls, and there it is, done. What you don't do is *go* there. So...what is it, buddy? Are you having an existential crisis? A *mid-life* crisis a decade or so early? Or...it's a woman."

I stood up and paced the width of the expansive travertine back patio. "Definitely a crisis of some sort. Coming here was...impulsive. I've been expanding into

the restaurant industry lately—I have three new properties in New York. It's a different field with new challenges. And I guess I wanted something different, so
Elara and I chose this portfolio. They're a different kind
of people and they run their business in a very unique
way. A traditional approach to investment or acquisition wouldn't work. And, to be honest, I was bored and
needed a change of scenery. So, here I am."

Givey laughed. "You're bored."

"Shut up," I muttered.

"No, no. Tell me more, mister world's most eligible bachelor, who has literally anything and everything
he could ever want or need at his fingertips."

"Exactly!" I shouted. "In the world of business, I've
done it all. I've conquered every Everest. At least, those
that interest me. I have no interest in competing with
Meta or Google or whoever. And I have no interest in
the literal Everest—I'm not a thrill seeker. But yeah, I'm
bored. I'm bored with business. Bored with life. Bored
with women. This is a challenge."

"And her name is…."

I huffed, annoyed that he knew me so well. "Delia
Badd."

"Does she know who you are? Because if I was a
betting man, I'd wager you're trying to go incognito,
lying about who you are and what you really want."
There's a subtext of laughter in his voice.

"Shut up."

He did laugh out loud, then. "I'm right! God, I

know you too well." Another laugh. "That's why you called to ask me about what I call you. You're telling her something like 'my friends call me Hawk.'" He dropped his voice into a rough, mocking growl that sounded nothing like me. "Tell me I'm wrong."

"You're fucking obnoxious is what you are."

He sighed. "Hawk, buddy. You're a fucking mess."

"Gee, thanks, ol' buddy old pal." I dropped back into the chair and sipped the scotch again, only to grimace and put it aside again. "Fuck, that's not great."

"What isn't?"

"This scotch I'm drinking. Delia gave me some scotch her uncle brought back from Scotland, and now this stuff I had Elara stock my new house with tastes like dog piss in comparison."

Givey just laughed. "What's she like?"

"Fuck, man. A wildcat. A siren. No, she doesn't know who I am, but I get the sense she wouldn't care if she did."

"That must really tickle your pickle," Givey said. "A woman who doesn't immediately throw herself onto your dick? What? Does such a woman even exist? I've known you since before you were Hunter Hawkins, billionaire. Women have always thrown themselves at you, billions or not."

"She doesn't. She wants me, but she's fighting it. And I honestly don't know what to do. Not that she's playing hard to get or whatever, but because it's a conflict. I really do want their bars."

"Why?"

I blinked. "Why? Why what?"

"Why do you want these bars in particular? What is it about them?"

"I don't know. They're different. It's *family-run* but very successful. Simple, as in uncomplicated, but quality. I like the way they do business."

"And when you appreciate something, you have to own it. Or control it in some way." Givey's voice was serious, then.

"Dude. Are you a psychoanalyst now?" I demanded, pissed off.

"Of you, yeah. Look, man, you're my best friend—you're like a brother to me. I'm on your side, ride or die, you know that. But you need to look at your motivations. Do you want the woman, the business, or both? Because I'm not sure you can have both."

I sighed. "I know. They're a big, complex, proud family, from what I can tell. And Delia seems to be in the thick of the business, although I'm not sure where she fits into the hierarchy. And yeah, she doesn't know who I am. I don't think."

"Well, let me spell something out for you, okay? You keep lying to her, it's gonna bite you in the ass. Women hate that shit. Obviously, I don't know the first thing about this chick, but if she's like everyone I've ever known, she probably has some kind of trust issues. And if you suddenly one day come clean, like hey babe, oh by the way, I'm actually Hunter Hawkins, the

world-famous billionaire playboy philanthropist genius…
it's not gonna go well."

"That's a misquote. And yeah, I know." I sighed
again, pinching the bridge of my nose. "I told her I never
lie outright, but I do lie by omission a lot. Hopefully,
that buys me enough leeway that when I do tell her
the truth, it won't feel as much like I was lying to her."

"If you tell her that *after* you buy her family's company that they've spent the last how many years building, I'm not sure it'll matter," Givey said.

"Forty years. Two generations."

Givey laughed. "Ah, fuck, man. You do know how
to pick 'em."

"Go on IG and look at Badd's Bar—B-A-D-D."

Silence as he did so. A few moments later, he whistled. "Quite a family, man, holy shit. You're *sure* you
know what you're walking into?"

"Absolutely the fuck not."

"At least you're aware. I mean, some of those dudes
look like they could snap you in half without breaking
a sweat." He chuckled, sighing. "Hawk, brother. You
need to think hard about this, okay? You'll be fine because you know that if this goes south, it won't affect
you. Your money, your status, your reputation, your
livelihood—none of that is threatened if this goes bad,
business-wise or personally. But these people? This is their
life. This is two generations of blood, sweat, and tears
you're messing with. You're not a monster, and you're
not some soulless, heartless, robotic, grasping, villainous

overlord. But if you're not fucking careful, that's exactly how you'll seem to these people. To this Delia chick, especially. And honestly, I don't know how the fuck you're gonna walk that line."

"Me either, Givey. Me either."

"If you're asking me, I'd focus on the girl. You can find a business challenge anywhere. You don't need these particular bars. You don't *need* anything. You could sign over control to the board and go float on a yacht on the Amalfi coast the rest of your life."

"I'd lose my goddamned mind."

"Yeah, I know. My point is, you don't *need* them. And I'm not sure they need you. Where's the benefit for anyone?"

"I just got here today. I don't know what they do or don't need. I'm still assessing the situation." I stood and paced some more.

Givey just snorted. "I've said my piece. You're gonna do what you're gonna do. Just don't fuck this family over, Hawk. Please?"

"Oh fuck you. I'm not gonna fuck anyone over."

A pause. "You have before." His voice was low, hesitant.

"Fuck you," I snapped. "I was young, arrogant, and stupid. I don't do things that way anymore." I hated the burn in my gut at the memory his words brought up.

"I know you regret it, Hawk—why do you think I brought it up? To remind you. You're not that guy anymore. Marissa's family didn't deserve what you did to them, and you only did it because of what she did to you. Which was shitty. I get it. But you ransacked her whole family's life—tore it to pieces out of pure vindictiveness. And I do *not* want to see you go back down that path, not a single step."

"This is *not* that, Givey. It's not. For one, I don't think Delia would do what Marissa did."

"You didn't think Marissa would do what Marissa did," he said, huffing a humorless laugh.

"Why the fuck are you still talking about this? That was almost ten years ago. I apologized to them. I made it right." I had to grip the phone until my knuckles hurt to keep from hurling it across the backyard.

Givey sighed. "I wouldn't be your one and only true friend and advisor if I didn't caution you. You can't always get what you want. Which is what you're used to. You may not be able to get both the business win *and* the relationship win. You may have to pick." A pause. "And you need to clue her in to your real identity sooner rather than later."

"I know. I know. I will."

"The longer you delay, the harder it'll be. I say this from experience."

"I hear you, Givey. I do."

"But will you listen? That's the real question."

We ended the call, then, and I sat outside until past dawn, thinking.

I spent the next few days avoiding Delia, mainly. I told myself I was investigating the rest of the Badd operation, which I was. But really, deep down, I was avoiding Delia. I spent time at the original Badd's, as well as the nightclub one, and I even took a *two-day* trip up to Anchorage to check out that location. Which was a bit of a mess, even to my inexpert eye. The servers didn't know the menu, the food came out slow and wasn't hot, and it just overall didn't have the same feel as the Ketchikan locations.

The simplest explanation I could find is that it didn't have a Badd family member managing it. Which didn't bode well for my plans. If the secret sauce that made the Ketchikan locations successful was the direct, *in-person* input and management of the Badd family, then my getting involved would only result in more of the same—franchises would fail because the family couldn't be everywhere. They didn't seem to want to leave Ketchikan to manage their own franchise.

Where did that leave me?

I asked questions.

Who managed Badd's Bar and Grille? Who managed Badd Kitty? Who managed Badd Night? Sebastian Badd, the eldest of the eight brothers, was the CEO of the Badd's empire, such as it was. The rest of the family helped out here and there, but most of them had their own businesses. Roman, Delia's uncle, owned Badd Kitty on paper, but it seemed Delia was the GM, and Roman…I wasn't sure what he did, day to day.

It isn't clear whose child Delia is. I felt like Sebastian, but I had to be careful of asking too many probing questions, especially personal ones. As it was, I already got some distrustful looks from the staff at the Ketchikan locations. The Anchorage staff just seemed lost.

Eventually, after almost a week of avoidance, observation, assessment, and pages of notes and thoughts, I was no closer to knowing how to approach the whole thing than I was when I first arrived.

It was a weird place to be. I always know what to do. It's not always right, but right or wrong, I'm typically very decisive.

Delia is the difference.

She's in my fucking head.

I could have made her come, that night in the back of her truck. And fuck, I wanted to. I've never had a woman literally run away from me like that before, and I don't know what to do about it. Givey was right—I *am* used to women throwing themselves onto my dick. I mean, sure, I wasn't always a billionaire, but my family was, and is, extraordinarily wealthy. So it wasn't always just me, my looks, my personality. It's always been about who I am and who my family is. What we have. What I have.

Delia didn't seem to know me or recognize me, so her reaction, as far as I can tell, was genuine.

And genuinely conflicted. Why? Fuck if I know.

If she's not conflicted because of who I am, then what's her issue?

Why wouldn't she let herself have anything to do with me? Why get angry when I turned her on?

I understand nothing.

Only that she *is* attracted to me, and I to her.

Beyond that? I don't know a goddamn thing for certain.

Which was, ostensibly, why I found myself bellied up to the bar at Badd Kitty at one thirty in the morning, sipping that fucking amazing scotch, and watching Delia dance gracefully and efficiently behind the bar. She pretended not to see me at first, and then, finally, after a full ten minutes of sitting there like a doofus, waiting, she finally poured me a finger without a word and went back to work.

I sipped. Watched sports replays I didn't give a shit about. Watched Delia work. Which was, in a word, a masterclass in bartending. She never hurried, even when the bar was *standing-room-only* and customers were shaking credit cards and cash and empties at her. Yet, despite never seeming to hurry, she worked consistently, quickly, and without fumbling.

I let her work. When I finished my drink, she poured another, again without a word or even eye contact.

Two o'clock came, and the lights came up, and tabs were paid, and the floor cleared out. No one bothered me, even though I never saw Delia confer with anyone regarding me.

The male bartender with the long black hair cleaned up while Delia vanished into the back. *Two-thirty* came, and the male bartender shut off the lights, leaving me bathed in darkness only cut by the dim red glow of the exit sign and the faint yellow from the office, visible through the kitchen doors.

"Put your chair up," he told me. "And make sure she's safe before you leave."

"Got it."

Another ten minutes later, I heard the office door close and the light shut off. I slid off my stool, put it up, and put my empty glass on the service side of the bar with a *hundred-dollar* bill inside it.

Delia came out and found me leaning in the door-less entryway between the bar area and the kitchen. She looked exhausted. Pale. Dark circles under her eyes.

"Figured when I *flat-out* ignored you, you'd get the picture." She jerked her head toward the kitchen. "C'mon. Exit is this way."

"You weren't ignoring me," I said. "You were working. And I was content to wait."

Through the kitchen—stainless steel counters, shelves, and appliances; cold stoves and grills and ovens; racks of utensils and cookware, racks of buns and bread, racks of paper and plastic products. A narrow back area with *walk-in* fridges and freezers, at the far end of which was a door, over which glowed an exit sign.

We came out into the alley, where the only vehicle was her purple pickup.

"What do you want, Hawk?" Her eyes were distant. "Any questions you'd like to ask me directly?" When I frowned at this statement, she narrowed her eyes at me. "You've been asking questions. Makes me wonder what you're really doing here."

"I told you the truth. I'm in Ketchikan on prospective business."

"Badd's is not for sale." She turned away from me, unlocking her vintage truck with the key. "So if that's the prospective business, you can go back to wherever it is you came from because that's not happening." She shoved her door open but whirled on me. "And I do not appreciate being fucked with."

I stepped closer. "I wasn't fucking with you. I'm *not* fucking with you."

"You show up, act all interested in me, and then you ghost me, poke your nose into my family's business, asking questions. You even went to fucking Anchorage?" She flipped me off. "You're fucking with me. Not interested."

"Delia, wait. Please." I never asked; I ordered. So that felt weird.

She sighed, hanging in the V between her truck's body and door. "What, Hawk? Or whatever your actual name is."

"My interest in you is separate from my business

interests." I held her eyes, hoping she'd see the truth in them.

"*Uh-huh.*"

"It's the truth."

"Then why go dark on me for a week? If you're interested in me as a woman and a person, and not just because my dad owns the businesses you seem interested in buying, then why vanish on me?"

"Because you confuse me."

"I confuse you?" She laughed. "That's rich. How?"

"You're nothing like the women I usually date. And I don't know what to do with that." I stepped closer, my feet carrying me to within a foot of her; she turned into me, staring up at me with a fierce *I-dare-you* spark in her eyes.

"A man like you is never confused by a woman. Try the fucking truth."

"A man like me?" I asked. "What does that mean?"

She plucked at my *black-and-blue* flannel shirt. "You're not fooling anyone with this shit, or the truck. You're about as Alaskan as…" she shook her head. "Fuck, I'm too damn tired to finish the fucking metaphor. I don't know. You're as Alaskan as I am a New Yorker."

"What does that have to do with me being confused by you?"

An annoyed roll of her eyes. "You're a player. Everything about you screams it. Your arrogance. The things you say. The way you say them. The way you touched me. You know the effect you have on women. I do not confuse you. But you still acted interested and then vanished for a week. Try the truth. I don't expect the full truth from you since, as we established last time, you're a master of lying by omission. But at least give me *something*."

I sighed, bracing my hands near hers on the roof of her truck and the upper rim of the door. "What I said *was* the truth, Delia. You're unlike any woman I've ever met. And I don't know what to do with you. And yes, my business interests do involve your family. I was asking questions. I went to Anchorage. But I swear to you, when I came here and walked into that bar," I pointed at the back door, "I had no idea who you were or what your connection was to anything. My interest was, and is, genuine. And yes, I avoided you on purpose because my interest in you does absolutely conflict with my interest in your family's business."

"Well, let me settle that conflict for you." She grabbed the front of my shirt and pulled me close, lifting up to put her mouth and nose inches from mine. "Fuck...off. We aren't for fucking sale, asshole."

I couldn't resist. How was I supposed to? She was right there.

I kissed her.

Not a little bit—not chaste, or sweet, or innocent, or exploratory. I kissed like I wanted to fuck her.

Because I did.

I grabbed her long, thick, dark red hair—burnished

to a *black-silver-purple* by the light of the full moon, wrapped the length of it around my fist, and jerked her against me, slashing my mouth onto hers. Her body bumped flush against me, tits smashed flat, hips pressing into mine. She gasped in shock at the sudden violence of the action, her hands bracing against my shoulders, pushing me away.

"Fuck—" she breathed.

And then my lips hit hers, and my tongue slid along her lower lip. She tasted like vanilla and cherries. Her mouth was soft and warm as she opened it to mine, another, softer gasp escaping her as she involuntarily melted against me.

I was just as shocked as she was.

I didn't know I was going to kiss her—I just did it, unbeknownst to the both of us.

But now that I was kissing her, I couldn't stop.

Vanilla and cherries.

Her tongue danced against mine and then dipped into my mouth, and her hands ceased pushing me away. Instead, her fingers curled into fists, bunching in my shirt—and then she pulled me closer, tugged me down. She moaned into my mouth, and one hand skated over my shoulder and cupped the back of my neck and dug into my hair.

The woman can kiss—goddamn.

My head spun as her lips warred with mine and her tongue darted and danced and slashed against mine and in my mouth and along my lower lip. She writhed against me, pushing her hips against mine. My cock stood hard as a fucking tent pole behind the zipper of my jeans, and she ground against me.

I pulled away first, panting, still gripping her hair in one hand, the other wrapped low around her waist, holding her hips against mine.

"You," she finished, on a shuddery breath. "Fuck you."

Arousal seared through me. Need. Desire. Hunger.

She blinked up at me from a distance of inches, fire in her eyes and desire written in every line and curve of her lush, glorious body.

I looked for words and found none. I held her gaze and gripped her hair tight in my fist, tugged her head backward gently but firmly, tipping her chin up so she couldn't look away. There was nothing to say—my arousal was undeniable. My need was written in my eyes—I know she saw it, and I know she understood it because her eyes sparked fury, even as her mouth fell open, begging me silently to kiss her again.

So, I did.

And this time, I let my hand slip down to explore her ass. And god, what an ass. Even hidden behind tight denim, it was full and round and firm. As I kissed her mouth and cupped her ass, she whimpered and gasped, tipped her hips against mine and clung to the back of my neck.

Fuck, I needed more.

I pressed her against the seat, and she instinctively

hopped up onto it sideways, and her thighs locked around my waist.

"Hawk," she breathed.

This wasn't exactly aligned with the advice Givey had given me, but I was lost to need. Lost to my attraction to this woman, sucked in by her fire, her ferocity. Teased by her ability to confuse me, surprise me. Obsessed by her beauty, her lush curves.

I've never been great at restraint, and she wanted me. I felt it. Tasted it in the way she kissed me.

Even still, I moved slowly, telegraphing my intent as I released her hair and slid my hands down to her hips. She tilted backward, grabbing my shirt and taking me with her as she lay backward on the bench seat of her truck. I bent over her, half in the vehicle, and kissed the unholy hell out of her.

And my god, she gave as good as she got.

I groaned as her tongue swept my mouth. She huffed openmouthed into the kiss and then slid her tongue into my mouth and tugged my shirt up to slip her hands onto my bare back. Scratching her nails down my spine, she arched into me, moaning as I crushed against her.. I mirrored her moans and groans at every turn, gasping when she sucked my tongue into her mouth, groaning when she swept hers into my mouth, hissing when she raked her nails in rough circuits across my back and shoulders.

Her hips tilted against mine, begging for more.

Who am I to deny a woman's want?

I freed the button of her jeans and lowered the zipper.

She broke the kiss, peering up at me, eyes *heavy-lidded*, mouth open, lips swollen. "Hawk, what are you…"

I nipped her lower lip and then tongued where I bit as I hooked my fingers into the waistband of her underwear and jeans and slowly dragged them down together.

For a moment, she did nothing—no resistance, but no help, either.

I pulled away from her, my eyes locked on hers as I *oh-so-slowly* drew her jeans and panties down—inch by inch, past her hips, and then sticking at the plump, generous swell of her buttocks. I left them there, just above the crest of her ass, her belly bare, a sprinkling of dark stubble peeking above the elastic of her *bubblegum-pink* panties.

"Hawk?" she breathed. A question.

I answered silently, pushing her *T-shirt* up past her navel. Bent, my eyes still *laser-focused* on hers as I slowly bent and pressed my lips to her stomach above her cute, shallow little belly button.

At the touch of my lips, she gasped, and her eyes squeezed shut. "Oh."

I drew her jeans down further, momentarily leaving her panties in place. Pink briefs with a tiny little white bow centered on the waistband. I scented her, then—arousal. Drawing her jeans past her knees, I ran my hand up her bare thighs, to her hips. Nuzzled her belly, kissing her navel. The tender slice of skin between navel and underwear.

Her hips tipped. Flexed.

She gasped again as I slid the elastic down an inch, my lips sliding over skin as I exposed it.

"Oh…god," she whispered. "Hawk."

I hooked my fingers in the elastic and pulled, but only enough to draw the waistband lower, not enough to pull the underwear off anymore.

"I need to taste you," I murmured. "Need to taste you as you come all over my mouth."

She was panting, gasping, belly sucking in and swelling firm with each hard breath, chest rising and falling.

She clutched at my arms, clinging and squeezing. "Hawk. Fuck."

"You have to say yes, Delia." I slid my nose against the cotton of her underwear, pressed my lips to her seam, smelling her arousal dampening the fabric, darkening it with her desire. "Tell me yes, Delia. Tell me I can make you shake. Make you scream. Say yes."

"You…" she trailed off, her hands going to my shoulders. Pushed me lower. "You can try."

FIVE

Delia

I'M SO DAMN PATHETIC.

I know he's lying to me.

I knew he was, and is, hiding something from me. He's after my family's business. He didn't deny it. He didn't give me the whole truth, but he didn't deny that much.

And then I fucking *kiss* him?

What the hell is *wrong* with me?

I mean, sure, he kissed me first, but did I stop him? No. Did I tell him to fuck off? Yes, but he didn't. And I didn't make him.

And now I'm on my back on the bench of my truck, and he's got my pants half off, asking if he can fucking taste me as if he's sampling wedding cake or some shit.

And I'm about to let him.

"You can try," I heard myself whisper.

"I should make you beg, but I can't wait any fucking longer." His words dropped like hot stones against my sex, breath steamy against my seam despite the cotton barrier.

Make me beg? Fuck that. I don't beg. Men beg *me*.

But god, I was close to begging. Not that I would, but I wanted to come so goddamn bad it hurt. Work has been so busy lately I haven't had time to give myself the O I need—that shit takes time. And snacks. And power tools.

I *need* to come.

And god, but this man had me writhing, had my core pulsing, my clit aching. I wasn't sure what dark magic he possessed or what deal he made with the devil to get it, but he had me more turned on than I've been in...I wasn't even sure. A long, long, *long* time.

Maybe ever.

Again, not that I'd admit it. I'd never give this man an inch. I wasn't sure what he wanted from me, but I'd take an orgasm if he was, in fact, capable of giving me one.

"Try?" He sounded almost offended. "Delia, I'll do so much fucking more than merely *try*."

My fingers, the traitorous bastards, feathered into the hair at his nape—longish, in need of a cut, beneath that ridiculous, *out-of-place*, *ratty-ass* red ballcap. Fuck that thing. I raked it off his head and scraped my hands through his hair.

"Then shut up and show me what you've got," I snapped, falling back on attitude and anger.

Instead of merely yanking my underwear off, as I expected, he reached down and pulled off my big, ugly, practical, *slip-on*, *non-slip* shoes and tossed them to the footwell of the passenger side. My socks.

What the hell was his game?

Before I could wonder any further, he yanked my jeans completely off, leaving me in nothing but my work tee and pink briefs. And my god, if I'd known this was going to happen today, I'd have worn sexier underwear.

A thong, maybe.

Or nothing at all.

But no, I was wearing pink panties. Cute and comfy and my favorites because they stayed in place and didn't ride up—getting a wedgie when you're on display behind the bar sucks.

Before I could say anything, my breath was stolen when he tugged the elastic down an inch further, baring more of my pubic area—which he then kissed.

God, the teasing. It's gonna fucking kill me.

My core pulsed with frustrated, *pent-up* need. I gritted my teeth to keep from begging him. I dug my fingers into his thick, hard shoulders, gripping and pushing. He resisted easily, his lips dotting kisses from right to left along the line of my underwear's elastic waistband, from hipbone to hipbone. He tugged the elastic down over my hip and kissed the exposed skin. Fuck.

The other side.

I drew my heels up the backs of his thighs, letting my knees splay wide—as much of an invitation as he was gonna get.

He ignored it.

Pulled my underwear lower, and now the very keyhole tip of my sex was bared, as was the fact that I hadn't waxed or shaved in a while. I wasn't rocking a bush, but again, if I'd had any clue this was going to happen, I'd have shaved.

He didn't seem to mind, his lips skating over stubble. Kissing. Touching. Tongue tasting flesh.

He had a choice, now. Or rather, I did. My legs were around him, making it impossible for him to take off my underwear or even lower them any further.

He answered the question by lifting my leg over his head and resting both of my legs on one shoulder. In one smooth pull, my underwear were off completely, gone as if by prestidigitation. My bare sex wept, the cool night air bathing my hot flesh.

My leg went back over to rest on his shoulder, splaying me open for him. I felt his gaze on me. I forced my eyes open, forced myself to look at him.

The look on his face…fuck me.

Reverence.

"Beautiful," he murmured. "Absolutely fucking beautiful."

Goddammit, that wasn't fair. The way he said it, as if he hadn't intended to say it out loud, or as if unaware that he had.

He sank to his knees right there in the alley, and his broad shoulders wedged my thighs apart.

I've never felt so exposed.

In public, in the alley, open to the sky and the stars and the whole universe.

Naked.

Sex soaked with my desire for him to taste me.

Hawk curled his hands around the outside of my thighs and pulled me to the edge of the bench seat until my ass hung out over space, until I was utterly at his mercy.

He breathed on me. Hot breath on hot flesh. A cool breath, then.

His hands spread over my belly, carving inward to my pussy. Big thumbs tugged me open.

His tongue dragged upward, fat and flat, licking. He groaned. "Fuck, you taste good."

My desperate need for orgasm was at a boil. I felt myself panting raggedly and forced my lungs to slow, to pull in long breaths. It didn't help.

When his tongue swiped upward again, I whimpered.

"Tell me why you said *try*," he murmured.

I'm not a liar, by omission or otherwise, so I told him the truth. "It's hard for me to come."

"Always?" The question huffed against my sex.

"Always."

He fused his lips around my clit and suckled. A ragged cry left my mouth, and my hips bucked upward.

"Can you make yourself come?" he asked.

"Sometimes," I admitted. "Takes a long time. Not always worth the effort."

"Boyfriends make you come?" He kissed my pussy after the question, and then suckled again, until I gasped and bucked once more.

"Not usually."

"So you fake it?"

I shook my head. "No. I never fake it."

"Never?"

"*Your* ego isn't *my* fucking problem," I snapped. "If you can't make me come, I'm not gonna stroke your little ego by faking it."

He laughed at that, a rough chuckle that I felt as much as heard. "So, can I ask you a dumb question?"

"You just did," I panted.

Another of those raw laughs. "Fair enough."

"What's your question, goddammit?" I knotted my fingers in his hair, infuriated that he kept fucking *talking* instead of giving me the orgasm I was now on the verge of begging for.

I felt his grin against my sex. "If you can't come, do you still like sex?"

He lifted his head and met my eyes, his full of hot humor and unveiled desire and *razor-sharp* male appreciation. Before I found the words to answer, he buried his face between my thighs and sucked my clit into his mouth, and when a spasm of pleasure rocked me into him, he slid a finger inside my clenching channel.

"Oh—*FUCK!*" I cried. "Yes! Yes, I like sex. I fucking *love* sex."

"Tell me," he murmured, licked, suckled, and licked again. "Tell me what you like."

"Make me come first, goddamn you," I snapped.

He licked, once. "Tell me what you like. Tell me what turns you on. Tell me what makes you fucking crazy." Another slow, fat lick. "The more you talk, the busier my tongue will be."

"Everything!" I shouted, fingers knotted into his hair and pulling him against me.

He ghosted his mouth against my lips, growling wordlessly. "Not gonna cut it."

I ground my sex against his mouth, but he pulled away, teasing his *tongue-tip* against my seam. "*FUCK!*"

"Tell me, Delia." A lick.

I spasmed from the quick, simple touch of his tongue to my clit, the seeds of an orgasm taking root in my belly.

God, I wanted to beg. Demand. Plead. Order.

"Tell you what, you sadistic fuck?"

"What you like. What you want. I want to know what makes you horny. What makes you come? What makes this hot, tight little pussy drip, Delia?"

Ah...fuck.

Words tumbled out of me, ripped free from the

depths of my soul by the raging need boiling in my veins.

"Forearm veins. Big arms. A good, sharp *V-cut*. A big cock wagging inside gray sweatpants. Witty banter. Intellectual stimulation. A really good massageOhhhh-hhhh*fuck*," I groaned, as he slid a finger inside me once more, and his tongue slid up my seam.

"Keep talking," he ordered.

"Strong hands. Sexy hair. Eyes. The right eyes really turn me on." I had to pause for breath because he wasn't lying—the more I spoke, the busier his tongue was. "Oh fuck, oh fuck. Foreplay. Kissing. *Tongue-fuck* me just right and I'll be all over you, even if I don't get an orgasm out of it. Someone who can take control without—fuck, fuck—without…oh god."

"Without what, Delia?"

"Without making me feel weak."

"Do you feel weak right now, Delia?"

"No."

"What else?"

"Making a man lose his mind."

"How?"

"Sucking him off. Teasing him until he doesn't know who the fuck he is." My ass lifted off the bench as he slid his finger deep, mouth fusing around my clit.

"Favorite position?"

"Cowgirl."

"Why?"

"Control. Angles. I like hands on my waist pulling me down. I love having my tits played with while I fuck."

"Do you have sensitive nipples?"

"Find out for yourself."

"Oh, I will. Count on that." He stilled his thrusting finger and flitted his tongue tip against my clit. "Do you?"

"Yes!" I cried, furious and desperate. "Yes, goddammit. My nipples are stupid sensitive."

"Yet you have a hard time coming?"

"Yes."

"You get close but can't always get there?"

"Yes."

His lips moved against my seam as he spoke, alternating licking and suckling with speaking. "I don't think you have a hard time coming. I think you have a hard time letting go." Lick. Suck. *Finger-fuck.* "I think you don't trust. I think you get in your own way." A quick series of *tongue-flicks*, his finger deep and curling. "I think I can make you come harder than you ever thought possible. Right now. You want to come, Delia?"

"Fuck you."

He just laughed. "Such a filthy mouth. I bet you can do some incredible things with that filthy mouth of yours, can't you?"

"Wouldn't you...like...to know?" I panted, writhing on the bench seat, refusing to beg, no matter how badly I wanted to.

"I would like to know. Very, *very* much." He teased

my clit, twiddling it with his tongue until I gritted my teeth on a scream, hips bucking upward. "And I think you want to show me. Don't you? You want to do bad things to me with that filthy mouth?"

I wrenched my eyes open and glared daggers at him. "If that was a joke about my name…" I clenched my thighs around his head and squeezed until he grunted in surprised pain. "I will crush your head like a motherfucking egg."

"Wasn't," he gasped.

I released the pressure, and he gasped, blinking and working his jaw.

"Jesus *Christ*, woman," he rasped, his voice hoarse. "What a way to fucking die."

I couldn't help grinning down at him, applying a little bit of pressure. "Yeah? You liked that?"

He suckled on my clit until I spasmed again, my thighs involuntarily clenching and shaking around his ears, and this time, he didn't tease or slow, but brought me to the quivering edge.

And *then* he stopped, his finger slicking in and out slowly. "If I died between your thighs, Delia, I would die a happy man," he whispered, his free hand cupping my ass and holding me up as if offering me to himself.

"Shut the fuck up and make me come, goddammit," I hissed. "Fucking tease."

His laugh only fueled my desperation and my anger. "Such a filthy mouth."

"Fuck you."

"I bet that filthy mouth would feel like heaven wrapped around my cock." He licked. Licked. Licked. Spasms wracked me, even as the edge of orgasm shivered just out of reach. "You want to taste me, don't you?"

My god, yes. "No."

A laugh. "Liar. I thought you didn't lie?" Lick, lick, lick. "You're so close, Delia. I could probably take you over the edge right now. I could make you beg for it."

"I dare you to try." Please don't; I'm about to as it is.

"Oh, I'll make you beg one of these days, just to prove the point. But right now, I'd rather you admit that you want my cock in your mouth."

"Not happening." God, please.

I bet it's huge. Thick and veiny and long. I bet he'd turn to a puddle of mush the second I get my lips around his fat cock.

"No?"

He crooked his finger inside me, and I jolted, and then his lips fused around my clit and he suckled and licked, thrashed my clit side to side until I was bucking and writhing and panting shrill gasps, hovering seconds away from sweet blessed release.

And then he stopped, everything, all at once, the bastard.

"FUCK!" I screamed. "You sadistic fucking monster! I hate you!"

"The truth shall set you free, Delia." A lick—and

I spasmed, so close to coming I could feel it like a balloon about to pop.

"What? *What*, goddammit?" I demanded, nearly ripping his thick, dark blond hair out by the roots. "Yes! Okay? Yes, I've fucking daydreamed about your cock. I woke up in a sweat this morning, gagging for it, dreaming about it. Is that what you want to hear?" I cried out as his lips sealed around my slit and his tongue began to circle my clit. "Let me come right now, Hawk, and I swear to fucking god, I'll suck your cock so good you'll see your fucking ancestors."

His lips moved, his words felt as much as heard. "Look at me, Beautiful."

I cracked my eyes open. "What, goddammit?" I snapped.

"*Now*…you can come."

As if his words were a trigger, I exploded from the inside out. He thrashed my clit with swift, aggressive, ravenous circles and *side-to-side* and *up-and-down* movements of his clever, relentless tongue, and his fingers—one, and then two, and then three of them—fucked in and out of me hard and fast.

At first, it was just an orgasm. A release of pressure and heat in my core, billowing upward and outward from my sex to my belly to my toes and fingers and scalp, everything tingling and spasming.

But when I reached the apex of my climax—or what I thought was the apex, because it was quite easily the hardest I've ever come—it turned out he wasn't done.

And apparently, therefore, neither was I.

Hips bucking wildly, grunting shrill screams through gritted teeth, I clutched his head and rode his mouth and fingers, expecting him to stop. He didn't. He kept going—same pace, same rhythm.

And I kept coming.

And coming.

Harder…and harder…and harder.

My lungs gave out and I couldn't scream anymore, and my hips flexed upward and froze there, my ass and thighs bunched and taut and quivering as lights burst behind my eyes and heat smashed through my convulsing sex.

"Hawk—fuck, fuck, fuck," I gasped, panting raggedly as wave after wave of *mind-melting* climax shattered through me. "Oh god, stop, stop—I can't take…I can't take any—any more."

His mouth pulled away, and he slid me onto the bench so my spasming, trembling lower half could rest. "Yes. You can. And you will."

Now, instead of his tongue, he used his other hand to strum my clit like the strings of a guitar, flicking rapidly up and down while his fingers inside me thrust in and out at the same pace, and then….

Something broke inside me.

I screamed like a banshee, my whole body arching helplessly upward, my hands fisting in Hawk's hard shoulders, my feet digging into his back with my knees splayed wide. The breaking became a shattering, my lungs empty, stars bursting behind my eyes.

A stream of something hot and wet sluiced out of me, but I couldn't find it in me, at that moment, at least, to care. I barely noticed, so lost in the wild paroxysms of pleasure.

He growled hungrily, pleased, as I came and came, the hot stream subsiding finally as the waves of orgasm slowed to a trickle, and then a halt.

Gasping and panting and whimpering, tears burning in my eyes and embarrassment in my throat, I could only lay there on the bench of my truck, shivering and trembling and mortified, as overwhelmed sobs battered at my gritted teeth.

I spasmed all over again as he slid his fingers out of me. My eyes wouldn't open, and I couldn't make my muscles work to sit up.

I felt Hawk's gaze on me. I cracked one eye and looked at him—and immediately regretted it.

Smug.

Arrogant.

Satisfied.

The fucking bastard.

"Help me up," I mumbled, wishing it had come out with more force.

At least I hadn't tacked on a "please."

His strong hands cradled my shoulders, and he helped me sit up—I had to grasp at the steering wheel and the back of the seat to stay upright, a gasp hissing out of me as an aftershock shuddered through me, forcing me to double over.

Naked from the waist down, I stared at Hawk. "What...the *fuck*...was that?"

He was soaked from neck to belly. He passed his shirt sleeve over his mouth and chin, grinning at me. "An orgasm."

"No. *Uh-uh*. I've had orgasms before. That was... something else." Dizzy, I closed my eyes as the word swam, and another aftershock quaked through me. "Fuck, fuck." I glared at him, embarrassment making me angry. "I *squirted* on you."

His grin widened. "Yes, you fucking did." He leaned close to me, and I could smell myself on his breath, his stubble, his clothing. "And it was the hottest thing I've ever seen."

Another aftershock hit me, this one weaker than the others. "I fucking *peed* on you, Hawk. Aren't you grossed out?"

"Fuck no." He braced his hands beside mine, on the wheel and seatback. Lips close to mine. Eyes leonine and wild and ravenous. "Now that I've had a taste of your sweet, pretty little pussy, I'll never be able to get enough. Making you squirt might be my new obsession."

I was lost at sea.

My head swam and my body was loose and jellied and hot. My thoughts were scattered to the winds and my emotions were all over the place, and I was tired and wired and wrung out.

"Need to go home," I mumbled, blinking as my eyes crossed and tried to shut.

Can you actually come so hard you pass out, but minutes after the actual orgasm?

If that's a thing, then that's what was happening.

"You okay, Delia?" Hawk's voice came from the end of a tunnel.

"Tired."

Darkness closed in.

"Delia?"

I tried to answer, but all that came out was a soft grunt.

"Fuck, she's out." He sounded equal parts amused and annoyed.

The last thought I had was: You've only got yourself to blame, buddy.

I woke up to bright warm yellow sunlight and the scent of coffee.

My bed was not this firm.

My blankets were not this heavy.

My bedroom faced sunset, not sunrise.

Nope, nope, nope. I wasn't facing whatever this

was. Not yet. I rolled over, pulled the lovely, warm, heavy blankets higher around my ears, and snuggled in.

Dozed off, maybe.

My bladder woke me again, and once that happens, there's no going back to sleep.

"Dammit," I muttered.

I forced my eyes open and took stock. The bedroom was huge—that was the first thing I noticed. The ceiling was knotty pine and soared at least twenty feet overhead. The light was coming from not one but two walls of glass, facing east, with a breathtaking view of rural Ketchikan—mountains, fields of wildflowers, and the Passage. The bed was a *four-poster*, the posts massive logs as big as the ones holding up the ceiling. The bed was what some called an Alaskan King—so massive I'd need a train to get to the far side. Thick white down comforter with impossibly high *thread-count* sheets against my skin. Pillows that were soft yet supportive.

A cute little seating area near one of the glass walls and leather armchairs with a low round table between them. On the table was a glass *pour-over* coffee maker thing full of steaming, aromatic *life-juice* with a single mug beside it.

I kicked away the blankets, only then realizing I was wearing a gigantic pair of gray sweatpants. The waistband was cinched as tight as the strings would allow, and still I could probably fit another of me in there with me. But I was covered, and I was still wearing my work tee and bra.

It seemed Hawk had brought me here, put his clothes on me, and put me to bed.

And made me coffee.

I slid off the *five-acre-wide* bed and padded to the coffee—the sweatpants fit sort of like Aladdin's pants in the Disney movie, but despite that, they were soft and warm and cozy.

You've heard of wearing your boyfriend's *T-shirts*, hoodies, and boxers; now get ready for...boyfriend sweats. Patent pending.

Not that Hawk was my boyfriend.

If he was my boyfriend, that orgasm he gave me would guarantee him blowjobs for life. Like, no questions asked. Home from work? I'm on my knees.

It was that fucking epic.

My legs still feel shaky.

I fucking *squirted*. I thought that was a myth. Or, more likely, fake. Like, porn stars wait until they have to pee and then just cut loose and act like it's normal. All part of the show, folks; nothing to see here.

Nope.

That shit took me by surprise. Like, it just ripped out of me. I couldn't have controlled it under threat of death. Or worse, having Mom and Dad involved somehow. Like, "Hey, Mr. and Mrs. Badd, your slut of a daughter squirted all over the alley behind your cousin's bar. What do you have to say?"

I have to laugh, though. Because knowing my parents, Dad would growl something about not *slut-shaming* his daughter, and Mom would *throat-punch* the person asking the question.

Still, let's leave them out of it.

I sat in one of the chairs, poured myself a cup of coffee, and sipped it while appreciating the view.

As I did so, I couldn't stop my brain from spinning out about Hawk and last night.

He made me come.

Harder than all of my previous orgasms combined, and then some.

With no more than his fingers and mouth.

In a matter of minutes.

In my truck, in an alley, in fucking public.

And I let him. Shit, I damn near begged him.

I *did* beg him. Sure, it was disguised as a demand, but we both knew I was begging.

Also, I'm pretty sure I promised him a blowjob so good he saw his ancestors. I guess I owe him that.

The first cup of coffee disappeared in a blink, and I poured a second one. It could use some Splenda, but I recognized *ultra-high* quality, *super-expensive* coffee when I tasted it.

Whoever Hawk was, he had an eye for the nicer things in life.

I can't stop puzzling over why he seems familiar, though. It's like I *should* recognize him, but I can't place him. I mean, I'm not exactly a connoisseur of current events. I don't give a shit about which celebrity is fucking whom, who's in rehab, who's divorced, and who

went on a racist tirade. I just don't care. Maybe it's growing up with Aunt Low and watching her struggle with
fame. I don't know. I just know Hawk's face niggles
something in my hindbrain. I'll figure it out someday.
Maybe I'll just ask him.

I finish my second cup and pour a third, and carry
the mug and the Chemex out of the room, hoping this
house isn't a maze.

Thankfully, it's not. A short hallway brought me
into a den—supple brown leather couches around a
coffee table made out of driftwood with a glass top, a
massive, *soot-stained* natural fireplace, and glass sliding
doors on three sides; the fireplace was *double-sided*, so
you could enjoy it inside or outside on the sprawling
stone patio.

The kitchen was gigantic—everything about this
place was oversized. Was it designed for giants? The
counters were higher and deeper than normal. Instead
of a refrigerator, even a *high-end* one, there was a *walk-in*
fridge and a *walk-in* freezer side by side next to a pantry you could play football in, stocked with every kind
of foodstuff available, from health food options to
Twinkies to enough canned goods to last you through
an apocalypse. A *regular-sized* refrigerator with a glass
door contained nothing but beverages—mostly canned
sparkling water in every flavor imaginable, plus six different kinds of beer, half a dozen bottles of champagne
and white wine and rosé, almond milk, and bottles of
flat water.

Mind-boggled, I helped myself to a bagel from the pantry and then went on a hunt for a toaster. Because this level of rich doesn't just leave toasters out where you can find them. Oh no, you have to hide them because…reasons.

I became increasingly frustrated as I rooted through cabinets, bagel in hand, muttering to myself about rich assholes and hidden toasters.

I was on my knees digging in the back of a shockingly deep corner cabinet, my front half mostly in the cabinet, which meant my back half was sticking up and out.

"As much as I appreciate the view of your very fine ass from this angle, Delia," I heard Hawk's amused voice say from above and behind me, "I must ask…what in the *ever-loving* fuck are you looking for in there?"

"Your tiny prick, you overstocked *cock-waffle*." I wiggled out and to my feet, shoving my *now-squished* and still uncut and untoasted bagel in his face. "Something to fucking toast this with," I snapped. "Why can't you just put your fucking toaster on the fucking counter like a normal fucking person?"

He just smirked at me, his lips twitching. "Because I haven't been able to fucking find it either, that's fucking why."

"Oh." The wind of anger having been let out of my sails, I winced at him. "Sorry. If I don't get carbs within half an hour after waking up, I'm kind of a bitch."

He bit down on a grin. "Noted."

I lifted my mug of *now-cold* coffee. "But thanks for this. It was very thoughtful of you." I plucked the sweatpants. "And these. And for bringing me here." I blinked, biting my lip as I tried like hell to keep my next words on the inside…and failed. "And for the best and craziest orgasm of my entire fucking life."

He just stared at me, his gaze going hot. I waited for him to remind me of the reward he was promised, but what he did wasn't that. "Now imagine what I could do if I had you naked and tied to my bed."

Well…fuck.

"I'm not into being tied up," I said.

He arched an eyebrow. "Have you been?"

"No. Because I'm not into it."

He moved to stand in my space, towering over me, *green-streaked* eyes piercing, daring me. He wrapped my hair around his fist and jerked my head back—a sharp but not exactly painful tug that elicited a shocked gasp from me. "What if I told you, Delia Badd, that if you trusted me, if you let me tie you to my bed, I could make the orgasm I gave you last night seem like a sneeze?"

I frowned up at him. "A sneeze?"

"Haven't you ever heard that old thing about how sneezes are *one-eighth* of an orgasm?"

"That's bullshit," I said.

"Of course it is." He kept my hair in his grip, my head tipped back, and his lips bruised my ear, his voice hot and low and making my core shiver and go slick and wet. "The point is, what I did last night?" He nipped my earlobe, and my pussy spasmed like a greedy, silly, horny idiot. "It would utterly pale in comparison to what I could do to you if I had you tied up."

"Bullshit," I whispered, as my legs trembled and my knees threatened to give out entirely.

"Remember when you begged me to let you come?" He turned my head to the side and kissed my throat, my jawline, and then went back to whispering in my ear. "I could make you beg me to let you *stop* coming."

"Bullshit," I whispered again, dipping deep into my reservoir of creative comebacks.

"Do not challenge me, Delia. Did you learn nothing last night?"

Oh, I learned plenty.

Such as, the man had a wicked, talented mouth and devilishly clever fingers.

Didn't mean I was going to just lay back and let a man I'd just met tie me up. Do you want to end up on Dateline? Because that's how you end up on Dateline.

"There's a massive difference between letting you go down on me and letting you tie me up, Hawk. And you have absolutely fucking not earned my trust enough that I'm gonna let you tie me up, no matter how many orgasms you might give me." I grabbed his crotch, feeling his *semi-erect* cock through the fabric of whatever it was he was wearing. "You did, however, earn one thing. Do you remember what it was I promised you if you let me come?"

"I believe your words were you'd suck my cock so good I'd see my ancestors." His voice was low and rough with desire. "But I don't play *tit-for-tat* when it comes to sex. I eat pussy because I like doing it. And Delia, babe, your pussy is the most delicious treat I've ever had. I'll eat your sweet little pussy until I get fucking lockjaw, and I'll never ask for a single thing from you, unless it's to hear you say six words."

"What words would those be?" I couldn't help but ask.

"'Please sir, may I have another.'"

"Fuck." My knees shook. "I could work with that," I said. "Still not tying me up, though. I may or may not have trust issues. And no, it has nothing to do with my father. My dad is the best, and I trust him with my life. My trust issues come from the fact that every man I've ever dated has been a lying, cheating piece of dogshit."

"That's fair," he said. "But how about I make you a deal? I'll give you six orgasms before I let you so much as *see* my cock. And in the meantime, you let me earn your trust."

"You'd have to tell me the truth for that to work," I said, mentally trying to tally up how far back I'd have to go to tally six orgasms. "And I doubt you'll do that. You're hiding something, and I know it. You won't ever have my trust if I know you're hiding something from me."

"You're right. I am hiding something from you." He grabbed my hand and pulled it away from his groin. "I promise to give you the full truth. Not now, but I will, before my time in Alaska is over. You have my word of honor on that."

"Will the full truth involve your actual name?"

"It will involve me answering, fully and without prevarication, any and every question you care to ask."

I held up my pinky finger. "Pinky promise?"

He snorted. "Pinky promise." He hooked his pinky around mine.

"So in the meantime, I'm just supposed to accept the fact that you're acknowledging that you're lying to me about something. You won't tell me what, but I have to assume it has something to do with why you're here and why you're asking around about my bars. And I'm supposed to set that aside mentally while you and I have hot monkey sex all over Ketchikan?"

"Precisely. I'm glad you understand." He tightened his grip on my hair, tugging my head back until I was off balance, and he cupped the side of my face, rubbing the rough pad of his thumb across my lips. "Now. Let's count last night as one. Are you ready for number two?"

SIX

Hunter

WHAT THE ACTUAL BRAINDEAD FUCK WAS I DOING? Playing with fire, that's what.

But she was addictive. I couldn't sleep last night because the smell of her pussy was all over my face, even after washing it. And fuck, that smell. Sweetest sugar, like the finest honey and wine and nectar. And the sounds she made when she came? A symphony of ecstasy.

All I could think of as I tossed and turned for hours was how badly I wanted to get her naked and play with her. Lick her sweet pussy until she wept. Sink my cock inside her. Bend her over my bed and fuck her senseless.

God, just thinking of all the things I want to do to

her had my cock stiffening into rebar behind my workout shorts.

And she felt it.

She sank her teeth into my thumb, biting hard enough that I jerked my hand away with a hiss. "I wasn't exactly keeping count last night," she whispered, her deep, wild blue eyes sparking fire. "But I think I came at least six times."

Uh-oh. My plan to keep her from asking questions I wasn't ready to answer by means of a ceaseless parade of orgasms may not have been very well thought out.

I wasn't sure exactly what happened. All I knew was that one second, I had her hair in my hand and her body flush against mine, and then my wrist hurt and I was stumbling backward, *off-balance* and Delia was prowling after me, her mane of auburn hair wild and tangled around her shoulders and face. She kept her eyes locked on mine and scraped her hair up onto the top of her head, slipped a hair tie off of her wrist, and bound her hair into a messy bun.

My cock knew what she was implying with that move—it hardened until it hurt, aching and throbbing.

"When I said six, I meant six separate ones," I said, backing away from her like a fool.

If I let her touch me, it would be over. I was already addicted to tasting her. But if she showed me what she could do with that sassy mouth of hers, I knew damned well I'd never get enough.

She ran her tongue across her lower lip, her eyes

raking over me. "Jesus, Hawk. Where does a busy, important, rich motherfucker like you find the time to maintain a body like that?"

"Dedication," I answered, my ego swelling at her awed praise. "And the fact that I've never needed more than four hours of sleep."

I'd caught my four hours—from the time I finally fell asleep at three or four until about *seven-forty-five*, which was pretty late for me. I'd just finished working out, which meant I was wearing a pair of gym shorts and nothing else, and the sweat was still cooling on my skin.

Her eyes skipped greedily over my pecs, arms, and abs, and that cute little pink tongue swept across her lower lip again as her gaze fixed on my extremely prominent erection—the tip of which was *this* close to poking out of the top of my shorts.

Desperate to keep control of the situation on my side, I backed up again—because as badly as I wanted to feel that mouth wrap around my cock, I knew if I let that happen, I'd be handing control over to her.

"Delia." I caught up against the counter. "I don't need you to do anything. I got exactly what I wanted just by making you come."

She grinned, crushing her chest against mine, nipping the point of my chin. "I know."

"And I said six, meaning separate. Last night was one."

"Except I'm the one keeping count, and I disagree."

She cupped me over my shorts, her eyes widening. "You can't tell me you don't want this."

"Fuck, woman. Of course I do."

She rubbed me, still over my shorts. "Then what's your problem? Never had a man run away from a blowjob."

"I'm not running away."

She just laughed, her palm cupping my erection and sliding up and down over the fabric of my shorts. "Scared, Hawk?"

"Don't be ridiculous."

"You *are*." She ran her other hand over my chest and abs. "You're scared of how bad you want it, aren't you? You can tell how good it's gonna feel to shoot your load down my throat, can't you?" her voice was a soft, sultry whisper.

"Fuck," I hissed. "No."

She trailed her fingertips down my centerline from throat to belly button and then slid her fingers under the waistband. She met the tip of my cock there, and a greedy grin lit her face. "What have we here?" She brushed her thumb over my slit, smearing precum.

Fuck, fuck, fuck.

She put her thumb in her mouth, eyes never leaving mine. "Mmmmm. Tastes like you want it."

"Nope." I'm an excellent liar. I can pass any lie detector test on the planet, and my heart rate won't so much as blip.

But that lie? About as plain as the nose on my face.

She just grinned, rubbing my tip with her thumb until my knees went weak, and I had to grip the counter to stay upright.

She saw the move, and her grin widened. "I expected you to be a better liar, honestly."

"I usually am." I closed my eyes as I realized what I'd just said, but she was still rubbing her thumb all over my *precum-weeping* tip, which was making my brain go haywire. "What I mean is, I'm not lying."

She just laughed. "Okay, buddy, tell another one." She slid her whole hand inside my shorts, grasping my cock and caressing down to the root, thumb and forefinger first. "Let me guess…you thought you could control me via plentiful orgasms? You would be partially correct."

"Partially?" I asked, gritting my teeth to keep from whimpering like a little boy at how fucking good her hand felt.

"Partially, because two can play at that game."

She stroked me slowly, her eyes on mine, hawkishly watching my reactions.

Hawkishly.

Ha.

Fuck.

I'm delirious.

My knees dipped, and my eyelids involuntarily shuttered and flickered, and my eyes rolled back in my head. When she slid her soft, warm, small hand down to cradle my balls, a rough groan was torn out of my throat.

She laughed. "You like that, do you? I haven't even seen it. What if I just made you come like this? When was the last time you came in your pants, Hawk?"

"Never." When I was thirteen, looking at a Playboy Magazine stolen from my dad's office.

"It's tempting, Hawk, I have to say." She stroked me from tip to root and then palmed my balls again, playing with them with her fingertips, and precum threatened to become the full show. "Make you make a mess all in these cute little shorts. Would you? Or would you beg me to keep my promise? Hmmm? I'll let you choose, Hawk. How about that? All you've gotta do is ask me nicely."

I clenched my teeth and locked my knees, gripping the counter so hard my knuckles turned white. "Not gonna happen."

She grinned wider than ever, clearly enjoying the hell out of our little game. "No? You'd rather hold onto your pride? Fine by me. I mean, I'm having fun." She pressed her lips to my chest, kissing my pec and then flicking my nipple with her tongue—I flinched, and my cock twitched in her hand. "Seems silly to me, though. If you say 'Delia, will you pretty please suck my cock?' You never know what'll happen. I might just feel inclined to take pity on you. I might drop to my knees and wrap these pretty little lips around your cock. You've got a pretty big dick, so I don't think I can take all of it down my throat, but I'd damn sure be willing to try. How's that sound, Hawk?"

I squeezed my eyes shut as she continued to plunge her soft hand down my cock, dragging it back up and twisting around the head, smearing precum, and then stroking down all over again. "Fuck, fuck, fuck," I hissed. "Never begged for anything in my life. Not about to start now."

"Asking nicely isn't begging, Hawk. It's just manners. I *could* make you beg. I could edge you until you promised me your firstborn if I wanted to. You haven't had my mouth on you, so I don't blame you if you don't believe me. But you should know that I'm really, *really* good at giving head."

"I don't doubt that."

She smirked up at me. "You're getting close, huh? About to blow your load. I can feel it. You're trying like hell, though, I'll give you that."

I gritted my molars until they threatened to crack. "I won't ask."

Her eyes blazed. "Remember how you warned me about challenging you? Well, Hawk, I happen to be viciously competitive. Two brothers and countless cousins. I hate to lose. So now you've thrown down the gauntlet."

Fuck.

My resolve was legendary in Manhattan business circles. I'd walked away from a *five-hundred-million-dollar* deal over a minor sticking point in the contract that I wasn't willing to compromise on. I've stared down the wealthiest and most powerful men in the world without flinching.

This sexy firecracker of a woman damned well might be my match.

I groaned and threw my head back when she sank to her knees in front of me, withdrawing her hand from my shorts. "You don't have to prove anything."

"Oh, but I do. After last night, I absolutely have something to prove." She cupped the backs of my calves in her hands, sitting on her feet on the hard floor. "Don't move."

I couldn't if I tried but didn't bother answering—I just watched as she went into the den, snagged a throw pillow, and brought it back into the kitchen, tossed it onto the floor in front of me, and knelt on it. Fuck—she's serious as a heart attack.

Not a funny turn of phrase—my heart was pounding out of my chest so hard I worried that, for as fit as I was, I might just have a coronary trying to pretend I wasn't one wrong touch away from coming in my shorts.

She ran her hands up the back of my legs, up under my shorts and palmed my ass. "Mmmm…nice butt."

"Thanks." I glared down at her, pissed at her for being every bit as good at this game as I am.

After a moment or two spent playing with my butt, which I have to admit felt pretty damn fantastic, she slid her hand back down my thighs, around to my quads, and then upward. Under the shorts once more, palms passing to either side of my cock. Which twitched and leaked in anticipation of her touch. The damned thing didn't understand the stakes of the game—the upper hand in this contest for control.

I was losing.

For a second, she just caressed my quads and hip-bones and belly, avoiding my cock. And then, without warning, she yanked my shorts down. Without think-ing, I stepped out of them, and she picked them up. Turned the front inside out to show where my precum had stained the fabric. Her tongue flickered out and touched the shorts, a grin crossing her face. "Mmm. I bet your cum would taste amazing." She touched her lips to my hipbone on the left side, and then my belly, and then my right hipbone; with her eyes on mine, she stuck her tongue out and touched it to the tip of my cock, licking away a bead of precum. "Yummy."

My eyes rolled back in my head at the quick soft flick of her tongue. "Fuck."

She laughed. "I barely touched you, Hawk. Don't tell me you're gonna come already? I barely got to play."

"Not even close." I was actively holding back, try-ing to picture my *fourth-grade* teacher, Mrs. Ellis—who resembled a bullfrog and had the personality of a rabid chihuahua—while using every Kegel exercise I knew.

She sank lower and nuzzled my groin, my cock lay-ing against her cheek, kissing and kissing upward, her eyes casting up to mine. Her lips parted, and her tongue slid out. Fuck, so close. All I had to do was say please, and she'd have mercy on me.

I threw my head back and growled through gritted teeth. "Not...happening."

Her hand wrapped around my erection, and I almost whimpered, at the last second turning the pathetic sound I almost made into a clearing of my throat. Not that either of us believed my little performance.

A slow stroke of her hand. "You can lie to yourself, but you can't lie to me. You're gonna come for me, aren't you?" Her tongue swept over my tip again, and my knees buckled. "Only question is, where is it gonna go? My face? My hands? My tits?"

Please fuck, don't talk about your tits.

If she pulled those things out, it was fucking over. I would beg shamelessly.

And...yep. She could read me like a book, obviously, because she grinned an evil, knowing grin. Crossed her arms over her middle and peeled the shirt off, tossing it up into my face. She was wearing a black bra—nothing particularly special, just a *run-of-the-mill* black satin *full-coverage* bra. But fuck, her tits spilled up out of the cups and threatened to escape entirely. I literally bit my tongue so hard I tasted copper in an attempt to stop myself from giving her the plea she wanted— and I wouldn't be begging her to suck me off, but to merely let me get a glimpse of those big, pale, perfect tits.

She read every thought on my face. "I'm not

playing fair, am I?" She cupped her breasts and lifted them. "If I got these big puppies out, you'd do anything I ask, I bet, wouldn't you?'

Abso-fucking-lutely. "Not a chance. Seen better."

She giggled, the saucy minx. "You have not. Mainly because you haven't seen them yet. But also because I have it on good authority that my tits are the best in the state, at least."

"Whose authority is that?"

"Every man and boy who has ever seen them."

"Boy?"

"I wasn't always an adult. Plus, there *was* that time I was trying on bras at Target and a *fifteen-year-old* boy accidentally walked in on me because I'd forgotten to lock the door. Most women would have screamed."

"Not you?"

She shook her head, reaching behind her back to unhook the bra. No, no, no. Don't do it. All I had to do to keep the edge of control was not beg. If she got those out, I'd be begging in a split second.

"Nope. I asked him if he liked what he saw."

"You did not."

"Did too. And *then* I told him to get the fuck out."

"I guarantee you he jerked off to you every day after that. Probably still does," I said.

She grinned, holding the cups against her chest. "Oh, I'm sure. I don't mind. He was a sweet, dorky little fella. Stood there like a deer in the headlights. No clue what to do."

"Probably never saw tits in real life before that," I said, "Lucky kid."

She gave me a look that was pure mischief. "I have a conundrum now, Hawk. See, if I keep hold of the bra, I can't use my hands to touch you. Hmmm. What to do, what to do." She grinned at me and ran her tongue up the underside of my shaft from root to tip, pulling a ragged groan out of me. "I could just use my mouth."

"You could," I agreed.

"But in order for me to let the bra go *and* use my mouth, you're gonna have to use your very best manners. I'll make it even easier for you. Two words: please, Delia." She licked again and then let the cups fall away a bit, enough to give me a tantalizing glimpse of more of her breasts. "I can make all your dreams come true, Hawk. Right here, right now. Don't you want that?"

Fuck.

I couldn't make myself say no. The lie simply wouldn't come out.

"Fuck!" It was a hiss of frustrated rage.

Not even Mrs. Ellis could bring me back from the edge. Mainly because all I could see, even with my eyes closed, was Delia, on her knees, tits taunting me, lips glistening with hints of my precum, willing to give me an orgasm I knew I'd never forget.

"I'm losing interest in the game, Hawk," she warned. "I have shit to do. Ask me now or I walk away."

She would, too. I knew it.

She was playing hardball. God, she'd be a fucking shark in the boardroom.

I bit down on my tongue and closed my eyes, because apparently I'm prideful dumbass.

Two words.

But it was the capitulation they represented that I hated.

They represented losing.

I didn't lose.

Ever.

To anyone.

I would walk away instead of conceding. Ask anyone who's ever faced me in the boardroom—I didn't back down from anyone about anything.

Delia shook her head, sniffing a laugh. "Damn, okay. You're serious." She stood up, snagged the pillow, and touched my chin. "You win." She kissed my lips, a quick touch, and I tasted myself on her lips. "Bye, Hawk."

She walked away, clutching her bra against her chest. God, her bare back was fucking sexy. What is it about a woman's bare back that's so insanely erotic?

Fuck, fuck, fuck.

"Wait." The word flew off my tongue unbidden. "Delia, wait."

She was halfway across the kitchen by the time my mouth betrayed me. She stopped, pillow in one hand, bra pressed to her chest with the other. "Yeah, Hawk?"

That look. Those eyes. Sultry. Hungry. Predatory.

She knew damn well she had me where she wanted me. And she loved it. Fuck, the arousal on her face was plain to see. She wanted it. She wanted me. She wanted to lose—her tongue slid across her lips, as if already tasting me.

I swallowed hard, grinding my jaws together in one last valiant but pointless effort to keep the words on this side of my teeth. My cock ached painfully, harder than it's ever been, leaking precum. I watched her eyes flick to it, widening, and she bit her lower lip.

Her eyes went to mine again. "Hawk?" It was a quiet whisper. Barely a word, yet full of promise—say the words. It was all I had to do.

Fuck.

"Please." I dropped my head, knowing I'd lost. "Please, Delia."

To her credit, she didn't gloat. She didn't laugh. She did grin, still biting her lip, and then dropped the bra.

I nearly came.

God, they were glorious. Absolutely massive, real, natural, and perfect. Huge teardrops, swaying subtly with each breath. Wide, dark areolae, big thick, hard, pink nipples that begged to be suckled. I'd need both hands for each breast and then some. On her otherwise slender frame, the effect was downright shocking.

"Fucking hell," I whispered. "You're incredible."

"I am, or they are?" She asked.

"Both."

She hooked her thumbs in the waist of the

sweatpants she was wearing. "I know how hard it was for you to say those words. I think you've earned a little bonus."

She wiggled out of them, tossing them aside to stand naked in front of me. And my god, incredible didn't begin to cover it.

I pushed off the counter but didn't make it a single step.

"Nope," she snapped, "you stay where you are. You haven't earned touching me yet."

I sank back against the counter, soaking in her perfect beauty greedily. The aforementioned giant tits, a soft belly that wasn't quite flat—beautifully so, in my opinion—generous hips, thick thighs, tight waist.

"Fucking gorgeous." It was a prayer, a whispered ode in two words.

She prowled toward me, those wide hips swaying. Fuck me—why had I wasted so much time chasing skinny little models with no ass, no hips, and tiny tits? She was fucking incredible. My cock went even harder at the sight of her naked body, and I had to grit my teeth and flex every muscle in my body until it hurt just to keep from coming.

She wasn't smiling anymore. Her gaze fixed on my cock. "Not to feed your ego, which I doubt needs any feeding, but god*damn*, Hawk. Your cock is *amazing*."

I couldn't manage words. Not when she was placing the pillow on the floor and kneeling on it in front of me. Not when she looked up at me from beneath thick dark batting eyelashes, erotic promise written on her beautiful face.

"Are you close, Hawk?" She whispered. "Truth, now. It'll cost you nothing. I just want to know."

"Can't you tell?" I asked.

She grinned. "Yeah, I can." She ran her hands over my abs. "Are you gonna blow the second I put my mouth on you?"

"Gonna try like fuck not to."

"Good. That'll make it more fun. See how long you can last. I bet you don't make it fifteen seconds."

"Thirty."

"If you make it to thirty, I promise I won't argue next time. I'll go along with whatever you want, within reason."

"Deal," I said.

She slid her hands around my waist and cupped my ass, gazing up at me. "Better start counting."

She parted her lips, eyes fixed unwaveringly on mine, and took me into her mouth.

"*Fuck,*" I breathed, because I knew I wasn't making it thirty seconds. I wasn't sure I'd make it five.

She made a sound of appreciation in her throat as she slowly slid her mouth down my shaft, tongue swirling and flicking and tasting. She dug her fingers into the meat of my ass and pulled, encouraging me to go deeper. Not that I had a choice; she was in control. I gripped the counter, head hanging, struggling to keep my eyes open as her hot wet tight mouth took my cock inch by inch.

And she didn't stop.

I groaned, watching in disbelief as she kept taking me and taking me until her nose touched my belly. She never took her eyes off of mine.

"Ohhhhh...fuck," I breathed, stunned. "Fuck, Delia. Jesus. Don't—don't hurt yourself."

She only moaned again, her eyes glinting with arousal, and pulled away, mouth open, flicking the tip of my cock with her tongue, and then driving down again, taking all of me in a single smooth slide. Once her nose touched my belly, she stayed there, swallowing around me until I hissed, flexing every muscle in my body in an attempt to keep from blowing my load.

I was counting mentally, and I hadn't even gotten to ten.

She teased another slow, *tongue-swirling* slide of her mouth up my shaft to the tip. She paused, grinning at me. "Ready?"

"For what?" I asked, my voice shredded as if I'd swallowed razor blades.

"This."

This was her proving that she'd been playing around. Toying with me. Teasing me. Now, she went down on me in earnest, pulling at my ass, encouraging me to move. She slid her lips down my cock, reached the bottom, and wiggled her mouth and throat around me, and then pulled up, bobbing on my tip, and then down again. And again. Harder. Faster.

My hips flexed helplessly, thrusting into her mouth; she moaned when I thrusted, pulling at my ass.

Her wide dark blue eyes blinked up at me, eager, hungry, aroused; she took me from tip to root again, her eyes on mine, erotic glee evident in her gaze as my knees buckled and a growl ripped past my teeth.

Fifteen seconds—although I'd blanked out a few times, which meant my count was suspect.

She reached up and grabbed my wrists and brought my hands to her head and pushed down.

"Fuck," I snarled. "That's how you want it?"

"*Mmmm-hmmm,*" she hummed, and the vibrations were nearly my undoing.

I cradled her head in my hands and guided her down my cock, thrusting at the same time. "You want it like that, huh? Want me to fuck your pretty little mouth?"

"Mmm!" she moaned, agreeing.

"Ahhh god, fuck, ohhhhhfuck," I grated, everything inside me pulsing, pounding, straining to let go. Not yet. Not yet.

She cheated.

She cupped my balls in one hand and squeezed gently, one long finger sliding along my taint and pressing, massaging. She clutched one ass cheek in her other hand, nails digging in with a sharp bite, pulling at me.

I couldn't stop myself.

I lost it.

Twenty-two seconds by my count, and I was gone.

I let loose a harsh shout and pulled her down while thrusting into her throat. She tasted my release the moment it began and groaned eagerly, and then began fucking me with her mouth. Her bun flopped and began to come loose, so I held her hair up out of the way and tried to keep up with her pace, which was fast, and then faster, and then all I could do was thrust my hips forward helplessly and lift on my tiptoes and grunt wildly as my orgasm ripped out of me.

Stars flickered and burst behind my eyes and my brain twisted into a pretzel and everything went taut and tense, and heat swirled in my belly and burst out of me in a flood.

I heard her gulping frantically and wrenched my eyes open to watch. She held my gaze as she swallowed around me, eyes wide as my release pounded out of me. She was forced to break for breath, mouth hanging open as she gasped, cum and saliva string from her mouth to my shaft. She gripped me and pumped hard, swallowing frantically and gagging for breath, and another rush of climax spasmed out of me, this one wracking me with such potent force that my knees buckled, and I had to catch myself on the counter. My cum splattered across her chest and trickled down her tits.

"Holy fuck," she breathed. "You're *still* coming?"

She sucked me into her mouth again, this time wrapping both hands around my shaft and pumping me, swallowing and suckling around my glans, tongue swirling.

I'd thought I was done. I'd already come so hard I was dizzy and barely keeping my feet. But when she put her mouth on me again?

Impossibly, I kept coming, or came again—I'm not sure which.

She made a surprised sound as she swallowed more and more, pumping and stroking my cock with both soft, clever, greedy little hands.

Even when the rush of cum subsided, she didn't stop. She just kept sucking, kept stroking. A ragged groan shuddered out of me, and I quaked, spasmed, helplessly clinging to the counter as my legs gave out completely. Dizziness washed over me, and darkness occluded my vision.

Finally, as my strength abandoned me at last, she released me with a loud *pop*. I sagged to the cold tile floor, panting as if I'd run a hundred meters flat out. My head thunked against the cabinet as I fought for coherence. Shit, I couldn't see straight.

When my vision cleared, Delia was kneeling on the pillow, hands on her lap, eyes fixed on me. She was smirking.

"Jesus," I breathed.

She just held her pose, letting her *shit-eating* smirk do all the talking.

"Shut up," I muttered.

"You goobered my tits," she said.

"Sorry?" It came out a question, for some reason.

I was still disoriented, dizzy, *light-headed*, weak, and stupid.

She just giggled. "I'm not. It was kinda hot. Never had anyone come as much as you just did, though. I mean, *holy shit*, you came like a fucking gallon."

"Been a while."

"I guess so. *Self-imposed* celibacy?"

"Something like that."

"Bored of all the women throwing themselves at you, were you?" She grinned, quirking an eyebrow at me.

I frowned at her. "How the fuck could you possibly know that?"

She laughed. "I didn't, but you just confirmed it." She cupped her breasts and craned down to lick my cum off her tits, where she could reach, at least. "Mmm. Yummy."

"Fuck," I sighed. "You're gonna be the death of me."

She just giggled—and fuck, the giggle was too much. Cute and sexy and erotic all at once. "Not all cum is the same, obviously. But yours?" She closed her eyes, kissing her fingers. "Delicious."

"Glad you like it." I shook my head. "That was... fuck. I don't know what it was."

"Did you see your ancestors?"

"I saw God, I'm pretty sure. And I'm not a religious man."

That fucking giggle again. "Told you." She rose onto her knees and crawled onto me. Straddled me, arms around my neck, tits in my face. "Taste it, Hawk."

"Fuck no."

"Aren't you even the least bit curious?"

"No."

"I know when you're lying." She cupped her breasts, offering them to me. A bead of cum glistened just above her nipple. "You know you want to."

"Fuck." My hands gripped her waist, slid up her belly.

She grabbed my wrists with shocking strength and stopped me before I could touch her tits. God, she was strong. I could overpower her, but not without risking hurting her.

"I haven't permitted you to touch me yet, Hawk." She leaned closer. "Taste yourself. It's right there. On my tit. Taste it, and these are all yours."

"You drive a hell of a hard bargain, Delia Badd." I already said I'd do anything.

I suckled her nipple into my mouth, and she gasped, releasing my wrists to clutch desperately at my head. I cupped her breast and lifted it to my mouth and ran my tongue over her hard nipple, and then higher. A burst of smoky, salty, slightly sweet flavor exploded on my tongue, a thick, pungent taste.

She clutched my head and looked down at me. "I'm almost always right, Hawk. You should get used to that now. Listen to me, and everything will be that much easier for both of us."

"You're impossible." I had her tits in my hands, and I was in heaven.

So soft, so heavy. She let me play with them for a minute and then pulled out of my reach, shifting backward off my lap.

"Too bad you won't tell me the truth right now," she said. "I'm so horny, you don't even know. I'd fuck your brains out, Hawk."

Goddammit.

"I can't. Not yet."

She sighed. "I know." She stood up and backed away. "Shame. You and me, Hawk? We'd fuck like gods."

And with that, she turned and walked away, big beautiful ass swaying to unheard music, bare back sensuous and enthralling.

She shut the door to the guest room I'd put her in, and a minute later, I heard the shower turn on.

I slid down to lie on the kitchen floor, groaning.

"I'm so incredibly fucked," I said out loud.

SEVEN

Delia

WHATTHEFUCK, WHATTHEFUCK, WHATTHEFUCK.
Why did I just do that?

What is *wrong* with me?

I collapsed against the wall of the shower, letting the scorching hot water batter my spine and shoulders. My thoughts whirled, my feelings coruscated, and my desires crashed up against logic and reason.

The man had every intention of giving me *another* orgasm.

Six of them…without asking me for a damn thing.

All I had to do was go along with it. Let the man have his way.

Did I do that?

No, I did not.

I turned the whole thing into a damned game. One I most certainly will not win. Because there won't be a winner. It's not a game anyone wins. It's playing chicken. It's stupid and immature.

But fuck, is it fun.

For a guest bathroom, this one sure is well stocked—quality shampoo and conditioner, good soap, clean washcloths and towels in a warmer. Even a *spa-quality* bathrobe. The shower itself is fucking magical. Acres of marble and glass, a rainfall showerhead with absolutely incredible pressure, and sprayers on the walls shooting hot water from a dozen different directions.

For a few minutes, I set aside everything that had just gone down and focused on getting clean. Shampoo twice, condition once. Scrub. Rinse. There was even a razor and moisturizing shaving cream—I would bet heavily on the fact that whoever stocked this guest bathroom was a woman. This raised questions, but that's for later. I shaved my legs, pits, and lady bits, a job that was long overdue.

Thusly clean, smooth, and smelling good, I reluctantly got out of the shower and dried off with the delightfully warmed towels. A drawer beside the sink held new toothbrushes and a tube of toothpaste as well as a package of flossers, which meant I even got to brush my teeth.

Even after my teeth were clean, though, I still tasted hints of Hawk's cum. Which shouldn't make me horny, but did. Because I'm weird like that, apparently. It's not normal, by the way. I mean, under most circumstances, yes, I do enjoy giving head. A lot. I like giving pleasure. Since I have trouble reaching orgasm myself, I get enjoyment out of providing the most pleasure for my partner as I possibly can. And I'm good at it.

But with Hawk? Things are very, very different. The norm for me is out the window.

I wrap myself in the bathrobe and hunt through the drawers and cabinets; I owe whoever stocked this bathroom a hug and a glass of wine because she thought of everything. There's a very expensive hair dryer, a brush, and a new package of hair ties. Magical!

I brush and blow dry my hair and try to figure out the best approach moving forward.

What's done is done—he gave me the best orgasm of my entire life. He was willing to keep giving them to me without expecting anything in return. Why? Out of the goodness of his heart? An ulterior motive? I'm not sure it matters. I circumvented his intentions and blew the whole situation up.

And I enjoyed the fuck out of it.

My pussy tingled just thinking about Hawk's cock. It was…in a word, perfect. Huge, but not so much that I was worried about it fitting. Or, well, I knew it wouldn't, but in all the right ways. I've been with *well-endowed* men and those not so blessed. And truly, it's really all about the individual, the motion of the ocean, and all those other stupid, trite sayings that are nonetheless true. I've enjoyed both ends of the spectrum. But speaking for myself, there is a just right, and Hawk is that. I desperately want to feel him inside me. If he can make me come that hard with just his mouth and fingers, what can the man do with that giant magical dong of his?

A lot of very *high-quality* fucking, that's what.

But he scares me.

I have a sneaking suspicion as to the reason for his presence here in Ketchikan, and I don't like it. Other investors and buyers have, over the years, come sniffing around, hoping to get a piece of the Badd's Bar action. Dad has always sent them packing without so much as a *how-do-you-do*. We're not for sale. We don't want or need investors. We're happy. We're content. We're growing.

But Hawk...he's different. I get the sense that he's the boss...and someone very important. I don't know how I know that, but I do. I'd wager my Ranger on it, and that truck is my baby. Who he is, I don't know. What precisely he's after, I also don't know.

But the fact that he's *flat-out* admitted that he's keeping something from me, but won't say what? It's weird. What do I do with that? I can't get pissed at him later, if and when he tells me the truth because he's been up front about his dishonesty, or at least his lack of transparency.

He's exciting. That's the problem. He's unlike anyone I've ever met. He's arrogant, but so far, he's backed it up, which makes it just *well-deserved* confidence instead of hubris.

He's fine as fuck, also.

I'd put him at about thirty, which is eight years older than me—about my cutoff for dating older guys.

Not that I'm dating him. Which is the conundrum.

What are we doing? What does he want? Is he using me somehow? Or am I just a target of opportunity?

Have I mentioned that he scares me? Or rather, my fascination with him worries me. The depths of my attraction to him. I mean, shit, our sexual compatibility alone is a worry, because he's not from here. He's not staying. There can't be anything between us. I have no intention of leaving Ketchikan, ever. I love this place. It's my home. My past, present, and future. Sure, I'd love to go on vacation to cool places, but I'll never *live* anywhere else. And Hawk? He's a New Yorker through and through. I hear it in his voice, see it in his mannerisms. He's a captain of industry, a *hard-charging*, *take-no-prisoners*, *win-at-all-costs* type. He's probably worth more than Badd's Bar has ever and will ever earn combined.

The idea that this undeniably combustible sexual chemistry between us could ever result in something real is *straight-up* laughable.

I don't want to be in love.

The Badd Family Love Charm can go fuck itself.

It's not real, and if it is, it's not gonna work on me. And certainly not with Hawk.

But good lord, the man can eat pussy.

And his cock is…well, let's just say that now that

I've had a taste, he's gonna be a happy man for as long as he's in town, because I'm already jonesing for more.

I don't think I'll fuck him, though. As much as I want to, it wouldn't be smart. I'd probably get attached. I'm starting to feel silly woman things. I've started to think he'd never feel the same way when it's just good sex.

So no. We'll play our little game, and we'll give each other some killer orgasms via oral and manual sex, and my heart will stay firmly out of the whole stupid situation.

I nod at my reflection, content with my decision.

"We aren't fucking Hawk," I tell the *sex-crazed* woman in the mirror. "You can suck him off till he doesn't know his own name, but you're *not* riding that big, thick, tasty dick of his. No matter how good it would feel."

My reflection didn't look convinced.

I had to talk to Emerson. She was the only one who could talk sense into me. I didn't tend to listen to anyone, myself least of all.

Hair done, clad in the thickest, softest robe I'd ever put on, I went in search of my clothing. The guest bedroom held nothing.

Sigh.

I had to find Hawk.

I left the bedroom and went back out into the kitchen, hoping like hell that Hawk had sufficiently recovered from my…erm…ministrations and had at least put on pants.

Because that cock, if it was out, was gonna eradicate what little *self-control* I had.

I found him at the stove, wearing nothing but those stupid little shorts again, scrambling eggs. His back was a rippling field of muscle, each movement of his arm doing delicious things to the defined musculature. His hips were narrow and hard, his ass a firm bubble straining against the fabric. Thick, powerful, hairy thighs. Big, firm, toned arms—not bodybuilder huge, but big enough that my mouth watered. He even had that little vein running along the center of his bicep—I saw it as he turned to greet me, spatula in hand.

His abs.

Jesus.

Good arms and sexy abs are my kryptonite, and the man had both. A smattering of hair dusted his chest, thickening into a line down his center and disappearing under his shorts, which hung just low enough to reveal an absolutely absurd *V-cut*.

Every other time I'd seen him, he was wearing that *ratty-ass* ballcap. Now, though, the hat was absent, showing me his hair. And my god, even his hair was fucking fabulous. He'd had a very expensive haircut at some point in the recent past, but he'd neglected it since, allowing it to grow a little shaggy around he ears and neck. Thick and dark blonde, it trailed across his forehead in *sweat-damp* curls and teased the shell of his ears and the back of his neck, begging my hands to bury in it and hold on as he dove between my thighs and…

"Ahem." Hawk's eyes told me he'd read my thoughts, something the obnoxious man seemed to have a freakish affinity for. "You good? Want to take a picture for later?"

"I'm looking for my clothes." I ignored his dig, ripping my eyes away from his stupid, glorious body.

"In the dryer. I ran them through a quick wash. Should be dry in about half an hour." He gestured at the stove. "Made a lot. You want some? You never got your bagel."

The gleam in his eyes told me he was thinking, as was I, about the distraction that had led to me not getting my bagel.

"Uh, sure. You ever find the toaster?"

He laughed. "Yeah, I just had to call my assistant, who had to call the realtor." He pointed the spatula at an appliance built into the wall near the double ovens. "Apparently, that's a toaster oven. Your bagel and mine are in there toasting right now."

The appliance dinged right then, and I slid the four bagel halves onto the nearby plate. He already had butter and a knife out, so I buttered them while he finished the eggs. A coffeemaker burbled and hissed as it finished brewing a pot.

"Sit." He gestured at the island.

I thought about arguing just for the sake of it, but my stomach rumbled, so I decided discretion was the better part of valor and sat my ass down. Hawk divvied up the eggs *sixty-forty*, which was fine with me. He was a big dude and needed more calories than I did. Bagels, forks, and fresh cups of coffee arrived next.

"Need anything for the coffee?" he asked.

"I wouldn't hate it if you had Splenda."

He rolled his eyes. "That shit isn't good for you. I have something better." he rummaged in a cabinet near the coffeemaker and brought me packets of something else—an alternative natural sweetener.

I added it, stirred, and sipped. Tasted sweet and black, just how I like it.

We ate in silence for a while.

"So, Hawk."

He arched an eyebrow at me. "So, Delia."

"I have to admit, I'm a bit shocked at your domestic skills. Laundry, cooking. You just don't seem the type." I expected an annoyed comeback or something snarky.

Instead, he just laughed. "Understandable. And generally, I'm not. I have people to do just about every-thing." He took a bite of bagel, washed it down with coffee, and then rolled a shoulder. "I grew up with a silver spoon in my mouth. Beyond privileged. Butlers, house staff, cooks, drivers, maids, groundskeepers, the whole nine yards. But my dad was insistent that I not be a spoiled little shit, so once I was thirteen, I was ex-pected to learn how to care for myself. I was taught how to do laundry and was expected to do it myself until I could prove that I was capable of it. It's the same with cooking. I spent two hours every Saturday morning with Ramona, our chef, learning how to make the basics. How to scramble eggs, make an omelet, fry them, boil them. How to make some basic pasta dishes. Steak, chicken, fish, and pork. I had to make my own breakfast and lunches, and had to prep, make, and serve three meals for myself, Mom, and Dad."

I blinked at him. "Wow."

He shrugged. "Yeah. I hated it at the time. I thought it was so fucking stupid. Like, we have all this staff, so what's the point in doing it myself? I knew I'd always have money, so why would I ever need to know how to cook for myself or do my own laundry?"

I laughed. "I have teenage brothers. We don't have a staff, but they still bitched when Mom cut them off from laundry services and expected them to start fending for themselves instead of having Mommy make their breakfast and pack their lunches."

He laughed with me, nodding. "Now, I'm glad. And honestly, I enjoy fending for myself. In my daily life, I have a herd of people who want to follow me around and do my every bidding. Which has its perks, I admit. But at home? I just want to be a normal person. To a degree, at least. So I have someone who comes and cleans the house for me every day because I don't want to be *that* normal. But I cook for myself, and I do my own laundry. Sometimes it piles up when shit gets busy and I'm traveling or whatever, and I'll have Marta help me get caught up, but I do most of it myself."

"Surprisingly plebian," I said. "How noble of you."

"Oh, fuck off," he said, laughing.

"I do have one question, though."

He nodded. "Okay?"

"Was it your girlfriend who stocked the guest bathroom or what?"

He arched an eyebrow at me. "I don't have a girlfriend." He spoke over me when I started to speak. "Or a fiancé, or a wife, or a mistress, or friends with benefits, or a Rolodex of booty calls, or an escort service on speed dial. I am not currently seeing, dating, talking to, or sleeping with anyone."

"So then, who was it?" I asked.

"My assistant."

I rolled my eyes. "I see."

He set his fork down rather noisily. "Look, yes, it has been that way in the past. I will be the first to admit that I used to fuck every assistant I had. I hired them, fucked them until things got messy when they inevitably began to think things were something they weren't, and then I fired them. Rinse and repeat ad nauseam."

"But things are *definitely* different now, right?" I said, my tone dripping with sarcasm.

He sighed, pinching the bridge of his nose. "I understand your skepticism, Delia. Truly. But yes, they are."

"What changed?" I asked. "What made you stop dipping your willy in the PA pool?"

He picked up his fork and spent a few moments

eating while he considered his response. "My secretary, Harriet."

I snickered. "Your secretary? Surely you see how this is not an auspicious beginning to your defense."

He rolled his eyes at me. "Harriet is in her sixties, spent almost forty years in the Marines, half of which was as the personal attaché to a *three-star* general in the fucking Pentagon. She's a grandmother. Most of my staff calls her Harriet the Hatchet. I have had a wandering dick, I will not and do not contest that. But even if I was inclined to do so, which I assure you I am not, were I to make a move on Harriet, I'm quite certain she would castrate me with a stapler."

I spluttered a laugh. "I see." I gave an imperious hand wave. "Continue with your defense, counselor."

"Not a lawyer," he said.

"You talk like one, sometimes."

"Because, unfortunately, I have to deal with them on a daily, if not hourly, basis." He sighed, pushed his now empty plate away, and leaned back in the chair, coffee mug clutched in both hands. "Now. Where was I?"

"How your secretary, Harriet the Hatchet, convinced you to stop fucking your assistants."

"Right, right." He sipped and frowned into his mug. "Fucking cold." He tossed it out into the sink and poured fresh. "If it's not burning my mouth, it's cold. There is no *in-between*."

I laughed. "I've been known to forget my coffee for an hour, find it, and keep drinking it. My best friend and adopted sister, Emerson, says I'm a freak like that. I hate iced coffee, but I'll drink *room-temperature* coffee."

Hawk looked at me with outright disgust. "That's a mortal sin against all *coffee-kind*, if you ask me."

"I didn't."

A sigh and a roll of his hand. "Anyway. After a particularly dismal quarter, Harriet told me she needed to have a serious talk with me. This was…oh, five years ago. Thereabouts, at least."

"When someone with the nickname 'The Hatchet' needs to have a serious talk, I'd be afraid," I said.

He laughed. "Fuck yes, I was scared. Harriet, you see, was hired by my father, who plays golf with the general she worked for. When she decided to retire from the Corps, Dad poached her and sicced her on me. I guess he figured I needed a firm hand to keep me in line."

"I'm thinking he wasn't wrong." I couldn't finish the last few bites of egg, so I nudged the plate toward him. "I can never finish eggs, no matter who made them. The last bite or two just…turns, every single time. I don't know why. It's not you—they were delicious. Thank you, by the way."

Hawk chuckled, taking the plate and finishing them off. "No, he wasn't wrong. A firm hand was absolutely a good thing. And I've come to rely on Harriet in just about every way. So, when she said she needed to talk, I reserved us a table at my favorite place in Little Italy, got a bottle of wine and some good pasta, and told her to make her case."

"Which consisted of 'maybe stop banging your PAs?'"

"More or less, yes." He took the plates to the sink and *hand-washed* them while speaking, and my lord, a man who does the dishes? Girl, I'm *D-O-N-E*, done. "She came with fucking charts and graphs, Delia. See, apparently, there was a pattern. I'd hire a new PA, I'd spend her first week seducing her while Harriet tried to train her, and then we'd start fucking, and it would be all—what did you call it earlier? Hot monkey sex?—for a few weeks, maybe two months. They rarely made it past eight weeks. Usually, according to Harriet's fucking PowerPoint presentation, around the *six-week* mark is when things started to go sideways. I'd get bored of whoever the latest flavor was, and she'd get annoyed that my attention was slipping away from her and back to, you know, work, and she'd start bitching and whining and acting like a jealous, clingy girlfriend." He put the plates and forks in the drying rack and put his butt to the counter to look at me. "And look, I set things out very fucking clearly. I had a whole spiel."

I rolled my hands toward myself. "Hit me with it."

"The spiel?" he said.

"Yes, the spiel. Pretend I'm your latest PA. Hit me with it."

He sighed. "Hmmm, let's see if I can remember it. I haven't given it in a few years." He shrugged. "I still give a version of it to whoever I'm seeing, I suppose. Um. Okay, here. It went something like this." He cleared his throat, smoothing his face into a blank, expressionless mask, and then adopted a very convincing smile that communicated decency and honesty. "I really enjoy spending time with you, Delia. You're a very lovely girl, and I like you a lot. I'd like to keep spending time with you the way we have been, but I probably need to make sure we're both on the same page. I'm just not at a place in my life where I'm looking for a serious, committed relationship. What we have, it's fun. It means something to me; truly, it does. But I can't commit to you. I can promise you that while we're spending time together, there won't be anyone else, and I hope you'll promise the same thing. While we're spending time together, the only thing I'll ever ask of you is that you don't speak to the press, do not distribute, sell, or share photographs or videos of us together, and that you do not treat me like a sugar daddy. This is a relationship, albeit a temporary one. I will spend money on you, gladly, and a lot of it. But it is *not* transactional. As long as we can agree to those terms, we can have all the fun in the world together."

I stared at him, absorbing what he'd just said. "Wow. I…um. Wow."

He sighed heavily. "I hope you understand that I wasn't, you know, saying that to you. You asked for the spiel, so I delivered it as if I were giving it to you. But I wasn't."

I laughed. "Yes, I got that."

"I thought I was being fair. Magnanimous, even. I

never had anyone sign NDAs, despite my lawyer's advice that I should. And honestly, it worked. Until it didn't. The second the girl started to act like she had some sort of...I dunno...input in or claim to my life, my business, or my time, it was over. If she got too clingy, it was over. If she started thinking she was more than the PA I was having sex with, it was over. And it always, *always*, ended up being one of those things."

I blew a sarcastic raspberry. "Gee, Hawk, I wonder why? Hmmmmm." I couldn't have been any more sarcastic if I tried.

"Yeah, yeah." He waved a hand. "What Harriet pointed out with her graphs is that in the two, three weeks I always had between PAs, revenue and efficiency increased. When I was dallying, as Harriet put it, everything dropped off a cliff."

"She appealed to your pocketbook," I said. "Smart lady."

"To my pride, really. I had lofty ambitions, especially back then. I was still making my mark on the business world, and I had a chip on my shoulder about it. I was determined to prove that despite my privileged upbringing and the rank nepotism that got me my start, I was going places. I was young and ambitious. Stupid. Thinking with my dick. And my work was suffering for it. So, Harriet told me in no uncertain terms that if I wanted to succeed, if I wanted to make my ambitions a reality, I'd have to separate work and personal life. Personal assistants were there to work, not play to my ego and pander to my *out-of-control* sex drive. As long as I dallied in the workplace, I was hamstringing myself and everyone who worked for me. She would be glad to arrange things for me outside of work if I wanted, but she wasn't going to continue working for someone who wasn't serious."

I made an impressed face. "It took ovaries of steel to confront your rich and important boss with something like that."

"Absolutely. Meet Harriet and you'll understand—that's what she did. She did that for men who saw combat, men who led thousands of soldiers, men who were in charge of the safety of the entire country. Confronting a selfish, *self-important*, horndog boy with more dick than sense? I doubt she lost even a second of sleep over it."

"And that was that, was it? No more workplace dalliances?" I asked.

"Correct. I put her in charge of hiring my PAs from then on and resolved that when I was at work, it was work only. I have not had a personal or sexual relationship with anyone connected to my business in five years."

"So this assistant…"

"Elara."

"Elara. Right. She, what? Came here and personally stocked your fancy new Alaska home?"

"More or less. She didn't come here, but she was in charge of the whole process. The fridge, the pantry, my wardrobe, everything. I just showed up here." He shrugged. "Why? Did she miss something?"

I laughed. "God, no. The opposite. I was convinced it had to be your wife or girlfriend because the attention to detail is impressive. There was everything a girl would need." I arched a wry eyebrow. "I suppose she was foreseeing exactly the situation that occurred, however."

"Meaning?" he said, a leading statement.

"Meaning, a dalliance. She was making sure your guest room was stocked with whatever your flavor of the week might need while you're here."

Hawk pushed off the counter and stalked toward me. Braced his hands on the counter opposite me and gave me a hard, steely glare. "Let's get one thing straight, Delia. Whatever this thing between us is, it's not a *flavor-of-the-week* situation. If it was, I'd say so. The fact is, I don't know what the fuck it is. I've never met anyone like you, and I honestly don't know what to do with you or how to feel. When I decided I was coming here, I told Elara to pick a house for me to stay in and see that it had everything I'd need. I left it at that and never bothered to check her work. If there was something missing, I'd get it myself or call her. I had no idea she'd stock a guest bathroom I've never even set foot in with everything a girl might need. I'm glad she did because you were able to take a shower and have what you needed. But it was *not* a premeditated act." He leaned close. "We clear on that?" His voice dropped to a growl.

"Clear," I whispered.

Why did I whisper? I'm not easily intimidated—see also my father, my seven giant, scary, successful uncles, and my three *whatever-an-uncle-cousin* is called, and the five *uncle-cousins-in-law*. No one scares me. No one intimidates me. No one. Ever.

But something in Hawk's eyes, something in his voice…he wasn't fucking around.

Also, why did that growl make me all squishy and hot in my nether bits? Why did I answer so meekly?

Sorcery.

It's the only possible explanation.

Somewhere in the distance of this magnificently oversized house, the dryer sang a cute little digital song, announcing the completion of the drying cycle.

"That's your clothes," Hawk said. "Be right back."

He swaggered out of the kitchen and returned a few minutes later with my clothing in a neat, folded stack—jeans, shirt, socks, underwear, and bra. "I didn't wash the bra because I wasn't sure what the deal was there. I just know the few times I've had anyone stay over at my place for more than a day or two and she did laundry, she didn't wash her bra."

I can't help a grin. "That's fine and very thoughtful, Hawk. Thank you." I took the stack of clean, warm clothing from him as I stood up from the counter. "Well, as lovely and domestic as this has been, I probably should go home so my parents don't think I was kidnapped."

Hawk frowned at me. "You live with your parents?"

I sighed. "Yes, Hawk, I still live with Mommy and

Daddy. Because why not? I could get my own place, but I'd rarely be there. I'm only ever home to sleep. I'll have a meal with the family now and then, but I live my own life. I'm a fucking adult, okay? It's just easier, cheaper, and more convenient to stay there. I've got no one I'm trying to impress, especially not with something as trite as 'Look, I've got my own place like a big girl.'" The last part I said in an obnoxious, breathy, *high-pitched* voice, the one I thought of as my influencer impression.

Hawk held up his hands, palms out. "I wasn't judging."

I snorted. "Okay, buddy. Yes, you were."

"Okay, fine, I was a little." He ran his hands through his hair. "I know you're not supposed to ask this, but… how old are you, anyway?"

I had to, okay? It was too good an opportunity to pass up. And he was setting himself up for it. "Seventeen. Almost eighteen."

He stared at me. Hard. *"Bull-fucking-shit."*

I blinked at him, *wide-eyed, doe-eyed*. My eyelashes all but went "tink…tink…tink."

"I am! I'm not supposed to be behind the bar, legally, but as long as no one reports me, it's fine. Right?"

Hawk's jaw clenched. "Delia, do *not* fuck with me on this. Please. I could call Harriet right now, and in fifteen minutes, I'd know more about you than you do. I asked an honest question. Please do me the most basic favor of answering honestly."

I shook my head, snorting. "Jesus, so serious. I'm

twenty-two." I couldn't help a laugh. "Worried you were gonna catch a case?"

"I knew there was no way in hell you were a fucking minor. But yes, that is a concern." He still wasn't laughing.

I sighed, rounding the island to pat his beefy bicep. "You're okay, Hawk. I'm legal and then some. And if you knew anything about me or my family, if I was underage and we'd been *dallying*, if I was you I'd be more worried about my dad and my very many, very big, very scary uncles."

"You have many big scary uncles?"

"No. I have *very* many, *very* big, *very* scary uncles. And they're *very* protective."

"I see. And I should be more scared of them than the law?"

"Well, yeah. Because in order for the law to handle the case, there'd have to be enough of you left to prosecute. You may be rich and important, Hawk, but around here, we do things a little differently. If you fuck me over, it's them you'll answer to. And trust me, buddy boy, you do *not* want that." I grinned up at him, lifting on my toes to kiss his cheek. "That's not a threat, by the way. Just letting you know how things stand."

And with that, I went back to the guest room to get dressed. Hawk drove me back to the bar—a short, quiet drive.

Before I got out, I took Hawk's hand and looked

at him. "Truly, Hawk, thank you for taking care of me last night. And this morning."

"You're welcome." He frowned thoughtfully. "About last night and this morning—"

"Nope," I interrupted. "We can talk about that another time. That's a whole conversation by itself, and I very honestly do not have the time right now."

He sighed, nodding. "Got it."

"You know where to find me, though." I winked at him. "Let's just say that a good time was had by all, on my end at least, and I'm definitely not ruling out some additional...dallying."

A grin spread across his face. "Delia, you're something else, you know that?"

I got out of his truck, paused in the doorway, kissed my fingertips, and blew it at him. "I know."

EIGHT

Hunter

WHAT A FUCKING MESS I'VE MADE OF THIS WHOLE STUPID situation.

I spent the last three days doing a deeper dive into the finances of the Badd's Bar company. I looked at their financial structure. The particulars of their LLC. I went through every last piece of publicly available information my team could dig up and a few things that may not have been exactly publicly available.

All signs pointed to a healthy, successful, thriving business, and a growing one. Which wasn't good news for me. Because that meant I had very little leverage. Why should they need me? They didn't. I didn't need them either, but I wanted them. I've spent a lot of time in their bars in the last couple of weeks. I like the ambiance. I like the food. I like the entertainment. Whatever the secret sauce is, it's working, and if we can put their talent and my money together, we could do some really good business.

I grinned—I just found my pitch. Funny—I haven't been the one to make a pitch in years. Usually, I'm the one being pitched to. And if I decide to invest in or outright purchase a company, I don't *pitch*. I give them the facts and present it as a *fait accompli*.

This is why I'm here, though. It's a challenge. I'm nervous. Worried I might mess up and lose the bid. It's fun. Exciting.

But then…there's Delia.

The daughter of the man I have to pitch to. And she seems to have a lot of sway. I intentionally haven't looked into her role in the company, but I suspect she's being groomed by her father to take over. Why else would a *22-year-old* be the GM of a busy, thriving bar?

She's impressive as fuck, is what she is. And I'm not talking about her body. Her—-the woman. The bartender. She makes a job I imagine isn't easy look… well, easy.

And I was developing…I'm not going to say feelings. But something. For her. I'm thinking about her all the time.

Yes, I dream, and daydream, and fantasize in the shower about that mouth of hers, and what she can do with it. Because good and holy goddamn, that blowjob deserves some kind of award, or title, or accolade, or something. Would it be shitty of me to have a plaque made for her? "Best blowjob ever, awarded to Delia Badd" with the day's date and an eggplant emoji or something.

I've been the recipient of a *lot* of BJs. The whole PA under the desk thing? Yeah. On the daily. While on the phone, typing emails, or signing paperwork. Or just because. So I'm somewhat of an expert, I'd like to think.

And what Delia did to me?

Fuck.

There aren't words to describe it. Not sure why—there's only so much technique involved, you know? At the end of the day, it's all pretty much the same act with minor variations. But something about her, the way she touched me, what she did, how she did it…left me in a literal puddle on the floor, speechless, paralyzed, and all but drooling on myself.

So yeah, I dream about that shit.

I also dream about tasting her again. Because that was just as good for me. Feeling her, watching her? Making her come apart for me? Especially when she told me she doesn't typically come easily, it made me feel about ten feet tall, knowing I did that for her.

I just don't know what to do with her and with the whole situation. She knows why I'm here, to a degree; or, at least, she suspects. I know damn well, and not just because she told me so, that the Badds are *not* interested in bringing anyone from the outside into their business. So me coming here and sniffing around their livelihood, asking questions, and generally being a nosy outsider…and then I start showing interest in her, tell her I'm fucking lying to her…

I can see how it looks bad. Because it is. How am I supposed to keep those two angles separate? I've become quite adept at keeping personal and professional separate since that dinner with Harriet. I don't date anyone who may be within two degrees of connection to my business—I won't date the daughter of someone I'm interested in doing business with; I won't even date that daughter's friend.

But here I am, playing a weird, *fucked-up* game of sexual chicken with Delia Badd, while planning to pitch a buyout or investment to her father.

I stared at my phone and the very short list of important contacts: Mom, Dad, Givey, Harriet, and now Elara. The only people I trust.

Elara I'm still developing trust with—but she'll never be the person I call for advice or to rant to. Same with Mom and Dad—I love them, I'm grateful to them, and I make an effort to stay in touch with them even if I'm not especially close to them. That leaves Harriet and Givey.

Harriet, technically speaking, is my employee. But over the years, I've given her more and more leeway in how we interact and more responsibility within the company, and I've come to rely on and seek out her advice regularly. Just…not on personal matters, typically.

Givey? My only real friend. The only person who

doesn't give two shits about my last name, net worth, or political and cultural influence. To Givey, I'm just Hawk, his oldest friend. We tell each other everything. I was there for him when his girlfriend came up pregnant during freshman year of college—and it was my money that paid for the PI who proved not only was she not pregnant, but if she had been, it could have been anyone's because she was a cheating, lying skank. He was there for me when Yasmin Utrecht recorded us having sex, doctored the footage to make it look like I assaulted her, and then tried to blackmail me for ten million dollars. What Yasmin didn't know was that finance was Givey's career, but his hobby was photo and video manipulation. Some guys do fantasy football, others join a rec hockey league, or bowl, or play online poker. Givey? He creates doctored images and videos and trolls the internet with them. Harmless, funny stuff, nothing political or culturally offensive. The point is, he watched the video and knew immediately that she'd fucked with it, and was able to work some sort of digital magic to prove she'd fucked with the footage.

The question facing me now is, whom do I call? Givey will sympathize. Harriet will offer logical solutions—even if, and especially if—that solution is what I don't want to hear.

I dialed Givey because I wasn't ready to hear what Harriet would tell me.

He answered on the third ring. "Dude, some of us have jobs and lives, Hawk. I'm not your goddamned PA.

It's *five-thirty* on a fucking Friday evening and I have a deadline I'm not gonna hit, so make it fuckin' snappy."

"I may have fucked up."

A long, stunned silence ensued. "Give me an hour," he said. "I'll call you back as soon as I finish this."

"Sounds good, bud. Talk soon." I hung up and tossed the phone onto the table.

I spent the next hour and a half working on my pitch, putting together my projected numbers, working up ideas for expansion, and determining how to identify and reproduce the *family-owned* feel on a larger franchise scale.

And honestly, it felt good to get my hands dirty, so to speak. Do the creative work. Most of what I do on a *day-to-day* basis is *boring-as-fuck high-level* admin shit. Overseeing the overseers, so to speak. Top down, *thirty-thousand-foot* overviews of the Hawkins Group Corporation operations.

It's been a long, long fucking time since I've done anything creative like this, and it's enjoyable as hell.

Makes you think a little bit.

I pushed those thoughts aside for later and put the finishing touches on the pitch, closing the laptop when my phone finally rang.

"Sorry, my boss wanted to see my work before I left for the weekend," Givey said; I was on speaker as he drove home out of the city.

"All good. Thanks for calling me back, man."

"So, you fucked up? What, is she pregnant?"

"Dude, no. Jesus. I'm more careful than that, you know that. And plus, we haven't actually even fucked yet." I paused. "Wait, how'd you know it was about her?"

He snorted. "Oh, fuck off. What else would it be about when you call me and say you fucked up? You don't make mistakes in business. Therefore, it's personal. And since you don't have a personal life outside of which model, actress, pop star, influencer, or socialite you've managed to piss off with your intimacy avoidance issues, it has to be about a woman."

"Intimacy avoidance issues?" I echoed. "The fuck are you talking about? I do not have intimacy avoidance issues."

Givey literally laughed in my face…metaphorically speaking. When he recovered, he sighed, and I could all but see him wiping tears of laughter from his eyes. "Oh, man. Wow. Good one, Hawk. I needed that laugh."

"Fuck you, man. I do not need this shit. I come to you with a real situation and you fucking laugh at me."

"Hunter, buddy. You have a textbook case of intimacy problems. Do you really need me to bust out my psychology minor on you right now?"

"Well shit, you know it's serious when you call me Hunter," I said. "Please, though. Enlighten me."

He sighed, still working through the throes of laughter. "Don't say that unless you mean it, Hawk."

"I'm serious, *Jonathan*. Enlighten me as to my intimacy avoidance issues."

"Oooh, the full first name. We're getting down to brass tacks now." He cursed floridly. "Hold on, let me get around this jackass going sixty in a *seventy-fucking-five*. Fuck you, you *slow-ass* bucket of dicks. I have shit to do besides wait for you to find the fucking accelerator."

I laughed. "You know, sometimes I miss driving myself everywhere. But whenever I'm on the phone with you and I have to listen to you and your road rage, I'm reminded of how lucky I am to have a professional driver. All I have to do is sit in the back of my limo and let him worry about traffic while I sip *thirty-year-old* scotch and get my dick sucked."

"Fuck you. I hate you."

"You're just jealous," I said.

"Yes, I am. Therefore, asshole, I'm gonna let you have both barrels."

"Hit me, big boy."

"Big boy? What are you? A stripper named Candi with an I?" He laughed. "Here we go—you ready?"

"I was born ready. Get on with it, peasant."

"You have mommy issues."

I waited, but nothing else was forthcoming. "That's it? That's your big psychoanalysis?"

"Oh, you want the deep dive? Fine, but don't bitch at me when your *widdle feewings* get hurted." He paused, muttering curses under his breath. "I do not have road rage, also. I just don't have patience for bad drivers."

"Which, according to you, is everyone."

"Exactly. Glad you get it." A groan. "*FUCK*! An

accident? Goddammit. I'm never getting home. Anyway, you want it? You got it. Yes, you have intimacy issues that stem from your complicated relationship with your mother. You were cared for, meaning she fulfilled her essential duties as your guardian, but she…how do I put this, since I still have to have dinner with the woman once a month?"

"This is between you and me, Jon," I said. "All jokes aside, I *do* want to know what the fuck you're on about. The monthly dinner with our folks at the country club will not be affected by anything, you say. You have my word."

"Fine. She's cold, man. You were cared for but not exactly loved. Your dad was the master of tough love. He meant well, and he gave you tools to succeed in business, obviously, but he didn't exactly show you any love but the tough kind. And your mother? Can you recall the last *non-sexual*, utterly platonic hug you got? From anyone?"

I rocked back in the chair, mind whirling. "Hug?"

He snorted sarcastically. "Yes, Hunter, hug. You know, that thing where someone puts their arms around you just to show you that they care about you?"

"Third grade," I said, after a moment of consideration. "After a science fair. My model of fault lines won first place in the *all-city* elementary science fair, and Mom gave me a hug and told me she was proud of me."

For some stupid reason, my throat felt tight.

"Jesus fucking Christ—you remember the *exact* moment?" Givey sounded utterly shocked.

"It was a Friday. March fifth. I was eight."

"And no one has hugged you since?"

"*Non-sexual*? No."

"Fuck, man. No wonder you're such an insufferable asshole to everyone all the time."

I coughed in shock. "Wait, hold on. Now I'm an insufferable asshole to everyone all the time, *and* I have intimacy avoidance issues, *and* mommy issues?"

"No, you're an insufferable asshole to everyone all the time *because* you have intimacy avoidance issues, which you have in large part because of your complicated relationship with your mother."

"This is a very enlightening conversation," I said. "Please, elaborate."

"You crave attention and affection. Love. You don't get it, and that makes you cranky. You look for it via sex with objectively attractive women you have absolutely no intention of letting past the front door, emotionally speaking. Most of the women you date are lucky to get all the way onto the porch, emotionally speaking. Most of the time, they're stuck on the sidewalk."

"And, according to you, this is my mother's fault?"

"According to psychology, yes. And it's more complicated than that, but if you want to boil it down, yes, basically."

"Mommy didn't hug me, so I use women for sex

and treat everyone around me like doormats, is what you're saying."

He sighed. "Hawk, you're like a brother to me. You know I love the shit out of you. But…yes."

"Well…fuck." I rubbed my face with both hands. "Lovely. Call for advice and find out I'm a monster."

"Not what I said, bro, Jesus. Come on. You're not a monster. We all have issues, Hunter. Everyone. Yours just happen to affect more people since you're such a *high-profile* person. One second, I'm getting off the free-way." He came back a moment later. "So. How'd you fuck up? Talk to Givey."

"Only if you promise never to refer to yourself in the third person ever again." I groaned. "This whole Alaskan restaurant project has gotten twisted, and I'm not sure how to proceed."

Givey was silent for a long beat. "I've never heard you say those words before—that you didn't know what to do."

"Quit busting my balls."

"I'm not. I'm being serious. You always know what to do. You're not always right, but you're always confident in your decisions."

"This girl I'm involved with. Well, woman. Young woman? I don't know. She's *twenty-two*, but she's—"

"If you say 'mature for her age,' I'm hanging up," he cut in.

"Fuck off. She is. She's the daughter of the owner of the company I'm looking at. She manages one of their locations, and she's damn good at it. But she knows why I'm in town, loosely speaking. She knows I'm not telling her everything about myself or why I'm here. I have no leverage in the situation because this family is kicking ass. They can tell me to go take a hike, and I'd have fuckin' dick to come back with. That's one side. The other side is that this thing with Delia…it's complicated."

"It's never complicated. It's usually very simple, you just don't want to accept the very simple path forward." He sighed. "You're involved with the *twenty-two-year-old* daughter of the man whose business you're trying to buy—a business you yourself admit doesn't need you. Yeah, Hunt, y'done fucked up, son."

"Thanks. Helpful."

"Not sure what you expect me to say. You're thirty, which is eight years her senior. You're a billionaire. You live in New York. You run a global corporation worth billions. Stocks rise and fall when you post on social media And she's barely an adult, lives in fucking *Alaska*, and runs a bar. I'm sure she's hot and nubile and shit, but you're on two very different wavelengths, Hunter. Honestly, you want my advice? Pull the plug on the whole fucking thing. Come back home. Buy a fucking restaurant here and find some other challenge. Shit, I don't know—take up skydiving, or rock climbing. Sell your whole company and start over. Get into acting. Start a band. Find a woman whose age and social status are appropriate, marry her, and have kids. I genuinely do not know what the fuck you're doing in Alaska in the first goddamn place, Hunt. Other than putting yourself in a compromising position for very little benefit, personally and professionally."

"You don't know what she's like, Givey."

A pause. "I see. So tell me, Hawk. What's she like?" Before I could answer, he cut over me. "And do not reference sex. What's she like as a person?"

"I'm more than just a skirt chaser, *Jonathan*. You act like all I give a shit about is sex."

Another sigh, this one annoyed. "Jesus, you're extra touchy today. Quit being a little bitch, Hunter. Tell me the last woman you had anything approaching a real relationship with. Someone you connected with. Someone you enjoyed spending time with—clothed, I mean."

"Um."

"Harriet doesn't count."

"I wasn't going to say Harriet." I so was.

"Think harder, buddy. I'll wait."

"Courtney Alberforth."

"Oh, fuck me. Do *not* bring that crazy ass lunatic into this, Hunter Hawkins."

"Before she went apeshit, I really did connect with her. We talked about everything. I truly enjoyed talking to her. Until she had her…episode."

"That thing you so quaintly call an *episode* nearly caused a national security crisis."

"How was I supposed to know she was the

estranged daughter of a diplomat? Or that she was off her meds and on the run from an involuntary psych hold?"

"Oh, I don't know, when she showed up at your penthouse at three in the morning wearing nothing but a pair of heels and a smile?"

"That was hot and quirky at the time. I didn't realize what a red flag it was."

"Because you saw those *G-cup* silicone knockers and lost all critical thinking faculties."

"They were *not G-cup*."

"Sorry, H."

"Wrong direction."

"You're missing the point. That was not a real connection."

"Fuck you, yes it was. Until the, um, incident, she was a great conversationalist. We really did talk a lot, fully clothed. Yes, she had the most absurdly oversized *bolt-ons* I've ever seen in real life, and yes, they were very fun to play with. But on my end, it was absolutely one hundred percent a real, personal connection."

"Until she went apeshit on your yacht in international waters and nearly got you killed by the SAS. And y'know, I'm still not clear on how they got involved."

"Me either. Neither are they, according to the official *after-action* reports I saw."

He sighed. "As fun as this stroll down memory lane is, it's only proving my point."

"I've forgotten what your point is."

"I asked you to tell me what this Delia chick is like as a person."

"Then why are we talking about Courtney fucking Alberforth?"

"Hunt. Focus. Your ADD is showing."

"Fuck you. I do not have ADD."

"Tell me about Delia and why it's complicated with her."

"Because I feel things, Jon. That's why. She's *whip-smart*, *hard-working*, and driven. She doesn't take my shit, and gives it back in equal measure and then some. She's the only person I've ever met who feels like my equal."

"That's concerning and insulting at the same time. Your hubris is breathtaking, also."

"I don't mean that everyone else is beneath me. It's just that most people can't keep up. They get intimidated. They see the name, the money, the magazine covers and hit pieces and puff pieces and that whole sexiest man alive *runner-up* bullshit."

"You only think it's bullshit because you lost to Henry Cavill."

"The Lord Jesus himself would have lost to Henry Fucking Cavill."

"My Sunday school teacher once told us that Jesus was probably ugly. Something about a verse implying that he wasn't attractive."

"Missing the point, Givey." I spun around in the office chair until my head swam—a secret habit of mine.

"I think about her all the fucking time. Let me repeat—I *feel* things."

Givey gasped, a *pearl-clutching* gasp of faux shock. "You…*feel*…things for this girl. As in *emotions*? Do tell."

"You're a real cockmuncher, you know that?"

"But a funny one."

"Debatable."

"For real, though. You're developing feelings for this *twenty-two-year-old* Alaskan chick? Like actually? Feelings for her personality, not just her rack?"

"Her rack is epic, and I do have feelings for it. But yes. We've messed around a few times, but we haven't had sex. And I'm honestly not sure if we will. We have this whole game we're playing, and I think the point of it is that we both have intimacy issues, and we both are feeling things we're not sure how to handle, so we're being stupid about it."

"When you say epic…"

"I've never been as physically attracted to any human being in my entire life as I am to her, and that was true before I saw her naked. She's fucking stunning. But her attitude, man. The sass, the sarcasm. Her wit is razor sharp and she's lightning fast with the comebacks. She knows exactly how to push my buttons and enjoys doing so. She's left me speechless—literally dumbstruck, Jon. And again, that was *before* we did anything."

He was quiet for a while. "You've never talked about anyone this way. You have my attention."

"I'm questioning my own motivations. I haven't

told her the truth—she doesn't know who I am. How, I don't know. But I truly believe she has no clue who I actually am. Which is a whole other situation, because I can be a version of myself with her that…that even I wasn't sure existed. And as soon as she knows who I am, that's gonna go away."

"You don't know that."

"It's not inevitable, but highly likely."

"Shake the magic eight ball again."

"You know how rare it is to meet someone who doesn't know who I am and doesn't care what I have or what I can do for them?"

"Yes, I do."

"Yeah, you do. So you have to know how I'm gonna feel about it."

He groaned. "Fuck, man. You *did* fuck up." He spent a few moments thinking. "So tell her who you are, make your pitch, and accept the consequences. I mean, really, bro, what options do you have? Pull the plug and run, or shoot your shot and take what comes."

"I'm emotionally invested in seeing this project through. That's what has me fucked up. I'm bored, Givey. All I do all day every day is put out fires, sign shit, read shit, and decide shit. It's dull. Every day is the same. There's no challenge, no creativity." I closed my eyes and set myself spinning again. "Honestly, bro, when you said sell everything and start over…I might actually consider that."

"Dude, you're having a *full-blown* existential crisis."

"Dude, yes, I am."

"You're really fucked up about this, aren't you?"

"Absolutely."

"I think we're exceeding my pay grade as your best friend, Hunter. I'm not qualified to tell you what to do in this situation. You're in uncharted territory."

I groaned a harsh, raspberrying sigh. "Wonderful. Some advisor you are."

"I'm a confidante, Hunter, not an advisor."

"Oh."

"I told you what I think. Shoot your shot, man. Put all your cards on the table and see what happens. Worst case, you lose a restaurant deal you don't need and a girl you've known two weeks doesn't want to be with you. You'll get over both."

"Sounds simple on paper." I opened my laptop and flicked through my pitch deck again. "Bid first, girl second, or girl first, bid second?"

"Bid first. If she's involved in the company on a management level then she'll be part of the pitch, most likely. So if that doesn't go well, the relationship angle might very well be settled that way, whereas if you try to settle things with her first and then the pitch gets fucked up somehow, she'll be forced to pick between her family and you, and that's a shitty position to put her in."

"Good point."

"That's why you pay me the big bucks as your advisor. Oh, wait. You don't pay me. In fact, I think *I've* paid the last several bar tabs."

I snorted. "You're bitching about a few hundred bucks in bar tabs? You're not exactly hurting for cash, Givey."

"I'm fucking with you, man."

I pulled up my bank app and transferred him some money.

A few seconds later, I knew he'd gotten the notification. "Hawk, what the fuck?"

I laughed. "Payment for services rendered as my confidante and advisor."

"A hundred grand is overkill for the joke, I think," he said.

"It's proportionate. Normal people would send what, five bucks? Twenty? A hundred grand, to me, is the same, roughly speaking, as twenty bucks to everyone else."

"You're a dick. I don't want your money. I was fucking with you."

I just laughed even harder. "If you were struggling for money, I can see how it would be insulting. You're not, therefore, it's a joke between friends. If you really don't want to take my money, donate it or some shit. I don't give a fuck."

He sighed. "You're impossible. Have I ever told you that? I should write a book: How to be Friends with a Billionaire—a comprehensive guide for penniless peasants."

"Not sure how much of a market there is for that, man."

"No shit. I'd be writing the book I wish I had. Dealing with your ass is a *full-time* job."

"Yeah, but you love me."

"Try as I might not to, yeah, I do." He chuckled. "Okay, well, this has been a *wild-ass* conversation, but I'm home now and I've got leftover pizza, the newest season of The Traitors, and a bottle of Blanton's calling my name, so I'm gonna have to let you go."

"Sounds good. Not the reality show; you're a loser for that. But the pizza and the whiskey sound great to me."

"You don't know what you're missing, buddy. That shit is quality entertainment."

"If you say so."

"Shoot your shot. And don't call me again until you have, yeah? I do have my own life to live."

"You do? You're watching reality TV alone on a Friday night."

"I'm on a break from dating."

"You mean Lisa dumped you."

"Fuck off."

"Yeah, you too," I said. "Talk later, buddy."

"Much later, you needy little bitch." He hung up before I could hit him with my comeback.

I tossed the phone onto my desk, poured myself a glass of scotch, and took it outside.

Shoot my shot, huh?

I would if I knew what that looked like.

With Delia, I mean. The pitch I have handled. If

they don't go for it, fine. I get it. I won't push it. Delia, on the other hand? Not a fucking clue.

It's a weird feeling for a man as decisive as me. Scary. Unnerving. I shouldn't be scared of shooting my shot with a *twenty-two-year-old* girl. But I am.

Because I care about the outcome.

And I don't know if she feels the same way.

NINE

Delia

MONDAY, JUST PAST NOON. DAD AND I WERE HUDDLED together in the family booth at Badd's, going over the latest numbers.

Dad had his readers on, which cracked me up to no end; I just didn't dare laugh at him out loud—he was sensitive about needing reading glasses. He scanned the P&L from the previous quarter as well as the numbers so far this quarter, scratching at his thick, *brown-gray* beard.

"Badd's Bar Anchorage is…" He tossed his readers on the table, sighing. "A problem."

"Yeah," I said. "It's just not catching on the way we'd hoped."

Dad stared into space, thinking. "Same decor and

ambiance, same menu, drink specials, killer happy hour deals. It's all the same as here. We've got good music lined up, karaoke, trivia night…we just can't seem to make that place turn a steady profit."

My mind goes to Hawk. The niggling sense that I should know who he is. The questions he's asked. The fact that he's been upfront about the fact that he's keeping his true identity a secret from me.

He's sniffing around our business—I know it. The question was, do I tell Dad?

Dad refilled our mugs from the *stainless-steel* carafe, leaned back against the booth, and sipped the scalding coffee with the nonchalant ease of a man who has long since scorched away all the heat receptors in his mouth. "Spit it out, Dee."

I blinked at him. "What?"

He arched an eyebrow at me. "You've been chewin' on something all damn morning. You're distracted. Come to think of it, you've been distracted for a couple of weeks." He sipped again, staring at me across the rim of his mug through a haze of steam. "I try to stay out of your love life unless you come to me with somethin', so you know I'm only askin' because I'm worried. So. Out with it, kid."

I sighed, staring into my coffee as I stirred Splenda into it, involuntarily remembering Hawk's words about Splenda being bad for me. "It's complicated."

"Bullshit." Dad said this with his lips on the rim of the mug, about to pull a sip.

I frowned at him. "What do you mean, bullshit? It's complicated. It is."

"I mean bullshit. It's never complicated. You may not want to talk about it, but that don't make it complicated." He set the mug down and wrapped both big hands around it.

I considered the issue for a minute. "Normally, I would agree with you, but in this case, it really, actually is sort of complicated, personally *and* professionally. And I honestly don't know where to begin. It is weird to talk about the personal side with you, but it's all mixed up with the business aspect too, and there's a lot I'm not sure about, but it potentially affects you, too, so—"

"Delia." Dad cut in over my rant. "Stop." My mouth clicked closed. "Deep breath." I pulled in a long breath, held it, and let it out slowly. "Now. Tell me everything. Or, perhaps I should specify, everything within reason. I do *not* need to know *anything* about your sex life."

I rolled my eyes at him. "Thanks for clarifying that, Dad." I rubbed at my face. "That's why it's complicated, though." I closed my eyes and rested my head against the booth's back. "A few weeks ago, this guy came into the Kitty. Clearly a cheechako, and a rich one, trying to look less like a tourist."

Dad snorted. "Which works about as well as a tutu on a tugboat."

I blinked at him. "What the actual fuck does that mean, Dad? A tutu on a tugboat? Are you drunk? It's barely noon."

Dad just sipped coffee. "Keep talking."

"He had this sense of…I don't know. Importance. I wish I could explain it better. I get the sense that he's someone I should know, but I can't place him. And I've *flat-out* asked him, and he told me he doesn't want me to know who he is and that there are things I don't know about him that would make a difference if I knew them."

Dad blinked owlishly at me, processing. "So, he's being honest about lying to you."

"Yes, exactly."

"I take it back—that *is* complicated."

"Right?" I rubbed my face again, and sat forward, clutching my coffee as if the heat of the mug will give me the words to explain this shitshow to my father. "He…I….we've…um, messed around a little bit. This is the personal part that I have to share some of with you because it intersects with the professional. He bought that big fancy log place that was in the magazines."

Dad snorted and rolled his eyes. "Which immediately calls his taste into question—that place is everything that's wrong with modern design aesthetic."

"Which you're clearly an expert on," I said, smirking.

"Don't sass me, child." He drained his coffee and toyed with the empty mug. "Why do I need to know that you're messing around with some *out-of-town* businessman who may or may not be someone of some kind of importance?"

"Because Kelly called and said someone matching his description was in Badd's Bar Anchorage asking suspiciously specific questions."

"Like?"

"How many employees we had, which distributor we used, if anyone from the family is ever up there managing, and how profitable business is."

Dad frowned. "Sounds like he's sniffing around to see if we're for sale." He eyed me. "And what'd you say to him?"

I blushed, remembering, and ducked my head to hide it. "I yelled at him. Told him we're not for sale."

"But he's still around." It wasn't a question.

"Yes."

"And you're still…involved with him, to one degree or another."

"Yes."

"But you're not any closer to knowing who he is or what exactly he wants."

"No. I suspect very strongly that he's looking at buying or investing, and he probably thinks that I'm not in a position to decide whether we sell or whatever, since I'm only *twenty-two*. I don't know what he does or doesn't know about our operations or my place in the company. And I don't know what to do about any of it."

Dad did what he always does in situations like this: stared into space, silent and thoughtful. I knew better than to push him—he'd speak when he was ready, and what he had to say would be worth waiting for.

"Set the business aspect aside for a second, babe."

I wrinkled my nose at him. "Dad, don't call me babe. You call Mom babe. It's weird."

He rolled his eyes. "I call a lot of people babe. It's a generic term. You're my daughter. I'm gonna call you babe—get used to it." He waved a hand. "Anyway. Set aside the work aspect of the whole thing, and let's just focus on the personal. You said you've messed around with him a few times. But you haven't slept together?"

I covered my face with both hands. "DAD! I thought we weren't talking about my sex life?"

"You said you were confused. I don't need details. Just yes or no."

"Yes. Correct. We have not." I spoke through my palms. "Moving on!"

"Not quite yet. Why not? You're attracted to him, obviously."

"Yes," I muttered. "Dad, can we please—"

He rolled his eyes at me. "Oh, grow up, Dee. We're both adults here. You said yourself that this affects me. It affects the business. You're involved with this dude who's got an interest in our family's livelihood—your career. So it matters. I'm not asking for a *play-by-play*. We're discussing the facts of the case."

"It's not a *case*, Dad. This isn't Dateline."

"Situation. Whatever. Don't parse words with me." He poured more coffee. "Look, honey. I only ask this because it matters, okay? I'm not here to judge, trust me."

I went beet red in anticipation of whatever horribly

embarrassing thing he was about to ask. "Oh, Jesus. What?"

"It's unusual for you to be involved with a guy this long—you said weeks, right?—without sleeping with him. Do I have that mostly correct?"

Hands over *red-hot* face. "Yes. That would be correct. It is a very unusual situation all around."

"So why the hold up?"

"Um, because he's lying to me? Yes, I'm attracted to him. He's like no one I've ever met. He has this confidence that's…well, it's arrogance, just straight up. But he backs it up, so it's…I dunno. *Well-founded* arrogance. And it's hot, even if it is infuriating at times. He's insanely smart. Easy and fun to talk to. Our banter is… peak."

"But?" Dad prompted.

"But he's sniffing around the business, and he's admitted that he's keeping things from me and that while he'll never straight up lie to me, he told me he's an expert in lying by omission. I…how do I get any more tangled up in that? What could it possibly become? I…I guess part of why I'm so intrigued by him is that he's utterly unlike any of the guys I've dated or been with, and that's a good thing. I'm tired of…the game, I guess. My last few relationships have been…frustrating. But he's not from around here, to say the least. Plus, he's a liar."

"But…?"

I sighed, fidgeting with the tip of my braid. "But I don't know. I can't get him out of my head. And…"I swallowed hard. "The time we have spent together has been…crazy. We avoid talking about the work stuff since I know he won't answer."

"Complicated." Dad scratched his beard. "You were right—it *is* complicated. I guess…what do you want, Delia? What do you *really* want?"

"I don't know! I love my job. I love being part of this. My goal hasn't changed—I want to take over when you retire, and I want more responsibility and authority in the business in the meantime." I sighed, shaking my head. "But Hawk, he…god, how do I put it? He challenges me. Look, I'm a lot. I know this. I'm loud, opinionated, and independent. I'm high octane. Everything about me just revs higher than most girls. Which means most guys don't know what to do with me. They can't keep up. They can't match me. But he does and then some. I guess this is where it's hard to talk about it with you because you're my dad. I just…part of me wants to tell him to fuck off and get lost forever, but another part of me just as strongly is like, 'no, no, we *like* this one.' And I don't know what to do."

Dad nodded. "I get that. The few of your boyfriends I've ever actually met haven't seemed to quite match your energy, I guess I could say. They're just not your equals. And I don't mean that like you're better than them, they just…" he trailed off, shrugging.

"No, you're right. I get what you mean. And that's what's different about this guy is that he does match me. I've never had that. It's…I like it. But he's lying! But then again, he told me he is, which is just confusing. Who does that? And what am I supposed to do with that? How am I supposed to feel about it?" I shook my head. "There are no easy answers that I can see."

"You're not wrong," Dad said. "I need to meet him. Hear what he has to say for himself. See if you can put together a meeting between the three of us—a business meeting between me, the CEO, and you, my protege and *second-in-command*, and him, a prospective buyer. We aren't selling, but it costs nothing to hear him out. We can get that aspect of the situation sorted out, and you can then set that aside and figure out the personal stuff. Make sense to you?"

I smiled at him. "Yes, it does. Thanks. I'll set something up and call you."

We wrapped up the weekly *check-in*, figured out the schedules, *double-checked* inventory, and all the other fiddly bits of running four bars.

I didn't have a phone number for Hawk. But I did know where he lived, and I could probably safely assume he'd show up at his *now-usual* spot at the bar at the Kitty at some point soon.

Two more days went by without me hearing from or seeing Hawk, and I was getting annoyed. I knew he was avoiding me while he did business things, whatever those were, in preparation for making whatever move he had planned.

I tried calling Sunni about everything, but she was too busy to talk for long—she promised to call me the moment she had more than five minutes of alone time.

Finally, I was fed up with waiting. So, on a slow Thursday evening, I left Zeke in charge and clocked out early. I absconded with a bottle of Uncle Roman's favorite scotch that Hawk was so impressed by and drove out to his house.

When I got there just past nine, the house was dark except for a single light on the main floor. I parked in the massive gravel circle, shut off my lights and engine, grabbed my purse, and headed for the front door.

I rang the video camera doorbell and waited…and waited…

There was a glass door around the side of the garage, which I peeked into: his truck was there, which meant he was there. Ignoring me? Doing something that made him unable to hear the bell? I went back to the front door and rang the bell again twice more and waited almost five minutes.

Fuck it.

I tried the front door: locked. Garage side door: locked. I went around the side to the back patio—the kitchen and den were both dark, and the door was locked also. Where was the one light I saw? Upstairs—his bedroom? How did I get in? Hopefully, he wasn't the type to keep a gun under his pillow. I went down to the *walk-out* basement where the pool and hot tub were— lights burned down here, and a trail of drying footprints led from the pool to the door. I tried the door: unlocked.

I poked my head in. "Hello? Hawk? It's Delia."

No answer.

There was a small puddle just inside the door where he'd dried off, and then increasingly smaller footprints leading upstairs. All the lights were off, so I couldn't really make out much but shapes and outlines, so I left my curiosity on read and headed for the stairs. All the lights on the main floor were off, so unless he liked to sit in total darkness, he wasn't there. I went up. The huge house was silent and still, and my heart pounded—I was intruding. This felt illicit, although probably not dangerous.

Right? Right. Hawk didn't strike me as a *gun-toting, shoot-first-and-ask-questions-later* type.

Hopefully.

Upstairs, the landing opened to a sitting area with a stretch of *built-in* bookshelves; to the right was a short hallway with three doorways, all closed—bedrooms; to the left, the owner's suite, a pair of French doors cracked slightly ajar. Light spilled through.

Taking a fortifying breath, heart pounding, hoping like hell I wasn't about to walk in on something I'd regret seeing, I nudged the door open and stepped in.

Hawk was on a huge Alaskan King bed in a nest of pillows, dressed in thin, light gray sweatpants and nothing else, noise cancelling headphones on, laptop on his lap, and stacks of papers and legal pads filled with scrawled notes surrounding him. He had a pair of glasses on—*blue-blockers*, if I had to guess. And fuck me, the glasses gave him a *nerdy-sexy* look that had my pussy sitting up and taking very intent notice.

Gripping my purse strap in one hand and the bottle of scotch in the other, I stood in the doorway just watching for a minute.

His focus was absolute. I couldn't see his screen, so I had no way of knowing what he was doing, but whatever it was, it took up every bit of his attention. He had a pen pinched between his *rolled-in* lips, and he flipped between glances at his pages of notes, the stacks of papers that he would sort through, and his screen, occasionally typing obscenely fast or using the tracking pad to swipe, pinch, or tap.

Not wanting to startle him and get punched by accident, I fished an old protein bar out of the bottom of my purse and lobbed it underhanded at him.

Most unfortunately, my aim was a little *too* good because it landed directly on his junk, causing him to toss his laptop aside, double over, and groan in agony.

"Oh, fuck! Hawk!" I said, hurrying over. "I'm sorry!"

He pawed his headphones off. "What...the.... *fuck*?" He rasped, peering at me in agonized confusion. "Delia?"

I perched on the edge of the bed beside him and pulled his head onto my lap. "Hawk, god, I'm *so* sorry—that was an accident. You were so focused that I wanted to get your attention from a distance. Are you okay?"

"What? How?" He groaned again, cupping himself. "Jesus fucking Christ. That hurt like a motherfucker."

"I'm so, so sorry, Hawk. I'm sorry."

He rested his head on my lap, groaning, for a minute. Eventually, he let out a harsh breath. "Fuck, that hurt." He levered himself upright. "Delia, what the hell? How did you get in here? What are you doing here?"

"To answer your second question first, I needed to talk to you. I rang the bell like five times and waited like five minutes, but you didn't answer. I knew you were home because I could see the light on and your truck is in the garage, so…I, um, went around back and came in through the basement." His hair was damp and messy, and he smelled freshly showered.

"And your first thought was, 'lemme throw a protein bar at his dick?'" He wiggled further upright, whimpering pathetically as he cupped himself.

"God, no, I just…It was supposed to hit your chest or something, not… there. It was an accident, and I'm so, so sorry." I covered my face with both hands. "I feel awful, Hawk."

He groaned a laugh. "I'll be fine. Probably. Eventually." He grabbed the offending protein bar and ripped it open.

"I wouldn't eat that," I said. "I don't know how old—"

He took a bite, stopped before his teeth had made much of an imprint, and then pulled it out of his mouth. "Holy shit that's stale."

I winced. "It's probably been at the bottom of this purse for…god, I don't even know. The store where I got it doesn't even stock those anymore."

He pulled the wrapper up around the *half-bitten* end and set it aside. "So you didn't just throw a protein bar at my junk, you threw a stale, *rock-hard* protein bar at my junk. I know things are weird between us, Delia, but that seems a little harsh." He scooted over on the bed to make room for me. "So. What brings you, uninvited, into my bedroom at…shit, it's after nine already?"

"You were very focused."

"Most people would take the fact that the lights were off and I didn't answer the door as a sign to come back another day," he said, with a wry arch to his eyebrow.

"Yeah, well." I shrugged. "I'm not most people."

"That much is evident." He gathered his papers and notebooks. "So. It's after nine on a Thursday and you broke into my house and threw a stale, *rock-hard* protein bar at my dick…why?"

"I didn't *break* in," I said, my tone arch and prim. "The door was unlocked. I let myself in. There's a difference."

He lay back against his headboard. "Delia."

His laptop was still open, and I blatantly stole a look at the screen. He had several things going on at once—a spreadsheet, several different graphs and charts, and a long document with changes marked in red.

"Hoping for clues as to my identity?" he said, eyes closed.

"Yup," I answered. "I'm a shameless snoop. Don't leave me alone around anything you're sensitive about."

"Why are you avoiding the question? Why are you here? Not that I'm unhappy about you being here—the opposite, in fact, dick injury aside. But this is a new de-velopment—you seeking me out."

I sighed. "We need to talk."

"Nothing good ever comes from those four words," he muttered. "Do I need to get dressed for this?"

"No," I answered, mainly because Hawk, in noth-ing but gray sweatpants and glasses, was a *turn-on* like nothing else. "It's not bad. I just…I don't know where to start."

"Just rip off the *Band-Aid*, babe."

"Babe," I muttered. "What is it with men calling me babe?"

"Not a fan?"

"I dunno. My dad called me babe earlier this week, and he was like, It's not weird, I call everyone babe, which is true. My mom, my adopted sister slash best friend Sunni, my aunts, everyone is babe."

Hawk shrugged. "I get that. Babe is not the same as baby. Babe is generic." He opened his eyes and turned his head to look at me. "You're changing the subject."

"Fine!" I snapped. "Fine. My dad wants a meeting."

Silence.

"Your dad wants a meeting as your father, like hey buddy what are you doing with my daughter? Or your father, CEO of Badd's Bar Enterprises, would like a formal meeting with me to discuss my proposal?"

"You have a proposal?" I asked.

He bobbed his head to one side. "I wouldn't classify it as a *full-on* pitch, like something I'd bring to a Fifth Avenue boardroom full of execs. But I do have a proposal that I'd feel comfortable bringing to your father on a *quasi-formal* basis."

"And to me," I said. "Because I'm VP of Badd's Bar Enterprises."

He regarded me for a long moment. "Delia Badd, VP of Badd's Bar Enterprises at *twenty-two* years old. Impressive."

I rolled my eyes. "No nepotism here."

"No, there's not," he said, the statement void of humor. "It's a family business. You're his oldest child and next in line to inherit the reins."

"I guess that's true."

"People tend to get their panties in a twist over nepotism, and I've never gotten it," He said. "I mean, when you're talking about some CEO forcing his useless shit of a kid into a role he's clearly unqualified for, yeah, that's a problem. But a parent using their resources and connections to give their kid a leg up in whatever industry, I don't see the issue. If I ever have kids and they show interest in the business, you bet your ass I'm gonna give 'em a headstart. I'm not gonna put them right into the corner office, but I'm gonna help them get started."

"Is that how you got started?" I asked.

He tipped his head side to side. "More or less. My father gave me five hundred thousand dollars the day I graduated high school. I had—have—a trust fund set up by my grandparents, but I've never touched that. I started investing and saving the money my parents gave me for living expenses when I was in junior high, with my granddad's advice and assistance. I started my first company when I was a junior in high school. By the time I graduated, I had plans for the business I wanted to start—Dad's seed capital was enough to get me started. I grew it all on my own from there. So, a half million dollars isn't nothing, I recognize that. But I didn't use any of my family's connections, and my business is totally separate from what my father and grandfather did and still do. They're proud of me, for sure, but also a little annoyed that I didn't take the reins of what they assumed would be a family company."

"I see," I said. "So, when your father and grandfather die and or retire, that's the end for that business?"

He shrugged. "Not necessarily. I've been toying with the idea of buying them out and folding them into my portfolio."

"So you're successful enough that you can buy out your family?" I asked.

He nodded. "Oh yes." He sat forward, raking his

hands through his messy, damp hair. "So. The meeting? When and where?"

I shrugged. "Whenever works for you. Dad and I are flexible. Before the bars open would be best. We could do it at Badd's."

He nodded again. "Works for me. Tomorrow?"

"Sure. I'll let him know. Let's say ten tomorrow morning at Badd's? The original location."

"Ten tomorrow. I'll be there." He picked at his thumbnail, not looking at me. "Delia, about you and me—"

"Nope." I slid off his bed. "I'm not here for that. I don't have a number for you, which is why I showed up like this. Otherwise, I would have just called or texted."

"I haven't been avoiding you, I've just been—"

"Hawk, no. Stop. For one, yes you were. And I get it. You're working. And work, in this case, is my family's livelihood. And listen, we're giving you a chance to be heard, but don't expect a warm or eager reception. My dad has run Badd's Bar for over twenty years—he and my family grew it from one little local dive bar into what it is today, and we're damned proud of that. I said it before and I'll say it again—we're not for sale. We don't want or need a corporate partner or sponsor."

"Delia, I understand and respect all that—truly, I do. And all I'm asking for is what you're offering—a chance to be heard, and I'm grateful for the chance."

"As for you and me," I started.

It was his turn to interrupt. "Delia, I…I think it's best if we put all that aside until after tomorrow."

"Me too," I said. "That's what I was going to say."

"I know." he looked at me. "That's not what I want, though."

I stared at him. "This is me *not* asking what you want, Hawk."

"I want to forget all about the business. I want to throw you onto this bed and devour you until you don't know your own name." He slid off the bed in a lithe, predatory movement and stalked toward me. "I want to know what you feel like wrapped around my cock. I want to lock that bedroom door and not come out for a week."

My knees shook. I locked them and swallowed hard, looking for the fire that usually sees me through every scenario. In its place, I only found pathetic, trembly, needy desire. My breath was caught in my throat, and my hands shook. "Hawk," I whispered. "We're not doing any of that."

"No?"

"No."

He reached for me, but his hand stopped short—I didn't miss the minute tremble. "What was it you said? We'd fuck like gods."

"I know," I whispered. "But we can't. I can't—I *won't*."

"You won't?" he echoed, making it a question.

"I won't. Not with you. Not until you've told me the truth." I threaded my fingers into his, palm to palm. "It's hard for me to set that boundary, Hawk. It's not what I want. I want everything you said. I want it all, and

I want it now, and I don't want to ever stop. That's how I am around you. It's nuts." I turned away, shaking my head—it was too hard to look at him; my desire was too strong. If I looked at him, I'd break. "I've never wanted anyone the way I want you. Which scares me. But it's because of how much I want you that I'm not going to let myself go there with you. I can't. For myself."

"I get that," he said.

"I don't know if you do or not, and that's part of the problem." I turned to face him but held my hands out. "Just…stay over there, please. Fucking gray sweatpants." I rubbed my face. "I don't have the best track record when it comes to relationships, Hawk. I'm not good at them. I always pick the worst guys. Sunni says I do it on purpose, but that's a topic for another day. I just…I really do like you. But I don't know who you are, and things are messy and complicated, and you're…not lying exactly, but holding things back from me. And I can't start something with you under those circumstances. And…and once upon a time, very, very recently, I would have been okay just fucking you for fun. But it's not that between us. It's not just fun, Hawk. You know it, and I know it. So…yeah. When business is settled, however that looks, and you decide you want to fill me in, we can talk. Until then, I need to hold onto this boundary."

Hawk stood with his hands at his sides, regarding me with an unreadable look on his face. "I respect that position a whole hell of a lot, Delia. And much as I hate to, I have to agree with you. Because I feel the same way."

"You…you do?" I asked.

"Absolutely. I'd wager my track record with relationships, if you can call what I've engaged in to be relationships at all, is probably far worse than yours. I'd come to the same conclusion, and that's what I was going to say."

"Then…what was all that about the things you want?"

He shrugged. "The truth. That *is* what I want. But for once in my life, I'm trying to listen to what's right and what's best, *long-term*, not just what I want in the moment."

We locked eyes for a long time, unspeaking, unmoving.

"If you don't leave right now, Delia," he said, taking a step forward toward me, "I can't be held responsible for what I do to you."

My entire being yearned to throw itself at him. Rip his clothes off and do unspeakably sinful things to him. Let him tie me to his bed and have his wicked way with me. Ride his rugged, handsome, beautiful face like a rodeo bronc. Suck him. Fuck him. Hold him. Lick him, kiss him, touch him, snuggle him…

Claim him.

Instead, I fled.

I didn't so much as look back, either.

I left through the front door this time.

TEN

Hunter

WHEN WAS THE LAST TIME I WAS THIS NERVOUS?
Nothing comes to mind.

This is stupid. I should not be nervous. I do not need this deal. They do not need this deal. But it matters more to me than possibly any deal I've ever done, with the sole exception of the very first one I ever did back when I was nineteen and had ambitions of world domination. Or at least an ambition of acquiring an absurd amount of money and power.

I've been up since six, tweaking and *fine-tuning*, writing and rewriting, adding and deleting. Obsessing. Acting like a *wet-behind-the-ears* intern about to make his first pitch to the big boss.

It's 9:55, and I'm in my truck out front of the bar,

laptop and notes on the console beside me, trying to center my mind and calm my nerves.

Jesus, is this what my people feel every time they have to pitch to me? Holy shit.

On impulse, I dial Elara.

"Good morning, sir," she answered, far too chipper. "How can I help you?"

"Love that attitude, Ms. Joseph. Good morning. Quick question—answer it immediately and without *follow-up* questions."

"Yes sir."

"What advice would you give to someone about to make their very first pitch and they're so nervous they're about to puke?"

"Square breathing, sir," she answered immediately. "Breathe for a *four-count*, hold it for seven, and exhale for eight. Focus on the strengths of your pitch. Go over the numbers a million times until you know them cold, forward and backward. Never let them see you sweat. Someone wise once told me that last one."

"Square breathing, huh?"

"Yes sir. It works. I, um, I suffer from panic attacks, and that's one of my primary tools when I feel one coming. Grounding myself is the other one."

"What does that mean?"

"Focus on the present. The here and now. What can you see? What can you smell? What can you taste? What can you feel? Name five things you're grateful for. Four things you're proud of. Three things that make you happy. Two positive habits. One thing you love about yourself."

"Panic attacks, Ms. Joseph? Have you ever had one at work?"

"Yes sir, almost every day."

"Jesus," I mutter. "We're gonna have to talk about that. For now, however, I have to go. Thank you."

"Good luck, sir."

"I wasn't talking about me, Elara."

Her tone was amused. "Of course not, sir."

I ended the call without saying goodbye, simply as a matter of exerting authority, just because I could. A minor dick move, but I'm in a weird place right now.

I collected my things, put them into my leather satchel, let out a breath, and exited my truck. I paused outside the entrance and then entered the bar. Lights up, chairs and stools up, it was a different place.

The thought that percolated in my head as I made my way across the bar for the booth near the kitchen where Delia and her father were seated was whether or not her father would recognize me. I figured the chances were high. A girl—woman—of *twenty-two* can be excused for not keeping track of the list of billionaires and eligible bachelors in Manhattan. A man Sebastian Badd's age? If he didn't know who I was, well…that would be weird, and I don't mean that in a hubristic sort of way.

I wasn't hiding myself. I wore a pair of jeans, my boots, and a plain black polo. I'd shaved, my hair was slicked back in my usual style, and my *Ray-Bans* were tucked into the neck of my shirt rather than hiding my face.

They saw me coming and both stood up. I saw recognition light up Sebastian's face instantly, followed by anger.

Fuck.

Delia seemed unsure how to greet me, so I set the standard of formality. "Ms. Badd, it's nice to see you again. Sebastian Badd, good morning. Thanks for meeting me." I intentionally didn't introduce myself.

Delia glanced at her father, at me, and then back at her father, reading the anger on his face. "Dad, I thought we were going to hear him out."

Sebastian glowered at me. "Not going to introduce yourself? Why's that? Hmm…*Hawk*? Figure either we don't know who you are or you're hoping to avoid the subject so you can keep my daughter in the dark a bit longer?"

"A little of both, if I'm being honest," I said, standing my ground as Delia's father—a big, muscular, *hard-looking*, tattooed, bearded man—infringed on my personal space.

"Oh, if you're being honest, huh?" He got in my face. "Why don't you be honest about who the fuck you are?"

I lifted my chin, meeting his hard, angry stare. "I've never met you, Mr. Badd. I've never been to Alaska before. I have nothing but respect for you and the business you and your family have built. So I'm not sure what I did to piss you off other than exist. But if this is how the conversation is going to start, with you pissed off and in my face, then there's no point in continuing. Delia, thanks for arranging this. I'm sorry it couldn't work out."

I turned on my heel but only made it a few steps. "Hawk, wait. Just...stop." Delia's voice halted me, and I turned around but didn't *re-close* the gap. "Dad, stop. Take a breath, please. I'm fully aware that Hawk isn't being fully forthcoming as to who he is. If you know, please share. Otherwise, you need to let me decide how to handle Hawk's dishonesty. I don't need you to be pissed off on my behalf. I can do that on my own, thanks very much."

Sebastian let out a disgusted breath. "You really don't know who this motherfucker is?"

Delia rolled her eyes. "No, Dad, I do not know who this motherfucker is."

"And you call him Hawk?" he pressed.

"Yes."

He glared at me, and I waved at him. "Go for it. I assumed it would come out today. I was never planning on hiding it forever. Just until I figured out the business end of the equation."

Sebastian shook his head. "No. You need to be the one to do it. Not me."

Delia growled, an adorable, sexy, and funny sound of frustration. "Ugh! Men and their idiotic *dick-measuring* contests. Someone just fucking tell me!"

I let out a breath. "My name is Hunter Hawkins."

Delia's eyes bugged out. "Wait…for real?"

"Last I checked, yes." I slid my wallet out of my hip pocket. "Would you like to see my ID?"

She had her phone out and was googling my name. I saw my photo pop up—a telephoto shot of me taken by a pap. In it, I was on a yacht in the Caribbean with a flavor of the week. I looked horrible. It was right after that whole thing with Courtney, so I'd tried to drown myself in the bottom of a bottle and between the legs of as many women as I could. I'd gone on a *two-week* bender, and by the time this photo was taken, I'd been awake and drunk for three days, fueled by coke and rage. I hadn't eaten, and I'd have liked nothing more than to fall off the boat and drown.

And when you google my name, that's the first fucking photo that pops up. I've tried for years to have it scrubbed from the internet, but asshole trolls online keep reposting it just to spite me because I had the gall to get rich via hard work and a lot of luck.

Delia's lip curled at the photo. "Wow. Flattering."

I said nothing.

She looked at me. "Hunter Hawkins. Hawk to your friends."

I snorted. "Friend, singular. Givey—the guy I called. He's my only friend and the only person, other than you, now, who calls me that."

"What does everyone else in your life call you?" she asked.

I shrugged. "Sir."

She laughed until she realized I wasn't kidding. "I'm not calling you sir, Hawk."

A joke bubbled up and died behind my teeth, emerging as a twitch of my lips that I know she caught.

"No, no, no. Nope." She snickered. "This is business."

"I said nothing." I bit my lip.

She snorted a laugh. "Shut up. This is serious."

Sebastian eyed us both in disgust. "Glad you two find this humorous."

She scrolled and then tapped on my Wikipedia page. She followed a link to an interview with a finance magazine I'd done a few years ago where I'd told the story about my father's five hundred grand.

Her eyes went to mine, surprised. "That was true?"

I didn't try to disguise the hurt. "Of course it was. Everything I've told you is true. The only lie I've told you is the omission of my real name." The hurt was good—it put the armor of ice around me; I met her father's eyes. "Now that that's out of the way...shall we? I can make my pitch in five minutes. I've timed it. I am fully aware of what your answer is going to be, but my trip here will have been wasted..." I paused for a split second. "Professionally speaking...if I don't at least present you with my idea."

Sebastian stared hard at me, assessing me. "Fine. Five minutes." He tugged his phone from his back pocket, set a *five-minute* timer, sat down, and started it. "Better get going, Hawkins. Time is ticking."

Delia touched my wrist. "Hawk, I just meant—"

I pulled my hand away and slid into the booth across from her father. "I know. Later, perhaps. Your and your father's time is valuable, I'm sure, as is mine."

Sebastian snorted. "Yeah, no shit. You earn what…a few million an hour?"

"No clue," I said, already tired of his animosity. "Never bothered to calculate something so pointless."

I opened my laptop, got out my phone, arranged my printouts facing them, and set my laptop to mirror my phone's screen, turning the laptop to face them while using my phone to manipulate my presentation.

"Badd's Bar and Grille, where we are now, was established over forty years ago by your father, Liam Badd. Please correct me if my information is incorrect or incomplete. During your father's tenure as owner and operator, he took it into the black within five years, which is remarkable on its own. By the time of your father's death a little over twenty years ago, it was a successful operation, beloved by locals and tourists alike. I'm unfamiliar with the particulars as it's not publicly available information, but upon your father's death, he left the bar to you and your seven brothers. Your ownership of it took it to the next level of success, likely due to the draw of you eight, along with the advent of social media marketing. Your cousins showed up at some point and opened their own bar, which should have been competition. Instead, you somehow parlayed that into a resounding success for the eleven of you. Am I correct so far?"

Sebastian grunted. "So far. I know my own history—what's your point?"

I ignored his question. "Having gone into business together, you opened a third location, Badd Night, a nightclub and live music venue. Most recently, you opened Badd's Bar Anchorage, which I'll address in a moment. A few years ago, you turned control of your socials over to someone new, which, in my rather expert opinion, was one of your best moves. Whoever is running your social media is fantastic. I'm not sure if you've seen the metrics, but if not, I've put them together for you." I clicked on the first slide, a graph of their total earnings with a marker indicating the likely date of the socials takeover. "As you can see, your earnings saw a steep increase as your socials manager began campaigns focused on presenting Badd's as a lifestyle choice—simple, attractive, professional photographs and short video reels of the Ketchikan locations featuring you all, the owners, your family, with relevant hashtags and catchy music. Your various family members all have their own careers, with the exception of the two of you and, possibly, your wife and Kitty. But yet, you all make regular appearances on the socials. Obviously, whomever is in charge of this has watched the metrics and is aware that posts which do not feature a member of the Badd family sees on average *thirty-eight* percent less engagement."

Delia, I noticed, looked increasingly uncomfortable as I went over the social media aspect of my pitch. Understanding dawns.

"Ah." I grinned at her. "It's you, huh?"

She shrugged. "Yeah. Aunt Eva was handling it for a while since she's a photographer, but she hated the social media aspect. So I took over, since…you know… social media is kind of my generation's whole thing."

I nodded. "Makes sense. And the truth is, when I first was made aware of Badd's Bar, your socials were the first thing I looked into, and I was seriously impressed. I say that with professional detachment, Delia. I had no idea who you were then, and I was impressed."

"Kiss ass," she muttered.

"Not at all. Simply telling the truth."

"And your point is what?" Sebastian asked, his expression still stonily blank.

"Which location is the least performing?" I asked, instead of answering.

"Anchorage," Delia said. "By a lot."

"Dee," Sebastian said, annoyed. "C'mon."

She rolled her eyes at him. "It's not exactly classified information, Dad."

"Anchorage," I said. "On paper, it makes sense. You picked a prime location. The drinks and food menus are largely the same as the other three locations. Good specials, ambiance, everything. There's no reason it shouldn't do as well as the others. But it's just not. Do you have ideas why not?"

Sebastian hesitated. "I mean, we can't be there *full-time*."

"Precisely. It doesn't receive the same promotion on social media simply because none of you are there. As a result, it feels a lot like any other bar. And if I'm being honest, it's not run particularly well, at least the time I spent there. The servers seemed lost and confused, the manager wasn't much better, and the food often came out wrong or cold or both."

Sebastian nodded reluctantly. "We've gotten the complaints. We know."

"And what are you doing about it?" I asked.

Neither of them answered.

"You're not sure what *to* do, are you?"

"And this is where you offer to buy it from us, I suppose?" Sebastian said. "No thanks."

"Dad. Hear him out."

"No, as a matter of fact," I said. "I'm not interested in buying anything from you. I considered it, of course, but aside from the fact that I knew before I ever left Manhattan that you'd never sell, my time here has proven that even if I did convince you to sell everything to me outright, it would be a wasted venture. The whole thing would tank within months, at best."

Sebastian and Delia frowned at each other. "And why do you say that?" Delia asked.

"Because the secret sauce that Anchorage is missing is *you*." I pointed at her. "I mean, not *just* you—the physical presence of someone from your family. A guid-ing hand."

They were silent at this.

"And your proposition is what?" Sebastian asked.

"Look, from what I can tell," I said, "only Delia is at a location on a daily basis. Sebastian, you're at least partly retired, doing most of the CEO work remotely from home or wherever. I imagine you still like to tend bar now and then, as does Kitty. But the locations here can run on their own successfully without one of you on the premises at all times. Why is that, do you suppose?"

Delia stared at nothing, thinking hard. "Because we spent time there when we opened it. We promoted it on socials. Spent time there so customers could come in and see us. Anchorage never got that. We spent a few days there around the grand opening but that's about it. We're rarely there in person." She looked at me. "So, again, what are you proposing?"

"A drastic move," I said. "You shut it down, fire ev-eryone, rehire, do some cosmetic updates, and someone spends six months to a year up there, in person, running it. And more importantly, training the new staff to very rigid standards. Slowly back off your presence there—work, open, and be gone before the rush. Take a week off here and there. Wean the clientele off of seeing a Badd family member there in person."

They looked at each other.

Sebastian frowned at me. "A lot of problems with that suggestion. We can't afford to lose the income we're getting from that location, number one, or at least not for the time it would take to do what you're suggesting. Two, who goes? I need Delia here, running Kitty. And Kitty, the only adult family member with experience in the industry, I suppose. My boys, her younger brothers, are still in high school, and I'm not sure what their plans are beyond that. Everyone else has lives and careers; they just pitch in a shift here and there. The bulk of *day-to-day* operations are run by Dee and me. I'm sure as fuck not spending six months to a year away from my wife and kids. Number three, the cost of firing and hiring a whole new staff, redecorating, and arranging a grand reopening? We don't have that kind of liquidity just lying around. So, appreciate the insight, and what you're suggesting would probably work; we just can't do it."

I arched an eyebrow at Delia. "You must get your brains from your mother."

She clapped a hand over her mouth, stifling a shocked laugh. "HAWK!"

Sebastian growled, very much like a *pissed-off* Kodiak bear. "I'll break you in fucking half, Hawkins. Fuck off."

I just laughed. "I didn't come across the entire country and spend almost a fucking month here to give you a free consultation, Sebastian. As you pointed out, my time is extraordinarily valuable. I told you I'm not interested in buying you out. I'm interested in being a silent partner. I'll provide the upfront capital for a percentage of the profits. And if we're successful in *re-launching* Anchorage, we look at expansion under the same model. And to be clear, I only take a percentage from the locations I help fund. My name will not appear anywhere. Badd's Bar Enterprises will remain a Badd family operation, I'm just interested in helping you bring your vision to more people."

Sebastian rocked back in the booth, crossing his mammoth arms over his chest. "Surely there are more profitable ventures for you to stick your fingers into than our couple little bars, Hawkins. What's your angle? Even if we did go with your proposal, we're not giving you a huge percentage. You're not gonna make a ton of money off this. So, honestly, I'm asking—what the fuck are you after?"

I shrugged. "I have money, obviously. When I first started out, yeah, my goal was to make as much money as possible as fast as possible. And I'll be the first to admit I ran roughshod over anyone and everyone who got in my way. I was fucking cutthroat."

"But now you're different," he mused, dry and roll. "Right. Pull the other one, Hawkins."

I sighed. "It's true. Look, you want the brutal truth? I'm fucking bored. Within a few years at most, my net worth, minus any assets from my father or grandfather, will pass the billion mark. That's without doing a damn thing—all properties, investments, companies, and subsidiaries left exactly as they are, no additional movement. I have holdings in every major industry or very nearly. I'm in tech, medical, transportation, manu-facturing, entertainment, and communications. I've ac-quired, via various means, corporations worth billions, just because. I've done VC work in Silicon Valley. I have a successful production company producing content for all the major streamers, and we're attracting top talent from all over the world. I have hundreds of millions of dollars invested in medical *R-and-D*, focusing on cancer and Alzheimer's research, primarily. I'm working on…" I waved my hand. "Look into it if you're interested—most of it is publicly available if you know where to look. If not, ask me—I'll tell you just about anything."

"What's your point, Hawk?" Delia asked.

"My point is, I've run out of challenges. *Day-to-day*, I do very little of any real value or importance—any competent executive can do the work I do. I'm an in-novator. I like a challenge. I enjoy hard work. I enjoy the challenge of bringing the best out of my employ-ees. I'm not doing any of that. I got into the food ser-vice industry because it was different; it was something I had no experience with beyond eating at restaurants and drinking in bars. I invested in a few places and took an interest in seeing what my money did. I bought a few places and took an interest in watching the professional restaurateurs take over and rebuild. I paid attention. And I'll tell you this much: I didn't get where I am by being a dumbfuck—I'm good at what I do. Damn good."

"And now you want to take things a step further," Sebastian said. "Get your hands dirty."

"Exactly. I enjoy meaningful work. I could have picked any of the thousands of restaurants and bars in New York alone, let alone from around the country. My PA and secretary came up with a list of possible investment opportunities—several from New York and then yours. How they picked yours, I don't know. But what you're doing interests me. The fact that you wouldn't just sign over your company if I offered you a dump truck full of cash interested me. The fact that you're out here, somewhere I've never been and know nothing about—that interests me."

Sebastian's expression had softened into interest—skeptical, but interested. "And now that you've met my daughter, you're *really* interested."

"DAD!" Delia snapped. "What the fuck?"

I let out a breath. "Sebastian, you do not know me. You only know what the tabloids tell you, and *ninety-nine-point-nine* percent of what the media reports about me is either taken out of context, inaccurate, or just plain made up. I understand and respect your skepticism. I understand and respect your desire to protect your daughter. But I'll thank you to not form opinions of my character without taking the time to get to know me." I leaned forward. "Yes, I am attracted to your daughter. I enjoy her company. She's smart, *hard-working*, talented, funny…and she keeps me on my toes. She may not have known who I was, but I'd like to think it wouldn't have made a difference. Yes, I'm older than her. Yes, I have a somewhat sordid history, romantically speaking. But at no point did my interest in her color my interest in being a part of what you're doing. Ask her. I never discussed your business with her. The time I spent with her was purely personal."

Sebastian looked at his daughter. "Dee?"

She shrugged. "He's telling the truth. The only thing he wasn't honest about was his name. And he told me *flat-out* that he was keeping it from me. And I guess I get why, to a degree."

"Why?" Sebastian asked.

"Being famous isn't easy," I answered. "When a large percentage of the world knows you on sight, knows who you are and what you do and what you're worth and who you've dated, it can be hard to meet people. When you're as wealthy as I am, it's hard to trust people. Are they interested in you because of who you are or because you can pay off their student loans with a credit card? When I came to Ketchikan, my hope was that I'd be able to fly under the radar for a while. I was hoping that a place like Ketchikan would have enough people who don't give a shit about me that I could come here as myself and see what was unde tected…for a while, at least. The *best-case* scenario is that I grossly overestimated my own fame. Which, so far, has been true. No one gives a shit—Delia least of all. Which is fucking fantastic."

Father and daughter traded glances.

"That much I do understand," Sebastian said.

"Forgive how this sounds, but…how so?" I said.

He chuckled. "Got a few family members who are sorta famous themselves."

"Oh, right. Myles and Lexi. I talked to Kitty about them the first day I spent here," I said.

He nodded slowly. "Yeah," he drawled. "Them, too."

"Who else?" I asked, frowning.

"Harlow Grace. She's married to my brother, Xavier."

"No shit?" I shut down my presentation and relaxed my posture. "Xavier Badd. He's doing some very interesting things with Valentine Roth in the aerospace field. And I mean, Harlow Grace is…well, I don't have to tell you, I guess."

Sebastian stared at me for a long, silent beat. "We'll talk about it and get back to you."

I nodded, gathering my things. "Very good. I look forward to hearing from you." I hesitated and then dug one of my cards and a pen out of my bag; I wrote my cell number on the back of the card and handed it to Delia. "That's my personal cell. I think maybe six people in the world have that number, by the way." I smiled at her. "So next time, just call me?"

She turned red. "Rude." She made a face somewhere between a wince and a smile. "You, uh, feeling okay?"

"Yeah, I'm good."

Sebastian watched this exchange between us with curiosity on his face but said nothing. I slid out of the booth, slung my bag over my shoulder, and extended my hand to him. "Sebastian. Good to meet you."

He shook my hand without standing up—a nice power move. "You too. Probably."

I snorted at this and then turned my attention to Delia. "We'll talk later?"

She had my card in her hand, running a thumb along one edge while staring at me. She nodded. "I'll call you. Unless I show up unannounced instead."

"Maybe just call.

"Probably not."

I bit down on a laugh, shook my head, and left without another word.

I drove back to my giant empty monstrosity and utterly failed to accomplish anything whatsoever, despite the monumental list of tasks I've been putting off for the last few weeks.

All I could think of was Delia.

Fuck the proposal. Fuck my entire company. Fuck everything.

I just wanted to know where things stood between Delia and me.

ELEVEN

Delia

I WATCHED HAWK—HUNTER HAWKINS, BILLIONAIRE businessman—saunter confidently out of the bar. Once he was gone, I pulled out my phone and opened up the browser tab with his Wikipedia page and went back to the original Google search. Pulled up the images and scrolled.

An old headshot, likely from his LinkedIn profile. Dozens of photographs from tabloid magazines—him with a rotating bevy of women, most of them famous to one degree or another; models, actresses, pop stars, influencers, and whatever the fuck a "socialite" is. Photographs of him getting into and out of limousines, usually with a phone to his ear and sunglasses on his face, wearing a *three-piece* suit like he was born in it.

Professional photographs of him from interviews, with soft lighting and digital retouching to unnecessarily perfect his already perfect facial structure, on folding chairs in blank industrial spaces.

So many photographs.

"How the fuck did I not recognize him?" I whispered out loud.

"Wondering that myself, hon," Dad said.

I shook my head. "I don't know. I mean, I know who he is. But…like, who cares? He's some billionaire businessman. Had he been Henry Cavill, obviously, I'd have known who he was. A lot of people way less famous than him I'd have recognized. But I don't follow pop culture all that much, and he's not…he's not pop culture anyway. He's famous because he's hot and rich."

Dad snorted a laugh. "I suppose that makes sense. To me, he's just one of those people who have been photographed so much it's hard to fathom anyone not knowing him on sight."

"I know, I know," I said, and then moaned in embarrassment, thunking my head down onto the table. "I feel stupid. I guess I just…we're in Ketchikan fucking Alaska. Why on God's green earth would Hunter Hawkins be *here*? It just didn't occur to me that he would turn out to be…*him*."

Dad patted my shoulder. "I wouldn't waste any more time on that aspect of this whole situation, honey. You didn't know. Now you do. What's next?"

I sat up rubbing my forehead because I'd thunked

a little too dramatically. "Fuck if I know, Dad." I looked at him. "What do you think about his proposal?"

Dad thought for a while before answering. "Honestly, as much as I hate to admit it, his points about Anchorage make a lot of sense. We set it up, got it going, and assumed because it had our name on it that it would just...*go* the way the locations here do. I mean, like he said, you're the only family member who can regularly be found in any of the bars here these days. I pop in here to do paperwork and whatever a few times a week, and I pull three or four shifts a week bartending, but I'm nowhere near as present as I was even a few years ago. But business is as good as ever."

"I'm just gonna play devil's advocate for a second here," I said. "Why do you say, 'as much as I hate to admit it?' And be honest with yourself about it."

He scratched his beard. "I dunno, actually, now that you ask. I guess I'm preconditioned to dislike guys like him."

"Meaning?" I pressed.

"Richer than god. Stupid *good-looking*. Had everything handed to him on a silver platter his whole fucking life, acting like he owns the whole world."

"But Dad, you spent less than half an hour with him, and he spent most of that on his presentation. How do you know anything about him?"

"Presentation is a strong word for that. So is pitch, for that matter. He had a few slides and some *half-baked* ideas."

"Which he came here himself to present to you. Dad, he's Hunter fucking Hawkins. He owns a *whole-ass* skyscraper in Manhattan. Anyone else would have sent some lackey with a fancy, *spit-polished*, *picture-perfect* pitch that we both would have hated. He came here himself. He did *in-person* research. He put together the pitch or whatever you want to call it himself and presented it himself."

"So you're saying I'm not giving him a fair shake because of what I've read and heard about him in the media, is that it?"

"Yes," I answered. "Exactly. Look, I'm trying really hard to keep things separate. But at this point, I don't think I can, and I don't know that it makes any sense to try. I've spent a good bit of time with him over the last few weeks, Dad, talking, hanging out, and…a little bit of other stuff that you don't want to know about. My estimation of the man that I've come to know is that he's smart, creative, funny, and interesting. He didn't have everything handed to him on a silver platter, either. Yeah, he grew up very wealthy. But his dad gave him five hundred thousand dollars the day he graduated high school and basically told him to figure it out himself. He hasn't used any money from his trust fund or inheritance to build his business or live off and doesn't consider himself really a billionaire because he hasn't passed that threshold solely on his own merit. He's only considered one if you count assets from his family."

Dad huffed. "Five hundred grand is a lot, especially

for an *eighteen-year-old*. But I guess I gotta give him re-spect for building a hell of a successful company out of that."

"Exactly. So, put your personal feelings aside, mainly because your personal feelings seem predicated on...I won't say it's a false premise, but it's pretty close. Look at his proposal objectively. Anchorage is not doing well. We've known that for months, at least. We've got-ten a pretty steady flow of complaints from customers, and the tweaks and changes we've made haven't done diddly squat. We fired the manager and hired a new one. Set guidelines and best practices. Nothing has changed. Anchorage is still floundering."

"I know, I know," Dad said, running his hand through his hair. "A shutdown, redo, and reopening does make sense."

"And the only way we can afford to make that hap-pen without leveraging assets or something—which, like, how would that even work? I'm *twenty-two*, I don't fuckin' know—is to bring in outside money. Right?"

Dad nodded. "Right. We'd have to take out loans or leverage the equity we have by owning this place outright. We're doing well. We have money. Three out of four locations are in the black. But the kind of cash we're talking about to totally shut down Anchorage, fire everyone, the time it would take to scout and hire management, supervisors, *front-of-house* staff and *back-of-house* staff, remodel, and do a grand reopening? It would put us in a bad position financially. Unless we pressed family for cash, but I wouldn't do that unless it was an emergency. Which, I mean, Anchorage *is* failing, so it does feel pretty critical to fix that one way or another."

"Agreed," I said. "So…?"

He let out a long, *lip-flapping* sigh. "Fuck. He's our best option. It's a sound proposal. He's not asking for a percentage across the board, only from the locations he provides funding for. That's fair. I mean, I'm sure the percentage he's gonna want will hurt, but…I guess that could be negotiated." He looked at me. "There's just one element I'm not sure how to get past."

"Someone has to be in Anchorage *full-time* for at least a year. He said six months to a year, but I think realistically, to make sure things are done right and all, a year is minimum." I tapped the tabletop with my fingernails, thinking.

"Agreed," Dad said. "But who? I can't. Mom can't. Kitty can't. The boys can't. Your other aunts and uncles are all busy with their own lives and careers. They like pulling a shift here and there for fun, but Badd's is our baby, Dee."

"I know. Which means it'd have to be me."

"And who would run the Kitty?"

I shrugged. "Zeke. I wouldn't have to move there for a few months, assuming we signed a contract today and got started tomorrow. But that stuff takes time to put together. So give me a few months and I could get Zeke ready to manage the Kitty. That's not an issue. You may have to spend some time there regularly to keep an eye on things till you trust him, but Zeke is good. He closes for me all the time."

Dad nodded. "Right, okay. So...you'd consider it, then?"

I rubbed my face with both hands and then covered my face with them, sighing, thinking. "Yeah, I would. I wouldn't want to live there *full-time*, forever. My home is here. But to get Anchorage running correctly? I could do a year—more likely a year and a half. It's not *that* far, either, so I can come back and visit regularly."

"It's pretty far, babe. Driving is like, what, almost forty hours nonstop? You'd have to fly if you're gonna do it regularly, and that adds up."

I didn't want to say what popped into my head because it was patently ridiculous—the thought had something to do with Hawk and a private jet and the perks that would come from being a billionaire's girlfriend.

See? Ridiculous. I'm not gonna date someone for the perks. I don't even know if I wanna date that man.

Lies. I want that man in my bed, and I want to handcuff him there and never let him leave.

Kidding, mostly.

Dad and I sat quietly for a while, each lost in our thoughts.

"So we're considering his proposal?" Dad said after a few minutes. "This obviously can't be a unilateral decision I make. I've essentially made you VP of Operations of Badd's Bar Enterprises. You're the one who'd have to relocate to oversee the expansion. And from what he said, he'd want to eventually do more locations. Which would mean more relocating for you." He fixed me with a serious look. "You need to think really hard about if that's what you want, Delia."

I nodded absently. "Yeah, I guess I've got some thinking to do."

He rubbed my back. 'Why don't you take the day, sweetheart? I'll handle things here and at the Kitty."

"Yeah, good plan. Thanks." I turned and hugged him. "Love you, Dad."

He kissed the top of my head, squeezing me gently. "Love you too, kiddo."

I slid out of the booth, got in my Ranger, and headed north for my thinking spot. Once there, I did what I always do when I have a major life decision to make: I called Sunni.

She answered on the fourth ring, panting. "Let me call you back in fifteen, yeah? I'll have time to talk."

"Okay," I said. "Talk soon. But it is pretty important."

"You okay?"

"I've just got a lot to fill you in on," I said.

"Fifteen minutes and I'm all yours."

It was more like twenty, but whatever. My phone burbled with an incoming video call. I answered, and Emerson popped up on my screen, her hair wet from a recent shower, the wall of her room behind her.

"So, talk to me," she said. "What's going on?"

"You first. My shit will take a lot of time to go over, and I want to know how you are. How's your man? How's life now that camp is over?"

She grinned. "Hayden is great, and life is great. I made the team!"

I squealed. "Of course you did! I'm so fucking proud of you, babe!"

She did a silly little dance, and I joined her until we dissolved into laughter. "For real, though, I'm so geeked. It was pretty brutal, but it was good. Those bitches are competitive, Dee. It's cutthroat as fuck out here." She sighed. "I'm a team player, you know? Like, I'm out here to win, yeah, but I want the *team* to win, not just me. So I had to sort of put on my bitch hat."

"*Sunni-girl*, you don't have a bitchy bone in your body."

"It turns out I do. A girl twisted her ankle and I was glad because it meant one less person to compete against." She waved a hand. "Hayden was so supportive, though. I just love him so much, it's silly." She lit up just talking about him. "We have some time off coming up, so we're gonna spend a few days up there."

"I can't wait! I feel like it's been ages since I've seen you."

"Right?" She clapped her hand. "Okay, so you're caught up on me. Now. Spill. I need to know everything."

So, I spilled the tea. I told her about meeting Hawk, that first kiss, the insane fucking orgasm he gave me, everything we'd talked about, the question of his identity, the business aspect, his proposal, everything. The only thing I didn't tell her was his name.

When I was done, Sunni was quiet for a while. "So he's hot, rich, has a great cock, gives you orgasms that literally make you pass out…am I missing anything?" she asked.

"Yeah. He kept his identity from me until today."

"But he told you he was."

"Right."

"And he didn't try to leverage your personal relationship for an advantage with the business deal he's proposing?"

"No. When we're together, it's purely personal."

"And he's not an asshole."

"So far, no."

"No wife, girlfriend, kids?"

"Nope."

"How do you know, though?" she asked. "I mean, you don't have the greatest track record with guys being honest about that. And also, when are you going to tell me his fucking name?"

"I know he's telling the truth because of who he is." I sucked in a breath, held it, and let it out slowly. "He's…ummm…his name is Hunter Hawkins."

Silence greeted this.

And then: "Shut…the *fuck*…up."

"Facts."

"Hunter Hawkins—*the* Hunter Hawkins—went down on you? You sucked Hunter Hawkins' cock. You slept in his bed. You broke into his house? He made you breakfast!"

"Yes, Emerson."

"How did you not recognize him? He was on fucking Time magazine! TMZ does features on him like every other week."

I sighed. "I'm not sure, honestly. I mean, you don't expect someone like him to show up in Alaska, right? Like, he was just there at my bar. I always had this niggling idea that I should know who he is. I guess if I'd taken a picture of him, I could have reverse image searched him and figured it out, but…"

"You wanted him to tell you, so you intentionally kept yourself in the dark. Because you have trust issues when it comes to romance."

"Correct." I slid off the tailgate of my truck, went down to the edge of the water, and sat down. "I don't know what to do, Em."

"What do you want?" she asked.

"I don't *know*!" I shouted. "I don't know."

"Buuuuull shiiiiit," she sang. "Yes, you do."

"I…" I laughed a sigh. "Yeah, I guess I do. I want him. I want things to be real with him. I want…I want the Hawk I've gotten to know to be the real him. But how do I reconcile that with him investing in my family's business? Especially if we do go into business with him and I end up living in fucking Anchorage for a year?"

"Do you *want* to move to Anchorage?"

I laughed. "I don't even fucking know, Em. Legit, I don't know. I mean…no? But yes."

She cackled. "Wow. That clarifies things."

"No, because Ketchikan is home. My whole family is here. Everyone I know is here. I know zero humans in Anchorage. I'd be totally alone, and that doesn't sound particularly nice." I shook my head, sighing.

"But?" She prompted.

"But also…I kinda do want to do it. I've only ever left Ketchikan a handful of times, and never alone. It would be an adventure, I suppose. It would be a lot of responsibility, and if I want to take over for Dad sooner rather than later, I need to know I can handle it. I guess…I mean, I live with my parents. I've never had to stand totally on my own two feet. I'm a *grown-up*, but…not totally, you know?"

"I do. I get it. It sounds to me like the reasons *to* go to Anchorage outweigh the reasons *not* to. And I mean, it also seems like the consensus from what I'm hearing is that you and Dad—" She blinked hard at that, paused to clear her throat, still emotional about the whole adoption thing. "You and Dad have pretty much decided that Hunter's proposal is the only real option you have. It's that, or it goes under, or you have to ask everyone else for money. Which, you know they'd all give you everything you need and then some, but that's not really the point."

"Yeah, that's pretty much the lay of things at the moment."

"So, I think you should do it." She set the phone down so all I saw was the ceiling, and then she picked it back up again.

"You do?" I asked.

"Absolutely. It would be good for you. It won't be easy, Dee, make no mistake. It'd be a lot of work, and you'd get homesick and lonely. But at the risk of sounding trite or cliche or whatever, it'd help you find yourself."

"Yeah, you're not wrong." I chewed on the idea of moving to Anchorage and found myself not hating it but feeling a little excited with a decent helping of trepidation. "And what about Hawk? What do I do about him? I mean, is there even a point? He lives in Manhattan. He dates movie stars and models. I…how do I fit into the man's life? I don't."

"Isn't that for him to decide? If he wants you to fit into his life, he'll make a way. And shit, honey, he certainly has the resources to make it happen. He could probably afford to fly out to see you every weekend. I mean, he has to have a private jet, right?"

"Honestly, I don't know. I don't know much about Hunter Hawkins. I know Hawk, but I guess I get the distinct feeling, based on absolutely nothing concrete whatsoever, that Hawk is pretty different from Hunter Hawkins." I sighed, hating how shaky and emotional I sounded—and felt. "Am I just getting caught up in the sexual, Em? Because we haven't fucked. Did I say that yet? We've only messed around. And, like, is that messing with me? Am I creating a connection that's not there because I'm anticipating how crazy intense the sex would be?"

"I can't answer that, babe. I haven't met the man or seen you two together."

"I know. I know, I just…" I flopped backward on the bank, groaning. It feels real. And…" my eyes watered—it was Emerson, so I didn't bother trying to hide it from her. "I guess I finally want something real. Is it him? Or am I just tired of the losers I've wasted my life on up until now? Is it the Badd Family Love Charm?"

"Answer your own question, Dee. No thinking— first answer that comes to mind: Are you in love with Hunter Hawkins, or do you just want to find out if the sex is as good as you're imagining it would be?" When I hesitated, she yelled at me. "Quick! Answer! Right now!"

"I'minlovewithhim," I blurted and then clapped my hand over my mouth. "Fuck."

Emerson was stunned silent for a moment. "Wow. Okay. That's a development I didn't see coming."

"That makes two of us," I said. "Holy shit. How did this happen? I barely know him. What the actual *fuck*, Sunni? What do I do?"

"Talk to him. Give him a chance." Emerson laughed. "I would like to take this opportunity to say I FUCKING TOLD YOU SO! I called it. I told you you were next. And here you are!"

"I hate you," I said. "You jinxed me."

"I know," she said. "But really, you love me. And

just to point out the facts and the logic here, I didn't *do* anything. I'm not in charge of the Badd Family Love Charm. You're just its next victim."

"I guess I need to go talk to Hawk." I let out a wordless scream just for the hell of it. "Fuck! This is crazy, Emerson. I fell in love with Hunter Hawkins and I didn't even know it."

Emerson just laughed. "I know it's scary, especially this part where you have no fucking clue what's going to happen, but just try to remember that no matter what does happen, you'll be fine. You've got dozens of people who love you and support you, and if this whole thing does go sideways on you, we'll be there for you, and we'll help you pick up the pieces. And if it goes well, we'll be there to cheer you on as you and your *hot-as-fuck* billionaire boyfriend make a life together."

"Hot as fuck billionaire boyfriend," I echoed. "I guess I could get used to that."

"When you do fuck him, I'm gonna need details, yeah?"

I giggled, covering my face as the giggle turned into spluttering laughter. "You know I'd never leave you hanging, sis."

She was silent a beat. "Well?"

I frowned at the screen. "Well what?"

"Why are you still on the phone with me? Go! Your billionaire awaits!"

"Yeah, but I'm scared."

Her voice was soft. "That's how you know it's real. You wouldn't be scared if you didn't truly, deeply care."

"I know. I'm not sure I like it," I said. "It was easier when my feelings weren't involved. Just sex and fun and that's it."

"Yeah, but how many of those boys ever made you come so hard you passed out?"

"Zero."

"And how many of them were as honest as he's been? And Dee, babe, in a weird, backward sort of way, the fact that he told you he wasn't being forthcoming about his identity was in itself a bizarre kind of honesty. And he had pretty valid reasons for it. If you'd have known who he really was, would you have given him the time of day?"

"No," I answered, miserable. "Not likely. I'd have judged him for what I think I know about him. I'd have made assumptions."

"Exactly. Dee, honey, from what you've told me, he seems like a good and decent man. Looks or wealth aside, that's something."

"And if anyone could understand and accept his dating history, it's me."

"And vice versa." She let out a breath. "Look, babe. You can sit here all day and all night thinking and over-thinking this whole thing. But you won't ever know what's gonna happen till you give it a chance. So hang up, pull up your big girl panties, and go talk to the man."

And so, that's what I did.

TWELVE

Hunter

I WAS CRAVING A GYRO FROM MY FAVORITE HALAL STREET vendor, who always set up his cart near the side street entrance to my building. I'd have Kenny, my driver, stop just inside the entrance to the garage so I could hop out, get my gyro, and eat it on the way up to my office. The main reason for eating it in the elevator is that I always stuffed a napkin into the neck of my shirt while I ate to protect my shirt and tie from any stray drips of tzatziki sauce. I looked like an idiot, so I liked to make sure no one saw me like that.

Vain, I know, but I find it unlikely that any employee who has seen their boss with a napkin stuffed into his shirt like some overweight good ol' boy at a plate of ribs will have trouble seeing that boss in the same respectful light.

I was fixating on the gyro craving because otherwise, I was going to go fucking nuts.

We'll be in touch.

Fuck.

The waiting was excruciating. I found that I did, in point of fact, care very much whether they accepted or not. It had nothing to do with the money—I'd make peanuts on the deal. So why did I care?

Gyro. Shaved lamb, tzatziki, onions. Simple and delicious. No drama. I'd hand Iannis a fifty and tell him to keep the change; the way his eyes lit up every time, even though I've been doing it for years, never ceases to hit me. He's always grateful. He never assumes, never expects. It's a very simple exchange we have. I ask him about his wife and daughters, and he tells me the latest drama—his wife is feuding with a cousin over something idiotic, and his eldest daughter is dating a real... something offensive in Greek, I've never quite figured out what he's saying or what it means...and his middle daughter wants to go to college in California and his youngest daughter is still young enough to think her daddy is cool and he's holding onto that phase for as long as it lasts. I just let him talk, and good god, the man can *talk*. He takes 10 minutes to make my gyro because he stops to talk every few seconds, but I don't mind. It's a little thing I do every day, and I enjoy it.

I can only think about gyros for so long. I doubt

there's anywhere in town I can get one, and if there is, I doubt very much it'll be even half as good as Iannis's.

Which leaves me spinning out about...well, everything.

I skipped half of what I'd planned to say, as well as most of my slides. I didn't panic or forget, I just realized I had to pivot. Sebastian Badd is no one's fool and wasn't going to be swayed by fancy graphics or impressive projections. Nor would Delia.

I have no clue how it landed. Sebastian didn't seem to like me. Delia was a little all over the place, to be honest. Neither of them gave much away regarding their thoughts. Just...we'll be in touch.

It's been hours. No call from Delia.

God, Delia.

The idea of going back to New York alone leaves me feeling...honestly, panicky. I don't panic. I don't get nervous. I don't spin out or spiral. I decide and follow through. I do what has to be done. I win. I succeed. I get my way.

Except in this case, I might not. Delia may not feel for me how I feel about her. Which is...what? What do I feel?

I don't fucking know.

I mean, obviously I want to fuck her. *Need* to. But that's...for the first time in my adult life, that need, that desire is not paramount in my *decision-making*. Or even in my mind.

I crave her company. In the weeks I've been here,

the time I've spent in her presence has been unparalleled. I enjoy talking to her. She makes me laugh. She teases me, and Givey is the only one who's ever done that. She doesn't take me seriously. She's not impressed or intimidated or scared. She's never asked me for anything.

Now, however, she knows who I am. Will anything change? I feel like it has to.

I groan, shooting up to my feet and pacing my living room.

If they accept my proposal, I'll have to come back to Alaska regularly to see things through. What if Delia doesn't return my feelings, whatever the fuck those feelings even are? What if it was just a bit of fun? Seeing her would be torture.

What if she does have feelings for me? How does that work?

My phone rang. "Givey, what's up?"

"I can feel you spiraling, brother."

I laughed. "You're spying on me, aren't you?"

"Yes, absolutely. I secretly flew there, snuck in, and planted a bunch of spy cameras in your...um...plants that I'm sure you have."

I cackled. "So many plants here, Givey. It's a regular fuckin' jungle. A real *ficus-fest*."

He laughed, I laughed—there was much levity.

"For real, though. You puss out on telling her how you feel?"

"No, asshole, I didn't puss out. I gave her and her dad my pitch this morning."

"And?" I heard him chewing, the bastard—he knew how much I hated listening to him eat while we were talking, yet he did it all the time.

"Could you quit fucking eating? So gross. Damn." I pulled the phone away from my ear when he smacked into the microphone. "You're such a dick, dude."

He laughed. "Alright, alright, I'm done. Sorry, some of us have jobs with limited windows for lunch. Unlike *some people*, who can afford to take a *three-hour* lunch."

"Oh, fuck you. I don't take *three-hour* lunches. I work. I usually eat at my desk while working."

"But you *could*."

"Givey, with love, shut the fuck up. I'm in no mood."

"No?"

"No."

"Pitch didn't go well, then?" he asked.

"Hell, if I know! They didn't say. They told me they'd be in touch."

"Oof."

"Yeah."

"And Delia?"

"We talked last night and agreed we needed to figure out the work aspect first. She actually came here. Scared the actual shit right out of me."

"You had those headphones on, didn't you?" he asked.

"No. Maybe."

He laughed. "A plane could crash right in front of you and you wouldn't notice when you're in that zone, wearing those things."

"She let herself in through the basement."

"Bold. Was she naked?"

"No, Jonathan, she was not naked. She came to talk. And that's all that happened."

"You're a mess, aren't you?"

"God yes," I sighed. "I care what happens. What's happening to me?"

He cackled again. "Awww shit, it's over. The great Hunter Hawkins has developed feelings."

"Take that back, you monster." I scrubbed my face while groaning. "For real, though. Caring what happens is, like, hard."

Givey laughed. "Le shock. Welcome to the shit-show as enjoyed by the rest of us plebian assholes."

"Why are you so mean to me?" I said, laughing. "All jokes aside, I don't know what to do. Wait for her to call? Go find her? What if she doesn't share my feelings? What if she does? I live in New York, she lives in Alaska."

Givey sighed. "Hawk, are you really that obtuse?"

"What are you talking about?"

"You can do whatever you want, man. You can leave your business to run on its own for a while or indefinitely. To be quite honest with you, man, I'm not sure why you're there in the first place. Like, you could buy Boeing and start a space company just for fun, but instead you're…investing in a bar in Alaska no one's ever heard of? Are you having a *third-life* crisis?"

I sighed. "I'm tired of explaining myself about this."

"You don't need to, Hawk. You forget, I know you. I've known you your whole fucking life." He paused for dramatic effect. "Hunter, you're *bored*. You've climbed every mountain, metaphorically speaking, and now you're looking for something to do. Why Alaska? That I can't answer."

"It sounded interesting."

"The point is, if this girl you're in love with pulls off the impossible and falls in love with your grumpy ass, you do whatever the fuck you want. Move to Alaska for a while. Fly back and forth on your *private fucking jet*. That's the easy part, brother."

"I'm not in love with her."

"Okay, buddy," he guffawed. "Lie to yourself if you want, but you can't lie to me."

I halted in my pacing. "I'm not in love with her. Am I?"

"Tell Dr. Givey about your feelings."

"Well, you're a twat, for starters."

"That's not new. Tell me something I don't know."

"The thought of going back to New York alone makes my stomach hurt. The thought of dating any more vapid, clueless models and *rail-thin* influencers with the IQ of a gravy boat makes me nauseated. My big, empty condo, the empty houses all over the world…what does any of it mean? What is any of it *for*?

I bought all this shit...why? Because I have the money, and I gotta do something with it all, I guess? It's what you do when you're wealthy—you buy houses and cars and yachts. But aside from you, who do I have in my life? If my plane crashed on the way home, who would truly mourn? You. Harriet. My parents, for like five minutes. Everyone else would be looking to see how my fortune gets divvied up and how they can get a piece."

Givey was silent. "I didn't know you felt that way, Hunter."

"Neither did I, till recently."

"And what prompted this epiphany?" he asked.

"Delia."

"The woman *single-handedly* altered your outlook on your entire existence in less than a month, and you haven't had sex with her." Dramatic pause. "But you're not in love with her."

"Fuck. You're right."

"Of course I'm right. I'm always right. The question is, what are you gonna do about it?"

At that moment, my phone alerted me that I had an incoming call—an unknown number, Alaskan area code. "I've got another call coming in, Givey. I think it's her."

"Then why are you still talking to me, dipshit?" He hung up, then.

I answered the incoming call. "Delia?"

"How'd you know it's me?" she asked.

I laughed. "Only my parents, Harriet, Elara, and Givey have this number. Oh, and my driver, Kenny. And now you. And you're the only one who has this number that's not saved in my phone, and you're calling from an Alaskan number. Not a difficult deduction."

"Oh. Well, open your front door. I'm here."

Like an idiot, I took the phone with me, still connected, to the front door. Sure enough, there she was, dressed in pale tight blue jeans and a plain white *V-neck T-shirt*. Her dark red hair was down and curled into loose spirals, and she'd put on bright red lipstick.

She took my breath away.

"Hi there, beautiful," I said. "Come on in."

"Actually, I was hoping we could go somewhere."

I shrugged. "Sure, where?"

"I dunno, anywhere. A date. Take me on a date."

I stepped into her space and cupped her face. "How's Paris sound?"

She rolled her eyes and snorted. "Yeah, okay. We'll just hop a flight to Paris for the day."

I grinned. "Maybe a few days." I brushed her lips with mine. "Not sure if you know this or not, babe, but I'm Hunter Hawkins. I can take you anywhere you want to go."

Her eyes widened. "You're for real?"

"Try me. Anything you want, I'll make happen, right now."

She blinked at me, frowning. "But Hawk, I don't care about your money. You don't need to impress me or buy me gifts."

"Need to? No. Want to? Yes." I swallowed hard. "*Are* you here for you, or...?"

"You're dying to know if we decided something, aren't you?"

I snorted. "Absolutely. Being on this side of the wait is traumatizing."

She laughed. "Poor baby." Her gaze went serious. "We're gonna do it. I'm going to Anchorage. I just...I hope you're serious about this. Like, you'd better not get bored again in six months and leave us swinging."

"I see things through, Delia, always. Regardless of our personal connection, I'd never leave you swinging. When I commit, I commit completely."

"Are you talking professionally, personally, or both?" she asked.

"Both," I said.

She looked up at me, blue eyes searching my face. "Hawk..." she shook her head. "Or should I call you Hunter?"

"Either. Givey calls me Hawk most of the time and Hunter when he's serious about something."

"Where does this leave us?" she asked.

"You tell me."

She pulled out of my arms and pushed past me into the house; I closed the door and followed her through the foyer and into the living room. She sat on the couch, tossed her purse aside, and let out a long, shaky breath. "I don't know, Hunter." She rested her elbows on her knees and her face on her hands, exhaling shakily again.

"I don't know. I thought I'd feel more…sure about things once I knew who you were and we were past your whole sales pitch bullshit. But…" she trailed off, shaking her head.

I sat down on the coffee table opposite her and took her hands in mine. "But what, Delia? Tell me what you're thinking. Tell me what you're feeling. Please."

"A million fucking things!" she shouted. "Everything! I'm confused and pissed off that I didn't know who the fuck you were to begin with. I feel like an idiot for prancing around like a fool, messing around with one of the wealthiest and most famous people on the planet, and I had no fucking clue."

"I'm not one of the wealthiest or most famous people, Delia. I'm not even in the top ten wealthiest and not anywhere on any list of most famous. Most people couldn't tell you what I do or why I'm famous other than for having a lot of money and dating a certain type of woman."

"And I'm not that type of woman, Hunter!" She yanked her hands away and shot to her feet, pacing away, raking her hands through her hair. "I'm not skinny. I'm not rich. I'm not famous. I'm not an actress or a model or an influencer or a pop star. I'll never be any of those things. I don't *want* to be. I like who I am, and I like my life. I'm happy in Ketchikan. I'm happy tending the bar. My ambitions stop at taking over the company whenever Dad is ready to retire fully, which probably won't be for a while yet."

I stayed where I was and let her rant.

She stopped and looked at me. "And you…you live in Manhattan. You own entire fucking buildings. You're just getting started, Hunter. As much as you've done already, it's obviously just the beginning. And I…I don't fit into that. I'll never fit into that."

I went over to her. Grabbed her wrists and tugged her against my chest, body flush to body. Her eyes flew wide, wet with emotion. "You done?"

She blinked at me, puzzled. "Wha…? Am I…am I *done*?"

"Yes," I repeated patiently. "Are you done?"

"With what?"

"Ranting."

"I'm not ranting, *Hunter*. I'm *communicating*. You should try it sometime."

"Oh, I think you'll find I'm an expert communicator, Delia. Just…not always with words."

She swallowed hard, wide blue eyes shimmering and deep and uncertain. "Then please, elucidate."

"I thought you'd never ask."

I grasped her wrists in one hand, slid my other to the back of her head, and leaned down to capture her mouth with mine. I ravaged her mouth, giving way to the full force of my need for her, letting my lips and tongue do the talking. I swept my tongue across her lips, and she parted them for me, accepted my tongue and danced hers against mine.

I felt her knees buckle. "I've grown tired of those types of women, Delia," I whispered.

I backed her up against the sliding glass door, which rattled as she caught up against it. I shoved her hands up over her head, pinning them against the cold glass. She gasped, eyes blazing with arousal while still laced with trepidation.

"Ask me why," I murmured.

"Why? Why are you tired of those types of women, Hunter?" She struggled against my hold, trying to free her hands.

I gripped hard enough that it was clear she'd never escape my grip unless I allowed it, but not hard enough to hurt. "They're boring," I said. "They have no wit, no class, no charm. The conversation is…beige at best. Flat. Lifeless."

"Conversation can't be a color," she whispered.

"Sure it can. I said so, so therefore it is." I touched her *kiss-swollen* lips with my thumb. "Kissing them is like kissing a dead fish. They've got no passion. To them, I'm nothing more than a gift dispenser with a nice dick. It's transactional. I give them diamonds and cars and trips to Geneva and weekends in the Aegean on my yacht, and they pretend to enjoy my company."

"Sounds awful," she said. "So why keep doing it?"

"An excellent question." I ran my hand down her side to her hip. "You know why else I'm tired of them, Delia?"

"No, Hunter. I do not. Why else?"

I pressed my hips against hers. "They're all the same. Same faces. Same botoxed forehead and same lip fillers, same hard little *A-cup* tits, same narrow hips and taut little asses. Same washboard abs from eating nothing but kale and birdseed."

"What's wrong with that?" she asked, her voice a delicate breath I could barely hear.

"Nothing, in and of itself. It just turns out that I'm attracted to a somewhat different body type."

"What type would that be?"

"Sexy redheads with foul mouths, a penchant for brutal sarcasm, an ass that doesn't quit, and tits for fucking days."

"Weird," she murmured, a tiny smile curving at the corners of her mouth. "That kinda sounds like me."

"It does sound like you, doesn't it? We had better be sure, though, shouldn't we?"

"Probably a good idea."

I pinched a spiral of hair between my finger and thumb. "Red hair, check. Sexy as hell, check. Foul mouth, check."

"Just checking things off your little list left and right, are you?" she snarked. "Reducing me to a checklist. How very efficient of you, asshole."

I grinned, nipping at her lower lip. "Brutal sarcasm, check." I kissed the corner of her mouth and then her throat. "Two items left to check off."

"I have a question before we move on to those last two items," she said.

"What's that?"

"Does this checklist have a title?" She struggled against my grip on her wrists, breathing heavily, eyes flashing with amusement and arousal. "Because all good checklists have a pithy title."

"It does have a title," I said. "Would you like to know what it is?"

"I think I'd better."

"It's tentatively titled 'My Dream Girl.' Although, I've been toying with 'The Perfect Woman' as an alternative."

"I feel like those are a little vague."

"I'm open to suggestions."

"You could call it 'Reasons I'm Wildly Attracted To Delia Dru Badd In Particular.'"

"That's somewhat on the nose, but accurate." I slid my hand over her hip and then cupped her buttock. "The last two items on the list require somewhat… deeper…investigation and research, I'm afraid."

She rubbed against me, panting softly. "Is that so? What manner of investigation do you propose, Mr. Hawkins? The committee must vote before any action is decided upon."

"Well, we at the Hawkins Group Corporation take *R-and-D* very seriously, Miss Badd. We research *very* thoroughly before taking any product to market. In this particular case, the subject of our research has, unfortunately, been obscured by several intervening layers of textile obfuscation, preventing an *in-depth* analysis."

"Is that so? What is your proposal in this case, Mr. Hawkins? As the subject, we are very invested in ascertaining whether we meet the standards herewith established."

I tried to hold back my laugh, resulting in a coughing splutter. "Herewith?"

"Shut up and go with it. I skipped corporatese class in high school."

"Very well then, Miss Badd. As head of *R-and-D* for this project, I have decided that the most efficient method of investigation is to remove the obscuring textile layers which have, up until now, prevented our research from commencing in a timely manner."

"I see, I see. Well, speaking in my official role as the Chairwoman of the Orgasm Acquisition Department, I hereby order you to commence your research." She lifted on her toes and nipped my lower lip in her teeth, tugged my lip away, sucked it into her mouth, and then slanted her mouth against mine, thrusting her tongue past my teeth. "Posthaste, if you please."

I grinned, wolfish and hungry. "Yes ma'am. Commencing."

THIRTEEN

Delia

I EXPECTED HIM TO DROP TO HIS KNEES RIGHT THERE. BUT, he surprised me, as usual.

He released my hands and bent at the knees, scooped his hands under my ass, and lifted me into the air. My legs went around his waist, and my arms around his neck, my fingers trailing through the hair at his nape. I took the opportunity to taste him: I kissed his jaw, his cheek, his throat with soft slow kisses with a flick of my tongue to taste the salt of his flesh. I sucked on his earlobe, breathed into his ear. Cupped the back of his head and kissed the corner of his mouth, his chin, the base of his throat.

I felt his erection nudging against my ass as he carried me up the stairs—climbing effortlessly, as if my weight was insignificant. He took me to his room, kicking the door closed with a slam.

He set me on my feet beside his mammoth bed. "Do you trust me, Delia?"

I frowned up at him, taken off guard by the sudden and serious question. "I…I'm starting to. Why?"

"Because I want to do something with you, but it requires you to trust me."

"Will it hurt?"

"I'd never hurt you," I said. "At least, not beyond some light spanking and maybe a bite here and there."

"No videos or photographs, nothing goes in my ass, and no gags."

"Perhaps we can revisit the first caveat in the future, but rest assured, I would never, ever, *ever* allow any sensitive materials to be discovered, shared, or disseminated. I am not a man who likes to share. And where you're concerned, I shall be very, *very* selfish indeed."

I let out a breath, nervous to discover what he had in mind. Nervous…and eager. "Then I shall choose to offer you my trust, Mr. Hawkins." I swallowed hard and searched his eyes with mine, knowing full well mine were probably all shimmery with emotion. "Please take care of it, Hunter. I do not trust easily. I've…I've been burned. Badly. By pretty much everyone I've ever dated. So…this is…it's hard for me." I fidgeted awkwardly with the hem of my shirt and shoved my hands into my pockets to stop them from the nervous fidgeting.

His smile was beautifully gentle. "Delia, please

believe me when I say that I understand completely. Everything I do will be focused entirely on your pleasure and enjoyment. Your trust is the most precious thing I could ever have. And, not to brag, but I own an original Renoir, among others."

I couldn't help laughing. "I get it, you're rich."

"Sassy."

"Bet your ass I am. And you love it."

"I do. I very much love it. I'd like to do very bad things to that smart, sassy mouth of yours, though."

I grinned, cupping him over his zipper. "You would, hmm? Such as?"

"You're about to find out, sweetheart. Wait there— don't move."

"Okay...?"

He vanished, breezing past me in a swirl of *Hawk-scent.* "Close your eyes."

I did, and my ears immediately attuned to him. I heard a rustling and his soft footsteps on the carpet as he moved behind me. Something soft and cool and slippery touched my eyes and was tied behind my head, a necktie most likely.

"Can you see?" he asked.

I opened my eyes, but everything was black. "No."

"If at any time you get uncomfortable and want to stop, just tell me. But don't say it if you don't mean it, Delia."

"I don't play those games, Hawk. Hard to get, no

means yes, saying I'm fine when I'm not…that shit isn't my style."

"Good." Soft lips and scratchy stubble brushed my jaw; a hand swept across my lower back. "All you have to do now, my lovely Delia, is stand there and be perfect."

"I can do that," I breathed.

Fingers ran along the waist of my jeans, paused at the button closure, flicked it open, and then traveled to my belly button, lifting my shirt with it. Up, up, up went my shirt. Cool air wafted across my bare stomach.

He worked the shirt off, careful not to dislodge my blindfold. I'd worn my favorite bra and panties set— crimson lace and silk, comfortable as hell and sexy as fuck. The bra was a bombshell pushup, and the cups just barely covered my nipples. Since, as we've already established, I have rather large breasts to begin with, the overall effect tends to dumbfound those I've blessed with a viewing.

Hunter, going on the stunned silence, was no exception. A full minute passed, by my count, before he found his tongue.

"Jesus Christ on crutches, Delia."

I smirked in the direction of his voice. "What?" I asked, endeavoring to sound innocent.

"You. Just…you. You fucking stun me, woman."

I expected his hands on my tits, or his mouth. Wanted that. That's not what I got, though. I got a hot wet kiss to the round of my left shoulder. A palm grazed my belly. Fingers teasing just under the elastic of my underwear. Stubble scraped my jawline, and then lips ghosted across mine, gone before I could claim the kiss I so badly wanted.

My knees shook, and my hands trembled. I wanted to be touched. I wanted to be kissed. I wanted *Hawk*. I needed him. I had finally allowed myself the realization that I was in love with him, and I wanted to feel safe enough to say so to him.

I didn't.

I was scared.

And that wasn't on him—or not entirely, at least.

But this?

The teasing? The blindfold? I hadn't expected this. I was *off-balance* and unsure what to expect. Every time he touched me, I flinched, gasped, expecting him to claim my erogenous zones.

Was this a game? A test? I wanted him to kiss me and make love to me and convince me to do life with him.

Because truthfully, I needed convincing. I wanted it—or, I wanted something. I just didn't know what. I just knew I wanted more, and with him.

Breathing shakily, I waited for his next touch.

Lips between my shoulder blades, my nape, the ridge of one shoulder and then the other. Hands circling my waist to cover my bare belly. Fingertips divoting under my panties, teasing downward...I swallowed hard, involuntarily sucking in my stomach.

His touch retreated millimeters from my sex,

leaving me whimpering, knees quaking. "Hawk," I whispered.

"Yes, gorgeous?"

"You're teasing me."

"Yes, I am."

"I don't like being teased."

"You will."

"Mmmm. Vaguely threatening verbal foreplay—my favorite."

His laugh was a rough sound against my shoulder, followed by a slow touch of his lips to the side of my neck. His fingers lowered my zipper.

Somehow, he managed to make the removal of my sneakers and socks enthralling and titillating, or maybe I was just horny as fuck and would have found a stiff breeze erotic.

I swallowed hard and waited for what he'd do next.

A tug at the leg of my jeans slid the denim down an inch, and then two, and then they stuck at the swell of my ass. Lips, warm and damp, touched my belly, stuttered down to kiss here and there, navel, curve of my side, the slice of skin between navel and underwear.

I gasped at his kisses, which dotted and danced across my belly, daring higher and higher while his fingers hooked into the belt loops of my jeans and drew them down and down. Past my ass, past the place where my thighs touched.

When the jeans pooled at my feet, I stepped out

of them. Stood blindfolded in just my lingerie, knees shaking and breath coming soft and fast.

"Fuck," he groaned, disbelief rife in his voice. "So fucking beautiful."

"God, Hunter."

"Love the way you say my name, Delia. I never really liked it until now."

"Hunter."

"Mmm." I felt the breeze of his movement as he circled me. "I just want to look at you. Memorize this moment. Burn the sight of you like this into my brain."

Hands rested on my waist, cupping the swell of my hips. Lips touched my spine just above my bra strap.

"Touch me, goddammit," I hissed, unable to hold it in any longer. "Please."

"Beg all you want, Beautiful, but I will not be rushed."

"I'm going crazy. Stop fucking with me."

He nibbled my earlobe, and when he spoke, his words were a hot breath, felt more than heard. "I'm not fucking with you, Delia. I'm researching."

"Enough of the games. Just get me naked and fuck me already."

I felt his amusement even if he didn't respond out loud immediately. "Oh no, I don't think so." He was in front of me, then, and I felt him towering over me; his lips slid over my throat, and his hand cupped my ass. "I'm going to take my time, Delia. You said you'd try to trust me. So...try. I promise you, when I finally give you what you want, the torture you're going through right now will be worth it."

"Done this a lot, have you?"

"Jealous?"

I swallowed. "Yes. A little."

"Only a little?"

"We're both adults. We both know we've had other partners. I just…I don't want to think that this, what you're doing to me, is part of some standard repertoire of yours. A move. A game." I felt my eyes prickling, hot and burning with pressure. "I want…I want to feel… special." My voice dropped to a tiny whisper at the end.

"Delia," he murmured. "Precious, beautiful Delia. You have no idea, do you?"

"About what?"

"How I feel about you."

"No. You haven't told me."

"You're absolutely right—I haven't. Neither have you, I might add." He cradled my cheek in one hand, his lips nuzzling mine. "You're all there is, Delia. Have I played with blindfolds before? Yes. But I'm not playing a game. I may be teasing you, but I swear to you, it will be worth it."

"I just…"

"Focus on me, sweetheart." Behind me, now, fingers trailing down my spine from neck to bra strap. "Talk to me. Tell me what you want."

"Touch me."

He grasped my waist. "Like this?"

"You're only teasing yourself, you know."

"Damn right I am. Do you have the slightest fucking clue how hard I am right now, seeing you in this?" He trailed those fingers along my bra strap. "Do you have the slightest fucking clue how badly I want to rip it off you and fuck you where you stand?"

"Hawk, fuck...please. I want that. Please." I was begging, now. Shamelessly.

My pussy was soaked, dripping with need. My nipples were diamond hard and aching. My skin tingled. One touch and I'd combust.

Yet he knelt behind me, hands on my waist, and kissed my back from shoulder blades to coccyx. He slid my panties down an inch...two, three, baring the upper swell of my ass, which his lips touched, kissed, paused upon, tongue darting and flitting across my skin. Another inch down, more kisses to the exposed flesh. Kisses, kisses while his hands glided up my calves and down my shins and up my calves once more to my thighs, palms pressing over my hipbones and my belly to rest just beneath my breasts, pausing, lips caressing the small of my back and the divot where my ass crack began, here and there and everywhere but where I wanted his kisses the most.

Quick, soft, short breaths escaped my lips as I struggled against the urge to plead yet again, fists clenched to keep me from grabbing him and shoving him violently where I needed him.

He asked me to trust him. So, trust him I would. Or, at least, I'd try.

My panties slid lower yet, bunched into a thin *roll-up* of silk and lace in the folds beneath my ass cheeks, the top of my sex bared. I felt his touch sweep across my belly once more, to the front of my thighs, catching the *rolled-up* underwear almost by accident and drawing them down past my knees until they drooped and then dropped around my feet.

He pressed a hand to the back of my knee, lifted my leg to step out, and then repeated the action on the other side. My sex was exposed now, soaked and hot and full of pressure and pulsing with need.

"Hawk," I gasped, as he palmed my ass in both hands, groaning in rough male appreciation as he squeezed, kneaded, and petted me. "More."

"Patience, Beautiful. You'll get all you want and so much more." He kissed the small of my back, my tailbone, one cheek and the other, and his hands slid around front to curl around my thighs, high and so close to my pussy. "Just let me worship you."

I shook all over as he palmed my thighs, and then at long last drew a fingertip up my seam, a silken soft touch along the lips. Again. And again.

"*P-please,* Hawk. Touch my pussy. Make me come. Let me come. *Please.*"

His laugh was almost malicious in its amusement. "Oh my sweet darling. I've barely begun."

"Fuck."

Another rough laugh. "Remember the first time I made you come?"

"*Y-yes*?" I was shaking so hard my teeth chattered, so potent was the need blazing within me.

"When I let you come, that will seem like nothing at all."

"I passed out, Hawk."

"Precisely."

I waited for the next touch of his lips, his hands. Instead, there was nothing. Only a sense of movement and a waft of air, and then I gasped as his lips touched my belly and his hands cradled my ass. My hips flexed forward in a silent, helpless plea.

He kissed my navel. My pudendum. Cupped my ass and caressed it, played with it, squeezing and lifting, patting and smoothing, scratching and slapping. And all the while, his lips kissed here and there of me: hipbone, quad, belly, the delicate fold where hip, sex, and thigh joined. His stubble was deliciously rough against my lips, and I rubbed myself against him, panting.

"Tell me what you want me to do, Delia. Ask me. Order me."

I buried my fingers in his hair. "*M-my* clit, Hawk. Lick it. Suck on it. Put your fingers inside me. Fuck me with them. Take off my bra and play with my tits. Suck on my nipples."

"Mmmmm," He growled. "That sounds like a lot of fun."

"Please, Hawk. Please. *Please*."

"Love the way you beg, sweetheart." His finger slid over my mouth. "Pretty red lips saying such sweet things. Begging me to make you make you come."

"Want me on my knees?" I said, knotting my fingers in his hair and tilting his head back. "Want me to beg for your cock? I need it, Hawk. I need your cock. I want it in my mouth. I want it between my tits. You wanna *titty-fuck* me? Bend me over the bed? You wanna come on my face? Or my tits? Anything, Hawk. *Anything.*"

"All of that and more, darling. You'll get my cock, I promise. However you want it…once I'm done playing with you."

He licked up my seam while sliding his hands up my belly, and this time, he didn't stop. He cupped my tits over my bra, and then yanked the cups down to let my heavy breasts bounce free. I gasped at the rough exposure, and then whimpered when his tongue, almost by accident, slipped against my clit. He kissed my pussy, then, lips to lips, kissing with such *self-evident* love that my heart clenched and the unbearable heat and pressure blossomed into something impossible, so potent and demanding that all I could do was gasp and whimper.

He pinched the clasp of my bra and then guided the straps down to my elbows, and the garment drooped off, and he tossed it aside.

Finally, I was naked for him.

His mouth covered my clit and his hands caressed my breasts, and I nearly sobbed in relief, even though I was still far from the edge of orgasm.

It wouldn't be long, I knew. I was so aroused, so fraught with climactic pressure that one errant lick to my clit and I'd combust, explode.

Hawk, it seemed, knew my body a little too well. He pinched my nipples and sent lances of heat billowing through me in a sharp line from nipples to clit, and his mouth slid over my seam and his tongue delved inward, retreating as it neared my clit.

Again, he pinched and licked, and my knees trembled, threatening to give out entirely before he'd even really begun.

I held onto his hair as my hips thrust against him. He cupped the weight of my breasts in his hands and his lips slid slow wet kisses along the slopes from chest to areolae, one breast and the other, back and forth, daring closer and closer each time to my nipples. When he finally suckled a nipple into his mouth, I gasped shrilly and arched my back to press deeper into his mouth. Held him there, panting as his tongue flicked and swirled. My sex pulsed as he gentled his mouth to a soft kiss, and then bit sharply enough that I cried out in shock rather than real pain. He pinched one and licked the other. I gasped again and again as heat built inside me with each kiss and each pinch to my hard, throbbing, hypersensitive nipples, and my knees dipped and my hips bucked.

No.

No way. It's not possible.

Yet, with each kiss and lick, each caress and pinch,

each twist and flick, the coruscating pressure and wild potent heat gathered behind my clit.

God, one touch and I'd come.

Just one.

Yet still he denied me, remaining focused on my tits, plying them with kisses and licks and pinches until I was gasping and dipping, bucking and panting, riding the ramping waves of ecstasy from nipple play alone.

I lost track of time, then, as dizziness washed over me and orgasm built inside me. I held him to my breasts and panted raggedly, so close now it hurt.

"Hawk," I rasped, my voice hoarse with need. "Please—goddammit, please. I'm so close."

"I know you are, darling. It would feel so good to come right now, wouldn't it?"

"Yes!"

"Say please."

"Please!"

"Perhaps just a little one."

I felt him rise, and his mouth ghosted across mine. "Hold onto me, sweetheart."

I wrapped my arms around his neck, burying my nose against the pulse thrumming behind the soft thin skin of his throat. "Please, Hawk. Please."

He drew a finger over my seam. Gripped my hair in his fist and yanked my head backward, a rough demanding jerk that left me gasping, and his finger delved inside my tight, hot, wet pussy as his mouth slashed over mine, tongue sweeping and demanding.

I came as he kissed me.

But, as promised, it was a small one, brief and aborted as he drilled a finger inside me and then swirled it against my clit just enough to trigger my climax, and then he stopped, pulling away entirely, leaving me shaking, whimpering, and about to collapse.

"Do you trust me?" he asked, his voice a hot whisper against my ear.

"Yes."

"Say it."

"I trust you."

"Say my name."

"Hunter."

"All together, now."

"I trust you, Hunter."

"Sweetest words," he whispered. "Almost as sweet as the words I dream of hearing you say to me."

"I'll say them, Hunter. I'll say them, and I'll mean them."

He was on the other side of me, now. "I know. But not yet. I wouldn't want to think you only said them to get an orgasm."

"I would *never*," I snapped, indignant. I softened my tone. "I couldn't. Those words mean too much to me."

He claimed my mouth again. "I know," he whispered, between kisses. "I know. Me too."

And then he scooped me up with rough hands on my ass, hefting me airborne, carried me a few quick steps, and tossed me. I shrieked in unfeigned fear and shock as I flew momentarily and then landed on the bed with a bounce.

Instead of pouncing on me, I felt...nothing. No Hawk, no hands, no mouth.

"Hawk?"

I felt the bed dip on my left side, and he knelt over me, pulled me up onto the bed, and positioned me on the pillows. The same soft, cool, slippery material circled my wrist, tightened, and then he drew my arm over my head—and the other. He bound my wrists together and tied them in place, so I only had a small amount of leeway.

"Hawk?"

His lips touched mine. "Hush, darling."

My ankle was bound, and the other. I was immobilized now. Helpless. And, honestly, equal parts turned on and terrified.

I panted, fighting panic. "Hawk. I...I don't know about this."

My legs were open, my weeping sex exposed. The air was cool on the drippings of my desire. My nipples throbbed. My heart pounded.

He didn't answer. I felt his weight on my left side. A kiss to my stomach—I flinched.

"I've got you, Gorgeous. Focus on what you feel. Focus on me."

I squeezed my eyes shut behind the blindfold and breathed through my fear—which was more about the lack of control than actually being tied up. I knew without a doubt that if I asked, he'd let me go immediately. I tugged at the bonds around my wrists and I knew if I worked at it, I could get loose. This knowledge soothed me—I did trust Hawk, I just...I had to know, for myself.

God, I *really* had control issues.

"I...I trust you, Hunter." I sank against the pillows, slowing my breathing.

Anticipating his touch, his kiss.

Lips touched my thigh. A hand grazed over my breast. I flinched, arched, gasped. A finger slid over my seam; a tongue flicked my nipple. Lips fused to a nipple, and that finger slid close and dipped inside. Slowly pushing into my channel, one finger curled inside me and he sucked on my nipple until I arched off the mattress and cried out.

He added a second finger and made love to my breast with his mouth. Two fingers drove into me and withdrew.

Orgasm rose within me, all at once burgeoning to nuclear heat, bucking my hips upward.

Again, those two thick fingers fucked into me, and I curled forward, pulling against the restraints as waves of ecstasy billowed through me.

He stopped, withdrawing his fingers right as I was seconds from coming.

"Hawk! Fuck, no, please, please...*fuck*!" I thrashed against the bonds, furious and desperate.

His weight moved, shifting down between my legs. Kisses trailed over my belly, hands cradled my breasts.

Lips covered my clit, and I cried out, ragged and raw. "Hawk!"

For long, unbearable, infuriating minutes, then, he toyed with me, teased me. Brought me to the quivering edge of climax, only to change up and pull me back from the edge.

Again and again, he edged me to the cusp of orgasm, teased me away, and then pushed me to the edge once more.

Before long, I was writhing helplessly, weeping openly with wild, crazed, unbridled madness. "HAWK!" I screamed. "Please, please. Fuck, please, baby. *Please*."

His lips brushed the corner of my mouth. "Baby?"

"I…I don't know where that came from," I admitted. "Never called anyone baby in my life."

"I like it," he whispered into my ear. "A fucking lot. Especially if it belongs only to me."

"It does," I answered. "Only yours. Like me, baby. I'm only for you."

"Promise?"

"Promise." I thrashed as he teased my slit with clever fingers. "Are…are you…mine?"

"Oh, my beautiful Delia." He slid those clever fingers inside me. Curled them against my *G-spot* until I quaked all over like a dry leaf in a long autumn wind. "You'll have to claim me, won't you?"

"How?"

"That's up to you." He fucked my slit with his fingers and rubbed his thumb over my clit, making me thrash and buck and growl like a trapped wildcat. "This is me claiming you."

"And then it's my turn?"

"Yes," he whispered, "and then it's your turn."

"And you'll submit to whatever I want? You'll trust me like I trust you?"

"Yes."

I rode his fingers, then, thrusting against them as a titanic climax swelled within me. "Promise? Swear to me, Hunter. Swear you'll trust me. Swear you'll give yourself to me."

Closer and closer I soared, and his mouth covered a breast, tongued a nipple, and then slid up my breastbone, kissed my throat, my chin, my mouth. "I swear it, Delia."

Fingers fucking, thumb rubbing, mouth kissing until I lost my ability to breathe, he brought me to the quivering edge of a climax so massive, so powerful, so divine that it terrified me—it would rip me in half, when it tore through me.

Could you die from an orgasm? Because this one, when it hit, might just kill me.

I shook and shrieked as he *finger-fucked* me and ravaged my mouth with his tongue and took me to the edge.

"Are you ready, Delia?" he demanded.

"Yes!"

The edge approached, a swift rolling tsunami of orgasmic intensity, and now he didn't slow, didn't change his pressure or his touch; his fingers slid through my pulsing, tightening pussy and his thumb circled my throbbing clit and his fingers pinched and squeezed my nipples in alternation, and his mouth plundered mine and he didn't stop, didn't slow as the beast within broke loose.

It hit me like a freight train.

White heat smashed through my body, synapse by synapse, *nerve-ending* by *nerve-ending*, swift as light and slow as molasses at the same time. Reality distorted and light burst behind my shut eyes. I was utterly paralyzed by the climax as it ripped through me like a lightning storm, lance after lance striking my core, and he thrust his fingers into me and rubbed my clit with the perfect pressure and speed, and when I couldn't make my mouth return his kisses because I was too busy screaming, he suckled my nipple between his teeth so the sharp bite of pain sent me into renewed paroxysms of frenetic, desperate, blinding release.

And it didn't stop.

Instead of multiple orgasms, he pushed me into one mad, wild, shattering climax, scream after scream shredding my throat until I was hoarse, my hips bucking and thrashing until I couldn't move.

It was endless—I couldn't breathe, couldn't move. I just kept coming and coming, wrenching my body into contortions of ecstasy that were pulled short by the silk restraints.

"*H-Hawk!*" I panted, sweating and breathless. "I—I can't. I can't. No more. No more."

Instead of heeding my plea, he palmed my breasts and fused his mouth to my clit, and now the endless orgasm shifted, twisting into something new all over again, freeing my lungs so I could cry out again, hot tears streaming down my cheeks as waves of climax surged through me, and my hips bucked helplessly as I kicked and pulled and bucked and thrust, coming and coming and coming against his mouth.

Sobs tore out of me, and the lightning struck and struck, and the heat billowed through me and the blinding light behind my eyes flashed and flickered, and still I came.

"*P-please*, Hunter," I begged, "no more."

"No?" he whispered.

"I can't. I can't take any more."

He released me from the throes of climax, then, slowly bringing me down to earth once more, his tongue's licking and his caresses to my breasts slowing until I was able to stop thrashing and spasming, and my lungs could pull a full breath, and the sobs could subside.

"Let me go now," I whispered when I could summon the powers of speech. "Please. It's my turn."

"I don't know," he murmured. "I kind of like playing with you like this. Having you helpless. Spread out and tied up for me."

"Hunter, you promised."

"I did. And I'll keep my promise. I just…it's so tempting to keep you here like this. I could keep you coming for hours."

"No," I hissed, desperate and crazed. "No. No. I want you. I need you."

"What is it you need?"

"Your cock."

"You need my cock?"

"Yes!" I cried. "I need it."

His weight vanished, and I heard rustling, and then the bed dipped under his weight, and I felt his hot flesh and solid muscle brush me. He knelt between my legs, hard thighs against mine, and his mouth stuttered up my belly and between my breasts, and his weight shifted upward.

He straddled my belly, and I felt something soft and warm touch my cheek. "This?" he whispered.

Oh, fuck—his cock. I opened my mouth, tongue out. "Yes!"

He slid it over my upper lip. "You want it, Delia?"

I tasted him with my tongue, soft flesh and salt. "Yes! I want it. Let me have it, Hunter. Fuck my mouth. Please."

I opened my mouth wide, tongue out, begging.

I tasted *pre-cum*, and moaned in pleasure as the flavor of him burst onto my tongue. "Mmmm," I hummed. "Love how you taste."

"More?" he whispered.

"More," I agreed.

The full thickness of him slid past my lips, and I stretched my jaw wide to accept him, moaning happily as he filled my mouth. I opened my throat for him, and he filled that too, and I swallowed around him, tongue working against his veins, and I sucked desperate breaths in through my nose and extended my neck and took more of him, nuzzling his belly with my nose.

"Fuck, Delia. Is that what you want?"

"Mmmmm," I groaned. *"Mmmm-hmmm!"*

"You like my cock, don't you?"

"Mmm-hmm!"

He pulled back, and I worked my tongue against him as he drew out completely, and I gagged on a desperate breath, gasping, panting. "Love how you take my cock, Delia."

"More," I whispered. "I want your cum, baby. Give it to me. Come for me. Come down my throat. Come on my face. Come on my tits. Please. I need it."

"Fuck," he hissed. "She's begging for it."

"Yes," I panted. "Please, Hunter."

"What if instead I did…" he whispered in my ear. "This?"

The blindfold vanished, and then he released my wrists with a single deft flick of his wrist, and then one foot, and then the other, and then I was free.

FOURTEEN

Hunter

I HAD BARELY GOTTEN THE LAST NECKTIE UNKNOTTED BEFORE I found myself on my back, disoriented and staring up at her in bewilderment.

She grinned down at me, auburn hair wild and loose around her face and shoulders. "My uncle Bax is an MMA coach. I know some killer takedowns and reversals."

"Clearly," I said, raking my gaze over her lush, beautiful naked body. "I don't even know what you did."

She knelt astride me, sex hovering over my belly, tits swaying over my chest, hips spread wide and begging for my hands. "Want me to demonstrate again?"

"Maybe later," I said. "Naked wrestling tutorial as foreplay."

"Sounds hot," she said, "I'm in. Definitely later, though."

I grasped her hips, squeezing a handful of flesh. "I may or may not be obsessed with this ass."

She grinned down at me, sitting tall on my belly. "As much as, more, or less than you're obsessed with my tits?"

"The phrase 'first among equals' comes to mind," I said.

She grabbed the *blue-and-white* striped necktie I'd used as a blindfold. Handed it to me. "Put this on."

"Turnabout is fair play, I suppose," I said, undoing the knot.

She sat on me, watching as I fitted the fattest part of the tie around my eyes. The moment the silk touched my face, I felt her soft small fingers circle my aching cock, pull it away from my body, and fit my head to her slit. I fumbled the tie, and she froze, One hand braced on my chest, the other grasping my cock.

"Tie it on, Hunter," she said. "What are you waiting for?"

She rolled her hips, sliding her seam against me. I'd been seconds from coming down her throat when I released her. I'm clearly a glutton for punishment, because I know perfectly goddamn well that she's about to torture me the way I did her.

I welcome it.

So, when she rolled her hips to rock her pussy against the *precum-leaking* tip of my cock, I jerked, the slippery hot slide nearly my undoing, making me fumble the tie again.

"C'mon, Hunter. I'm not fucking you till you're blindfolded."

I attempted to gather my focus, concentrating on the *should-be-simple* task of tying a stupid fucking knot. The moment I got the tie looped over itself and tugged tight, she grabbed my wrists and pushed them over my head. Rocked her pussy against me again, this time taking a tiny bit of my head inside her.

"Tying you up would be too simple," she said. "So here's how this game is going to go. Ready?"

"Fuck. Yes?"

Amusement laced her voice. "You aren't allowed to touch me until I say so. You aren't allowed to move your hands. You aren't allowed to move at all. If you do, I stop."

"I can handle that, I think," I said.

Famous last words.

I could *not* handle it.

I grabbed the upper edge of the headboard and waited.

I felt her shift, leaning forward; her hands punched into the pillow beside my face, and something soft and warm slid across my mouth, my chin, my cheeks, drifted across my eyes.

"Open your mouth," she ordered.

I parted my lips, and the soft warm something entered my mouth—her nipple. I sucked on it until she gasped, and then it was gone. Now damp, her nipple ghosted across my face again, and I sought it with my mouth, but she anticipated my movements and allowed me only a brief taste before taking it away again.

I groaned when she draped her heavy breast against my face, and then suckled her nipple when it slid between my lips; as I sucked and licked and tongued, she cupped my balls, and then stroked my shaft with her hand, drawing a ragged moan from me. She fit me to her pussy again, allowing just my glans inside her, and then her hands slid up my belly and over my chest.

I opened my mouth to beg her to take me all the way, but I bit down on the plea, wanting instead to see how she would let this play out.

I tasted her mouth and hungrily kissed her until we both broke with a gasp. "Fuck, I love kissing you," I breathed.

She circled her hips, working my throbbing cock in wide spirals. I clenched my teeth and groaned, refusing to beg, refusing to let my body do what I so desperately needed to do: thrust; move; take; claim—Fuck.

She grabbed my shoulders and held on tight, changing her angle, draping her tits against my face again and working the head of my cock between the lips of her pussy.

"Fuck, Delia," I hissed. "You're fucking killing me."

"What was it you just said? Turnabout is fair play?"

"I was an idiot. Have mercy."

"Like you had mercy on me?"

"Was it worth it?"

She touched her cheek to mine, her lips against my ear. "*Fuck* yes, it was worth it. My legs are still shaking from how hard I came." She nibbled on my earlobe. "Now it's my turn to tease us."

"I need to be inside you more than I need my next breath, Delia," I admitted.

"Then you'd better hold your breath," she said, "because I'm not ready to fuck you yet."

She slid me out entirely; my cock slapped against my belly, leaving me groaning. My hands tightened on the headboard until my knuckles hurt. Her weight vanished; I flinched with a loud grunt of surprise when her hot wet mouth closed around my cock and her tongue swirled against me.

"We taste *good*, Hunter," she murmured.

"Ohhhh *fuck*." It was all I could manage.

I throbbed, ached, on the verge of having to hold back already; she let me go, and her lips touched my navel, my hipbone, my thigh. Her soft, warm lips kissed the inside of my thigh. And then she suckled my sac into her mouth, tongue gently swirling and sliding; she grasped my erection around the base and squeezed hard, in direct juxtaposition of the delicacy of her mouth on my balls.

"Ohfuckohfuckohfuck," I hissed, feeling the edge well up within me.

She felt it and pulled away, leaving me pulsating

and aching with the blissful agony of hovering on the verge of release.

Unsure of what to expect next, I could only grip the headboard and wait.

She trailed her fingernails softly over my balls, teasing, tickling, making me twitch and groan, desperate for her to make contact with my cock—one lick, one stroke, one suck, one thrust, and I'd be done.

She sensed this and spent the next few minutes playing exclusively with my balls, cupping, scratching, kissing, licking, suckling, petting, teasing—all of it enough to keep me riding the knife edge of climax, but not enough to put me over.

When a finger trailed southward, my hips tipped up, ass cheeks clenching together. "Do that, and it's game over," I said.

She ignored my warning, palming my balls with both hands and extending a finger along my taint, pressing, massaging until I grunted with the effort of holding back.

"Fuck, fuck, fuck," I hissed. "You'd better stop unless you want me to come right the fuck now."

She giggled, sliding her palms upward on either side of my erection, licking up the underside of my cock...and rolling her mouth over my tip, taking me in, and down, and down, and down, swallowing around me until her nose nuzzled my belly and I felt my orgasm boiling in my balls, surging beyond my ability to restrain.

At the very last second, her mouth was gone and I was panting raggedly, desperately tensing my entire body to keep the orgasm back.

I felt her swing astride me, felt her pussy slide against my belly, her tits draping onto my chest. "Good boy," she breathed in my ear. "Hold it for me. Don't come yet, Hawk."

"Trying like fuck, baby. You make it difficult."

She nipped my earlobe. "Love hearing you call me baby."

"I'm not usually one for endearments. But you… for some reason, I can't seem to stop myself with you. Not sure why."

She laughed. Circled her arms under my neck to cradle my head, grinding her slit against my abs, lower and lower until my throbbing, *precum-leaking* tip nudged her opening. "Not sure why? Hmmm. Could it be…because you have feelings for me?"

I gripped the headboard with every ounce of strength I possessed in an attempt to stop myself from grabbing her hips and thrusting inside.

"Maybe. Seems like the likeliest answer."

She ghosted her lips against mine, a teasing *not-quite* kiss. "Only likely?"

"You gonna admit your feelings first, baby girl?" I asked.

She moaned. "Mmmmm. Baby girl, now, is it? I'm a sure thing at this point, Hunter. No need to butter me up with sweet talk. I'm gonna fuck you sideways. I'm just having fun claiming you first."

"I hope you understand how hard I'm working to keep my hands to myself and let you have your fun, Delia," I growled. "Because I fucking *need* to be inside you. I've been dreaming and fantasizing for fucking *weeks* about how it'll feel to have that sweet, hot, wet, tight little pussy wrapped around my cock. And now you're teasing me. Just a fair warning—I'm about thirty seconds from the end of my *self-control*. Can't promise I'll behave after that."

She rubbed her slit against me, the slick wet lips gliding over my cock. "Since when do you ever behave yourself, Mr. Hawkins?"

"Trying to, for you."

"I know you are. Trying to be a good boy for me, aren't you?"

I laughed, and the laugh turned into a groan as she pressed the very tip of me inside her. "Not sure how into the good boy kink I am, Delia. Taking all I've got to not put you on your hands and knees and fuck you till your pussy hurts. Calling me a good boy is liable to break the last thread of my control."

She pressed her lips to my ear and kept rubbing herself against me, shifting herself against me until the head of my cock nuzzled against her clit, and she writhed and ground against me. "That sounds like a good time to me, Hunter. I may just let you do *exactly* that."

"Keep teasing me and there won't be any 'letting' about it," I growled, my voice tense and rough.

"Promise?" She breathed, the undulation of her hips becoming frantic and frenetic, driving her clit against the ramrod of my cock.

"Gonna come for me like a good girl?" I snarled. "Come all over my cock, sweet Delia."

She bit my lower lip, gasping shrilly as her writhing pussy slid wet against me. "Oh fuck, Hunter. I'm gonna. You want it?"

"Fuck yes I want it," I snapped. "Come for me right the fuck now."

"Can you keep waiting?" she panted.

"Not long."

Her mouth went wide, quivering against mine, her breath coming in swift sharp gasps as she ground herself to climax. Her hips spasmed, and she shrieked, pressing her face against my throat as her orgasm seized her and set her to stuttering, staccato thrusts.

I groaned with her, every muscle in my body straining to the utmost as I tried to hold back my own climax. "Delia, fuck, I...I can't wait much longer, baby girl."

She whimpered as her climax reached a crescendo. "Tell me you're clean, Hunter."

"Promise I am. Always wrap it, and got tested a few months ago."

"I have an IUD," she whispered. "And I'm clean, too." She put her lips to my ear. "I believe you; I trust you."

"Delia, I...I've never been bare with anyone before."

"Never?"

"Never."

"Me either." She bit my ear lobe, panting, whimpering. "I need you, Hunter. Tell me you trust me. Tell me it's okay."

"I trust you, Delia. I need you. I need to be inside you."

She nuzzled her face into the side of my throat, one arm hooked around my neck, and with the other hand she reached between our bodies and grasped me, lifted me away from my body. I felt her tilt her hips, and the hot wet silk of her pussy wrapped around my aching cock.

"Ready, baby?" She breathed.

"Please, Delia. Don't make me beg anymore. Fucking please. I'm gonna fucking die in a second."

"You're gonna die without my pussy?"

"Fuck yes."

"We can't have that, can we?" Once I was notched just between the lips of her sex, she brought that hand up to my face and cupped my cheek.

She paused, hesitating, unmoving, panting.

My cock was so hard it hurt, so close to exploding that I didn't dare move, barely dared breathe.

The moment extended into infinity, seconds lasting for eons as I waited, breath lodged in my throat, my entire body locked, spine arched, desperately fighting to hold back my orgasm.

With a breathless gasp, Delia impaled herself on me, taking my cock to the hilt in a single long, slow slide.

"*FUCK!*" I shouted, and then the shout became a wordless roar as I clenched my ass and locked down my PC muscles and fought like fuck to keep from coming.

"Hunter!" She screamed, driving her ass down against my thighs to take me deeper. "Oh fuck oh fuck ohfuckohfuckohfuckoh*fuck* you feel...oh god, Hunter. I'm—I'm gonna—fuck, baby, I'm coming again. Give it to me, baby. Come for me. Come inside me, honey. Right now. Please, Hunter, fuck me. Fuck me as hard as you can, baby."

My hands shot to her hips and gripped the soft spill of flesh. Another wordless shout ripped out of my throat as I fought to hold back just a little longer, wanting to thrust at least once before I came.

She sat upright on me—I ripped the blindfold off and hurled it aside, blinking at the light.

"Fuck, you're beautiful," I snarled, as I drove a hard thrust into her, my eyes fluttering at the hot lush tight clutch of her pussy spasming around me as she came, screaming.

Heat built in the pit of my stomach, my balls throbbed, and my cock pulsed with the desperate need to come. I scraped my hands up her belly and cradled the heavy weight of her huge, perfect tits, and I fought for another breath, gave her another hard, ramming thrust—each time I pounded into her, she screamed louder, came harder.

And then I lost the fight.

I gave in, bellowing wordlessly yet again as an orgasm with the potency of a thousand detonating stars smashed through me. I lost all sense of time, of self, of place—there was only Delia and me. Only her tight wet pussy sliding around me, only her big soft ass slapping against my thighs, only the heavy weight off her tits bouncing as she lifted high on her knees and slammed down against me. Only our bodies united, only her voice and mind singing a hoarse, wild song of release.

When I came, it burst out of me so hard my eyes shuttered involuntarily and darkness swallowed me and dizziness twisted through me. I had no control over my body—none. I fucked her with everything I had, every muscle and tendon and synapse focused on her, on our joined bodies. She screamed and screamed and screamed as I fucked her, and I bellowed and roared and grunted wildly as she fucked me right back just as hard.

I came endlessly, each new wave of release more powerful than the last until I had no breath left to so much as gasp, and still she came all around me, riding me with everything she had, slamming down so hard I felt each thrust in my gut, felt each spasm of her pussy around me, felt her ass slap against my thighs.

Darkness slashed through me, dragged me under, dizziness washing over me.

"Hunter?" I heard her voice from a great distance. "Hunter!"

I battled against the darkness, groaning. "Delia?"

"You passed out, honey." Her voice was…faint. Shaken.

She was still straddling me, collapsed forward onto me, panting raggedly; I was still buried inside her to the hilt, still hard but fading. She was shaking all over.

I let my hands devour her curves, then, caressing her ass, her hips, her waist, her shoulders, her back. "Delia…that was…fuck, baby, I don't know what the fuck just happened."

She shook her head, her nose and mouth nuzzling my throat. "Me either."

I brushed her hair away, wild and tangled and sticking to her sweaty forehead, cheeks, and lips. I swallowed hard, emotions I couldn't name but couldn't fight or deny or hide welling up—as fraught and potent as the orgasm we just shared.

More so.

My eyes burned. "Delia, I…" I blinked hard. "That was…"

Her deep, dark blue eyes shimmered, met mine, searched. "I know." Her throat worked hard. "That wasn't just sex, Hunter."

"No," I rasped. "It most certainly was not."

She squeezed her eyes shut, but tears leaked out anyway. "Hunter…I…" she was breathing hard, now, panting, panicking.

"Hey," I whispered, gathering her hair in one hand, cupping her face in the other. "It's okay. I've got you. It's okay. breathe, baby."

She shook her head again. "I can't. I can't."

I kissed her cheeks and tasted salt. "Hey, whoa, whoa—talk to me, Delia."

She shook her head, pulling away from my touch— she pulled her hips forward and I slid out of her, and we both groaned at the loss. Before I could react, she was off me and scrambling off the bed.

"Delia!" I shouted, following her across my bedroom. "Wait!"

She slammed the bathroom door before I could reach it, and I heard the lock click. "I…I need a second, Hunter."

I slumped against the door, panting, my wobbly legs threatening to give out. "Delia, baby, what—what's wrong?"

"Just…fuck. *FUCK*!" her voice was tearful, shaking. "I can't—I fucking *can't*."

"Can't what?"

I heard the toilet flush and then the faucet turned on. A moment later, I heard her unlock the door, and then she opened it. Her eyes were *red-rimmed* and tears glistened on her cheeks. "I have to go."

I shook my head, frowning. "Go? Go where? Why? I…Delia, what we just shared was—"

She pushed past me and dressed so fast it was nearly an act of prestidigitation. "I can't. I can't. I…I have to go. I'm sorry, Hunter." She refused to look at me, and when I reached for her arm, she danced away. "Don't. I'm…just…please don't. I'm sorry."

"Delia, I don't understand. What's wrong? What did I do?"

She shook her head, fleeing for the stairs. "You didn't—it's not you. You're—god, you're *amazing*. That was—I'm just—" she shook her head again, tears streaming freely down her cheeks as she dug her keys out of her purse while trotting down the stairs.

I followed her, stark naked, outside to her truck. "Delia, c'mon. Just slow down and talk to me. I get that it was intense, but let's talk about it."

"I can't, Hunter. Just—just go back to New York." Her eyes were hazy with a flood of tears, and her shoulders shook. "I can't do this with you. I thought I could but I can't. It's just…it's too much."

"But Delia, I—"

She was gone in a roar of the engine and a squeal of her tires.

"…Love you," I finished, the words trailing after her like a dandelion seed on a long summer wind.

I went back inside, closed the front door, and slumped backward against it, jaw clenched as I fought the burn behind my eyes and the hot lump in my throat.

"Well…fuck," I said, to the walls and the ceiling and to nothing at all. "Now what?"

FIFTEEN

Delia

I FISHTAILED OUT OF HUNTER'S DRIVEWAY, FRANTICALLY blinking tears out of my eyes as I sobbed. A horn blared angrily; I jerked the wheel to get back in the correct lane and then gunned it. I barrelled north, away from town, away from everyone and everything, hating myself, hating Hunter, hating love, hating my body, hating the empty, gnawing pit in my chest where my heart should be.

My phone rang: Dad. I ignored it.

It rang again: Mom. Ignore.

Finally, it rang a third time: Emerson.

For her, and only for her, I answered. "I don't want to talk about it, Sunni."

Her laugh was amused. "I didn't even say anything."

I sniffled, trying to slow the sobs that wracked me. *"Th-then…*what do *y-you w-want?"*

"Wait, hold up, are you…*crying?"*

"Yes," I answered in a miserable little voice.

"What? Why?"

"I just said I don't want to talk about it."

"We don't have to talk about it, but you do have to tell me everything."

"That's fucking stupid. Telling you everything is talking about it."

"Darn. You caught me." She sighed. "Dee, *sugar-tits.* Talk to mama."

"You're not my mama."

"Yeah, but you didn't answer the phone when she called."

"So they *did* sic you on me."

"Possibly. I plead the fifth."

"Which means Hunter called my father, and they called you when I wouldn't answer."

"Ding-ding-ding." She sighed. "C'mon, Dee. Pull over and tell me all about it."

I groaned in frustration, but I knew she wouldn't stop hounding me till I told her—she'd fly up here if she had to. "Fuck—fine. Hold on."

I pulled off the highway and onto a scenic overlook. I shut the engine off and rolled the windows down, and then spent a moment trying to collect myself.

After a minute or two, I let out a shaky sigh. "We finally fucked, that's what happened."

"And this leads you to hysterically sobbing…why?"

"I…I don't know. I just…I freaked out."

"Where are you?"

"Hell if I know. North of town. I don't know. I just…I fucking ran, Sunni."

"You're gonna have to elaborate, sweetie."

"At first, it was…honestly, it was the hottest fucking experience of my life." I slammed my head back against the headrest. "That's not an exaggeration, Emerson. Our sexual chemistry is fucking *insane*. He can make me come so fucking hard, so fucking fast, so many fucking times…I swear it's sorcery."

"Okay…"

After putting the phone on speaker and resting it on my thigh, I covered my face with both hands. "And his cock? Em, you don't even know. I know you said Hayden is packing, and I'm happy for you, but holy Jesus, Hunter's dick is…god." I sighed, rubbing my face. "It's Goldilocks. I mean, seriously, if that man's penis was even a fraction bigger, and I'm talking length *or* girth, it'd be too big. As it is, I can barely get my mouth around it. I *deep-throated* him a few times and nearly gagged."

Emerson snickered. "You don't *have* a gag reflex."

"Exactly."

"Jesus. And…did you actually have sex with him?"

"YES! Why do you think I ran away?"

"It was too good?"

"I'll never be able to have sex with anyone else ever again."

"Okay, so…I'm not hearing a reason for running away. Not only can Hunter Fucking Hawkins, a famous billionaire, make you come, he can give you *multiple* orgasms, enjoys doing so, you have wicked chemistry with him, *and* he has a magical dong, *and* the sex was the best you've ever had."

"It was fast, Em. Like, the actual sex. The foreplay was…fuck, it was fucking insane, babe. But the actual sex? A couple of minutes at most. And I'm *fucking ruined*. He's not just the best I've ever had, he's the best I will *ever* have. Better than all the sex I've ever had, combined. *Plus* masturbation."

"You're not doing a very good job of selling your reasons for running away, Delia." Emerson sighed, a long, gusting, sympathetic breath. "You're scared."

"Fucking terrified."

"Dee, you know I love you, but *girl*—you're an idiot."

I gasped. "EMERSON!"

"You are! You're being stupid. Beyond stupid. Like, is there something you're not telling me? Did he, like, say something cruel? Call you an ex's name? Stealth you? Like, there has to be something. You've been looking for a guy who can give you orgasms and isn't a lying, cheating, *lame-ass* scumbag your whole adult life. Now you finally find one, who is, let me repeat, a *fucking*

BILLIONAIRE, and you have what was, according to you, the best sex of your life…and you *run?*"

I swallowed hard. "No, he didn't say anything mean. He didn't stealth me because we didn't use a condom in the first place. He's…he's amazing, Em. Smart, successful, hardworking, hot, sexy, confident…the list is endless."

"Wait, wait, wait. Girl—*GIRL!* You fucked the man *raw?* The *first* time you fucked him, you fucked him *bare?*"

"Yes?" I answered in a tiny whisper.

"As far as I know, you've never had bare sex in your life. You swore you never would until you met the man who you'd let put a baby in you." She sounded utterly shocked. "Did you tell him that?"

"No! Jesus. I didn't tell him that—I told *you* that when I was eighteen and no one else."

"I…I'm speechless. That was your one hard and fast rule." She blew out a breath. "What was it like?"

I sniffled. "I know. I…I was crazy, Em. He edged me until I was foaming at the mouth. And then I edged him until he almost came everywhere. I don't know what I was thinking. But my god, it felt so fucking good." I covered my face with both hands and screamed, stomping my feet on the footwell. "I don't know what I was thinking. I *wasn't*—that's what. I was out of my mind, legitimately. I mean, you ever fuck so good you enter a different dimension?"

"Delia…" she sighed. "Every time Hayden and I

have sex, that's how it is. And not to scare you even more, but it's better every time. You know why?"

"Are you gonna talk about the power of love? Because both Celine Deion and Huey Lewis already covered that."

She sighed. "Haha. Yes, bitchface, I am going to talk about the power of love, and you are going to damned well hear me the fuck out."

"I'm hanging up now," I said.

"I'll be on the first flight to Ketchikan and stalk your ass all the way to fucking Nome, If I have to. Don't test me. You know I will."

"Fuck, fine. Jesus. Pushy."

"Yes, I'm gonna be pushy because you're making a very serious mistake. You need to turn your *ho-ass* around and apologize to that man."

"Emerson, I am not apologizing."

"Yes, you are. You're going to get on your knees and apologize with your mouth."

"As opposed to apologizing with my elbows?"

"I meant blow him, *dumb-dumb.*"

"I know what you meant."

"Then don't play stupid. You're already on thin ice with me with this whole 'running away from the best thing that's ever happened to you' business."

"On thin ice? What does that even mean? Am I four? What are you going to do, spank me?"

"I'll leave the spanking to Hunter Hawkins."

I whimpered. "God, I'd love to be spanked by him."

"I bet he'd oblige in a New York minute. You just have to go back."

"I can't."

"Why?"

"Because."

"What are you, four? Yes, you can."

"No, I can't."

"Why? Fuck me, woman. Why not?"

"BECAUSE I'M IN LOVE WITH HIM AND I'M FUCKING TERRIFIED!"

"Well now we're getting somewhere," Emerson said. "Finally the truth comes out."

"You're so smug with your 'oooh I'm so in love,'" I adopted an obnoxious, wheedling tone.

She snorted sarcastically. "Yeah, because letting myself fall in love with Hayden was *so* easy."

I groaned. "I'm not you. And it's not the falling in love I'm scared of. I already am. I couldn't have stopped it if I tried. It's what comes next that I'm scared of."

"What? Being deliriously happy with the man of your dreams?"

"Emerson, you're making light of this. I'm for real here, okay? I'm scared. I don't know what to do."

She sighed. "I'm sorry, sweetie, I'm not trying to shit on your fears. But...look, I was scared. You were there, you saw. But I jumped. I took the risk. And it worked out, didn't it?"

"Yeah, but...Hawk is different. He's not like other guys. He offered to take me to Paris for a date. Like...

oh no big deal, let's just fly to fucking *France* for the afternoon."

"You can't fly to France from Alaska for the afternoon, babe. It's a *thirteen-hour* flight." She paused. "But let's put aside the minor issue of flight times and focus on the really important part: why are you not in Paris?"

I sighed. "Em, c'mon. Even if he actually was serious…why?"

"I haven't met the man, obviously, but I feel like maybe he's not the type to joke about trips to Paris," Emerson said. "And why? You're asking the wrong question. Why not?"

"I…" No rational reason came to mind. "I…"

"Exactly. Your honor, I'd like to enter this into evidence, proving that my best friend is, in fact, a bit of an idiot." She cleared her throat. "What are you going to do, Dee? Ignore the man? Pretend the last few weeks never happened? Go back to lame hookups with the same pool of liars, cheaters, losers, and assholes?"

"I don't know. I mean, no, that doesn't sound fun. I just…" I screamed again, just because. "I don't fucking know!"

"What are you afraid of? You still haven't clarified. What's the *worst-case* scenario?"

"I…" I fought back a fresh wave of tears. "I don't know."

"Dee," she scolded. "You absolutely *do* know, you're too chicken to admit it."

"Why are you being so mean? I thought you were on my side."

"I am, always. No matter what. But part of being on your side means calling your ass out when you're being an idiot, and you're being an idiot. You're in love with him. You had truly intimate sex for the first time in your life, and I'd bet my left tit that he's in love with you back. Yet you're alone on the side of the road in the middle of fucking nowhere because you're scared of being in love for reasons you've never adequately rationalized to me. And yet, you won't even admit *why* you're scared—to yourself, much less me, let alone to him."

Irrational anger barreled through me and took over my brain and my mouth—I heard the words coming out and knew they were bullshit even as I said them, but I was powerless to stop them, just as I'd been powerless to stop myself from running away from Hunter.

"Oh, fuck off, Emerson. I'm not afraid. I just don't trust him. He lied about who he is. Our lives will never line up. I don't fit into his life and he doesn't fit into mine. And the sex wasn't even that intimate. Hot, yes. Intimate, no."

Stunned silence greeted my *lie-filled* diatribe for a full thirty seconds.

"Wow," Emerson drawled. "You're really in denial, huh? All right. Well, babe, if you can't handle the truth right now, then there's nothing else I can say to you." A pause. "Look, Dee. I love you. You *know* I love you. You *know* I'm on your side. I've said my piece, so you know

how I feel, but I'll reiterate it for you as clearly and con-
cisely as I can. You are in love with Hunter Hawkins.
You're terrified of real, true vulnerability and intimacy
for reasons clearly not even you understand. You're running away from a relationship that seems to me to be
the best thing that ever has and ever will happen to you.
You're letting fear and pride deprive you of a joy of such
magnitude that you cannot comprehend it from where
you are. My advice to you is to turn Eggplant the Dick
Ranger around and lay all your cards on the table for
Hunter and see what happens. Worst case scenario, he
doesn't return your feelings, and you're heartbroken.
And guess what? You'll heal. You have a huge family
that loves you and will have your back and support you
through it if that were to happen—and to be clear, I absolutely do not believe that's what would happen. Now,
I have to go, babes. You're your own woman, and you're
gonna do what you're gonna do, and there's nothing I or
anyone else can say or do to change your mind. I know
that. But to recap: you're making a mistake if you let
Hunter go. A big, huge, colossal, massive, idiotic mistake. I say that with every ounce of unconditional love
I have for you, sister of mine. Okay, now for real, I gotta
go. Practice starts soon, and I need to get dressed still."

"Get dressed?" I asked. "It's…" I checked the time.
"*Twelve-thirty*."

"Let's just say it was a late start for Hayden and
me."

"I don't need to know the details."

"We were fucking. It was magical. He's been doing this thing lately where he—"

"HANGING UP NOW," I shouted. "You're no help at all and I loathe you entirely."

"You're welcome. Go talk to *Hunter-okay-bye*." She hung up before I could, which annoyed me further.

I stared out the window at the brilliant Alaskan sun glittering off the Inside Passage and utterly failed at any sort of valuable introspection.

Instead, I fixated on what I damned well knew was the wrong thing: Sex. Particularly, how fucking good it had been with him. And let's be clear: under any other circumstances, that would have been laughably short intercourse. I don't like fucking for hours, just to make the point. Just like I'm not a size queen, I don't want or need a *six-hour fuck-fest*. Or, at least, not nonstop—that's too long by, ohhh, five hours and thirty minutes, at least. I'm all about quality over quantity in most things, and sex is no exception. But with Hawk just now, actual intercourse had lasted all of two minutes.

And it was goddamned spectacular.

Why, though? The extreme foreplay in the form of edging? Obviously, that played a part. A big one, I'd imagine.

Something Emerson said echoed in my brain: "You had truly intimate sex for the first time in your life."

Bitch. Fuck you for being right.

Sorry, Em, I don't mean it. I love you.

I know Emerson is right on every count. I just…I can't convince myself to turn around.

I can't even convince myself to dig deeply enough into my own psyche to understand why I'm reacting this way.

Bawk-bawk—I'm a chicken. So much for being a strong, independent woman.

I did turn my truck around—which, yes, Emerson and I have, on numerous occasions, lovingly referred to as Eggplant the Dick Ranger—but I didn't go to Hunter's house.

I went to work.

I acted totally fine.

Aaaand best actress in a drama goes to…

Delia Badd.

A day turned into two. And then three. And then a week. I continued to act totally fine; Emerson, when we talked, pointedly refused to bring up Hunter or the entire situation, which annoyed me to no end and also for which I was grateful.

We signed a contract with Hunter's corporation. The contract was delivered by courier. Who knew we even had couriers in Ketchikan? I refused to think about the fact that even seeing Hunter's scrawled signature left me hyperventilating so badly I had to leave the office and do some square breathing in the alley.

A week turned into two, and I was turning into a total bitch. I snapped at Zeke for no reason...twice. When Dane teasingly *jumped-scared* me—a game he and I have played our whole lives, mutually—I nearly took his head off with a haymaker and then verbally eviscerated him so loudly and viciously that Mom had to intervene like we were little kids again.

I couldn't masturbate.

I was losing my appetite.

Even a sparring session with Uncle Bax didn't touch my shitty attitude.

I spent the weeks following the signing of the contract training Zeke to take over for me as GM of the Kitty, which, thankfully, was work enough to *almost* occupy my stupid mind.

I thought about Hunter constantly.

I found myself watching the entrance, hoping to see him swagger in and act like nothing had happened. I checked my phone obsessively, even though I couldn't remember if I'd even given him my number...not that that would stop a billionaire. If he wanted to get a hold of me, he would.

Clearly, he did not.

I told him to go back to New York, and he listened.

Good for him. He dodged a bullet by not getting involved with me.

A month and a half after signing the contract, we

received word via email from Hunter's secretary that it was time to start flipping the Anchorage location. We'd informed the staff of the plans so they'd have ample time to line up new employment—we gave them all a small bonus, as well.

So, the email came in. *Twenty-four* hours later, I was packed and in the copilot's seat of Uncle Brock's plane, on the way to Anchorage.

Dad and I had worked up a plan, did some designs and mockups for the cosmetic updates we had planned, and had a headhunter company line up interviews. I'd have to hit the ground running the second I landed because my *to-do* list was a mile long. Thank god for that—hopefully, I'd be too busy to miss Hunter, too busy to wonder if maybe Emerson had been right and I'd made the mistake of a lifetime letting Hunter get away.

"So…Rebecca." I smiled at the woman opposite me—black haired, blue eyed, a few years older than me, and absurdly hot. "Why Anchorage?"

She smiled back, but it didn't quite reach her eyes. "I needed a drastic change in my life, for a lot of personal reasons. I can't say Alaska was exactly on my radar, but I got an email from a recruiter, did a little research, and figured I'd give it a try."

"With your experience, you could work just about

anywhere. We'll definitely keep you busy, but I can't say you'd make the money here that you would in a big city in the Lower *Forty-Eight*. So, I guess I need to push on your answer a little bit. Why us? Why Anchorage?"

She met my gaze for a while, considering her answer. "Before I answer that, can I ask you a question?"

I shrugged. "Sure."

"You seem awful young to be the general manager. I guess...I don't mean to be disrespectful, but..."

"What are my qualifications?"

She gave a wincing smile and a shrug. "Yeah, basically."

"Well, I suppose the simplest answer is nepotism. My father and uncles owned and operated the original location in Ketchikan before I was born and for my whole life, I grew up behind the bar with my dad. Some of my earliest memories are of being behind the bar with my dad, watching him work. As soon as I was tall enough, he'd let me wash the glasses and stuff. When I was little, he'd set up a pretend bar for me in our basement playroom, complete with empty liquor bottles that he'd fill with water so I could pretend to pour drinks. Fucked up, I guess, but I loved it. I've worked my way up to this, Rebecca. My first official job was washing dishes. I bussed. I waited tables. I worked the line. I've done it all. Does that help?"

She nodded. "Yes, it does." She stared into space for a moment, blinking thoughtfully. "The truth is, I picked Anchorage because it's just about as far away from my previous life as you can get while still being in the United States. I'm not in trouble with the law or anything, I just…I needed to get away—far, far away."

"I appreciate the honesty, Rebecca." I went over my notes of the preceding conversation with her, tapping my pen idly against the legal pad. "Well, I have a couple other interviews for the position, but I will tell you that you're the *front-runner*, so far. I'll make a decision within *twenty-four* hours, okay? You're in Anchorage for how long?"

"Till the weekend," she answered. "And, for what it's worth, if you do decide to hire me, I can start right away."

I smiled. "I'll keep that in mind, thanks."

The next interviewee for the assistant manager position was a young man named Ernie. Yes, really. He was a sweet kid—and when I say kid, I mean someone who felt younger than me, even though he was actually a year older—with decent relevant experience, including a *two-year* stint as an assistant manager of a coffee shop in Seattle. He answered all the questions well and asked insightful questions—all in all, he interviewed quite well.

Except for one minor thing…

He never took his eyes off my boobs. And, for the record, I was wearing a fitted Badd's Bar polo and one of my more supportive and compressive sports bras, so it's not like I was busting major *side-boob* out of a tank top or something. Nope. He was just *laser-focused* on my boobs. Eye contact was minimal, at best. I'm not sure if he was even aware he was doing it, honestly, but that's just not something I can deal with on a daily basis with a coworker. Customers are gonna ogle you; I'm used to that. I've worked with my fair share of men—not related to me men, I mean—so I'm used to the occasional stare from the cooks when I'm in the back of the house. I've got big boobs, and men, generally speaking, tend to turn into prehistoric lizards when boobs of any size are around, but more so when monsters like mine jiggle into their line of sight.

It's fine. I get it. I'm not threatened or pissed off by it—just be discreet, dude. Get a good look and move on.

Ernie? He missed the "and move on" part of the memo.

I sent him on his way with a vague "we'll be in touch" *blow-off*.

The last interviewee was a stern woman named Georgia, who wore her *blonde-and-silver* hair in a severe bun, had reading glasses perched on her head, and answered all my questions with an expression that suggested she'd eaten an entire lemon mere moments ago. She talked down to me, clearly regarding me as a mere child, as if I was wasting her time by playing interviewer when the adults were talking.

I wrapped up my questions and set my pen down. "So, Georgia, do you have any questions for me?"

"Yes, as a matter of fact. When will your father or

one of your uncles be here to conduct the *follow-up* interview? I'd like to arrange that as soon as possible."

Oof.

I sighed. "I think we're done here, Mrs. Miller. Thank you for your time. We'll be looking elsewhere. Enjoy your stay in Anchorage."

I stood up, collected my pad and pen, and turned away.

"Excuse me, child."

I ignored her.

"I said, *excuse me*, child."

I whirled on her, my nerves frayed from a full day of interviews on top of overseeing the reno, which was becoming more extensive than originally planned and was seriously stressing me out.

"And I said we're *done* here, Mrs. Miller." I settled my features into an icy mask, letting my *pent-up* ire bleed through my gaze. "I am *not* a child. I am the general manager of this establishment. My father will not be conducting any interviews, ever. And certainly not with you. Nor will any of my uncles, most of whom rarely even set foot in our bars except to have a drink with family once in a while. You are rude, disrespectful, ageist, and, honestly, just plain unpleasant. And now, if you'll excuse me, I have things to attend to, so I bid you good day, madam."

I turned on my heel and stalked angrily to the office, seething. I shut the door behind me and tried to steady my breathing.

Which was when the hilarity hit. "I bid you good day, madam?" I repeated. "What the fuck was that? Am I an aristocrat in Victorian England? Jesus, I'm losing it."

When I was somewhat in control of my emotions once more—as much as I could be, lately—I left the office and went into the kitchen to assess the progress—we were opening the wall to create an open kitchen, which meant a total revamp of the kitchen. You see, Hunter's "people"—whatever that meant—had hired some company or other to conduct a survey of Anchorage residents, and the results had indicated that most wanted a more upscale, *semi-casual* dining experience rather than yet another sports bar. So we were pivoting—Badd's Bar Anchorage would now be rebranded as a restaurant rather than a bar, which meant a bigger overhaul and renovation. It also meant my job was harder—I knew how to run a bar. But an "upscale dining experience?" The fuck was that? I had a lot to learn.

This was where Rebecca would come in: her experience was largely in restaurants, mostly nice *sit-down*, *slower-paced* places with heavy, *three-page* menus, cloth napkins, and expensive silverware.

I called her and offered her the job, starting tomorrow, with five percent above her asking salary. She'd technically be my assistant manager, but in reality, she would probably end up being more like a *co-GM*. Which was fine by me—I just wanted the place to succeed.

I lost myself in the work—choosing appliances, silverware, linens, laundry service, a food distributor, getting all the necessary certifications and licenses, and narrowing down the menu with my newly hired head chef Anton. Yes, we had a head chef because places like this had chefs, not just mere line cooks. I put him in charge of hiring his own BOH staff.

Anton was in his *mid-thirties*, with tanned olive skin, *jet-black* hair, and a thick European accent that I couldn't place. His interview had been mostly him showing me the kinds of dishes he specialized in—classic Americana fare, but with a sophisticated European twist. Or so he said. It ended up being things like burgers with weird ingredients that somehow ended up being *mind-blowingly* delicious and lobster mac 'n cheese for the highbrow set. He'd put together a few dozen dishes, which were then tested by the same company that had done the survey; a poll was conducted, and favorites were selected. Once the kitchen was finished, we'd host tasting nights where the staff and a few locals would test and vote on the menu—subject to Anton's and my final approval.

It was all very *hoity-toity*, if you asked me, and not what I'd signed up for, but it was a challenge and a half, and it kept me working like a maniac twelve and sixteen hours a day. Which meant I had very little time to be a disaster about Hunter.

Who I may or may not have dreamed about six nights out of seven for the last…well, since the day I ran away from him. So…three months? Thereabouts. I've not been keeping track.

My heart hurts. I miss him. I miss talking to him. I

miss our witty banter. I miss his arrogant smirk. I miss his genuine smile, which, while rare, was breathtaking when it appeared. I missed his *green-flecked* tan eyes.

I missed his body.

I missed kissing him.

I missed his cock.

I just…missed him.

I wasn't ready to admit to myself that I had, in fact, committed a grave error. But…I was close.

It wouldn't matter if I did admit it, though. I may have accidentally googled him again, and I may have accidentally seen a tabloid article with photos showing him all cozy at some Manhattan bar with a glamourous, skinny *model-type* with perfectly round silicone tits and a veneered smile and a blowout that probably cost more than I make in a week.

He'd moved on.

And that was fine.

Just fine.

I was fine.

Ever see that meme of Ross, crying, a hand to his throat, claiming he was fine?

Yeah.

I'm *fine*.

SIXTEEN

Hunter

"SIR, I HAVE SEBASTIAN BADD FOR YOU ON LINE ONE." Harriet's voice came through my intercom.

Fuck. "Okay, got it. Thanks, Harriet." I closed the lid of my laptop, removed my blue blockers, rubbed the bridge of my nose with a finger, and let out a sigh. "Let's do this, I guess," I muttered to myself.

I picked up the phone. "Sebastian, good afternoon. How are you?"

His deep, gravelly voice was distant, meaning I was on speaker. "Okay, Hunter, and you?"

"Not too bad, I guess. What's on your mind?"

His voice came back close and clear as he put the phone to his ear. "Delia."

I swallowed a sigh, a curse, and a growl all at once.

"Ahhh, I see. Okay. Things in Anchorage seem to be progressing well. We're on track to open next month, I hear, and we're actually under budget."

"This is a personal call, Hunter."

"Oh." I cleared my throat. "Is she...did something happen?"

"You tell me, son."

I bristled at the *son*. "Sebastian, I'm not sure how I feel discussing Delia on a personal level."

"Too goddamned bad." This was growled—he was pissed.

"Sebastian, I—"

"I've made a habit of staying out of my daughter's romantic life, and that's been my policy since she was seventeen. She knows her mind, and when she sets her mind to something, there's no changing it. My approval or disapproval of her boyfriends made no difference to her. As long as she was safe and her boyfriends treated her well, I let her be. Only once have I stepped in, and that was...well, that wasn't her fault. The jackass was a *grade-A* sociopath, diagnosed and everything. I had to send him packing the hard way, and even then, she wasn't happy at my interference, lemme tell you."

"I can see that. Did he threaten her?"

"Oh yeah. See, my nephew is a computer whiz, and he didn't like this jackass either, so he did some not entirely legal investigation into his past and his record, and discovered he had a violent history."

"So you stepped in."

"Yes, I did. I told him if he didn't leave Ketchikan on his own, he'd be leaving it in pieces."

"Effective," I said.

"Especially since I delivered that threat with all seven of my brothers, my three cousins, and my uncle."

"He pissed himself, didn't he?"

Sebastian laughed. "Yes, he did." The laughter faded swiftly. "Son, listen—"

"Don't call me son, Sebastian. I have a father, and he's not you. I mean no disrespect, but I do not like that term."

"Fair enough." A pause. "I don't know what went down between you and my daughter. And unless you physically hurt her, it ain't any of my business."

"I can state without equivocation that I did not hurt her, physically or otherwise. And she will verify this, regardless of how she may feel about me." I let out a breath, unable to hold the sigh of pain in any longer. "Sebastian, can I be brutally honest with you?"

"Only way to be, if you ask me."

"*She* hurt *me*. That's what happened. We…I thought we had something. I was ready to…I don't know. Explore it, I guess. But the second shit got real, she bolted. Told me in no uncertain terms that she couldn't do this with me and that I should go back to New York." My throat closed up, hot and tight. "So, I did. And it killed me to do so, Sebastian. I cared about her—deeply. I still do. But I listen. She told me to leave and I left. We both agreed there would be no games.

I'm not going to chase her after she made it clear that she didn't want to be with me."

A long silence greeted this. Eventually, he let out a breath. "Well...fuck. That changes things, I guess."

"Not sure it does."

"It absolutely does, Hunter. She doesn't play games like that. But...shit, how do I put this? I'll just put it bluntly—she's a mess, man. She's a fucking disaster, and she has been ever since we had that meeting."

"So have I, to be honest."

"My intention in calling you was to get you to talk to her, see if you could sort things out. Because honestly, she's miserable, and I can't stand it anymore. Every time I talk to her, she's just...down. Flat. Sad. It's not her. I thought she'd snap out of it, but she's honestly never been this upset after a breakup before," he growled, annoyed and frustrated. "I know it's not my business, especially if she broke up with you. But...if you still have feelings for her, man, you gotta do something."

I was silent for a long time. "Sebastian, I...I don't know. I just don't know. She was very clear. She *flat-out ran* out of my house. The details are personal and private, but...let's just say she left after we shared a...um... very vulnerable moment together. It meant something to me, Sebastian. And to her. But she ran. She ran, and I don't think she wanted me to chase her."

Silence. "You close with your mother?"

I blinked, confused at the abrupt change in topic. "Um. Not especially close, no, but I see her a few times a year. They spend a lot of time in Europe now that Dad is retired. Why?"

"No sisters?"

"Nope."

"Ever been in love, son? I mean, Sebastian, sorry."

"I'd have said yes, before Delia, but now I'm not sure I knew what love was. Why? What is this line of questioning about?"

"Because you clearly don't know dick about how women operate."

I sank back in my Herman Miller office chair, pivoted to face the wall of windows overlooking Fifth Avenue, and tried to get my jaw to close. "I…"

"You may be hot shit with the types of girls you've always got hanging on your arm, but I'm guessin' you don't pay a lot of attention to their emotions."

"You don't know anything about my relationships," I snapped, pissed off, embarrassed, and feeling targeted.

"Maybe not, but I can guess."

"Guess away, then, Sebastian." It was not said kindly, I must admit.

"Hey, now, don't get your panties in a twist, kid. I ain't comin' for you, okay? But I don't fuck around. I don't play games. I'm concerned as fuck about my daughter, and I've got a feeling you're the only one who can do anything about it. So I'm gonna get under your skin and point a few things out to you since it don't seem like anyone else is willing to." He said something to someone else, muffled and distant, and then I heard a door close. "These New York chicks you date. You usually end things, or do they?"

"Things tend to run their course on their own, I find."

"Meanin' you two have your fun and then it's done, right?"

"More or less, I suppose."

"Don't mean this as a criticism, because before I met my wife, I was the same way, but....I take it you don't do relationships."

I cleared my throat. "Not...not so much, no. That's what was so different about Delia. I wanted it—I wanted something real with her. And the second it seemed like she might be willing to admit she did too, she bolted. Ghosted me."

"I'm getting to that, hold on. What I'm getting at is you don't have a lot of experience with women and strong emotions, amiright?"

I growled a begrudging sigh. "Yeah, I guess so. Strong emotions make me uncomfortable."

He chuckled. "I feel you, man, believe me. But the strong emotions? That's where the real shit happens. You have any guesses as to why Delia ran?"

"I mean, she said she thought she could do this with me, but she couldn't. It was too much, she said."

"Dig deeper. Why? Why would it be too much?"

I hummed thoughtfully. "Too many big emotions, I guess?"

"Bzzzt. Nope. Try again. Delia is all big emotions, Hunter. She doesn't do *anything* by half measures."

"Um. Fuck, man, I don't know. Just tell me."

"Nah, you gotta work this one out. Think. Think about yourself. Were you all in right away? Ready to tell her how you felt right off the bat?"

"Fuck no. I never told her how I truly feel—I would've, had she stuck around."

"Why didn't you, though? What stopped you?" He hesitated. "No bullshit, now."

I swallowed hard because I knew the answer immediately—it was just difficult to get the words past my clenched teeth. "Fear."

"Of?"

"Rejection. Heartbreak. Pain."

"Right. Heartbreak sucks. And Delia…she's seen all of us—me and her mom, and her whole crew of aunts and uncles—love each other hard. Big love. Lasting. Real. If I had to guess, I would guess that she's afraid of failing. She's my oldest and has a massive drive to succeed. She's seen dozens of role models stay married and in love for decades. Maybe it's deeper; I don't know. She keeps her shit close. I mean, we talk about things, but she keeps her relationships private. From me, at least. I'm her dad, so I guess it's hard for her to talk about that stuff with me—I don't know." He sighed deeply. "Fuck, man. All I know for sure is she's scared out of her mind but too proud and stubborn to do anything about it except hide behind *sixteen-hour* workdays in fucking Anchorage. Even Emerson is worried because she won't discuss what happened at all, even with her."

"Emerson?" I asked.

"Her best friend since childhood—whom we adopted over Christmas." He paused. "She tells Emerson *everything*, but this is *off-limits* even for Emerson."

"Fuck."

"Exactly. So…what are you going to do about it?"

I rubbed my face with one hand, groaning roughly. "I'll have to figure that out, it would seem. In my experience, when a woman says she doesn't want to do something anymore, tells me to leave, and then cuts off all contact, it's usually a pretty definitive end to things."

"I know, and I appreciate where you're coming from, Hunter, I really do. But I'm telling you, as her father and as her boss, she's not okay. She's miserable as fuck, and too stuck in her own head to know how to fix it. I'm not promising you anything. I don't know how she'd react if you…I don't know…showed up or something. I don't know. I just think it's worth a shot. Talk to her. In person, face to face. If nothing else, she might just need closure."

I growled wordlessly. "Fuck." I paused, but the flood of words in my throat came out anyway. "Watching Delia run away from me right as I was starting to accept how I felt about her…it was the most painful thing I've ever experienced, Sebastian. It fucking gutted me. I…I haven't slept the night through since I left Alaska. I work all day, but my productivity is in the shitter. I'm rude to my employees. I've had to apologize to my secretary and assistant several times each in the last few months, and I never apologize. I have no appetite. Even my workouts feel like a chore, and usually, they're the one thing that keeps me sane. I fucking miss her, Sebastian."

"Exactly, so—"

"I don't know if I can handle being rejected a second time. I was ready to give her my heart, and she fucking ran away from me. I get it—I was scared too, but I was willing to try. She fucking rejects me, sets my fucking world on fire, and I'm the one who has to hunt her ass down and offer up my broken fucking heart on a silver platter for her to shit all over again? I don't know, man. The ROI on that is feeble."

"Ever have anyone you were close to die on you?" Sebastian asked.

"Uh, no. Why?"

"My dad died when I was in my late twenties. Sudden. And here's something I learned through that that I don't talk about all that often. People say what you said all the time—I don't know if I can handle that again. Shit like that. But the fact is, you don't have a goddamn choice. Shit is gonna happen in this life. You're gonna get hurt. It's gonna suck. And yes, some people do choose to check out early because they don't see a way through. But there always is. Not always a good way, or an easy way. Sometimes it just means suffering through the suck."

"Wow, this is some seriously uplifting advice you're doling out, Sebastian."

"Shut the fuck up and listen to me, you *over-privileged* twat."

I rocked back in my chair. "Jesus. The last person who spoke to me that way was the CEO of a company I was buying when I was…*twenty-two*, *twenty-three*? I ruined his life."

"Yeah, yeah, I'm so scared. You gonna listen or what?" His growl was rough, hard, and low. This man did not give a shit who I was or the power I wielded.

"Fine. What's your point?"

"My point is, going through life avoiding things that bear risk of pain is weak, lazy, and shitty. Once upon a time, I'd have called you a pussy, but as my wife and daughter and a multitude of *sisters-in-law* like to point out regularly, pussies are strong, powerful, and amazing. So I'm not gonna call you a pussy. Yeah, she might reject you. Again. I can't do shit about that—she's her own woman. I just know that you'll resent yourself and her forever if you don't sack up and face the situation like a real fucking man." He grunted, a sound that was somewhere between a laugh and a sigh. "Look, kid, just answer me this: You love her?"

"Yeah. I mean, I can't get her out of my head, and all I want is for her to be happy, and I wish to fuck I could be the one to make her happy. If that's love, then yeah, I love her."

"Are you willing to risk getting hurt again for the

chance that you could make both of you happy?" he said. "Because that's what you gotta decide. Are you more afraid of getting hurt again or of missing out on your chance at real love because you were too scared to take another swing?"

"You make a compelling case, Sebastian," I said. "I guess I have some thinking to do."

"Guess you do. Just don't think too long. At a certain point, you just gotta accept that there is no certainty, and you just gotta jump without knowing where you're gonna land." He cleared his throat gruffly. "Alright, Hunter. I said my piece. The rest is up to you."

"Sebastian, I…" I started, hesitated, and then barreled onward. "Thank you. For calling, I mean. For being willing to hit me with the truth. People willing to speak the blunt truth to me are few and far between."

"Never been one to pull my punches, no matter who and no matter what," he said.

"Well, thank you. I do appreciate it." I swallowed hard. "I also wanted to say…um…" I'm not used to being *tongue-tied*, not knowing what to say, so this struggle was a tough one for me. "Delia is a remarkable and amazing woman. You and Dru raised a hell of a human."

A brief silence. "Thank you, Hunter. I appreciate that."

"Hopefully, Sebastian, this will be the first of many conversations."

"In that case, you'd better call me Bast."

"Bast?" I repeated.

"Yep. *B-A-S-T*. It's what anyone who knows me calls me. My youngest brother, Xavier, couldn't pronounce my name when he was little, so he called me Bast, and it stuck."

"Funny how that works," I said.

"Quick question, to appease my curiosity. Does anyone actually call you Hawk, or did you make that up?"

"My buddy Jonathan Givens calls me Hawk. We've been friends for...shit...fifteen years? Thereabouts. We met in high school. So, I didn't make it up, but he's the only one who does call me that."

"What's everyone else in your life call you?"

"Well, my folks call me Hunter, and everyone else calls me sir because they work for me."

"So let me get this straight. You have exactly one friend, parents you aren't close to, and employees who call you sir…"

"Yeaaaahhhh…?" I said, drawing out the word and making it a question.

"Sounds like a hell of a lonely life. You got a big fancy penthouse that you rattle around in like a marble in a maze?"

I snorted. "Now you're just shitting on me for fun, Bast."

"Nah, I just think you need some people in your life who don't give a shit who you are. Friends. Family. A support system. Someone who worries about you when you're obviously fucked up and miserable."

"Givey calls me pretty much every day to check in on me," I said.

"Well that's good. Alright, well, Hawk, I'ma let you go. But assuming you pull this shit off, bring your boy Givey up to Ketchikan with you, yeah? Trust me when I tell you no one parties like the Badd Clan."

"Assuming I pull this shit off, I will do that."

"Good. Go get the girl, Hunter Hawkins. Lay your heart on the line. I know my daughter, and I'd wager a full percentage of one year's profits that you won't regret it."

I laughed. "Bast, I wouldn't take you up on that out of financial principle, but I will say that I hope to fuck you're right. Because I've tried living without Delia these last few months, and it sucks ass."

It was his turn to laugh. "That's how you know it's right. If your emotions leave you no choice, then you'll do whatever it takes to work it out."

"Truth. Alright, well, I have a pile of work to do if I'm gonna be able to do anything, so goodbye for now."

He echoed my goodbye, and we ended the call. I hit the intercom and summoned Harriet and Elara into my office.

When they were both seated in front of me, I let out a breath, tapping my pen on the desk. "So, I suppose it's not exactly a state secret that I've not exactly been myself lately."

Harriet snorted. "With all due respect, sir, you've been an insufferable monster."

I arched an eyebrow. "Elara? Feel free to be blunt."

She grimaced. "Um…well, sir, you…err…as you said, you've not been your, um, usual cheerful self."

Harriet guffawed. "If Hunter Hawkins has been cheerful a single day in his life, I'm Mother Theresa."

I sighed. "Tell me how you really feel, Harriet."

She arched an eyebrow back at me. "Do be cautious in what you request of me, sir. You just might get it."

"That was sarcasm, Harriet. But if you have further truth to bestow upon me, you happen to find me in a receptive mood." I leaned back in my chair and steepled my fingers in front of myself, an obnoxious, pretentious, cliché habit I learned from my father that I've never been able to entirely lose.

She smoothed a hand over her skirt, let out a breath, and nodded. "Very well, sir. I do not know the details of what happened in Alaska, and I do not need them. But in my experience, when a man goes into a funk like you've been in since your return, it can only mean one thing: love gone awry."

"You would not be incorrect," I said.

She nodded, eying me while thinking. "Hunter, I care about you. I've worked for you since the beginning of your career. You've been singularly driven to prove something. I'm not sure what. That you're not your father? That you can succeed without his help? I'm not sure, and it doesn't matter. But you've never had much of a social life, as far as I can tell. I'm an old woman, and this is my second career. My husband and I are used to long periods apart, so I don't have a life, and nor do I want or need one. But you—you're a young man, just thirty. You have your whole life ahead of you, and you've already succeeded to a degree that very few other human beings, past, present, or future, ever will."

I rubbed my face with both hands—apparently, today was "lecture Hunter" day. "Again, you aren't wrong. What's the but?"

"But you're wasting your life. You're accumulating wealth, but you don't use it. You don't spend it. You donate to charities for tax purposes, and you attend the requisite social functions. But…what fulfills you, Hunter? What is important to you? Who do you share your life with?"

"You just said you and your husband spend a lot of time apart."

She nodded. "We do. But my career in the military meant I went where I was ordered. We talk on the phone, video call, and if I'm away for more than a few days, we send each other letters."

"Letters?" I echoed. "Like, physical letters? In an envelope with postage?"

She snickered. "Yes, Hunter, physical letters in envelopes with postage. It's a dying art form. One day, I'm going to put the letters we've sent each other over the years into a single, chronological volume and publish it." She shook her head and waved her hands. "My point is, that's how our relationship works. I love him. I'm committed to him. I'm comforted by him. He is my purpose, my reason, my logic, and my everything. You need that for yourself, Hunter. You're drowning. If you stay the course you're on now, you're going to end up a sad, fat, lonely old man with a vault of money and a wasted life."

I blinked. "Well…damn. Okay." I turned to Elara. "And you?"

"Oh, I couldn't, sir." She picked nervously at a wrinkle on her blouse.

"Well, now I insist," I said, "if only out of curiosity."

"You're already lonely," Elara said, her tone strengthening as she warmed up to her topic. "Obviously, you're not sad or fat or old, but you *are* lonely. I, um…I think you've substituted sex for companionship and intimacy, and…well, truthfully, sir, it shows."

I threw up my hands, left my chair, and faced my wall of glass. "Is everyone wiser than me?"

"Only a wise person would ask that," Harriet said. "But…yes."

I laughed. "Full of the zingers today, Harriet."

"Yes sir. I had an extra cup of coffee this morning."

I looked at Elara again. "How does it show?"

"One of the first things you said to me was that once upon a time, you'd have already had sex with me. And you said that without knowing a single thing about me, and you said it as if it was a virtue that you hadn't. That says a lot, to me, at least." She shrugged. "You're always working. You have one friend. Until Alaska, you had a constant parade of girlfriends, according to tabloids and the media, at least, none of whom were ever around for more than a few weeks. Plus, you're insulated from real life by your status as a famous billionaire. That on its own is a lonely place to be. At least, it seems that way to me, based purely on my observations."

I stared out the window again, thinking. After a few minutes, I let my ruminations unspool. "I'm considering a drastic change, as a matter of fact. I was thinking about it when I was in Alaska, before what happened... happened. Which, since I trust you both, is that I fell in love with a woman. Except she got scared and shut me out. And now I'm thinking I need to...talk to her. See her. And if things with her were to work out, I may very well transition the *day-to-day* operations of... well, everything...out of my direct control. Free up my time. What that would look like, I don't know. That's why you're both here. Harriet, you know more about the operation of this company than I do, I sometimes think. What do you recommend?"

She let out a breath but didn't answer for a while. "The bulk of the corporation's *day-to-day* management can be delegated. I would appoint someone to be the person in charge—create a new role, perhaps. A VP, or name a new CEO. You would still need to check in and be the deciding vote, sign things, et cetera, but except for a rare case, everything can be delegated or done remotely. I think we could have you transitioned away from your daily role within a few weeks, perhaps a month at most."

I nodded. "Who would you recommend?"

She thought hard for a moment or two. "Robert Halloway, senior VP of Marketing, is a solid choice. Eric Martinez from accounting is consistently reliable and has been with us nearly as long as I have. Or you could split the roles. Robert knows brand management and development, and Eric knows the numbers."

I nodded again. "Astute selections. You're missing one obvious person, however."

She frowned. "Who?"

"You."

She spluttered and began coughing. When she'd caught her breath, she shook her head. "Sir, you cannot be serious."

"I am. As a heart attack."

She looked at Elara, who just stared back blankly, and then at me. "Hunter—Mr. Hawkins. Sir. I'm your secretary. I can't...I can't be CEO."

"Sure you can—if I say so. It's my company. I can do what I want. Unless you're ready to retire."

She glared at me. "That's a dirty word to fling at me, Hunter. I'm old, but not *that* old."

"Then give me one good reason why you can't do the job," I said.

She blinked. "I..." a breath, a shake of her head. "Well, I...I suppose I *could*."

"Of course you could. You're Harriet the Hatchet. Mortals tremble in fear when you pass by."

A disgusted sigh. "I hate that nickname."

"I mean it with love, Harriet," I said. "Here's my proposal. You're CEO. Robert and Eric are your direct underlings—they're both smart, savvy, and trustworthy. As you said, Robert can help with image and such, and Eric knows the numbers. They report to you. Elara becomes your secretary. You consult me as necessary."

She rose and crossed to the windows and stared out for a long time. Eventually, she turned and slumped backward against the window. "Hunter, sir…are you *sure* this is what you want to do? I don't just mean me, I mean…everything. You've worked your whole adult life building this company. Are you sure you're ready to hand it over to someone else?"

I stood as well and went over to her. Took her hands in mine. "Enough with the 'sir' bullshit, Harriet. Regardless of what is decided about my role or yours, I…you're my friend. I have relied on you personally and professionally for nearly fifteen years. I should be calling *you* ma'am."

She squared her shoulders, cleared her throat, and blinked hard. "Hunter, it has been my honor to serve as your advisor."

"You mispronounced 'mentor,' Harriet." I squeezed her hands. "You are, as of this moment, unofficially the new CEO of the Hawkins Group Corporation. I'll convene a board meeting ASAP and make it official."

"And what will you do?" she asked.

I shrugged and shook my head, huffing a laugh. "Hell if I know, *long-term*. No, not restaurants. I need a bigger challenge than that, I think. *Short-term*, I'm gonna go back to Alaska and see about a girl."

Elara cleared her throat. "Mr. Hawkins, sir, may I provide a suggestion?"

I smiled at her. "Certainly, Elara. But only if you do so confidently. You have immense value to provide. Believe in it. Believe in yourself and be bold. People will listen when you do. Especially since it seems rather likely Harriet is about to make you her personal secretary."

"To start with, yes," Harriet said, smiling. "You have a bright future here."

Elara blinked hard and let out a breath. "Sir, assuming you're able to, um, sort things out with Miss Badd, you might consider asking her if she can get you a meeting with her uncle, Xavier Badd."

I frowned, confused. "Why would I do that?"

She frowned back, equally confused. "Because he is a business partner of Valentine and Corinna Roth of Valkyrie Extraglobal Solutions. Together, Xavier Badd and the Roths have not just transformed the aerospace industry but have singlehandedly created the concept of extraorbital construction in a very real, practical sense. If you want to challenge yourself, sir, put your money and ideas there."

I stared at her. "Xavier Badd is a business partner of Valkyrie?"

"Yes sir. Valkyrie provides the rockets, infrastructure, and personnel, and Xavier provides the software, hardware, robotics, and nanotechnology. They are equal partners, financially."

"No shit?" I said.

"I've always loved space, Mr. Hawkins. I'm a bit of an astronomy and *sci-fi* nerd in my free time. They've revolutionized spaceflight."

I sighed thoughtfully, turning to gaze out the window. "Interesting idea, Elara. Very interesting."

Harriet touched my arm. "Hunter, if you're going to consider that move, then you'll need capital to work with."

"What are you suggesting?"

"Sell off some of the tertiary companies and subsidiaries. Streamline."

"I hate that term—streamlining. It just means laying off hardworking people." I nodded, however. "But you are correct. Hawkins Group has become rather unwieldy over the years. Lots of income streams, which worked when I was running the ship—the plethora of subsidiaries are all things I've taken interest in. But if—when, rather—I pivot to a new project, it makes sense to sell them off so the core structure is…well…more streamlined and easier to manage."

"Precisely, sir. And, as I said, you'll need the capital to invest with because the sector you're considering requires a massive amount of *buy-in* capital." Harriet indicated Elara. "And since she seems to have more than a passing interest in and knowledge of that field, she should go with you. Nothing against her at all, but if I'm going to be CEO, I'll want to *hand-pick* my inner circle, and her skills will be best used elsewhere, in a field where her interests and passions will be an asset."

Elara's eyes lit up. "Oh, sir, that would be—gosh, that would be a literal dream come true. I was one of the first to own OpenBot—my father got me a proto-type for my birthday when I was a little girl, and I watch every Valkyrie launch. My computer at home has the live stream of their orbital construction project running *twenty-four-seven*."

I frowned at her. "So…why are you wasting your time interning here? Why aren't you at NASA or something?"

She sighed. "Because my father holds the purse strings. He considered space to be the silly hobby of a little girl, not a viable career choice for his only child."

I shook my head. "I hate that shit. So, I take it that, assuming I am able to shoehorn myself into their com-pany, you'd welcome the opportunity to be involved?"

"I would sell my ovaries for the chance, sir," she said.

"Well, thankfully for your future progeny, that won't be necessary. For now, you'll stay here and keep learning from Harriet. I'll need time to figure all this out. But you have my word, Elara—if and when I go into business with Xavier and the Roths, you'll be my *right-hand* woman. I'll need someone with the knowledge I lack to help guide my decisions, if nothing else."

She blinked away tears. "Sir, I…"

I pulled her into a rough, platonic hug. "If you cry, you'll see the old Hunter come out," I teased.

She resisted my hug for a moment and then softened, awkwardly patting my back. "Yes sir, sorry sir. No crying here, sir."

I laughed as I let her go. "Very good, Miss Joseph. Now, then. I'll need the board convened ASAP and a flight to Anchorage."

SEVENTEEN

Delia

I WATCHED THE FRONT OF HOUSE STAFF FROM MY FAVORITE vantage point behind the bar; three months after the signing of the contract with Hawkins Group, Badd's Fine Dining is finally operating smoothly.

Servers wafted gracefully and unhurriedly about the dining room; bussers smoothly and quietly cleared, cleaned, set tables, and delivered ice water and baskets of freshly baked French bread to new tables while the expo team delivered the dishes. Customers looked happy, digging into delicious food, chatting, laughing, and enjoying themselves. The kitchen staff was a *well-oiled* machine, hired, trained, and turned into a team by Anton.

Our menu was small, each dish handpicked by Anton, myself, and Rebecca. Our fare was a fine dining take on classic Americana cuisine: burgers, pasta, fish and chips, steaks, salads, and things like that, but done with a fancy, gourmet flourish.

The decor was simple and understated as well, with low ambient house lights supplemented by tealights on the tables, prints of famous paintings on the walls, and *rustic-chic* furniture.

So far, the reception has been overwhelmingly positive—our online reviews are glowing, and local critics are raving about the success of the revamp.

Professionally, I'm over the fucking moon. Dad spent a week up here for the grand reopening and praised me up and down. That felt good. I never thought I'd be the manager of a fine dining establishment, but it turns out I love it. I can still go behind the bar and sling drinks when I get the bug, but mostly, I get to spend my shift floating in the dining room, chatting with my tables, and stepping in if someone gets in the weeds. It's *slower-paced*, almost relaxing, compared to the frenetic frenzy of a *jam-packed* bar on a Saturday night when cruise season is in full swing. Not as exciting *day-to-day*, perhaps, which has taken some adjustment, but I still enjoy it.

Personally? I've been sort of a robot. I have a routine. Perhaps "ritual" is the better term.

I take a shower, get dressed in my fancy clothes—the GM of a fine dining restaurant can't wear jeans and a polo, so I've had to invest in slacks, blouses, skirts, and dresses, as well as fancy shoes and accessories, so I look *grown-up* and professional—and I put on makeup. The process is akin to putting on a suit of armor. As I gear up for my shift, I put my sadness, loneliness, and regret into a little box, lock the box, and shove it down deep inside. When I get home from work, I remove my armor, pour myself a glass of the scotch Hunter likes so much, and let myself pine over him for half an hour or so. I let myself Google him to see if there's any news, any new socialites or models attached to him. I let myself look at pictures of him. I let myself relive the delicious and unbelievable things he did to my body.

I let myself miss him for thirty minutes a day. I let me hate myself for being such a damn chicken.

Once I've had my thirty minutes of missing Hunter, I put it all back in the box, and the next day, I do it all over again.

I did try to hook up with someone once. It was a dismal failure. We met for drinks at a place he knew and had a good time. We chatted, flirted, and played the game. We went back to his place and had another drink. He kissed me, and I let him. It was a decent kiss. But the moment his hand went near my ass, I started panicking.

It felt like I was being unfaithful. I wasn't even with Hunter, and I couldn't have sex because my heart still claimed loyalty to the man.

I'd had to apologize with a stupid excuse not even I believed as it came out of my mouth, and bolted.

I masturbated in the shower the other day. Or, I

tried. But if I didn't think about Hunter, I couldn't even get close, let alone reach orgasm. Think about Hunter's mouth, his fingers, his cock? Immediate O.

Fuck me.

So, here I am, working on a Friday night because I have nothing better to do. Rebecca is officially in charge, so I'm helping out behind the bar as needed, and mainly just sort of…being in the way because it's better to be alone here than alone at home getting *scotch-drunk* and crying.

Why don't I just reach out to him? I could, through Dad. Once this place was up and running, Hunter basically vanished, content to take his percentage and go about his real life, back in New York with his skinny bitch flavor the week, or day, or month, or hour, or whatever the fuck. I mean, sure, other than that one photograph, which some claim was a repost from years ago, he's been radio silent from pop culture. No news articles, no interviews, no social media posts…other than "where has Hunter Hawkins gone?"

I don't know where he's gone. It's just easier to hate him and miss him than it is to wonder if he misses me, if he thinks of me. Because if he did, he'd call. Or text. Or DM me. Or come find me.

He hasn't.

So, neither will I.

Fuck it. I'll just be a lonely old *cat-lady* spinster. Except I don't have a cat, and I don't even really like cats all that much; I'm more of a dog person, but I don't have the time for a dog right now.

My phone vibrates in my pocket, alerting me to a new message. Since we have a strict *no-phones* visible in the dining room policy, I hurried into my office to check it.

It's from Emerson: DID YOU SEE THIS?

It's an article in Business Weekly. The headline? HUNTER HAWKINS DIVESTS 50% OF HAWKINS GROUP PORTFOLIO, STEPS DOWN AS CEO.

What?

I rapidly skimmed the article. It detailed the shocking move wherein Hunter sold off more than half of his company, stepped down as CEO, and appointed a new CEO. The article speculated on several unsubstantiated rumors of what he was planning to do next, which ranged from running for public office to going to space with Valkyrie's next launch to the Asgard Orbital Construction Platform.

It also discusses, again with breathless speculation, as to what prompted the sudden move and his subsequent disappearance from public life.

Emerson: He's coming for you.

Me: Bullshit.

Emerson: You really think it's coincidence that he sold his company, stepped down, and vanished within months of what happened with you two? Because I don't.

Me: He had months to make a move. He didn't.

Emerson: You rejected him, woman. Why would he come back for more? You'd call him a pathetic puppy or something if he'd followed you around begging for a second chance.

Me: I didn't reject him.

Emerson: Okay, fine. You didn't reject him. You pussed out. You ran away from him, literally, like a scared little bitch.

Me: Jesus, Em. That was harsh AF. I'm honestly hurt.

Emerson: Oh, fuck off. You're an idiot. You know I love you, you know I support you, you know I'm on your side no matter what, but I told you then and I'll you now. Men like him don't come along but once in a lifetime. You let him go. You're an idiot. And you've been a closed off, grumpy, miserable little bitch ever since. Everyone in your family is a talking about it. We're all sort of glad you're in Anchorage right now because none of us could handle dealing with your bullshit right now. This is me calling you out, Delia Badd. You had your chance and you blew it. Stop moping around. Accept the consequences of your decision and move the fuck on.

My eyes stung, burned, and blurred.

Me: Wow, okay. Tell me how you really feel. Some friend you are.

Emerson: I'll always tell you the truth, even if it hurts. I love you with all my heart, unconditionally, forever. But you hae to get out of this funk. If you won't woman up and call him, then you have to move on.

Me: I can't! I don't know how.

Emerson: No one can do it for you, babe. This is called heartbreak and you did it to yourself.

Me:. I do NOT feel any better. Thanks for the pep talk, BESTIE. I have to go to work now. Bye and thanks for nothing.

I silenced my phone, and then turned it off and left it in the office, muttering curses and imprecations under my breath.

I snapped at a server for no reason. Nearly caused a catastrophic collision when I failed to call out as I entered the kitchen. Messed up a drink order.

Eventually, Rebecca pulled me aside. "Delia, I… with all due respect, I think you need to go home. It's obvious to all of us that you have something on your mind. We've got this under control, okay?"

Eyes burning, I nodded, my throat too full of a hot, hard lump to manage words. I exerted every ounce of willpower I possessed, swallowed the lump, kept the tears in, and let out a breath. "Tell everyone I'm sorry. I'll see you all on Monday. Call me if you need me."

She squeezed my shoulder, hesitated, and then hugged me briefly. "If you need a friend to talk to, I'm here."

"Thank you, Rebecca. I'm going, now."

I had the staff put together a *to-go* meal for me, took it home, and ate it in silence; it tasted like ash.

I drank scotch until the world swam, and then I passed out on my couch, tears staining the pillow under my face.

I woke to someone knocking on my door.

I ignored it. They paused and then resumed insistently.

When several minutes went by and the knocking didn't go away, I realized I had to face the fact that whoever the fuck was bothering me on a Saturday morning wasn't going away.

So I lurched to my feet, stumbled blearily to the door, and yanked it open without checking the peephole first.

"The fuck you want? Jesus." I blinked one eye and then the other, realizing I may still be a little drunk.

"Ms. Delia Badd?" The insistent knocker was a tall, trim man with a shaved head and a *salt-and-pepper* beard, wearing an immaculate *three-piece* suit.

"Yes. Am I being served or something?"

"No ma'am. I represent Hawk Aeronautics."

"Never heard of it—you—them, whatthefuckever. What do you want?"

"Will you come with me, please, ma'am?"

"Fuck no. Go away."

He reached into the inside pocket of his coat—my

instinctive, *half-drunk* reaction was to think he was pulling a weapon on me, so I pulled a BJJ throw on him and had him on the ground beneath me before he could blink.

He gasped hoarsely. "Ma'am, please. I have a message for you."

I backed away from him and let him get up. "Sorry, sorry. My bad."

He got to his feet, wincing, and brushed himself off. Caught his breath. This time, when he reached into his suit coat, he did so very slowly, his other hand raised. "I'm getting my phone, ma'am."

He withdrew a sleek folding smartphone, unfolded it, cued up a video, and handed it to me. "Just press play, ma'am."

I pressed play. The background was a blank white wall. For a moment, nothing happened, and then a body crossed in front of the camera, too close to make out anything but black fabric and movement. And then Hunter filled the screen as he sat down facing the camera.

He grinned, and that grin took my breath away and caused tears to spurt into my eyes. "Hey, you. Did you punch my employee? I'm guessing you did. It's okay; I'll just pay him off to keep him quiet about the assault." Those gorgeous *green-flecked* eyes twinkled and then went serious. "You may have heard about my, um, business activities. Or maybe not. If not, here's the short version. I sold off most of my company, made my secretary the CEO, and left Manhattan. As in, I sold my condo. I am, as of last month, no longer the CEO of Hawkins Group." He paused and smiled. "What does this have to do with you, you ask? Well, I'll tell you: everything. I'm miserable without you, Delia. I can't eat, I can't sleep, and nothing that used to bring me even the slightest amount of happiness does anymore. Not without you. I've been bored for months, if not years. But being in Alaska, meeting you, getting away from the grind? It changed me, Delia. *You* changed me. I knew within weeks of trying to go back to my old life without you that it wasn't going to work. I was an asshole to everyone. Givey called me out, Harriet called me out, even my PA called me out on my shit. So, I decided to do something drastic."

"Get the point, Hunter," I muttered.

"I can hear you telling me to cut to the chase, so here it is. I never should have let you go. I should have chased you. I should have told you the truth—that I care about you." He swallowed hard, looked away, and then let out a sigh. "Saying that I care about you is the understatement of the century, but I won't say how I really feel in a video." He gritted his jaws and sighed again. "If you have any interest in finding out how I really feel about you, Delia, then accompany Bruce. He'll bring you to me. You don't need to take anything with you but your phone—but if it makes you feel better, pack a weekend bag."

I looked at Bruce. "Bring me to him…where?"

"It's intended to be a surprise, ma'am. I'm not allowed to say. But Mr. Hawkins did tell me to tell you, when you asked me this, that you don't have to trust me, you just have to trust him."

"How do I know this isn't some serial killer plot to cut off my tits and stuff me in a hole in the ground?" I asked.

Bruce blinked at me, puzzled. "Um. I just showed you a video of Mr. Hawkins?" He hesitated. "Also, ma'am, I'm gay. I'm not interested in your breasts."

"Oh." I frowned as I considered. "Fine. Come on in while I rinse off and get dressed. Are we on a schedule or anything?"

He shrugged and shook his head as he entered my apartment. "No schedule, ma'am. Take your time."

"In that case, I'm going to need a medically inadvisable amount of caffeine and something greasy to eat. I don't suppose I could convince you to run and grab me something while I shower?"

His smile was sweet and knowing. "No convincing needed, Ms. Badd. One hangover cure coming up."

He left, and I hopped in the shower. I meant to be quick, but the hot water felt so damned good that I got *shower-locked* and couldn't make myself get out. Therefore, it was nearly thirty minutes before I emerged from my bedroom, showered and dressed in my favorite black leggings and my oversized black Badd's Bar & Grille hoodie.

Bruce was sitting at my kitchen table with one of

those big boxes of coffee you get for a catering party and a white paper bag full of something that smelled greasy and delicious.

As soon as he saw me, he filled a paper cup of coffee, added two Splenda packets, stirred it with one of those sticks, and handed it to me.

I narrowed my eyes at him. "You know how I take my coffee."

He just grinned. "A little birdy told me."

"A little birdy, or a certain hawk?" I sipped the scalding liquid gratefully, hissing as I burned my lips and tongue. "Either way, thank you, Bruce. And knowing I like my coffee is enough to reassure me that you're not gonna cut off my tits and stuff me in a hole."

He snorted. "Good to know, ma'am."

I took another sip. "Call me ma'am again I'll be tempted to dump this on your head, Bruce. My name is Delia."

He chuckled. "Got it, Delia." He nudged the bag toward me. "We aren't on a schedule, but I do happen to know that my employer is rather impatient to see you."

I opened the bag and found a bagel, egg, sausage, and cheese breakfast sandwich from a *drive-through* place down the road. "Oh, fuck yes. You're an angel, Bruce." I took a huge bite and ate it with a moan of delight that was so sexual Bruce looked distinctly uncomfortable.

I grinned at him apologetically. "Sorry." I swallowed and took another sip of coffee. "I'm not really processing or coping with what's happening right now, to tell you the truth, so I'm not really emotionally…available, even to myself. I tell you this because you should be warned that once my emotions do catch up to me, there's a chance I could get a little unstable. So, I need coffee and this fucking amazing sandwich first, and then I can think about the fact that you're here on behalf of the man I… um. Have a complicated relationship with."

"I understand completely. When my ex dumped me last year, I spent almost six months at the bottom of a bottle trying to forget them. It didn't work. It took my brother and my friends literally forcing me to get sober and find a job for me to move on."

"Sorry to hear about your breakup," I said. "You're better now?"

Bruce nodded. "I am, yes. Thanks for asking."

"The truth is, Bruce, it's not really all that complicated, I'm just a chicken."

He laughed. "Oh, honey. We all are, at some point. My ex is a combat veteran, and they said that charging a machine gun nest was less terrifying than coming out to their former squadmates. I've been out since I was fourteen, so I've had my share of struggles. And let me tell you, sweetheart, matters of the heart are the scariest things you'll ever go through."

"Sounds to me like you may still have feelings for your ex," I said.

Bruce sighed. "Oh, yes. Very much so. I always will. But sometimes, it's just not in the cards." He smiled at me. "And sometimes, it is. You never know until you try.

You may get hurt, or even heartbroken, but speaking from experience, heartbreak is infinitely easier to heal from than regret."

I groaned a laugh. "God, how many times do I have to hear this same damn speech? Jesus! Okay, okay, I get it! Tis better to have loved and lost than to have never loved at all. I'm going, okay?"

Bruce's eyes went wide. "I—I'm sorry, Delia. I didn't intend to lecture you."

I rolled my eyes and shook my head. "Not your fault, Bruce. I've just heard some variation of what you said several times now. I know it's probably true and all, but it doesn't make it any easier on this side of things. I'm still scared out of my mind. And now I have the fact that I ran away from him to deal with on top of everything else! It just feels like an impossible situation. I know it's not. Logically, I know it's not impossible. But I can't help how I feel."

Bruce took my paper coffee cup when I emptied it and refilled it, added the Splenda, stirred it, put a cap on it, and handed it to me. "Just take it one step at a time. That's how I got over Sam. One step at a time. For now, just come with me. That's step one and all you need to worry about, okay?"

I crumpled the wax paper the sandwich had been wrapped in, threw it and the bag away, and washed my hands. "Sounds good to me. Thanks, Bruce. Let me grab my purse and phone and we'll be on our way."

I called Rebecca from the car—a sleek black electric Mercedes—and told her I'd be out of town for a few days. I received the expected response: *No worries, boss, we're good. We'll call you if anything comes up.*

I also informed my parents that I was going to be away from Anchorage for a while, that it was about Hunter, and I'd tell them more when I could.

With no information, clues, or hints to go off of, I had zero clue where Bruce was going to take me. I decided to try to just relax and trust Hunter—easier said than done. I closed my eyes, rested my head back, and tried to enjoy the smooth, quiet ride.

I must have dozed off because I woke up to Bruce opening the door. "First stop, ma'am. I mean, Delia."

I yawned and stretched and then clambered blearily out of the car and found myself on a tarmac at the Anchorage airport. A jet rumbled overhead, and another idled nearby with a powerful whine.

I scanned—there were several *run-of-the-mill* private jets nearby, but all of them were parked and clearly not going anywhere anytime soon.

Which left the…jet, I suppose you could call it…that was perched a few dozen yards away like an alien insect.

It was not any kind of aircraft I'd ever seen. Angular, low to the ground, sleek and streamlined, it featured a delta wing design. It was jet black and looked like something a James Bond villain might fly away in after delivering a cackling monologue about his plans for world domination while stroking a fat tabby cat.

I turned to Bruce. "What the fuck is *that* thing?"

"That thing is our ride," he answered with a grin.

"I was afraid you'd say that. Does it come with the James Bond villain?" I asked, forgetting that Bruce was not privy to my inner monologue.

He just laughed. "No, ma'am, no villains. It does come with a complimentary microfleece blanket and *eye-mask*, however."

"But…again, what is it?"

"It's an experimental hypersonic aircraft designed by Valentine Roth. It can go a touch over Mach Five."

"That sounds really fast," I said, having no clue whatsoever.

Bruce chuckled. "Yes ma'am, it is. Very, very fast. That means something like ninety minutes from New York to Paris."

"Are we going to Paris?" I asked.

"No ma'am. *We,* immediately speaking, are going to Texas. And from there, *you* are going somewhere rather more exciting."

"More exciting than *Paris*?" I asked. "Okay, buddy, tell me another one."

Bruce just grinned. "Having been to Paris, I can say it's a pretty damned amazing place to visit. But where are you going?" He shook his head. "Let's just say there's nowhere on earth that can come even close."

"Texas?" I asked, dubious.

This got me a belly laugh. "No, ma'am. Not Texas. That's just stop number two." He indicated the jet. "Ready?"

"I suppose," I said, following him.

The interior was as unexpected as the exterior. The walls, ceiling, and even the floor were wraparound screens showing the world beyond the airplane—which at the moment was tarmac, sky, and airport; the effect when airborne must be incredible, however. The seats were *zero-G* lounge chairs with *five-point* harnesses, able to sit upright for takeoff and landing and reclinable into something you could sleep in. Everything was airy and white, in shocking juxtaposition to the villainous black of the exterior, with quilted leather for the seats and *soft-touch* surfaces everywhere else. It looked to fit maybe twenty people max, but I was the only passenger.

I whistled as I took it all in. "Holy shit, Bruce. This thing is…I don't even know."

"Pretty remarkable, huh?"

"You could say that, yeah," I said. "How much does something like this cost, you think?"

"Well, considering that this is the only one in existence, I'd say 'priceless' is a pretty accurate estimate."

I blew out a shaky breath—this was getting real. "Hunter is really pulling out all the stops, isn't he?"

Bruce just grinned. "You ain't seen nothin' yet, ma'am."

"That sounds a little ominous, Bruce, not gonna lie." I sat in the nearest seat, clicked the harness together, and eyed the ground nervously. "Is the floor gonna stay like that the whole flight? Because I'm not sure if I can handle that."

Bruce shook his head as he buckled into the seat beside me. "No, we can turn it off. I had it on for the flight here."

He touched a button on his armrest, and a panel opened, allowing a small touchscreen to rise up out of the armrest. He tapped a few buttons, pressed his index finger to the screen, which flashed green as it scanned his fingerprint, and then tapped again. The floor went dark and opaque, becoming nothing more than a mere floor.

I breathed a sigh of relief. "Thank you. I've only flown a few times, so I'm a nervous flyer. Seeing the ground from however many thousands of feet? No fucking thank you."

Bruce laughed. "Yeah, it's not for everyone. I do *hang-gliding* and skydiving in my free time, so I think it's cool."

I shuddered. "Nope, nope, nope. My uncle is a pilot, so when I say I'm a nervous flyer, I mean commercial. I fly with Uncle Brock in his little seaplane all the time, but that's different."

I felt something, then—a lurch and a sense of movement. I looked—well, not out the window, because the whole thing was a window, essentially. You know what…I just *looked*. The screens showed that we were gliding away from the hangars and terminal, taxiing toward the runway. We made the turn onto the runway, paused for a minute or two, and then began rolling forward. The sense of movement was gradual at first. Just a nice little roll, and then the landscape was blurring a little, and then my stomach was protesting its passage up into my throat as we accelerated to the point that the horizon was one great blur.

And then…nothing.

The ground fell away and the clouds settled around us. We made a big, banking circle until we were heading south. With the ability to see in 360 degrees, I could see all of Alaska laid out beneath us as we flew higher and higher.

A male voice came from the ceiling. "Prepare for hypersonic."

Bruce reached out and made sure my harnesses were secure, and then his own. A moment later, I felt a giant fist press me into my chair, making it hard to draw a full breath. The crushing sense of acceleration lasted for several minutes.

Outside, huge banks of puffy, scudding clouds swept beneath us so quickly you'd miss it if you blinked. Far, far below, the ground was a quilt of green and brown and blue; from this height, the curvature of the earth was visible.

After the acceleration was done, the sense of momentum faded, and it once again felt like we were just floating along…except for the Earth speeding underneath us at a disorienting pace.

"I'm gonna turn the floor on for a minute. You

really should experience it, just once, just for a minute," Bruce said.

I swallowed hard and gripped the armrests. "Okay."

A few seconds later, the floor vanished, and I screamed, yanking my feet onto my seat, hyperventilating. "Holy shit holy shit holy shit." I was a bird, soaring miles above the earth. "Fuck me, that's wild."

"Breathe, Miss Badd. Put your feet down. Reassure yourself that you're safe."

I let out a tight breath and set my feet down—it did help, actually. The sense of vertigo was still debilitating, but by scanning the horizon and the sky as well the floor, it eventually lessened into something like breathless, but still vaguely terrified, wonder.

"Shall I turn it off?" Bruce asked.

"No," I breathed. "Leave it. It's…"

"Incredible, right?" Bruce said.

"Once I get over the abject terror, yes."

He laughed. "I'm used to being up high, and it still got me the first time."

We touched down smoothly, taxied, and halted. Bruce used another touchscreen to open the door; someone had attached one of those portable staircase thingies to the airplane, and I followed Bruce down to the ground.

"Um. This is not an airport," I said, using my Sherlock Holmes observational skills.

To wit: there was no terminal, no other airplanes anywhere around, parked or taxiing, taking off or landing. The runway was, at a rough guess, infinitely long, and there was just the one.

Another factor that featured heavily in my deduction that this wasn't an airport was the monstrous structure in the distance—a tower of girders and booms supporting a *rocket-spaceship-thing*.

"No ma'am, it's most certainly not," Bruce said. "This is Valkyrie's launch center outside Houston."

I stared at him. "So, um. Question. I'm not going on that thing, am I?"

Bruce grinned. "That's not for me to answer." At that moment, a black SUV made a turn to appear on the tarmac. It pulled to a halt beside me, the driver's door opened, and the driver circled to the rear passenger seat. A short, stocky Asian man in a black *three-piece* suit, the driver smiled at me. "Welcome to Valkyrie Extraglobal Solutions Launch Facility, Ms. Badd. I'm to bring to you Mr. Hawkins."

I smiled back, albeit a little weakly, since my nerves were firing on all cylinders. "Thank you, Mister..."

"Lin," he answered.

"Thank you, Mr. Lin," I said, climbing into the interior of the vehicle.

It was a short drive—straight for the rocket. My heart started pounding in my chest and then migrated northward and started pounding in my throat. I didn't bother asking Mr. Lin any questions because it didn't seem likely that he would answer if he even knew. Apparently, Hunter wanted this whole thing to be as mysterious and *nerve-wracking* as humanly possible, the jerk.

Up close, the rocket was *mind-bogglingly* gargantuan. As jet black as the airplane I'd just arrived in, it stood several stories high, bristling with bits and pieces I couldn't even begin to identify. The actual nozzles from which the fire emitted were so big they could fit a small *ranch-style* house inside with room to spare. The support framework—gantry?—featured an elevator cage; Mr. Lin parked the SUV, left it idling, walked me to the elevator, guided me inside, pressed a large yellow button with an up arrow, and then closed and latched the cage door. The moment the door was latched and locked, the gears started humming and whining, and the elevator rose smoothly and swiftly upward; the rocket was so close I could have stuck my hand out of the cage and touched it. I didn't, however, because that seemed a little unwise, and I'm not an idiot. Despite how fast the elevator moved, it still seemed like the journey lasted for an hour before the cage slowed and halted at a platform near the very top of the rocket. A man in a pale blue jumpsuit bearing the Valkyrie logo—a stylized winged woman wielding a sword and shield—and a yellow hard hat opened the cage door.

"Ms. Badd, welcome aboard the Brynhild."
Br-ihn-hild.

"Um…thanks? I have no clue what's happening."

He gestured for me to follow him along a catwalk within the gantry. "You're accompanying a resupply flight up to the Asgard, where you will meet Mr. Hawkins."

"The Asgard?" I asked. "And…how far up?"

"The Asgard is an extraglobal construction platform orbiting the Earth at a distance of a little over four hundred kilometers above the equator," he answered.

I halted in my tracks. "Wait. I'm going into outer fucking *space*?"

He nodded. "Yes ma'am."

"But…but…I'm not—I haven't…I'm hungover, wearing leggings and a hoodie, and also I'd like to point out that I'm not a fucking astronaut!" I may have been shouting by the end.

He just smiled. "Spaceflight tourism is at an *all-time* high. We make flights up to the Asgard every month, and we usually have a handful of civilians going up simply for the experience. You're the only civilian on this flight, however." He resumed walking, and since I had nowhere else to go but back down, I followed him. "You have nothing to worry about, Ms. Badd. It's perfectly safe. We'll walk you through everything you need to know, do, and wear for the trip up. I've been up myself, and it's…well, ma'am, it is frankly *life-changing*."

"If you say so," I muttered.

He led me along the catwalk another few dozen feet to a hatch in the side of the rocket. A gangway led up and inside—the walls were thicker than a bank safe; the gangway led to a small platform at the bottom of a stairwell, although it was more of a ladder than anything.

My guide climbed up before me, pausing after a few feet to glance back down at me. "Keep three points of contact on the ladder at all times, please."

Yeah, no problem there.

I followed him up, still trying in vain to swallow around the hammering of my pulse in my throat. At the top of the ladder, I emerged into a large circular room; the interior wasn't at all what I was expecting. I don't know what I'd pictured, but it was probably something like the images of spaceships from my school days—gray, industrial, and complicated, with a billion dials and buttons and switches. The walls bore racks of space suits, although these looked less like the bulky things that came to mind when I pictured a spacesuit. Instead, they were more of a beekeeper's suit or a hazmat suit. They were white, made of a thin, flexible material that was somewhere between rubber and leather. There were six of them spaced evenly around the circular room, and each rack held a *dome-like* helmet beside the suits. Another *hatch-door-thing* stood open across the room from the ladder, through which I could see suited figures seated at consoles and carrying out various tasks.

My guide went to one of the suits; he tapped a

touchscreen, which came to life with a glow of digital light. "Come over here, please," he said to me, indicating a green circle painted onto the floor near the rack. "Stand in the circle, arms at your sides. It's a simple laser scan. You won't feel a thing."

"What is it scanning me for?" I asked as I moved to stand as indicated.

"One moment, please," he said. He tapped and typed and swiped for a few moments and then turned to me. "These suits are customizable for each wearer. Nearly as much *R-and-D* went into the design of the suits as the rockets, shuttles, and the station itself."

A circular blade of green laser light swept down from the ceiling in the precise circumference of the circle in which I stood, paused at the floor for a beat, and then swept back up. LED lights in the rack lit up, which made me realize it was more than just a storage rack, but was actually an intricate piece of machinery. Things hummed and whirred, and lights blinked and flashed. Something hummed, and the suit slid away from the wall, held by a robotic arm. The back of the suit hung open from below the knee to the neck.

"Step in, please," the technician said.

"Just as I am?"

He nodded. "Yes ma'am. Just as you are." he frowned. "Actually, you should remove the sweatshirt. You'll be more comfortable."

I removed my hoodie and handed it to him, and

then I held up my phone and wallet, the only things I'd brought. "What about this stuff?"

He took them from me. "The suit has pockets, ma'am. Once you're sealed into the suit, I'll show you."

"Pockets?"

He shrugged, tipping his head to one side. "Technically, they're sealable pouches, not pockets, but the downstream meaning is the same. You'll see in a moment."

With a shaky breath, I stepped into the suit, leggings, *T-shirt*, and sneakers and all. The technician placed my hoodie into a small locker on the side of the suit rack. I placed my arms into the sleeves and my feet into the…boots? *Foot-places*? I don't know. I put my feet where they were supposed to go.

"Hold still for a moment." The technician tapped the screen, and the suit closed itself, the edges zippering together somehow—I couldn't see how since it was happening behind my back.

Once it was sealed up to my neck, the technician fiddled with the screen again for a moment; the suit was voluminous, way, way too big for me. It hung on my shoulders, sagged at the legs, and bunched around my chest. But then, a few seconds after he finished with the touchscreen, I felt it adjusting. It cinched around my legs and waist, belled outward to accommodate my chest, and tightened around my shoulders and arms. Once done, it felt like a second skin. Now, only my head and hands were bare.

The technician handed me a pair of gloves and the helmet. "You don't need these till launch time," he said. "Simply click the gloves into place and they'll seal on their own. Same with the helmet—don't worry about which way it goes, just put the helmet on your head and pull it down till you feel it click. The moment you hear the click, you should hear and feel oxygen flowing. It'll be a little cold and smell a little funny at first, but you should stop noticing it after thirty seconds or so."

He tapped the screen again, and the robotic arm holding the suit retracted and folded itself away within the *suit-rack* mechanism.

I took an exploratory step; it felt no different than wearing insulated coveralls and was actually a little lighter. I moved my arms and legs, testing my range of motion—zero restriction.

"Barely can tell I'm wearing it," I said.

The tech nodded, grinning. "That's where the *R-and-D* dollars went, ma'am, making sure it not only functioned the way it needs to, but functioned comfortably so you can wear it indefinitely."

I frowned. "Indefinitely? What about going to the bathroom?"

He chuckled. "Well, this flight is rather short, ma'am. You'll be able to take it off once you dock and board the Asgard, you just have to wear it for the flight as a precaution."

"Precaution against what?" I asked.

"Something going awry out of the atmosphere,"

he answered. "But please, don't worry. Nothing will go wrong. It's just standard operational procedure. We've done hundreds of flights without issue." He gestured at the suit. "Were you to be going on a longer flight, say to the moon or beyond, you'd be hooked up to a full recycling and reclamation system. Oxygen scrubbers, waste reclamation and recycling, a cooling and warming system, biometric telemetry, comms, the works. For this short hop, though, all you need are the comms, scrubbers, and temperature control."

"Tell me about the temp control," I said. "Please."

"Once you put the helmet and gloves on, the suit comes online. It'll measure your body temperature and respiration rate and will adjust accordingly, so you'll feel like you're at room temperature within the suit—not too hot, not too cold. It'll dispense the oxygen mix that lets you breathe in space for the flight to Asgard. The shuttle has atmospheric capabilities, but it only uses it on long trips." He eyed me. "Any other questions?"

"What if I have to pee?" I asked.

"Do you? Because if so, we need to handle that right now. There's a *porta-potty* on the gantry for that purpose. Otherwise, you hold it. If you have to pee during the flight and can't hold it, just go. The suit will turn on the reclamation system and process it. Your clothes will smell, but they'll be dry. But you launch in *T-minus…*" he checked a cheap digital watch. "Thirty minutes. The flight itself should last about five hours and thirty minutes, max."

I didn't have to pee, so I shrugged that question off. "Five hours? Is there an *in-flight* movie?" I asked, only partially kidding.

He laughed. "No ma'am. You'll be in space. Once you get up there, you'll forget everything else. You won't get bored, I promise."

"How long will I be up there?"

He shrugged. This shuttle is scheduled to return in *seventy-two* hours. You and Mister Hawkins will be returning on that flight."

"*Seventy-two* hours in outer space?" I shook my head. "I'm gonna have to have words with Hunter about springing this kind of thing on a girl."

"Ms. Badd, again, I promise you, once you're up there, it'll feel like far too short of a time. It's…well, magical is the only word I can think of." The tech gestured at the hatch leading to the cockpit. "Please, this way, ma'am."

I let out a breath and then headed for the cockpit, helmet in one hand, gloves in the other, and my heart in my throat.

Once again, my expectations were shattered. I'd been picturing inverted seats, you know? Like sitting upside down, facing the sky, with screens and switches and buttons. Instead, the cockpit felt more like the interior of a particularly technologically advanced electric vehicle. The windshield was a curved sheet of glass wrapping *three-quarters* of the way around the nose of the shuttle, providing a nearly *360-degree* view of the world around us. And, despite the fact that the rocket and shuttle were vertically aligned, as in pointing skyward, the cockpit was oriented "normally," as in I walked in as if I would into any other room.

In fact, the cockpit looked and felt like something out of a Star Trek movie, with curved stations around each of the five seats, with four more seats behind those, which didn't have a workstation. The seats resembled *zero-G* recliners, upholstered in the same material as the suit I wore. The armrests featured digital touch screens, headrests with bolters to prevent *side-to-side* head movement, and *stirrup-like* rests for the feet; it looked like your feet were locked in, somehow, like the pedals of expensive bicycles.

The five workstations were manned by the figures I'd seen earlier, and judging purely by what I could see from behind, at least two of them were women.

The tech ushered me further into the cockpit. "Captain Malcolm, this is Ms. Delia Badd, your passenger for this flight.

The stations were arranged, again, like the bridge from a Star Trek ship—one by itself in front, and the other four in two rows of two behind that. Captain Malcolm was at the station in the front.

Captain Malcolm was a short Black woman with long microbraids tied back behind her head, hanging down her back within the suit. She smiled warmly at me. "Welcome aboard the Brynhild, Ms. Badd. It's a pleasure to have you with us today." She nodded at the tech. "That'll be all, Mr. Thompson," she said, and the tech nodded, smiled at both of us, and exited the spacecraft.

Captain Malcolm took me by the arm, her warm smile still in place. "Your seat is here," she said, guiding me to one of the passenger seats. "Do you have any questions or concerns?"

I laughed. "I mean, considering I had no clue this was even happening until a few minutes ago, I don't...I don't know. Everyone's reassured me how safe this is, but in my experience, the more you have to reassure someone of the safety of something, the more suspicious I get."

She laughed with me. "That is entirely understandable, Ms. Badd. This will be my thousandth flight into orbit, and I've only experienced one malfunction in that time, and that was a *non-critical* system glitch, resolved with a simple reboot. These flights are, statistically, safer than anything you can do anywhere on the planet. It's safer than flying on a commercial airliner or cruise ship. It is absolutely normal to be apprehensive for your first trip up, but I assure you, you're in the best hands on or above the planet."

I let out a breath. "I guess I feel better, but...still. This is all very last minute for me."

"I'm aware," she said. "Now. Let me show you around a little."

The tour was short but interesting. She showed me the various stations—telemetry, guidance, biometrics for the crew and myself, and critical systems overwatch, as well as her captain's station, which featured the data from all four stations, as well as other data she said I wouldn't understand. She explained that the cockpit was actually a gimbal system, meaning the cockpit was sort of *free-floating*, so to speak, within the shuttle, so no matter the orientation of the shuttle itself, the cockpit remained oriented in whatever direction the guidance officer dictated. After the tour, Captain Malcolm eyed me, chuckling. "You look overwhelmed. Why don't you just take your seat and relax? We'll take off before you know it."

And she was right—only a few minutes after taking my seat, speakers in the cockpit announced T minus five minutes. Captain Malcolm helped me click my harness in place, used the touchscreen to bring my seat online—my feet did in fact click into place, which connected the suit to the seat's electronics system, bringing my telemetry online, communicating it to my seat, to the telemetry officer's workstation, and to ground control's system. Or, at least, so it was explained to me.

By the time the count was at two minutes, the whole craft was rumbling, and a deafening roar made my ears ring.

"Helmets and gloves on," Captain Malcolm announced.

I settled the helmet on, pulled down, and felt it click. Immediately, I heard a faint hiss, felt cool air rush upward into the helmet, and tasted copper and iron—the smell and taste faded quickly. I slid the gloves on, and they too clicked into place; once the gloves were sealed, I heard an electronic whine in my ears, and then Captain Malcom's voice.

"Comms check. Sound off."

"Telemetry online," a deep male voice said.

"Guidance online," a high, soft, female, *Spanish-accented* voice said.

"Systems Overwatch online," a rough but quiet male voice said.

"Biometrics online," another voice said—this voice was very quiet, very *soft-spoken*, and gender *neutral-sounding*. Or, at least, I couldn't immediately determine the gender of the speaker, and the heads I could see from behind gave no clues, since everyone's hair, except for Captain Malcolm, was cropped short.

T-minus thirty seconds, and the rumbling felt like an earthquake; the roaring was muted by the helmet.

I gripped the armrests until my knuckles hurt, gritting my teeth and staring up at the clear blue sky.

"Ms. Badd," came a voice in my ear—the biometrics officer. "You need to breathe. Your respiration rate is quite low. In through the nose, out through the mouth. Slow and even."

I didn't bother answering—I couldn't. It took everything I had to force my lungs to draw a breath, and the moment I did, my head swam. But the next breath felt better and came easier, and then I was able to keep my respiration nominal, as I imagined the biometrics officer would have said.

"Ten…nine…eight…" came the countdown.

Fuck, fuck, fuck.

I'm going to space? Hunter Hawkins, I'm going to kill you for this.

The rattling, rumbling, and shaking were *all-consuming*. My bones rattled in my skin. The noise was monstrous, even through the *noise-canceling* of the helmet.

"Five…four…three…two…one…"

For a moment, nothing changed.

And then a giant fist pressed against my chest, shoving me into the seat. I felt the suit tighten around my limbs, squeezing hard like a blood pressure cuff. The pressure increased until it was hard to draw a breath, and my head swam, and darkness floated at the edges of my vision. I tasted copper and iron as the suit worked to compensate for my low respiration. Above, the sky seemed to swell, to grow larger, brighter, bluer. A cloud scudded past faster than my eyes could track, a brief blur of white.

Blue gave way to black in an ombre shift, and the titanic pressure squeezed harder and dizziness washed through me.

And then…stars.

A countless trillion of them, everywhere, like being inside a snow globe full of sunlit diamonds.

White sunlight blazed brilliantly as we angled away

from the globe, and then the pressure of acceleration slowly subsided, and I could breathe and was no longer dizzy.

Holy fucking shit.

I'm in outer space.

EIGHTEEN

Hunter

I LET OUT A NERVOUS BREATH AS I WAITED ON THE GRAVITY side of the hatch. I've spent the last two weeks up here, and I'm still not used to the transition of going from the *zero-g* section to the *earth-normal* section. It's bizarre and disorienting at best. Good thing I don't need to spend much time in *zero-G*—it makes me queasy.

"Nervous, sir?" asks Commander Racine, the officer in charge of administrating the platform.

She's an older woman with a lifetime of experience in *large-scale* admin, *hand-picked* by Valentine and Xavier. I'm late to the party, so I had no say in the pick, but she's who I would have selected anyway. She's much like Harriet, and in my book, that's a damned good thing.

"Yes ma'am, Commander Racine, I am. I'm shaking in my boots, as a matter of fact," I said.

She laughed kindly. "Good. You should be." She noted my quizzical expression and laughed again. "If you're not nervous about the outcome, then you're not fully invested in the process."

I blinked at her as I processed this statement. "Casual wisdom from Commander Racine."

She patted my shoulder. "I proposed to my husband. This was nearly forty years ago when such a thing was very much *not* the done thing. I was extraordinarily nervous even though I knew what his answer would be."

I chuckled. "The problem is, I *don't* know what her response to any of this will be. She walked away from me. That was six months ago. She had zero warning that I was arranging this…meeting."

Commander Racine arched an eyebrow at her. "Wait, you sprung a *last-minute* trip to a space station on the poor woman?"

I cleared my throat. "Um. Yes?"

She laughed and shook her head. "Brave, brave man, and even braver woman, if she actually boarded."

"I have confirmation from Captain Malcolm that she is, in fact, on board the Brynhild," I said.

"Then I'd wager you have very little to be nervous about, Mr. Hawkins. If this woman is willing to wake up and go to outer space without, oh, say, several months of prep time and consideration, then she loves you."

We both heard and felt the *thud-thunk* as the Brynhild docked with the Asgard.

The Norse mythology naming system is cool but a little on the nose. Again, however, I'm late for the party, having just started investing in the last few weeks. Right now, I'm a silent investor only—I need to assess what they're doing, how, and why, and then figure out where I am best used. Valentine and Xavier both agreed to sell me a quarter stake in the project as a starter while I research and observe. Which is why I was on the first flight up here after wiring them the money— to get a *boots-on-the-ground* look at what's being built, how it is being administrated, how the public perceives it, how the ROI will shake out...neither Valentine Roth nor Xavier Badd are morons, obviously, but neither are they me. They brought me in because they felt I could add something.

What a fucking challenge this is.

My thoughts were interrupted when the signal lights above the hatch changed; red indicated the chamber was open to vacuum, yellow—the color it had just changed to—indicated that it was cycling oxygen in, and green indicated that it was safe to open the hatch.

Another several minutes elapsed—the chamber was rather large and required a lot of oxygen.

Finally, the light turned green, and Commander Racine placed her palm on the biometric pad beside the hatch; the pad flashed green as it scanned her palm, and then a lock thunked as it retracted, and then the hatch cracked open with a hiss.

A short Black woman with her helmet under her arm was the first through—Captain Malcolm. Her flight crew followed, making the awkward transition from the *zero-G* of the chamber to full gravity with the seamless grace of people who've done it regularly. Last in line was Delia, helmet still on, drifting slightly out of true to the orientation of the inner section.

"Oh dear," Commander Racine muttered. "Captain Malcolm, our new guest is not accustomed to *zero*-G."

Captain Malcolm halted and turned to look. "Oh! My apologies, Ms. Badd." She handed her helmet to one of the officers and reentered the chamber to help Delia. "Grab these handles on either side of the doorway. Good. Now, swing your feet through and let go."

Delia, looking a little pale but determined, frowned, grasped the handles, swung her feet forward and let go. She gave herself a little too much of a swing, however, because she landed heavily and toppled forward.

Right into my arms.

I grinned at her as I helped her to her feet. "Hi, you."

For a minute, she just stared at me. "Hunter," she whispered. "It's really you."

I unlatched and removed her helmet; her hair stuck to her cheeks. "It's really me."

She looked around and then backward at the *still-open* hatch. "Gravity. How?"

I shook my head. "The details are beyond me, but basically, this inner section, which contains the living quarters, mess hall, and common areas, spins, which creates gravity."

She looked back through the hatch. "So, then, I'm confused. If the inner section spins but the outer section doesn't…"

I laughed. "Hell, if I know, babe."

"Listen, Ms. Badd," Commander Racine said, "unless you're planning on a career up here, I wouldn't worry too much about the details of how things work. If one of us who does live and work up here gives you instructions, follow them. Otherwise, just enjoy the experience. You're one of very, very few people on the planet to visit the Asgard. It is an extraordinary privilege indeed, ma'am."

Delia shook Captain Malcolm's hand. "Thank you for the safe flight up here, Captain."

A nod. "Just doing my job, ma'am." She nodded at me. "Mr. Hawkins, sir."

She and the rest of the flight crew tromped down the corridor and vanished around a corner.

Delia let out a breath. "I can't believe I'm here. This whole thing is…surreal. That's not a strong enough word, but my brain is so scrambled right now I can't think of a better one."

"Believe me, I understand," I said.

She arched an eyebrow at me. "Oh, you do, huh? So *you* were woken up out of a hungover stupor, flown on a hypersonic jet from Alaska to Texas, and then boarded *a fucking rocketship to outer fucking space*?"

I winced. "A bit dramatic, I admit, but if I'd merely invited you, would you have come, knowing in advance where you were going?"

"A bit dramatic? *A BIT DRAMATIC*? You know, a lot of kids dream of being astronauts, Hunter. I get that, but I'm not one of them. A bit dramatic would have been a flight to Paris. Bringing me to a space station is....is...fucking insane, Hunter! That's what it is." She sighed and rubbed her face. "Sorry for yelling. It is called jet lag up here or, like, space lag? Is there a time zone in space?"

"The Asgard observes Greenwich Mean Time," Commander Racine explained. "So you're nine hours behind. But since there's no sunrise or sunset and since there are very few people up here, I doubt you'll feel much lag. It is normal to be exhausted after that trip, however, so if you needed a nap, no one would blame you."

Delia shook her head. "I'm physiologically incapable of napping. I'm way too *high-strung* for that shit." She looked at me. "So...here I am, in space with you, as requested. Now what?"

I shrugged. "All in due time. For now, let's get you out of that suit and I'll give you a little tour. I'll answer the questions I'm sure you have as we walk."

"If you'll accompany me this way, Ms. Badd,"

Commander Racine said, gesturing, "I'll assist you out of the suit."

A few minutes later, Delia was out of the suit and looking grateful. "You know, that thing is surprisingly comfortable, all things considered, but I'm glad to be out of it."

"Remarkable feat of engineering," I said. "The amount of *ground-breaking* tech in that suit is shocking. Everyone talks about the station itself, which, yes, is remarkable, obviously, but those suits are the truly remarkable step forward in space technology. According to your uncle, at least."

She frowned. "My uncle?"

I nodded. "Xavier? A majority stakeholder in this venture and the chief technological officer. He designed quite a bit of the tech, not just in the suits but everything else, as well."

She blinked. "Wow. I…I knew he was involved with Valkyrie, but I guess I didn't realize what that meant. He doesn't like to talk shop when he's around family. Mainly because he'll start lecturing, and he's aware that most people can't follow any of it." She looked back at the *now-closed* door that led to the suit room. "He designed the suits, huh?"

I tipped my head to one side. "As far as I'm given to understand, not the suits themselves. He refined and perfected the design already in the works when he joined forces with Valentine Roth."

She stopped short and stared at me. "Wait, wait,

wait. You sold off your company and vanished, and now you're up here…"

I grinned. "You're looking at a *twenty-five* percent stake shareholder in Valkyrie."

"So…this is what you're doing now?"

"Yes."

She regarded me carefully. "How long have you been up here?"

"Two weeks. I needed to see it for myself. I need to understand the business from the top to bottom, inside and out, so I can provide the best insight."

"But…you're a businessman, Hunter. No offense, but what do you know about outer space?"

We continued down the corridor—here, the corridors were *low-ceilinged* and narrow, with white, featureless walls and floors and LED lights overhead providing warm yellow light rather than the usual harsh white of most industrial spaces. A door here and there broke up the walls, each with a biometric lock to keep out the unauthorized—some of them, even I, as a *part-owner*, wasn't allowed in without an authorized crew member. Which was fine with me—you don't want to go monkeying with things you don't understand when you're hundreds of miles above the Earth in the endless frozen vacuum of space.

"I know absolutely nothing about space," I admitted. "Which is why I'm up here. Valentine is a businessman, too, though. Albeit, he's been designing jets for years, so he has a leg up on me in that regard. But at the end of the day, this is a business. It needs to make money so we can keep functioning. Valentine is focused on R&D with Xavier. They brought me on board to focus on the branding and marketing aspect, which is what I do best. I'm not the bigshot anymore. I'm not even a CEO. And you know what? I've never been happier. I can focus on what I do best."

"That makes sense," she said.

I showed her, briefly, the living quarters for the station and flight crews—small, sterile rooms with little more than a bunk, bathroom, and storage for personal effects. The mess hall was next, a huge space with portholes showing the vast infinitude of space; several dozen tables were scattered around the mess hall, with a traditional *galley-style* mess line. Next was the common areas—the lounge, with TVs and game consoles; a library with a limited selection of physical books and a large selection of *e-readers* stocked with every book imaginable; a rec room with a pool and foosball table, a golf simulator that lets you whack balls not just on simulated Earth courses but imaginary ones like Mars or the moon, with accurate gravity; and a VR room.

Last was what everyone on the Asgard affectionately referred to as The Fishbowl, a bubble of glass at the end of a long tunnel—since it was outside the inner section, the Fishbowl was *zero*-G but did have atmosphere. The tunnel was narrow and featured handrails to make it easier to pull yourself along. Since both of us were newbies, even that was a comedy of errors, with both of us either using too much or not enough force to pull ourselves along. We both ended up twisting around and drifting at awkward angles to each other.

I slipped past Delia to enter the Fishbowl first so I could catch her as she drifted in and then helped get her oriented *face-to-face* with me.

Her auburn hair floated around her head, wafting and drifting gracefully. She looked at me first. "Where are we?"

I gestured around us. "This is The Fishbowl."

Her eyes went up, first, and then around—the Fishbowl was so named because it was essentially that—a glass bowl providing a nearly *360-degree* view of space. There were benches and handrails around the bowl and at regular intervals.

I watched Delia's eyes widen, heard her breath catch. "My...*god*."

"Right?"

She tore her gaze away for a moment and met mine. "Hunter...this is..."

"Worth the trip by itself?"

She nodded. A tear slid down her cheek, unnoticed. "I...I'm speechless. It's..."

I guided us to a bench, which featured *vehicle-style* seatbelts to keep you seated, and latched us down. She spent several minutes in silence, just looking. I had to give her that time because everyone who comes to the Fishbowl for the first time has the same reaction.

It's one thing to see the stars from the ground, even

in a place like Alaska. But up here? You're not just see-ing them…you're *among* them. They're not *above* you; they're all around you. The moon is a dim gray ball in the distance, and Earth is…

Well, it's the most beautiful thing you can imag-ine. Words fail. Seeing photographs of the Earth from space doesn't do it justice. Nothing does.

Delia shook her head as if shaking herself out of a stupor. "No one will believe this," she breathed. "I don't believe it."

"You have your phone?" I asked.

She nodded. "Yeah, but it won't work up here, ob-viously. Right?"

I grinned. "Let me see it."

She fished her phone from her pocket and gave it to me—I connected her to the Asgard's dedicated sat-ellite system, which allowed smartphones to function nearly as normally as on Earth.

"There. Call someone. Your friend Emerson, maybe," I said, handing it back to her.

"What? How?"

"A special dedicated satellite system. You can video call her, just keep it brief. Data is not unlimited, although you're on my dime, so it may as well be."

A second later, her phone burbling; she held it close, so the camera only showed her face.

"Hey, bitch," came Emerson's voice. "Still mad at me or are we good?"

"Hey, hooker," Delia answered. "We're always

good. I was just salty. You know how much I hate it when you're right."

"I'm always right. You should know that by now." A pause. "So. What'd you decide about your grumpy billionaire? Have you moved on, or are you still sitting around feeling sorry for yourself for running away from the best thing that ever happened to you?"

"I'm not grumpy," I said.

"Uhhh," Emerson coughed. "You're with him?"

"Yes?" Delia said, making it a question and then turned the phone to face me. "Emerson, meet Hunter Hawkins. Hunter, meet Emerson, my best friend and sister, whom you may hear us refer to as Sunni."

I smiled and waved. "Nice to meet you, Emerson."

Emerson's eyes were wide. "Um, yeah. Hi, Hunter. Nice to meet you." Delia turned the phone back to face herself, and I heard Emerson squeal. "Did he take you to Paris? Where are you? Also, why do you have it so close? I can't see anything but your triple chins."

Delia pulled her chin and made a face, managing to look remarkably unattractive in a comical way. "There. That better?"

"Troll," Emerson said. "Where are you?"

"Not Paris," Delia answered. "Guess again. Although I warn you, you'll never get it."

"Better than Paris?"

"Much. Infinitely better. A shorter flight, though."

"Shorter flight than Paris and better. London? Prague? Caribbean?"

Delia burst into laughter. "I told you, you'll never guess. The keyword is *infinite*."

Emerson sighed. "Then just tell me, if I'll never guess."

"You wouldn't believe me if I told you," Delia answered.

A disgusted sigh. "Then...what? You're not making sense."

Delia pulled the phone away slowly and panned it around to give Emerson the full panoramic view, ending with Delia and me in the frame with the Earth in the background.

A long silence ensued. "I don't understand. Is that a, like...VR thing? Some fancy *techno-dork* thing in Vegas?"

"No, Em. It's the real thing."

"When you say the real thing...what does that mean?"

Delia tapped on the glass. "I mean, you're seeing what I'm seeing. It's not VR. It's real reality."

"But...but..." Emerson spluttered, leaning closer to her screen. "That's...Earth?"

"Yes."

"So...you're...on the moon?"

Delia cackled. "Not quite, babe. I think that's a bit longer of a trip than six hours."

"More like three days, I'm told," I said. "I haven't been there yet, although Valentine told me they're planning an excursion to survey sites in the next few months."

Emerson was silent. "But...but...*how?*"

"Apparently, when Hunter cashed and out vanished, this is what he was doing—investing with Valentine Roth and Uncle Xavier in Valkyrie."

"Okay, but how does that end up with you in outer space? I texted you *yesterday*, and you didn't mention, oh, I don't know...*spaceflight* as being on the menu."

"Because it wasn't. It was...sort of last second."

"*TO OUTER SPACE?!*" Emerson shouted. "Do you realize how fucking insane that is?"

"I do, since I'm the one who got strapped to a god-damn rocket while still hungover," Delia said.

"Again? Boo, you gotta quit that shit. The drinking isn't doing you any favors."

Delia frowned. "Can we not, right now?"

Emerson sighed. "Sorry, sorry. You're right. So... let's get back to the salient question. OUTER SPACE?"

I laughed. "I don't do things in *half-measures*, Emerson. If I'm going to make a dramatic gesture to get Delia back, it's going to be...well, *very* dramatic."

Emerson snickered. "I'd say so. Not sure anyone will ever top that as a dramatic declaration of love."

Delia seemed suddenly uncomfortable the moment her friend dropped the *L-word*. "Em, don't."

"Oh for fuck's sake, Delia," Emerson snapped. "The man brought you to *space*. Who does that? If you don't see it for what it is, you're the dumbest human on the planet."

"I'm not *on* the planet," Delia muttered.

"You know what I meant, *bitch-face*." Emerson sighed. "Why are you wasting your time up there talking to me? Hang up on me and talk to *him*!" She blew a kiss and waved at us both. "I'll make it even easier—like this. Bye!" The call cut out, going back to the FaceTime call screen.

"Your friend doesn't pull punches, does she?" I asked.

Delia shook her head. "No, she does not." Her voice was quiet. "Hunter, I…"

I took her hand. "We don't have to go there yet, okay? You just got here. It's overwhelming, being up here. Seeing…this?" I gestured at the vast infinitude of space beyond the Fishbowl. "We have *seventy-two* hours. We have time. It's okay."

She shook her head, sighing. "Emerson has been calling me out for how I walked away from you since I did it. She thinks I'm stupid for it."

"I don't," I said.

She jerked her gaze to mine, shocked. "You…you don't?"

"No. It hurt, obviously. It wasn't the reaction I was hoping for, obviously, especially after what we shared. But I get it. I've made a lifetime out of avoiding commitment. It's scary. And I don't have the legacy hanging over my head that you do." I took her hands in mine. "Like I said, we don't have to get into the deep shit right now."

She sighed in relief. "So…you don't hate me?"

I laughed. "Yes, Delia. I loathe you entirely. Clearly.

I bring people I hate to outer space at immense personal cost."

She blinked at me. "How much personal cost?"

I shrugged. "Well, we've been working on ways to bring costs down, but if you were just some random schmuck who wanted to pay to spend the weekend up here, you're talking a minimum of ten million. That's way down from the early days of spaceflight tourism where a single seat was something like fifty million."

Delia coughed. "*T-ten million*? Dollars?"

"No, Delia, ten million seashells." I rolled my eyes at her. "It's not exactly like hopping a 777 *red-eye* to Paris, babe."

"What about that jet?" she asked.

"Oh, well, those fancy jets of Valentine's are all privately owned, so there's no way to estimate a *per-seat* or *per-flight* cost. Once he finalizes the design and starts selling them, though, he anticipates they'll start at a hundred mil, with no real upper cap since they're essentially infinitely customizable."

Delia sighed. "Jesus. A flight to Paris really would've sufficed to get my attention, sweetheart."

My gut clenched at the endearment. I tried like hell not to read too much into it. "It wouldn't have sufficed for me. You're worth everything, Delia. The whole world." I touched her jaw. "If it got me you, I'd give up everything. I'd start over from scratch. You and me in a crackerbox loft in Astoria. It doesn't matter."

"Easy to say from your personal space station," she muttered.

I snorted. "It's hardly mine, babe. I'm not even a majority stakeholder yet."

"So, what's the business? Tourism?"

I let her steer us back to a less emotional footing. "No, that's going to be fractional. There aren't enough people who can afford the cost of entry to make that a profitable enterprise. No, the idea is that in order for exploration beyond the Earth to really make sense, we can't keep wasting time, money, and resources getting rockets out of the atmosphere. That's heinously costly and ineffective. Plus, you're inherently limited by the constraints of gravity."

She blinked. "I'm not following."

I twisted, pointing at a long gantry extending away from the actual construction platform itself. "See that? The long arm thing? We're going to build a ship there. But because it's being built out here and will never see the atmosphere, our design options open up drastically. It can be any shape and almost any size. Again, I'm not an expert in this stuff. My job is going to be helping market it and brand it to potential investors and clients."

"Okay, I follow that part. But what clients? What's the product you're selling?"

I shrugged. "Deep space mining, for one. There are asteroids not all that far away that have billions and trillions of dollars worth of minerals on them that we haven't been able to access simply because of how prohibitively expensive it is just to get out of Earth's atmosphere, into orbit, and then back safely. But if you have a station like this, you can send a *custom-designed* ship and crew to mine and only make the return voyage to Earth once in a while. That's just one possibility. Essentially, Valentine and Xavier saw the potential a long time ago and started building Valkyrie on a gamble that others would see the value and invest. It's still a gamble. The whole enterprise is still a long shot in the dark, but we've got investors and clients in talks. Plus, various governments will want a presence out here or on the moon. Maybe someday, there will be a colony on Mars. This is *sci-fi* come true, basically."

"And it's a challenge," she said.

"The biggest challenge of my life," I said. "Professionally speaking, that is."

Delia sniffed a laugh. "Me being the unspoken greatest challenge of your personal life."

I shrugged. "Nothing worth doing or having ever comes easily."

"Well, as we've established, I certainly do not come easily," she quipped.

"I haven't encountered that with you, as a matter of fact," I said, nuzzling her throat with my face. "Quite the opposite, rather."

She let out a shaky breath. "I'm getting a little disoriented," she said. "Can we go back down, or in, or whatever?"

"For sure."

We drifted out of the Fishbowl and I led her to the guest quarters, which were rather more luxuriously appointed than the crew quarters.

I showed her the door that led to her quarters and the biometric panel that was coded to her for the duration of her stay.

About the size of a suite in a *four-star* hotel, the guest rooms were also decorated to resemble a hotel room, with one major difference. Instead of curtains and a window to outside, the wall was a single digital LED screen that could be programmed at will to show a variety of scenes, from a *real-time* view of space as if the screen was a window to a view of Earth, or other select scenes from space, such as a composite of the Milky way or the Pillars of Creation. Otherwise, the room felt pretty much like a hotel room anywhere on earth, with a queen bed, a bureau, a TV, and a bathroom.

"My room is right next door," I told her, feeling oddly nervous. "I…obviously, I wasn't going to assume that you'd want to, you know, share a room with me right off the bat."

She smiled. "I appreciate that, Hunter. Thank you. And, if I'm being honest, I wouldn't mind a little alone time to decompress. It's been a bit of a whirlwind today, if you know what I mean."

"I sure do." I indicated the bathroom. "Let me show you one thing, though. The showers are a little different since hot water is a pretty precious commodity up here. Each room, meaning each person, is allotted a

certain amount of hot water per *twenty-four* hours."
I showed her the digital panel beside the shower stall.
"This shows you your allotment as it is now. Obviously,
you currently have your full allotment. So you can select increments—five minutes, ten minutes, and fifteen
minutes. If you do fifteen, that'd be your full allotment
for the *twenty-four* period. So, if you don't mind washing
your hands in cold water later, go for it. You can start
with five, and if you need more time, you can add it,
but once you go through the whole allotment, that's it
until it replenishes. And obviously you can always stop
it early."

"That's easy enough," she said. She turned to face
me as I paused at the door. "Hunter, I…"

I went back to her. "Hey, it's okay. You don't need to
say anything. You don't need to know how you feel right
now or what to say. Take your time. Decompress. Get
a shower." I indicated a *two-foot-by-two*-foot cupboard
near the bed. "This is a miraculous little device. It's a
coffee and tea dispenser. It can't do anything fancy—
plain black coffee and green or black tea. But it's hot and
damn near instant, right here in your quarters. Pretty
simple to operate. I stocked you with plenty of Splenda
packets." I showed her the small drawer full of her favorite sweetener.

She shook her head. "You're killing me, Hunter,"
she whispered. "Now go away so I can have the freak-
out I've been fighting off for the last six or seven hours."

"I'll be in my quarters right next door," I told her.

"I've got paperwork to catch up on, so take your time. And if that's in the morning, that's okay. If you wake up in the middle of the night and want to talk, that's fine, too. The lock panels beside the doors have a buzzer, like a doorbell."

She closed her eyes, sniffed a harsh breath, and let it out. "I'm glad I'm here, Hunter. I *can* tell you that much."

I couldn't stop myself from pulling her against me in a hug. Or from kissing the top of her head. "I'm glad you're here too, honey."

She pulled away. "Also, you're crazy. And lucky as fuck that I'm just crazy, because I don't know many other people who would've gone along with this bat-shit plan of yours."

"Plan is a generous term," I said. "I set it up and hoped. Until Captain Malcolm confirmed just before takeoff that you were on board, I wasn't sure you'd even want to see me, especially once you realized where I wanted you to go." I cupped her face, wanting desperately to kiss her. "And believe me, I know exactly how lucky I am."

She grasped my wrists in her hands. "Hunter…" she trailed off, eyes closing. "It's hard to know what to say, what I feel. I'm all mixed up and overwhelmed right now. But you need to know that I care. I care a fucking lot. I just need some time to sort out my head and heart."

I smiled at her. "I know." I leaned in slowly and

touched my lips to hers, softly, reverently, more a promise of kisses to come than a kiss in itself. "Go. Do what you need to do. Take the time you need."

I backed away, and she entered her quarters.

Once the door shut, I collapsed against the wall next to her door, shaking with hope.

NINETEEN

Delia

I OPTED FOR A *TEN-MINUTE* SHOWER. IT WAS, BY NECESSITY, AN abbreviated version of my usual showering process, but I was honestly too exhausted and mentally overloaded to bother with much more, anyway. By the time I emerged, my eyes were drooping. It took sheer willpower to towel off without falling asleep.

I discovered another little surprise left for me by Hunter: a care package of sorts on the bed. It was a stack of clothes, new with tags, in my sizes—leggings, solid color *V-neck T-shirts*, an athleisure style hoodie, a cardigan, a simple but very expensive linen dress, and matching bra and underwear sets, again in simple solid colors. None of it was fancy or ostentatious, but rather simple and of the highest quality. I didn't recognize the brand names of anything, but found myself not caring after putting the clothes on. Also included in the care package was a set of toiletries—a new toothbrush, flossers, toothpaste, mouthwash, deodorant (the brand and scent I favor, and I found myself wondering how he knew that), a hairbrush, a package of hair ties, and a silk sleep mask.

It was a thoughtful gift, especially because it was all practical and utilitarian. No lingerie or anything provocative. Not that I would've been upset had he gotten me something sexy, but the fact that he told me not to pack anything and then made sure I was taken care of spoke to a genuine sense of care and thoughtfulness that left my heart beating a little harder, made the walls crumble a little more.

I put on underwear and one of the *T-shirts*, turned off the lights, and slid the sleep mask onto my face.

I was asleep within seconds.

I woke up disoriented. I wasn't in my bed in Anchorage, nor in my bed at home in Ketchikan. There was no light, no sound.

After a moment of disoriented panic, I remembered the sleep mask. And then I saw my surroundings and remembered the rest.

Another item in the care package Hunter had left

for me was a pair of soft, supple leather ballet flats. I put on a pair of leggings and the flats and went to find Hunter.

I rang the bell at his quarters and received no answer; I was about to try and find my way to the mess alone when he rounded a corner. He was shirtless in a pair of very short shorts that clung to his thick, powerful thighs. His broad shoulders and hard chest and shredded abs glistened with sweat. He was more ripped than the last time I'd seen him—leaner and harder, as if he'd been driven to renewed extremes of fitness by strong emotion.

Fuck.

My mouth went dry, my palms clammy, and my lungs solidified in my ribcage.

He had a plain black ballcap on backward, his hair a little too long and messy and sticking to the back of his neck. He had earbuds in and he was intently tapping away at his phone as he did the *phone-zombie* shuffle toward his room.

Fuck.

I couldn't breathe, looking at him, remembering the glory of his body under my hands, his skin against mine, the lithe and powerful movement of his muscles as he drove into me…

I was in motion before my brain caught up. He was so intent on the email he was drafting that he didn't notice my approach—he'd stopped short of his door by a few feet, still panting a little, sweat droplets sliding down his nose.

Need blazed inside me, the inferno of my desire for this man roaring to life with such undeniable, irrepressible power that it took my breath away. It was beyond mere physical desire, however.

Yes, my nipples were diamond hard and pressing against the *T-shirt*—I'd not bothered with a bra, being more intent on finding Hunter so we could talk than with silly nonsense like wearing a *titty-prison*.

Yes, my pussy was soaked with need, and my whole body pulsing, aching, raging with arousal.

Yes, I needed to touch him more than I needed my next breath.

But it was more.

So much more.

More than flesh and blood, more than muscle and nerve endings.

It was a need in my soul. A requirement in the very core of my being.

I was starved and dying of thirst and the only thing that could sate my hunger or slake my thirst was Hunter.

His voice, his words. His scent, his touch. His kisses, his love.

Him.

I just needed…him.

I couldn't deny it—not within myself any longer. I couldn't deny his claim over my mind, my heart, my soul, and my body.

I couldn't deny my own claim over him—he was mine.

I stopped short of touching him, just barely. He was so shocked by my appearance that he fumbled his phone and nearly dropped it.

"Delia!" he said. "Holy shit, you scared the hell out of me, woman."

I found my tongue frozen to the roof of my mouth. Found words jumbled and scrambled in my brain and trapped in my throat.

All I had was touch.

I pressed my palm to his chest and pushed him back up against his door. Crushed my body against his, thighs to thighs, belly to belly, breasts flattened against pecs.

A greedy, hungry smile spread across my mouth as I felt his erection grow behind his shorts.

I grasped his wrist and guided his hand to the biometric reader; it flashed, and his door slid open—in what had to be an intentional homage to Star Trek, the doors were all automatic, hydraulic pocket doors, so when you touched the biometric reader, they slid inside the wall with a satisfying *sci-fi* whoosh.

He stumbled backward, and I followed him inside, giving him a gentle shove further inward. I'd expected his quarters to be at least a step or two better than mine since he was a part owner and a billionaire, so I was a little shocked to find he was staying in a mirror image of my quarters.

"Delia—" he started, plucking the earbuds from his ears.

I took them from him. Took his phone from him. Set them on his nightstand. Swept the backward hat from his head and tossed it aside.

"Delia, shouldn't we talk first?"

I shoved him back again, and he tripped, stumbling against his bed—the mattress hit the backs of his knees and he sat down hard. I insinuated myself between his thighs.

"No," I whispered.

"But, I…" he started.

I crawled onto his lap and circled his neck with my arms. "I know." I cupped his face. "I just can't think of anything else but this right now, Hunter."

He growled and ran his hands up my thighs, paused at the crease of my hips, and then slid them under my shirt. I lifted my arms, and he tore my shirt off and tossed it aside.

He cupped my breasts with a sound that couldn't be described as anything but a sigh of relief. "Dreamed of you, my love," he murmured, lifting the weight of one breast to his mouth and kissing the upper slope. "Dreamed of this."

"I did too," I whispered. "Every night."

I arched my back to press my breast deeper into the soft wet warmth of his mouth, into the delicate suckle of his lips, and I gasped, head tossed back.

Hunter groaned, letting go of my breasts so they

bounced free with a sway, and his hands slid up my back, cradling the back of my neck, and then his mouth found mine.

"Fuck, please," I whimpered. "Please kiss me, Hunter. Kiss me and never fucking stop."

His answer was another ragged groan, and his lips fused with mine and his tongue danced in my mouth, tasting me, claiming my mouth, my kiss.

Yet, the moment I began to return the kiss, he pulled back, hands roughly framing my face, keeping it close to his as he pulled back just enough that our eyes could meet.

"Will you run again?" he asked.

Tears spurted into my eyes, blurring my vision. "Hunter, I—"

"Will you…run…again?" he demanded, harshly now.

I shook my head as tears slid hot down my cheeks. "Hunter, no. No. Where would I go?"

"That's not fucking good enough. I didn't bring you all the way up here so you wouldn't have anywhere to go, Delia. I brought you here to share this place with you. To share something that's important to me."

A sob wracked me. "I *know*—I…I know, Hunter. I just…I meant—"

"If you don't want me, I'll let you go. If you don't love me, you don't even need to say so. If you want to run, I'll let you." His voice shook. "I'll fight for you, Delia. I'll fight for us. But I need to know it's what you want me to do. I won't play hard to get. If you run, I'll let you go. I won't chase you."

I shook my head again, blinding tears burning in my eyes. "No, Hunter. No. No."

"No what?"

"I'm not playing hard to get. I never was."

"You ran."

"Because I was scared!" I yelled, shooting to my feet and staggering away from him, scrubbing my face with both hands.

"So was I!" he yelled back. "But I fucking stayed."

"And I didn't!" I whirled away from him, sobbing so hard it was impossible to breathe. "I ran. I ran and hid. And yes, I wanted you to chase me, but only because I was too scared to—to—I don't fucking know! I don't know, Hunter! I don't know what I wanted, what I was thinking. I was scared. I still *am* scared. But I'm here, aren't I?"

"Delia—"

"I'm here," I whispered, my knees threatening to give out.

"So I ask you again." I felt him behind me, felt his bare, hard chest against my back. His hands went around my middle and he pulled me back against him but barely held me there, making a point of giving me freedom to pull away. "Will…you…run…again?"

I shook my head, crying too hard now to manage words.

"I need to hear it, Delia."

"No!" I shouted. "No!"

"No what?"

I turned in his arms. "No, Hunter, I will not run again."

"Why not?"

I frowned. "Why not? What do you mean, why not?"

"Just that—why won't you run again? What changed? What's different? You just said you're still scared."

"So did you!"

"But I never left, even though I was afraid."

"Can't you forgive me for that, Hunter?"

"Yes, of course I can."

I swallowed hard, looking up at him through *tear-hazed* eyes. "Will you?" I held onto his shoulders. "I'm sorry, Hunter. I'm sorry I ran away. I'm sorry I let my fears win. I'm sorry I hurt you."

"Delia, I love you." His voice was so tender, so soft.

I wanted to say it back; the words caught in my chest. I squeezed my eyes shut and fought to get them out. "Hunter, I—"

His lips quested across my cheeks, kissing away tears. "Don't fight it, Delia. I know I love you. I can say it easily because it's been obvious to me since before we made love in that ugly fucking house in Alaska. I love you. I'm in love with you. But I don't want you to have to fight yourself. If you're not there, that's okay. Maybe you never will be. Just..." he swallowed hard, his whisper shaky and emotional. "Just be real with me, Delia. Give me the raw, brutal truth, no matter what that truth may be."

I trembled all over, a billion fraught and confusing emotions whirling in the vortex of my heartspace. I loved him. I was terrified of loving him. Terrified of not knowing how to love. Terrified of not being able to love him well enough. Terrified of failing where everyone else in my family has succeeded. I know, I know—it's a stupid and pathetic thing to be so afraid of. But it's a very real pressure. I know I'm good at what I do at work. I know my place. I know my skills.

But love?

I have a terrible track record.

"I'm not good at it, Hunter," I whispered.

"At what?"

"Love." It wasn't even a whisper—it was a breath, barely a sound.

"You can't be bad at something you've never experienced."

"But, I—"

"Have you ever truly been in love?"

I realized, then, what he was saying. "No," I admitted.

"Well then. You're not bad at love. Neither am I—because I've never really been in love before either. This is new for both of us."

"You don't understand, Hunter," I protested. "Every man I've ever dated has been…problematic. I've been the other woman more than once. I've been with a man I *knew* was married. I've been lied to about—everything. About being married or in a relationship. About having kids. I've been cheated on repeatedly. I've been used for sex. I've used men for sex. I've had sex with strangers and never learned their names. I've dated so many fucking losers, Hunter. Not because there weren't any good men in Ketchikan. There are. A lot of them. I just lied to myself about that because it was easier than admitting that I was the problem. I've always been the problem."

"What do you want, Delia?"

"Is this going to be a *Notebook* moment?"

"Yes. Tell me what you want."

"You."

"You had me. You still have me." He shook his head. "I'm the problem for me, too, Delia. I'm a privileged, *out-of-touch*, selfish bastard. I grew up rich and got richer. I've always gotten what I want. Always. I used women. I always made sure they knew how it was, but that doesn't change the fact that I used them. I never had any intention of letting a relationship become anything real, and I'd still sleep with them even when I knew damn well they'd end up developing feelings for me. And when they inevitably did, I cut them loose. I walked all over anyone who stood in the way of my career. I ruined the careers of men who stood in my way."

I shook my head. "Hunter, this isn't a 'who's worse' competition."

"Good, because I'll win. I have spent my entire career thus far being the poster boy for faceless corporate villains. I've done terrible things in the pursuit of wealth I do not, have never, and will never need." He stared hard at me. "I don't deserve you. I don't deserve your love. But I'm still enough of a selfish bastard to want you anyway."

"So we're both awful? Is that what you're saying?" I asked.

He shook his head. "No. I'm saying—"

I slammed my mouth against his. "Oh, for god's sake, Hunter—shut the fuck up and kiss me already." I kissed him so hard our lips would be bruised later, probably. And then I broke away and whispered, lips moving against his. "We've talked this in circles. What does any of that matter? All that matters is now. Right? I'm here. I came because I was miserable without you. I worked until I couldn't stay on my feet anymore, and then I went home to my empty apartment and drank myself into oblivion because it hurt too bad missing you and knowing how wrong and stupid I was for running."

He closed his eyes, and his head tipped down, his forehead resting against mine. "So what are you saying, Delia?"

"I'm saying I'm done running—from you, from love, from what I really want."

"Which is what?"

"What my parents have. What all my aunts and

uncles have." I let out a shaky breath. "I'm just…I'm still scared of it, Hunter."

"What is it exactly you're so scared of?"

"Not being enough. Failing."

"Look, Delia. I don't have any examples of real love in my life. My parents aren't in love and never have been. They're friends and partners, but it's not love. My fear comes from that—I don't know what it looks like. And I know I don't want that—I don't what they have. I want something real. I want what your family has, too. And yeah, I'm scared of the same thing—I'm scared I'm not enough. That I'll fail. That I'll end up like my parents. They have all the money in the world, but at the end of the day, they go to bed in separate rooms."

"That's sad," I said.

"Yes, it is." His gaze was fierce. "The only way you and I can fail at this is by not trying. I may not know how to be a good boyfriend, let alone husband. But by god I'm willing to fucking try. I'm willing and ready to go all in on loving you. On being there for you. I'll do *anything* for you, Delia. This—" he swept a hand at… everything. "This was to prove that to you, I suppose. I'll give you the very fucking stars in the sky, my love."

"But I Hunter, I don't need the stars. I just need you."

"Then all you have to do is stay," he whispered. "Love me. Let me love you. Take it one day at a time. When I fuck up and do something or say something that hurts you or pisses you off, forgive me. When you want to run, don't. If you need time alone to sort things out,

I'll give you all the time and space you need, as long as you come back to me at the end of the day. That's all I need. That's all I ask. Choose me every day, because I swear to you, Delia, I'll choose you every day."

Love surged within me, so potent, so fierce it took my breath away.

Is that really all it is? Choosing someone, day in and day out, no matter what life throws at you?

"That seems so simple," I whispered.

"I'm no expert, but I don't think it was ever all that complicated. I don't think that means it's easy. It's just... not all that complicated."

"I think you're right." I touched his lips, smiling up at him, letting the love I finally allowed myself to fully feel shine through my eyes. "And I think there's only one thing left for me to say."

"What's that?" he demanded in a soft, growly murmur.

"Make love to me, Hunter. Please." I shimmied my leggings off and stood naked in front of him.

His eyes raked over me, eager, fierce, wild, and full of love. Unwilling to wait for him, I found the waist of his shorts and tugged them down. He kicked them away, toed off his sneakers and socks.

When he went to kneel in front of me, I caught him. "No, Hunter. I don't want that. Not this time." I crushed myself against him, hooked one thigh high around his hip.

He lifted me, and I caught his neck and found

my balance by claiming his mouth. Took his tongue. Devoured his breath. Whimpering, gasping, I reached between us and guided his erection to my seam.

"Delia," he whispered. "My love."

"Yes," I answered. "Yours."

I let my lips tremble against his as I fit him to my opening. "Mine," I said, the word a soft breath of wonder as I sank down on him. "Mine. You're mine."

"Oh god, oh god," he hissed, filling me, staggering as his knees buckled at the pleasure of our union. "Yes, yes—I'm yours, Delia. I belong to you."

We crossed the room as my sex swallowed his cock, taking him deeper and deeper inside me, and we caught up against the door. It was cold and hard against my back. He let my weight sag lower, until he filled me so deeply that I ached with him, the thickness of his cock stretching me to a perfect, delirious burn. I cried out with joy, clinging to his neck, settling lower until he could fill me no more.

"Love me, Hunter," I demanded.

He drove into me with a ragged grunt, and the force of his thrust ripped a cry from my lips. "I love you."

"Again," I snarled. "Harder."

He pinned me to the door with his body, cradling my ass in his hands, pulling me open for himself.

Another thrust—this one harder yet. "I love you, Delia."

My breath caught on a sob of delirious rapture. "Hunter!" I cried. "Again."

I clung to his neck and whimpered as he dipped at the knees to draw out of me, shaking all over with the orgasm I'd been denied for so long, for all the endless minutes, hours, days, weeks, and months since I last had him here, where he belongs—inside me.

His next thrust was everything I needed. He slammed into me, driving me against the door with a hard, powerful thrust, his cock filling me to bursting, angled to perfectly slide against my clit, his chest scraping against my sensitive nipples, his mouth crushing mine and his tongue claiming mine.

It was a thousand years of lovemaking in a single thrust.

I broke.

I came with a scream as he fucked into me.

"I love you, Delia," he growled, his voice shaking and ragged. "I love you so fucking much."

As I came, I clutched around him, spasming and squeezing. His knees gave out then, and he sagged to the floor, lying on his back, and I rode him down, wrapping myself up in him, draping myself over him. He was fully within me, pulsing with arousal as I quivered above him, gasping as I came, panting until I caught my breath.

And then I took over. I cradled his face in my hands and rolled my hips, thrusting against him—the action ripped a whimper out of me as it sent me to new trembling heights of ecstasy, but this was no longer for me.

It was for him.

For us.

When I felt him bottom out inside me, I braced my hands on his chest, lifting my hips and leaning forward. He gripped my ass and stared up at me. "Delia, I lo—"

I bit his lower lip. "Hush. I know." I sank against him. "I know, Hunter."

He groaned as I thrust against him again, gasping as he filled me.

Another thrust.

Faster.

"Delia," he started again.

I covered his mouth with my hand, riding him hard and fast now. My hips rolled in a blur, and another orgasm rose within me—I fought it off, however.

Faster.

He gripped my ass in his strong hands and helped me fuck him, lifting me up and crashing me down as he thrust with mad, ragged power, grunting against my hand. I rested my forehead on his, one hand on his shoulder for balance, the other clapped over his hand, silencing him until I found what I needed.

His grunts became a roar, and his thrusts lost their rhythm as he reached his climax.

Now.

I took his hands, threading our fingers together, and pressed them up over his head. Stretched out on his body, breasts crushed against his chest, I set the rhythm. I rode him with everything I had, slamming onto him with wild abandon, screaming hoarse and wordless as a climax ripped through me.

He bellowed through gritted teeth, and I pressed quivering lips to his mouth, stole his breath since mine was lost, snatched away by the furious intensity of our union.

"Hunter," I whispered, feeling him reach the precipice. "Say it again."

"I love you," he rasped. And with that, he came. "Oh—god. Oh god. Delia—Delia!"

He exploded within me, and my orgasm shattered, merging in a thousand pieces with his, and now all that I was became him, became us.

I devoured his protestation of love. I stole his breath. I rode him through my climax until I was breathless and mad, thoughtless and wild, a creature of primal frenzy.

"I love you!" I shrieked, the words ripped from the depths of my soul as he came inside me, as we came together. "Hunter—I love you, I love you—oh god, *I love you.*"

"Delia," he whispered, visibly shaken to the core. "Mine. My Delia."

"Yes," I breathed, "yours. Yours. Always yours. I love you, Hunter."

We moved together in slow silence, then, sliding against each other through the last shaky waves of mutual release, and I felt something damp against my cheek.

I pulled away and saw tears glistening on his cheeks. I kissed them. "Mine," I whispered, kissing tears as they leaked from his eyes.

"Fuck, I—" he started.

I silenced him with a kiss to his lips. "Don't cheapen it with an apology, Hunter."

He let out a ragged sighing snarl. "You make me feel things I didn't know I could feel."

"Same."

I hissed as I slid him out of me, rose to jellied legs and pulled him up after me. Drew him to the bed and lay down, taking him with me. I cradled his head on my chest and we breathed together for a time I didn't care to measure.

We dozed, then.

He turned the lights off and made the wallscreen show the *blue-green* beauty of Earth spinning gracefully in the vast black.

He kissed me—my lips, my throat, my breasts. Every inch of me. He kissed my sex until I came, and then he guided me to my hands and knees and slid into me from behind and made slow, deliberate, forceful love to me as we watched Earth, larger than life, the most incredible sight I've ever seen, spin as we delved into each other, braiding our souls together.

We slept. We conserved water by showering together, and he made me come again and again, whispering his love for me with each thrust.

I lost track of how many times we made love, there in the *half-light* of the glow of Earth.

I woke with my head on Hunter's chest, sore and sated and full of such unutterable and delirious joy that it was almost hard to breathe.

I peeked at him with one eye, drowsy still. "Hi."

He was toying with something that caught the dim, otherworldly light—it was small, round, and thin.

And glittered.

"Hunter?" I whispered.

"Your uncle and Valentine sent a probe to the asteroid belt, way back when they first started designing, building, and testing their reusable rocket and shuttle system." He was building up to something, so I held my questions. "It took samples—a lot of them. Only a handful of people know about that probe or the results it brought back. Which are minerals unlike anything we could ever find on Earth."

He showed me the object: a ring.

It was *silvery-gray* and iridescent—otherworldly. Despite being a simple circle, it was the most beautiful thing I'd ever seen.

"Hunter…is that…?"

"Made from minerals that the probe brought back from the asteroid, yes." He brushed his lips against mine. "Diamonds, titanium, platinum…anyone can have those," he said, turning the ring this way and that; each new angle made it gleam with a different sheen, showing new hues, new colors I'd swear don't exist on earth. "You deserve something no other human on the planet has ever had."

"Hunter," I breathed.

He took my left hand. "Marry me?" His eyes met mine, and I saw the fear, the hope, the love all written there plainly for me to see.

I slid my finger into the ring and kissed him. "Yes, Hunter. Yes. Yes, yes, yes. As soon as possible. Just… not up here."

He laughed. "No, not up here. Your whole family wouldn't fit up here. This station has a max capacity, and your family is too big."

"You really had a ring made out of space rocks?"

"I did. Although calling them space rocks sort of cheapens it, if you ask me. That ring is literally priceless. The minerals it's comprised of do not exist anywhere but that asteroid hurtling through space hundreds of thousands of miles from Earth. And since it'll be years, at best, before any real mining happens out there, that ring will be *one-of-one* for a very long time."

"I'd have been happy with a ring out of a Cracker Jack box, Hunter," I said.

"Which is exactly why you deserve that." He let out a breath. "I didn't really expect you to say no, but I was still nervous."

"Of course, I wouldn't say no," I said with a laugh.

He looked at me. "When you say as soon as possible...?"

I shrugged. "I mean exactly that. I don't want or need some big thing. I just need my family around me celebrating us. The earliest date we can get my whole family together is when I want to marry you. And I want..." I swallowed hard. "I want to marry you at home. My parents' home, in Ketchikan."

"As long as you're my wife at the end of it, Delia, it can be whatever, whenever, and wherever you want. I'll spend a billion dollars on it, or we can do it on a shoestring. Becoming your husband is all I care about."

"Then it's settled. In my parent's backyard, as soon as possible." I sighed. "I just have one question."

"Hmmm?"

"Where will we live?"

He shrugged. "I can do most of what I need from anywhere. I'll still have to make trips now and then for various business purposes, especially once Valkyrie starts taking clients."

I grinned. "I like that answer. Because what I'm hearing is you're building us a house in Ketchikan."

He laughed. "Sounds like I am. Because, good lord, I *hate* that place I was living in before. It is *so* godawful ugly."

I cackled. "Thank god you said that. I was worried you liked it."

"God no. It's the worst." He kissed me. "I have

two words for you, Delia, and they're two very simple words that you're gonna have to get used to hearing: unlimited budget."

I grinned. "You may regret that. I have expensive taste."

He just laughed. "Pauper me, my love. I dare you to try."

I nuzzled against him. "I'll do my best."

TWENTY

Hunter

THREE YEARS LATER

I PUT MY NOTECARDS ON THE PODIUM, ADJUSTED MY TIE, cleared my throat, and started my speech. "On behalf of my partners, Valentine Roth and Xavier Badd, I'd like to thank you all for being here. I'd be remiss if I didn't thank my partners for taking a chance on me, for letting me in on this exciting little project." There was a wave of laughter because there was nothing small about the project. "This is years of work in the making—mostly for Valentine and Xavier. But seeing as they're both too chicken to make speeches, it falls to me, so I'll sing their praises for them."

In the wings of the stage, Valentine gave me an

annoyed glare, and Xavier stared blankly, his version of an annoyed glare.

"It was Valentine's vision, first and foremost. He saw the potential, the future need, and gambled billions of his own fortune to make this a reality. Xavier joined him a few years later and added his technical expertise that helped Valkyrie really...take off." I grinned as the audience groaned. "Sorry, I couldn't help myself. My contributions have been minimal. The real attention needs to be on the dozens of incredibly smart and *hard-working* scientists, engineers, and builders who have made this whole thing possible. We provided the money and the ideas, but it's them who truly made it all happen, one day at a time."

I paused, focusing my attention on the massive screen, which showed a *real-time* feed of The Meili, the ship we were launching—named after the Norse god of exploration, whose name means *"Mile-Stepper."*

"This marks a new chapter in human history—the launch of the first ship to be built entirely outside the confines of our planet. The brave men and women aboard the Meili," *MAY-lee*, "depart today for a *year-long* excursion to Mars, with the *end-goal* of establishing a permanent waystation there. This is the first step in a wider exploration of our solar system, a stepping stone to mining and colonization. There will be many obstacles and challenges, but we will meet them all, as we always have. But let's not get ahead of ourselves. Today, we celebrate the launch of The Meili, and, hopefully, the beginning of many successful missions to come. Thank you."

I answered the endless barrage of questions, sticking to the talking points the science team gave me—even after all this time, I'm still far from an expert on any of the tricky stuff, so we leave those details to be published in the science journals.

As exciting as the event is, I'm more excited to be done so I can go attend the real event, in my eyes: the birth of our first child.

Over the last three years, Delia has been busy. The Badd family has opened a *half-dozen* new locations across the country—and no two are exactly alike. She spends several months at each new location, and while she's opening that location, her advance team is scouting for the next one. Once the new location is running smoothly, she takes a month off, and we retreat to our home in Ketchikan. We shut off our work phones, ignore our emails, and pretend we're nobodies with no responsibilities. We party with her family, ride our horses, and relax. And then, at the end of the month, we move to the next location, and the whole thing starts over. I work remotely for the most part, from wherever home is—Denver, Cleveland, Detroit, Chicago, Miami, LA, Atlanta. They're a popular chain, now, with a growing cult following. Each new enterprise presents a different challenge since she adapts the concept to fit the city and the specific location. The key, she found, is keeping the concept flexible and providing direct oversight during the first few months. She's constantly traveling, even after the locations are up and running, to provide her direct influence and presence. Her father also checks in regularly—now that he's mostly retired, he and Dru turn the site visits into extended vacations since they've never really left Ketchikan until recently.

But now, everything is about to change.

She's about to give birth.

To our son.

The first Badd grandchild—and Papa Lucas' and Mama Livvie's first *great-grandchild*.

This means Delia will be stepping back from work and travel for a while, and the barrage of new locations will slow, which has been the plan all along. We're going to permanently relocate to Ketchikan, and Delia is going to be a *full-time stay-at-home* mother—by her own choice, mind you. She'll keep tabs remotely, of course, and she'll be available if anything comes up, but things have been set up to run on their own for the most part.

The only sticking point for the Badd family lately has been the fact that Delia's brothers don't have much *long-term* interest in the family business. They've both put in plenty of hours helping out around the Ketchikan locations, but they've both made it clear that they will not be following Delia into the restaurant business permanently.

That's not the problem, though. The problem is that neither of them knows what it is they *do* want to do.

I applaud Bast and Dru, though—they're patient

and understanding, willing to give their boys the time and space needed to figure that out on their own.

Trust me, I'm taking parenting notes.

I've offered them both internships anywhere in any of my business ventures, both with Hawkins Group and Valkyrie, but so far, neither of them has taken me up on that.

Delia says she's not worried—Badds always find their way. And usually, it's the Badd Family Love Charm that provides the impetus.

I was mystified when she first explained what the love charm was, but then I took a look at her family and the absurd success rate of their marriages, and I understood. It also made a lot of sense as to why she was so scared to commit to me.

I guess we'll just have to wait and see what happens with Duncan and Dane.

I've become incredibly close to Delia's family over the last few years—Bast is somewhere between a father figure and a friend, someone I admire and look up to, and someone whom I simply enjoy spending time with. Dru is like a mother to me, as well, always hugging me, calling me out when I get grumpy, teasing me—as the whole family tends to do, which took some getting used to, as Givey is the only person who's ever been able to tease me. I've learned how to give as good as I get, especially with her very many, very big, and very scary uncles—who are in fact that numerous, large, and intimidating. In fact, the whole clan has sort of adopted me, and whenever we're in town, I find myself swept up in some new adventure with her brothers, cousins, uncles, and aunts.

I wouldn't trade any of it for the world.

I let my security team escort me away from the crush of the press circulating outside the event center and into the SUV, which whisks me off to the airport. The jet is waiting, and I board it. The flight back up to Ketchikan is short but feels way too long, especially with Emerson texting me updates every hour, letting me know how far apart the contractions are and how dilated she is.

I hated to be away so close to her due date, but she knew I had to conduct the press conference in person from the launch center in Houston. It just sucks that she went into labor literally five minutes before the conference started.

"JUST GET HERE SAFELY ASAP," Emerson texted me. "You know she won't let herself have this baby until you're there, so hurry your ass up."

I told the pilot to fly as fast as the hypersonic aircraft would allow, and we made the trip in record time.

I sprinted down the hallway of the hospital to the private birthing center we'd had built—a massive donation and a *much-needed* upgrade to the local hospital.

Delia laughed between groans of pain and exertion. "Slow down, Hawk," she said through gritted teeth. "You won't be any help if you break an ankle, old man."

Yeah, she's taken to mocking my age and the fact that I'm eight years older than her. Ha ha.

I ignored her teasing quip and stood next to her. "Where are we at, baby?"

"Well, no baby yet, that's where," she panted. "You're just in time. The doctor thinks he'll be here any time now."

"We broke Mach Six getting here," I said.

She frowned at me. "Reckless."

"I wasn't about miss any more of this. Not for a stupid press conference."

"It's not stupid," she said, and then paused to groan as a contraction hit. When it passed, she continued, panting, sweating. "It's the culmination of years of work, and it was important. You haven't missed anything but me screaming, cursing, and sweating."

"I should have been here," I insisted.

She glared at me. "You're here now. Stop arguing with the pregnant lady, honey."

Emerson, on her other side, grinned at me. "You *really* want to listen to her, buddy. Trust me."

The door opened again, and Dru poked her head in. "I'm here, honey. Want me in here with you or what?"

Delia rolled her eyes. "Like you'd miss the birth of your first grandbaby, Mom."

Dru grinned. "I mean, duh. But it's your birth. If you want me to wait in the waiting room with your father, I will."

"Just get over here," Delia said. "Emerson sucks at counting."

Emerson just laughed. "I'll forgive you since you're in labor."

Which was how I found myself at Delia's left hip, holding her leg with one hand and letting her crush my knuckles with the other as she bore down with a primal scream through the contractions that came hard and fast.

The doctor, clad in blue scrubs with a mask and plastic face shield, sat on a rolling stool between Delia's open thighs, shouting encouragement. "Here he comes! I see the head! One more big push, Mama!" She went silent, then, and I watched my son squirt out of his mother.

I know, I know, but 'squirt' really is the only word for it. If you know, you know. The doctor caught him easily, but my heart leapt into my throat—the cord was wrapped around his little neck, and he wasn't crying. She slipped a finger under the cord and tugged, and then the cord was free. She rubbed a knuckle against his little chest, muttering "C'mon, buddy" to herself.

"Hunter? What's happening?" Delia asked, her voice tight with panic.

Before I could come up with what to say, a sharp, angry little cry filled the room, and Delia burst into sobs.

Relief so potent I got dizzy rifled through me, and I nearly collapsed—a nurse nearby kept me upright long enough for me to regain my balance.

"You've got a healthy, beautiful boy," the doctor said; she wasn't our usual OB/GYN since this whole thing had happened unexpectedly, and I'd been late, so I never caught her name. "Dad, you want to cut the cord?"

I cleared my throat, struggling with the flood of emotion; my throat was hot and tight and my eyes burned. *"Y-yeah.* Yes."

The doctor fastened clips to the cord in two places and handed me a pair of weird scissors. "Right here between the clamps, Dad."

Dad.

That's me.

Holy fuck.

I could barely see and had to blink hard. I hesitated, meeting Delia's tearful gaze for a moment. All I needed was the love I saw in her eyes, and I was okay.

I cut the cord, and then our son was in his mother's arms, squirming and covered...stuff...and wailing like crazy.

I moved beside her as Delia held our son. "We're parents."

She nodded, too overcome to speak.

"You did it, honey. You did it. I'm so proud of you." I kissed the top of her sweaty head, watching her soothe our son.

"Hi," she whispered. "Welcome to the biggest, craziest family in the entire State of Alaska."

"Do you have a name picked out?" the doctor asked.

"Sebastian Drew Hawkins," Delia said—he's named after, obviously, Delia's dad, and his middle name is Delia's maternal grandfather's, now deceased.

Sebastian was whisked away then, for a few minutes of measuring and who knows what else, and then he was brought back cleaned up, wrapped in one of those ubiquitous hospital baby blankets, with an adorable little blue hat on his head and a tag with his name and Delia's on it.

Delia, sitting up now, cradled him to her chest. "Mom? You want to hold him?"

Dru sniffled tearfully. "Do I want to hold my very first grandchild? What kind of a question is that?"

Delia handed him off to his grandmother, who cooed and rocked him with the automatic expertise of a parent.

"Hi there, Little Sebastian. You are going to be *so* loved, you know that? You have so many aunts and uncles and *great-aunts* and *great-uncles*, and you're gonna have so many cousins to play with. But since I'm your grandma, I'm gonna be your favorite, okay? Sssh. Don't tell anyone else, though—it's our secret."

Delia and I laughed as she continued to whisper silly, loving nonsense to him. A few minutes later, Sebastian was in Emerson's arms—a bittersweet thing, since she and Hayden have had some struggles getting pregnant. Emerson wept as she held him, and such was the bond between the women that Delia didn't have to say a word—she just watched, crying with her best friend and adopted sister, understanding the depth of emotion Emerson was feeling.

The next few hours were a whirlwind as Delia's massive family came through in waves. My parents, predictably, were "stuck" on some island in the Aegean. I didn't mind.

I have everything and everyone I need right here in Ketchikan.

EPILOGUE

Rune

"C'MON, RUNE, JUST TAKE A BEAT, AND LET'S TALK ABOUT this!" Hayes followed me like the sad, pathetic, cheating sack of donkey balls he was.

I spun on my heel and threw a *cross-country* trophy at his stupid, pretty, cheating face. "FUCK YOU, HAYES WILLOUGHBY!" I shouted. "We're *done* talking."

He dodged the trophy, which was probably good since it would've done pretty significant damage to his face, seeing as it was a very large *first-place* trophy, weighed a lot, and I was an *All-State fast-pitch* softball pitcher.

"I made a mistake, Rune. Can't you forgive me? It didn't mean anything." He picked up the pieces of the trophy and stared at them. "Also, can you not throw my trophies, please?"

I threw another trophy at him—this one he caught. "Fuck—and I say this with the utmost disgust—you. Fuck you. Fuck off. Fuck *all the way* off." I took a break from trophy hurling and started yanking his clothes out of my closet and throwing them out the *second-story* window into the parking lot below.

"I was drunk, Rune," he said, watching his clothes flutter to the concrete. "It was an accident."

"Oh, it was an accident? And it didn't mean anything?" I adopted a tone so sickly saccharine you'd get diabetes just by listening. "That makes a difference, Hayes. Why didn't you say so before?" I wiped fake sweat off my brow. "Whew. Glad we worked that out. It was just an accident and it didn't mean anything. We're fine. It's all fine now, Hayes."

He looked so hopeful that I almost ruined the bit by bursting into laughter. "Really?" He even laughed in relief. "I knew you'd see reason."

"NO, YOU MORON!" I threw another trophy at his head. "My god, Hayes, have you always been this stupid, or did the cheating *skank* you *fucked* in *my bed* in *my condo* do something to *short-circuit* your brain?" I punctuated each statement by throwing another object at him.

"Rune, for fuck's sake, stop throwing shit at me!"

I threw a signed baseball at him. "Did you miss the part where I said fuck off? Because fuck off, Hayes. You come at me with excuses like 'ohhh it was an accident,' and 'ohhh it didn't mean anything,'" I snapped, in a deep, mocking voice. "You accidentally put your dick in another girl's vagina…on accident. You accidentally invited said girl over to—let me repeat—*my condo* where you live because I am, apparently, the world's most pathetic pushover. You plied said girl with *my* alcohol, in *my* condo, and then accidentally took off all your clothes, accidentally got into *my* bed, and accidentally put your penis inside her, repeatedly. Got it. It was all an accident. Like, what, you were possessed by a horny ghost? You tripped and your dick just sort of ended up in her twat?" I shook my hands. "You know what, let's say it was an accident, somehow. Okay, fine. Moving on to your next excuse: it didn't mean anything."

"It didn't! I love you, not her!"

My blood, boiling with rage, instantly went ice cold. I very carefully set down the very heavy, very *sharp-edged* trophy—this *man-boy-person-whatever-he-was* seemed to have an inexhaustible supply of the damn things. I put it down because if I didn't, I was liable to brain him with him, and then I'd go to jail, and that didn't sound fun.

I stalked over to him. "What…the *fuck*…did you just say to me?"

The dimwitted pile of cheating pond scum was not smart enough to recognize his mortal danger. "I don't love her, Rune. It didn't mean anything to me. I lo—"

I picked up one of his *balled-up* dirty socks from the floor and shoved it into his mouth. "Get out."

He tried to spit the socks out. "Roo—gah, ugh, nasty. Rune, wait!"

I shoved him backward, hard. "Get the fuck out. Get the fuck out before I do something we'll both regret, Hayes."

"But I—"

"No." I was calm—too calm. "Nope. You're done. This is done. In fact—you know what? I'm not gonna waste my time packing your shit. *I'll* leave; *you* stay. You pack your shit. I don't give a single solitary flying fuck where you go or what you do, as long as I never see you again."

"I don't understand—what—what did I say?"

I cackled. "What did you *say*? Are you really this dense? For a guy who graduated summa cum laude from Stanford, you sure are a dumbass, you know that?" I put my face in my hands. "Fine, I'll break it down for you. Number one, you don't accidentally fuck someone. You make a choice. I don't care how wasted I am. I would never, *ever* have sex with another guy when I'm in a relationship. Because I am *in control* of my impulses, Hayes. And you know what, I'll be real with you—I've been tempted. I have. Drunk and sober, I've been in situations where I've met a guy I was attracted to. I've even flirted, to the point that if I'd wanted to, I could've had sex with him. But you know what I did, Hayes? I chose not to. BECAUSE I'M AN ADULT WITH IMPULSE CONTROL! I don't let my vagina dictate what I do. I make choices, and since I am—or was—in a relationship with you, I chose *not* to cheat on you. Because I cared about you."

"Rune, I—"

"Shut the fuck up, I'm not done," I snapped. "Number two—it didn't mean anything. Really? Is that supposed to make it better? I'm supposed to feel better because you had sex with someone, but it didn't mean anything? Do you have any clue how insulting that is? It would be better, to some degree, if it *did* mean something. Like, I could get it a little bit if you'd fallen in love with someone else and just…I don't know… couldn't wait to break up with me or something. That's still shitty and pathetic, but at least you ruined our relationship over something that meant something. But *no*. It didn't. It was just random pussy for you. Meant nothing. You ruined our relationship over what? A few minutes of drunk, meaningless sex? It's *so* much worse, Hayes. So much worse. So yeah, fuck you for 'it didn't mean anything.'"

"Rune, fuck, please, I'm—"

"Shut up; still talking. I don't want to hear anything you have to say. Keep your apology, by the way, and shove it all the way up your asshole. It means nothing to me—much like the sex with that bitch meant nothing to you. The last thing you said, and the one that really fucks me up? You don't love her; you love me."

Finally, he seemed to get it. "Rune, I…I didn't mean—"

"We've been together for two and a half years, Hayes. Since sophomore year. Our lives are all tangled up. Your friends, my friends—they're all in the same social circle. Two and a half years of my life. And you know what you've never said to me, not once? That you love me. I say it. I've told you I love you frequently. And you know what you say, every single goddamn time? 'Me too.' Not 'I love you too,' but 'me too.'" My throat was tight, and my eyes burned, but this little boy did not get to see me cry over him, so I choked it all down. "And *now* you say it to me? In *that* context? You didn't love the random girl you got drunk with and accidentally fucked in my bed, in my condo. You don't love her. You love me. As I'm throwing you out—literally throwing your shit out the fucking window—you say that to me? Fuck you, Hayes. Fuck you till the end of time."

"Rune, I'm sorry."

I snarled and had to turn away before I punched him in the face. "I told you—shove your 'sorry' up your ass. I'm leaving. Get your shit out of my condo and fuck off out of my life—permanently."

I ignored him as I packed a suitcase, *carry-on*, and purse with enough stuff to last me for a few weeks.

The last thing I said to him before I walked out was: "My dad has keys. I'll give you the weekend to move out, and then I'll let Dad handle you. And I'll tell him what happened."

Hayes paled—my dad was *six-six*, a former professional strongman, and a BJJ black belt. And he *hated* Hayes. If I told him why I was breaking up with Hayes before he got a chance to skip town, there was a very real chance Hayes would spend a few months in traction.

I tossed my stuff in my car and drove away without a backward look. I didn't call anyone. I just drove.

North, out of LA for the first time in my life—not count-ing vacations, obviously.

I'd just graduated college, had no job, a lot of debt, and now…a broken heart.

I'd loved Hayes. Truly. He was sexy in an adorable way; he could be sweet when he wanted to be, and our lives aligned.

Or so I'd thought.

Two and a half years…and he cheats on me the week after we graduate. Who does that? The ink on our diplomas wasn't even dry yet.

I made it thirty minutes north of LA before I had to pull over and have my breakdown. Or, the first of what I assumed would be several.

This one was for me. A private breakdown, if you will.

Once I was able to get my shit together once more, I set out again, heading for who the hell knows where.

Anywhere but here.

SEATTLE, WASHINGTON; TWO MONTIIS LATER

"Linz, let me stop you right there," I said. "No. Just… no."

My best friend, Lindsey Snelling, let out a frustrated sigh. "It's one afternoon, Rune. You can handle it."

"Absolutely not."

"It's Raquel, babe. We love Raquel."

"We do love Raquel, but it's not just one afternoon. It's travelling there. Getting a hotel. She'll want to have the bachelorette party the night before." I swallowed hard. "And *he'll* be there."

"That's the real reason, Rune, and we both know it. It's been two months. Surely you can stomach seeing him for the duration of one wedding."

"Surely I cannot, Linz. Am I still all sad and heart-broken? No. I'm okay. But I never want to see his ass again. Not even for Raquel."

"You don't even have to see him. Not really. He'll be there, yes, because obviously Raquel's brother is his best friend. But you can avoid him. Better yet, find someone to bring with you, Rune. Let him see you happy."

I sighed. "Linz. Bring someone? Who?"

"I dunno. Go on Farmer's Only or something."

"Funny."

"Rune, you *have* to go to Raquel's wedding. She and Hamish are wonderful together and you'll regret it the rest of your life if you let Hayes Motherfucking Willoughby's dumb cheater ass keep you out of it. Please. On Raquel's behalf and my own, I'm begging you."

"Where is it again?" I asked. "Juneau?"

"Ketchikan. Supposed to be a really cool place, actually. I've done a little research. She has a bar crawl planned for her bachelorette party, and the crown jewel of the bar crawl is a place called Badd Kitty. It's supposed to be *the* place to go for young people our age."

"Badd Kitty? Really?" I let out a disgusted sigh. "What kind of a name is that for a bar?"

"I dunno, babe. All I know is that everything I've read online says it's amazing. The reviews on Insta are crazy. The guys who work there are supposed to be wicked hot."

"Wicked hot, huh?" I laughed. "Your Boston is showing again."

"Shut up," she said, playing up her natural accent. "Just come, Rune."

"And it's when?"

"A week from tomorrow."

"Why so last minute? Is she pregnant?"

"No, they just decided to elope since neither of their parents approve. They don't see the point in waiting. They had this backpacking trip to Alaska planned anyway, so they decided to make Ketchikan the last stop and get married there. It's gonna be small and simple, just our friend group."

"Which is so much worse, Linz—everyone knows what happened, but—"

'But you ran away like a chicken and you haven't talked to any of us about it," she interrupted.

"I talked to you about it."

"Well, yeah. But only me. Everyone else had to hear it secondhand from me."

I sighed. "I don't want to talk about it. That's

my condition. No one, and I mean *no one*, asks me a single fucking question about Hayes Motherfucking Willoughby."

"So you'll go?"

"Yeah, I'll go. But tell them all, Linz." I sighed again. "And I'm going to Ketchikan first. Maybe I can pick up a fake boyfriend or something."

"Or maybe you can pick up a real boyfriend or something?"

I laughed bitterly. "Not happening. I've had four boyfriends in my life, Linz. *Four*. That's it. And what do they have in common? They've all cheated on me. So, no thanks. No more boyfriends. I'm thinking of joining a nunnery."

"I don't think they call them nunneries, babe. I think that was just a Shakespeare thing." She laughed a little too hard. "Plus, you're not even religious. You swear more than my brother, and he was in the Navy."

"Fuck off, I do not."

She just cackled. "Fine. A fake boyfriend, then, little miss bitter."

"Glad you see it my way."

"What's the name of the bar, again?"

"Badd Kitty," she answered. "There's also Badd's Bar & Grille and Badd Night, all owned by the same people. Apparently, they're the best bars in Ketchikan."

"Oh! Do they own Reel Badd? The *movie-themed* bar in West Hollywood?"

"I think so?"

"That place is cool. Well, I'll check it out. The Kitty one, I mean."

"Pick a really, really hot guy for your fake boyfriend. That'll make Hayes Motherfucking Willoughby regret his life choices."

Linz and I had, at some point, come to an unspoken agreement that the only way we would refer to my *douche-waffle* of ex is as Hayes Motherfucking Willoughby.

I laughed. "I'll see what I can do, *baby-cakes*."

"You're Rune Rigby. You can do anything."

"Except pick men, clearly."

"Well, this one is fake. He just has to look the part for the wedding, so there's no pressure. You don't have to actually like him, you just have to pretend for a few hours." She laughed a little too gleefully. "Get into it, babe, you'll have fun."

"*Uh-huh*. Because fake relationships always work out *so* well in the romance books you make me read," I deadpanned.

"Um, yeah, they do by the end. Clearly, you're not actually doing the reading."

"I just read that shit for the steamy parts, since it's the closest I'm getting to actual action. The romance parts make me nauseous."

Lindsay sighed. "Because you're jaded as hell."

"Yes," I agreed. "I am. Very jaded."

"Just go to the wedding, Rune. Fake boyfriend, no fake boyfriend, you know I've got your back. If Hayes

Motherfucking Willoughby tries to talk to you, I'll throat punch him like Melissa McCarthy in that movie with Jason Bateman."

"I do not know your obscure movie references, woman."

"Heathen."

"I know. I know." I sighed. "Fine. I'm already in Seattle. I'll make the drive up to Ketchikan and check things out. See if I can find a really hot guy to *fake-date* for the wedding."

"That's my girl," Lindsay crooned. "I knew you'd come around."

"Because I am, as has been established previously, a pathetic pushover."

"No, you just love me and you can't say no to me because I'm your bestest best friend in the whole wide world."

I laughed. "That too."

"Okaybyeeeee," she *sing-songed*, drawing out the last "ee" syllable into, like, seven.

"You're nuts and I love you. Bye. Oh, and remember, we don't talk about Bruno, and in this case, Bruno is Hayes Motherfucking Willougby."

"Now who's using obscure movie references?" she teased.

Click.

The bitch—she loves to hang up on me, and it was always a game between us to see who could hang up on the other first. She always won.

The next morning, I punched Ketchikan into my GPS, tapped away the various notifications about the route, and headed north.

Apparently, you can't drive to Ketchikan. Who knew? Apparently, there's a *whole-ass* ferry involved? Which wasn't in the budget, but whatever.

I walked into Badd Kitty and was immediately impressed. The crowd was young, and everyone was wild and having a hell of a good time. There was a band playing—some old dude and his wife? Canary? I dunno. Good music—that's what mattered.

I spotted a big dude finishing his beer at the bar and paying his tab; I stole his stool the moment he left, pulled up my thread with Linz, and started texting.

"Welcome to the Kitty," a deep voice said. "What can I get you?"

"House white and Sprite, half and half," I said, not looking up.

"*Seven-Up* okay?"

"Sure."

A silent pause. I got the impression he was waiting for something, so I finally looked up.

Oh.

Oh *shit.*

He was fucking hot as balls.

He towered over me—I was sitting and he was standing, but still, he was *huge*. His arms made my mouth water, and his shoulders were…oof. *So* broad. But his eyes? And his hair? Fuck.

Brown eyes—molten chocolate. Puppy dog brown eyes that sparked with humor and intelligence and attitude.

His hair was *reddish-brown*, wavy and messy, but not messy on purpose—messy because he didn't care and it ended up looking like he'd just rolled out of bed. In a sexy way, to be clear.

Permanent *just-fucked* hair.

Sex hair.

Run-your-hands-through-it-while-screaming-his-name hair.

"What are you doing a week from tomorrow?" I heard myself blurt.

A sly, wicked grin spread across his absurdly gorgeous, *chiseled-from-marble* face. "You, it would appear."

BADD BABY
Coming soon!

ALSO BY
Jasinda Wilder

Visit me at my website: **www.jasindawilder.com**
Email me: **jasindawilder@gmail.com**

If you enjoyed this book, you can help others enjoy it
as well by recommending it to friends and family, or
by mentioning it in reading and discussion groups and
online forums. You can also review it on the site from
which you purchased it. But, whether you recommend
it to anyone else or not, thank you *so much* for taking the
time to read my book! Your support means the world
to me!

My other titles:

Forbidden Fruit

Wild Ride: Biker Billionaire

Delilah's Diary

Big Girls Do It:

Big Girls Do It
Married

Badd Luck
Badd Mojo
Big Badd Wolf
Badd Boy
Badd Kitty
Badd Business
Badd Medicine
Badd Daddy

Goode Girls:
For a Goode Time Call…
Not So Goode
Goode To Be Bad
A Real Goode Time
Goode Vibrations
Dad Bod Contracting:
Hammered
Drilled
Nailed
Screwed

Fifty States of Love:
Pregnant in Pennsylvania
Cowboy in Colorado
Married in Michigan
Christmas in Connecticut

Billionaire Baby Club:

Lizzy Goes Brains Over Braun

Autumn Rolls a Seven

Laurel's Bright Idea

Club Sin:

Rev

Kane

Chance

Silas

Saxon

Solomon

Blood Heir

Blood Heir

Blood Bonds

Blood Reign

Blood Bonds

Standalone titles:

Yours

The Cabin

The Parent Trap

Wish Upon A Star

Big Hose

Non-Fiction titles:
You Can Do It
You Can Do It: Strength
You Can Do It: Fasting

Jack Wilder Titles:
The Missionary

JJ Wilder Titles:
Ark

To be informed of new releases, special offers,

and other Jasinda news, sign up for
Jasinda's email newsletter.

www.ingramcontent.com/pod-product-compliance
Lightning Source LLC
Chambersburg PA
CBHW020828030726
47496CB00001B/149